THE
# BETTER
OF
# M<sup>C</sup>SWEENEY'S

*Vol. II*

McSWEENEY'S BOOKS
SAN FRANCISCO

www.mcsweeneys.net

Interior art by Michael Schall
Cover photo by Shay Levy

McSweeney's and colophon are registered trademarks
of McSweeney's, a privately held company with
wildly fluctuating resources.

ISBN: 978-1934781-52-4

# I UNDERSTAND

*by* RODDY DOYLE

### CHAPTER ONE

THIS MORNING, I stand at the bus stop. I have been in this city three months. I begin to understand the accent. I already know the language. How do you do? Is this the next bus to Westminster? I have brought my schoolroom English with me. There is no Westminster in this city but I know what to say when the next bus goes past without stopping.

—Fuck that.

People smile. One man nods at me.

—Good man, bud, he says. —Making the effort.

I smile.

I understand. This word, *bud*. It is a friendly word. But I cannot say Bud to this man. I cannot call him Bud. A man like me can never call an Irish man Bud. But I can say, Fuck that. The expletive is for the bus, the rain, the economy, life. I am not insulting the bus driver or my fellow bus-stop waiters. I understand. My children will learn to call other children Bud. They will be Irish. They will have the accent. If I am still here. And if I have children.

It is spring. I like it now. It is bright when I stand at the bus stop. It is warm by the time I finish my first job. Early morning is the best time. It is quiet. There are not many people on the footpaths. I do not have to look away. Eyes do not stare hard at me. Some people smile. We are up early together. Many are like me. I am not resented.

I polish floors in a big department store. I like pushing the buffer over the wooden floor. I am used to hard work but every machine and tool has its own pain. With the buffer, it was in my arms. It was like riding an electric horse. My arms shook for a long time after I finished. I felt the buffer every time I closed my eyes. I heard it. Now, I like it. I control it. It is my horse now and I am the cowboy. This morning, I push the buffer too far. The flex becomes tight and the plug jumps out of the socket. I have to walk across the big floor to insert the plug. It is a correct time to say Fuck that. But I do not say it. I am alone.

I like this job. I like the department store when it is empty. I like that I am finished very early. I wear my suit to the store and I change into my work clothes in one of the changing rooms. I carry my work clothes in a bag that I found in my room. It is a bag for Aston Villa. It is not a very good team, I think, but the bag is good. It is grand. I understand. How are you? Grand. How's the head? Grand. That's a great day. It is grand.

One time, the supervisor was outside the changing room when I came out.

—Make sure you don't help yourself to any of the clothes, she said.

I saw her face as she looked at me. She was sorry for what she had said. She looked away. She is nice. She is grand. She leaves me alone.

Every month, the window models are changed. This morning is a change day. Pretty women and men with white hair are taking out old models and putting in new ones. The new ones have no heads. I wait to see them put heads on the models, on top of the summer clothes, but they do not. One day, perhaps, I will understand.

I change into my suit and I go home. Today, I walk because it is nice and I save some money. It is warm. I walk on the sunny sides. It is not a time to worry. I eat and I go to bed for a time. The room is empty. My three friends are gone, at their works. Sometimes I sleep. Sometimes the bad dreams do not come. Most times I lie awake. There is always some noise. I do not mind. I am never alone in this house. I do not know how many people live here.

I get up in the afternoon and I watch our television. I like the programs in which American men and women shout at each other and the audience shouts at them. It is grand. I also like MTV, when there are girls and good music. They are also grand. Today, I watch pictures of people, happy in Baghdad. A man hits a picture of Saddam with his shoe. He does this many times.

I get dressed for my second job. I do not wear my suit. I do not like my second job but it is there that my story starts.

CHAPTER TWO

My second job takes me to the place called Temple Bar. I walk because the bus is too slow when other people are going home from work. The streets are busy but I am safe. It is early and, now, it is spring and daylight.

Temple Bar is famous. It is the center of culture in Dublin and Ireland. But many drunk people walk down the streets, shouting and singing with very bad voices. Men and even women lie on the pavements. I understand. These are stag and hen people, from England. Kevin, my Irish friend, explained. One of these people will soon be married, so they come to Temple Bar to fall on the street and urinate in their trousers or show their big breasts to each other and laugh. Kevin told me that they are English people but I do not think that this is right. I think that many of them are Irish. Alright, bud? What are you fucking looking at? But Kevin wants me to believe that these drunk people are English. I do not know why, but Kevin is my friend, so I do not tell him that, in my opinion, many of them are Irish.

Here, I am a baby. I am only three months old. My life started when I arrived. My boss shows me the plug. He holds it up.

—Plug, he says.

He puts the plug into the plug-hole. He takes it out and he puts it in again.

—Understand? he says.

I understand. He turns on the hot water.

—Hot.

He turns on the cold water.

—Cold. Understand?

I understand. He points at some pots and trays. He points at me.

—Clean.

I understand. He smiles. He pats my shoulder.

All night, I clean. I am in a corner of the big kitchen, behind a white wall. There is a radio that I can listen to when the restaurant is not very noisy. This night, the chefs joke about the man in Belfast called Stakeknife. The door to the alley is open, always, but I am very hot.

—How come you get all the easy jobs?

I look up. It is Kevin, my friend.

—Fuck that, I say.

He laughs.

Food is a good thing about this job. It is not the food that is left on the plates. It is real, new food. I stop work for a half hour and I sit at a table and eat with other people who work here. This is how I met Kevin. He is a waiter.

—It's not fair, he says, this night, when he sees my wet and dirty T-shirt. —You should be a waiter instead of having to scrub those fucking pots and pans.

I shrug. I do not speak. I do not want to be a waiter, but I do not want to hurt his feelings, because he is a waiter. Also, I cannot work in public. All my work must be in secret, because I am not supposed to work. Kevin knows this. This is why he says that it is not fair. I think.

The door to the alley is near my corner, and it is always open. Fresh air comes through the open door but I would like to perspire and lock the door, always. But, even then, it must be opened sometimes. I must take out the bags of rubbish, old chicken wings and french fries and wet napkins. I must take them out to the skip.

And, really, this is the start of my story. This night, I carry a bag outside to the alley. I lift the lid of the skip, I drop in the bag, I turn to go back.

—There you are.

He is in front of me, and the door is behind him.

—Hello, I say.

—Polite, he says.

I understand. This is sarcasm.

—Did you think about that thing we were talking about? he says.

—Yes, I say.

—Good. And?

—Please, I say, —I do not wish to do it.

He sighs. He hits me before he speaks.

—Not so good.

I am on the ground, against the skip. He kicks me.

I must explain. The story starts two weeks before, when this man first grabbed my shoulder as I dropped a bag into the skip. He spoke before I could see his face.

—Gotcha, gotcha.

He told me my name, he told me my address, he told me that I had no right to work here and that I would be deported. I turned. He was not a policeman.

—But, he said, —I think I can help you.

He went. Three times since, he has spoken to me.

Now, this night, I stand up. He hits me again. I understand. I cannot fight this man. I cannot defend myself.

### CHAPTER THREE

I am alone again in the alley behind the restaurant. The man has gone. I check my clothes. I am no dirtier than I was before I came out here. I check my face. I take my hand away. There is no blood.

He will be back. Not here. But it will be tonight. I know exactly what this man is doing. I am no stranger to his tactics. I go back into the restaurant. I work until there is no more work to do and it is time to go home. Every night, this is the time I do not like. Tonight, I know, it will be worse.

I walk with Kevin to the corner of Fleet Street and Westmoreland Street. He has his bicycle.

—Are you alright? he asks.

—Yes, I say.

—You're quiet.

—I am tired.

—Me too, knackered. Seeyeh.

—See you.

I will buy a bicycle. But, tonight, I must walk. It is later than midnight. There are no buses. I walk across the bridge. I walk along O'Connell Street. I do not look at people as they come toward me. I cross to the path that goes up the center of the street. It is wider and quieter. And, I think, safer. But never safe. It is a very long, famous street. I do not like it. All corners are dangerous.

This night no one stares or spits at me. No words are thrown at my back. No one pushes against me. Once or twice, I look behind. I expect to see the man. He is not there. This, too, I expect. It is his plan. Then I think that I will not go home. I will hide. But this is a decision that he would expect of me. He is watching. I keep walking. I do not look behind.

The last streets to my house are narrow and dark. Cars pass one at a time, and sometimes none at all, as I walk to my street. I walk toward a parked car. It is a jeep, made by Honda.

A cigarette lands on the footpath.

—I'm giving them up.

He is alone.

—D'you smoke, yourself?

—No, I do not.

—Four years I was off them. Can you believe that?

But he is not alone. Two more men are behind me and beside me. They hold my arms.

—In you get.

A hand pushes my head down, and protects my head as I am pushed into the backseat. I am in the middle, packed between these two big men. They are not very young.

The driver does not drive. We go to nowhere.

—Have you had a re-think? he says.

—Excuse me? I say, although I understand his words.

—Have you thought about what I said?

—Yes.

He does not look back and he does not look in the rearview mirror.

—And?

—Please, I say. —Please, tell me more about my duties.

The men beside me laugh. They do not hit me.

—Duties? says the driver. —Fair enough. That's easily done. You go to another place, here in Ireland, sometimes just Dublin. You deliver a package, or pick one up. You come back without the package, or with it. Now and again. How's that?

I cannot shrug. There is not room. I do not ask what the packages will contain. The question, I think, might result in violence. And I do not intend to deliver the packages.

—Do you have a driver's license? he says.

—No.

—Doesn't matter. You'll be getting the train.

The men laugh.

—All pals, says the driver. —We'll take you home.

It is a very short distance. The men at my sides talk to each other.

—So the doctor, says one man, —the specialist. He said, Put your fuckin' finger on that.

—Were you not out?

—Out where?

—Knocked out.

—No.

The driver turns the last corner and stops at my house. He opens his door and gets out.

—There's a 99 percent success rate, says the man at my left.

—Well, the wife's brother died on the table last year.

—But he was probably bad before he went in.

—That's true.

The big man at my left gets out. I follow him. The driver hits me before I straighten, as I get out. The other man is right behind me. He also hits me. The driver tries to grab my hair but it is too short. He pulls my shoulder.

—None of this is racially motivated. Understand?

I nod. I understand.

—Grateful?

I nod.

—Good man. And, come here. There'll be a few euros in it for you.

—Thank you.

—No problem, he says. —And, by the way, I know your days off.

There are no more blows. I am alone on the footpath. I watch the jeep turn the corner.

CHAPTER FOUR

My next day off is Sunday. But I know that, in fact, the man in the jeep will decide. My next day off will be any day he wants it to be.

I must wait. I must decide.

It rains this morning. I do not like the rain but I like what it does. It makes people rush; it makes them concentrate on their feet. It is a good time for walking.

I must think.

I can run.

I can run again.

I am very tired. The buffer controls me this morning. I follow it across the floor.

I will not run. I decided that I would not run again when I came to Ireland, and I will not change my mind. I ran away from my home and my country. I ran away from London. Now, I will not run.

It still rains.

But what will I do? What is my plan?

I stand at the service entrance behind the department store. The lane is one puddle.

I wait for the plan to unfold in my mind. I look, but the lane is empty. Perhaps the man in the jeep does not know about my early-day life. I do not believe this. The plan stays folded and hidden.

—God, what a country.

The supervisor has opened the door. She stands beside me. She looks at the water. She judges its depth.

—What made you come to this feckin' place?

Then she looks at me.

—Sorry.

I understand: she sees famine, flies, drought, huge, starving bellies.

—I like this, I say.

—You don't.

—Please, I say. —I do.

—Why? she asks.

I do not want to make her uncomfortable. But I tell her.

—It is safer when it rains.

—Oh.

I have not told the men who share my room. They have their own stories, and I do not want to bring trouble to them. I do not know what to tell them.

She has not moved yet. She looks at the rain.

—Busy? she says.

—Excuse me?

—Are you busy these days?

I shrug. I do not wish to tell her about my other work.

—Have you time for a coffee? she says.

I am stupid this morning. At first, I do not understand. Then I look at her.

—Please, I say. —With you?

Her face is very red. She is not beautiful. She laughs.

—Well, yes, she says. —If it's not too much bloody trouble.

She is, I think, ten years older than I.

—Forget it, she says.

—No, I say. —I mean. Yes.

—You're sure?

—Yes.

—Come on.

She tries to run through the rain but her legs are very stiff and her shoes are not for running. She stops after few steps and walks instead. I walk beside her. We go down a lane and then it is Grafton Street. I look behind me; I see no one. We enter the café called Bewley's.

She will not allow me to hold the tray. Nor will she allow me to pay for two cups of coffee and one doughnut. She chooses the table. People stare, others look quickly away. I stand until she sits. She takes the cups off the tray. I sit.

—Thank you.

She puts the doughnut in front of me. I feel foolish. Does she think I am her son? I did not ask for this doughnut. But I am hungry.

—People smell when it's been raining. Did you ever notice?

—Yes, I say.

Again, I feel foolish. Is she referring to me?

She lifts her cup. She smiles.

—Well. Cheers.

—Yes, I say.

I lift my cup but I do not smile. The coffee is good but I wish I was outside, under the rain. I think she is trying to be kind—I am not sure—but I wish I was outside, going home. It would be simpler.

—Any regrets? she says.

—Excuse me?

—D'you ever wish you'd stayed at home?

She tries to smile.

—No, I say.

I do not tell her that I would almost certainly be dead if I had stayed at home.

—I like it here, I say.

It is the answer they want to hear.

—God, she says. —I don't like it much and I'm *from* here.

I look behind, and at the queue at the counters.

—Am I that uninteresting? she says.

I look at her.

—Excuse me?

—Am I boring you?

—No.

—What's wrong?

—Please, I say. —Nothing.

—What's wrong?

I do not want this. I do not want her questions. So I smile.

—Fuck that, I say.

But she does not laugh. She cries. I do not understand. And now I see the man in the jeep. He is here, of course, without the jeep, but the keys are in his hand. He walks toward me. I hear the keys.


CHAPTER FIVE

The man stops at our table. He picks up the remaining piece of my doughnut.

—Tomorrow, he says.

He looks at the supervisor.

—Breaking your heart, love, is he?

She looks shocked. He laughs. He turns, and his car key scrapes my head. He goes.

She no longer cries but her face is very white, and pink—stained by anger and embarrassment.

—I am sorry, I say.

—Who was that? she said.

—Please, I say. —A friend.

—He was no friend, she says.

I look at her.

—Sure he wasn't?

—No, I say. —He is not a friend.

—What is he then?

—I do not know.

I stand up now. I must go.

—Thank you, I say. —Goodbye.

I am grateful to her, but I do not want to be grateful. It is a feeling that I cannot trust. I have been grateful before. Gratitude unlocks the door that should, perhaps, stay locked.

—Fine, she says.

She is angry. She does not look at me now.

—Goodbye, I say, again.

I go.

I go home. My three friends are gone, at their works. I lie on the bed. I do not sleep. I watch our television. American men and women shout at each other. The audience shouts at them. On the programme called *Big Brother*, a man washes his clothes. He is not very good at this. His friends sleep. I watch them.

I understand. I will see the man before tomorrow. He must let me see that the decision is not mine. I must know that there is no choice. I will see his violence tonight. I know this.

I know this and, yet, I am still hungry. I might die but I want a sandwich. I was hungry some minutes after I watched my father die. The hunger was welcome; there was no guilt. It made me move; it made me think.

I want a sandwich and I make a sandwich. In this house the choice is mine, as is the cheese. The bread, I borrow. I eat, and watch the *Big Brother* people sit.

It is time to go.

It rains. I walk. A drunk woman falls in front of me. I do not stop. She is very young. Her friend sits down beside her, in the water.

I walk through the restaurant. There are not so many customers. I go to the back door. I look out. There is no one there. I shake the rain from my jacket. I hang it up. I fill the sink. I start.

I welcome the heat of the water. I welcome the pleasure, and the effort that the work demands. I scrub at the fear. I search for it. The work is good. I am alert and useful. I have knives beside me, and in the water. I can think, and I cannot be surprised.

—Great weather.

It is Kevin. He is very wet.

—Fuck that, I say.

—I have a new one for you, he says. —Ready?

—Yes.

I take my hands from the water.

—Me bollix, he says. —Repeat.

—My—

—No. Me.

—Me. Bollix.

—Together.

—Me bollix.

—Excellent, says Kevin. —Top man.

He dries his hair with a tea-towel.

—Please, what does it mean?

—My balls.

—Thank you.

—You're welcome. I'm meeting some people after. Want to come?

I answer immediately.

—No. Thank you.

He sees my face; he sees something I feel.

—Sure?

—Perhaps, I say.

—Good.

He puts the tea-towel on my shoulder.

—Later, he says.

—Me bollix, I say.

—Excellent.

I resume the washing. The restaurant starts to fill. I am glad of this. I am very occupied. There is an argument between the manager and one of the chefs—the radio is too loud. A pigeon walks into the kitchen. I go out quickly to the skip with full bags, but there is no one waiting for me. It is a good night, but now it is over. I take a knife. I put it in my pocket.

—Are you coming? says Kevin.

—Yes, I say.

I do not want to bring trouble to Kevin, but I do not want to go home the expected way, at the expected time.

—Excellent, says Kevin.

Outside, it rains. The street is quiet. I walk with Kevin. He pushes his bicycle. We hurry.

We go to a pub.

—It is not closed? I ask.

—No, said Kevin. —It opens late. It's not really a pub.

I do not understand.

—More a club.

Still, I do not understand. I have not been to many pubs. The men at the door stand back, and we enter. It is very hot inside, the music is very loud, and it is James Brown.

I talk; I shout.

—James Brown.

Kevin smiles.

—You know him?

Now I smile.

And I see her.


### CHAPTER SIX

I see her, my supervisor, but she is not among Kevin's friends. She is standing at a different table, with other people. She sees me. She nods. I nod.

I am introduced to Kevin's friends. The music is loud. I do not hear names. There are five people, three women, two men. All shake my hand vigorously; all offer me space at the table. I stand between two of the women.

I look. She is looking at me. She looks away.

Kevin shouts into my ear.

—What are you having?

—Excuse me?

—Drink.

—Please, I say. —A pint of Guinness.

He moves to the bar.

The woman at my left side speaks.

—Guinness, yeah?

—Yes.

—Nice one.

I nod. She nods. I smile. She smiles. She is pretty. Her breasts and teeth impress me. I hope that she will say something else. I can think of nothing to say.

She speaks. It is exciting.

—You work with Kevin, yeah?

She shouts.

—Bollix to it, I say.

I shout.

She laughs.

—Yeah, she says.

She nods. I do not really understand but, looking at her smile at me, I am quite happy.

One Guinness is placed in front of me. A white sleeve holds the glass. I look. It is not Kevin. The man, a barman, nods at the next table. The supervisor is there. She lifts her glass. She has given me this Guinness.

She smiles.

I do not want to touch it.

The other woman speaks.

—You've an admirer, she says.

She is smiling.

So many smiling women.

—You'll hurt her feelings if you don't drink it.

I pick up the Guinness. I smile at the supervisor. I drink. I smile. I look away.

Kevin's friend, the other woman, is no longer looking at me.

No more smiling women. Kevin comes to the table with another Guinness for me. He sees that it is not the first, and is confused.

—What's the story? he says.

His friend, the woman, turns to us.

—He has an admirer, she says. —Amn't I right?

—Fuck that, I say.

I now have two pints of Guinness.

—It's good to be Irish, says Kevin.

She laughs at Kevin, and she smiles at me. I do not know which is more significant, the laughter or the smile.

—What's your name? she asks.

Perhaps the smile. I hope so.

—Tom, I say.

I have many names.

—Oh, she says. —I was expecting something a bit more exotic.

—I apologize, I say.

I smile. She smiles.

—Is Thomas more exotic? I ask.

She laughs.

—Not really.

I like this girl's teeth, very much. I like her smile. I like the sound of her laughter.

I have many names.

—And yours? I say.

—Ailbhe, she says.

—Oh, I say. —I too was expecting something more exotic.

Again, she laughs. Her open mouth is beautiful.

—Please, I say.

I shout.

—Spell this name.

Her mouth is now close to my ear. She spells the name, very, very slowly. If she does this because she thinks that I am stupid, for this time only, I am most grateful.

—Please, I say.

I shout.

—Does this name have a meaning?

Yeah, she says.

She shouts.

—It's Irish for The Slut Who Drinks Too Much At The Weekends.

She sees my shock. I see hers.

—Sorry, she says. —It's an old joke. Friends of mine. We made up silly meanings for our names.

She holds up her glass.

—I'm drinking Ballygowan.

I understand.

—And I'm only a slut now and again.

I think I understand.

—And it is not the weekend, I say.

—Well, yeah, she says.

I am grateful for the Guinness. I can hide behind it as I drink. I can think. I can decide. I like this girl. And I like her sense of humor.

It is a thing that I had forgotten: I, too, have a sense of humor.

I smile. And she smiles.

—Out for the night?

It is the wrong woman who now speaks to me. It is the supervisor.

—Thank you, I say.

—Ah, well, she says.

She shouts.

—This morning was a bit weird, wasn't it?

It was just this morning that we drank coffee in Bewley's? I am surprised. It has been a very long day.

I shrug. I am afraid to speak, but must.

—It was nice, I say. —Thank you.

—Ah, well.

I think that she is drunk.

—That guy, she says. —This morning. He was a bit creepy, wasn't he?

I do not want to talk about the man. I do not want to talk to her about him.

—D'you not think? she says.

I will leave. I must.

—Do you need rescuing?

Ailbhe's mouth is at my ear. She whispers.

—Please, I say. —Yes.

CHAPTER SEVEN

—God, she says. —You came a bit fast-ish.

—Please, I say. —You are very beautiful.

—You're good-looking yourself, she says. —But I'd planned on making the most of it.

—I—

—Don't say you're sorry. I'm only joking. Will we get into the bed?

I have not seen a bed.

—Yes, I say.

She stands. I stand.

I pick up my shoes. A bus passes. The headlights race across the wall and ceiling. She closes the hall door.

—That's better, she says.

She turns on the light.

I follow her.

I cannot remember her name. This is very strange. I want to run away but I also want to follow this woman. I like her. But, even so, her name has disappeared.

The hall light clicks off suddenly. It is dark but I see and hear her unlock a door.

—You do not live in the entire house? I ask.

—No, she says. —Just this place.

So, we made love in a public hall. Again, I want to run.

The door is open. She turns on the light. I enter. It is the room of a woman. I am glad that I am here.

It is not a big bed. We lie beside each other.

I like this woman. I wish that I could remember her name. She remembers mine.

—Dublin's a bit of a dump, isn't it, Tom?

—Please, I said.

And I remember.

—Avril.

—Who the fuck is Avril?

—You are not Avril?

—No, Tim, I'm not Avril.

She sits up.

—But call me whatever you like.

She leans down and whispers into my ear.

—Avril.

I like this woman.

I wake up.

I know where I am, but I am surprised. I slept. This was not my plan. The man with the jeep expects to meet me this morning. But I am here; I am not at home. I look at the curtains. There is strong daylight at its edges. I am not at the department store, at work.

She is beside me, asleep, this woman whose name, I am sure, is almost Avril.

I get out of the bed.

She wakes.

—Get back in here, you.

Please, I say. —I must go. To work.

—You work nights, she says.

—I have two jobs, I say.

—Poor you, she says.

She notices that I hesitate. She sees me fumble with my shoelaces.

—Give work a miss, she says.

I would like to do this, very much. I would like to take off my clothes and stay. I would like to touch this woman's warm skin and stay close to it.

But I cannot do this. The man might know where I am. He might be outside, waiting. He is not a patient man.

My laces are tied. I stand up.

—Goodbye, I say. —Thank you.

I open the door.

—Ailbhe, she says.

—That is your name? Ailbhe.

—That's it, she says. —See if you can remember it till tonight.

—I will remember, I say.

—We'll see, she says.

—My bollix.

It rains and, this morning, I do not like it. I am too far away to walk, so I must wait for a bus. I see no jeeps, parked or coming toward me. But I think that I am being watched. I want to move, to run away, but I wait.

The bus is very slow. It is full, so I must stand. I cannot see through the windows because of the condensation. But I do not need to see to know: the bus is not moving. I will be late. I will be late.

I am very late.

The service door behind the department store is locked.

I knock and wait. I try to hear approaching feet. I knock.

A hand is on my shoulder. A hard hand, grabbing, pushing me to the door.

—The very man.

The door opens as my head hits it. My face falls into the supervisor's jacket.

I get free and see her face. She is looking at the man and she is angry. She does not seem to be surprised.

—Go away, she says.

—I was just talking to Thomas, he says. —Wasn't I, Thomas?

He looks at me. He smiles.

—Yes, I say.

—He's doing a bit of work for me, he says.

He smiles at her.

—You know yourself. No questions asked. No visas needed.

He winks.

—I told you once, she says. —Go away and leave him alone.

And she stands between me and the man. The door is narrow. I cannot pass her. I do not try.

—And what if I don't? he says. —Will you call the Guards?

He laughs, and winks again.

—No, she says. —I'll do better than that.

He stops laughing.


CHAPTER EIGHT

The supervisor stares at the man. He tries to understand her. I can see it in his face: this woman must be taken seriously. And I can see him fight this fact. He would like to hit her. But he is worried. He is no longer sure.

I am ashamed. The woman stands between me and the man—he continues to look at her. And I do not feel safe. For now, he cannot reach me.

But she cannot stand in front of me forever, for more than five minutes. And I do not want her to stand there. I am not a child. I am not a man who will hide behind a woman. Or another man. I will not hide.

—Please, I say. —Please.

I realize now; I understand. I say *please* too often. The word is not often understood in this country. I am not weak.

—You must leave me alone, I say.

They look at me, the man and the woman. She turns. He already looks my way. They both look pleased, surprised, uncertain. They wonder: Is he talking to me? They had forgotten, perhaps, that I am there.

The man moves. She blocks his path.

Again, I say it.

—You must leave me alone.

She knows. I am talking to her. He knows. I am talking to him. She looks puzzled, then angry. He steps back. He knows that he will get me soon.

—I'm trying to help, she says.

—Yes, I say. —Thank you.

—He's dangerous, she says.

—Yes.

He is dangerous and he is a fool.

—I know his type, she says.

I nod. I also know his type. I have been running from his type for too many years. I will not run now. I will do this myself.

He is a fool because he has not seen me. He has not bothered to look. He sees a man he can frighten and exploit, and he is certain that he can do this. The men who made me fight when I was a boy, they too saw fear and vulnerability. They made me do what they wanted me to do; they made me destroy and kill, for ten years. I am no longer a boy. This man frightens me but I, too, am a man. I know what a hard man is in the language of this city. Tough, ruthless, respected, feared. This man looks at me and sees none of these qualities. He sees nothing. He is a fool.

The supervisor shrugs.

—Sure? she says.

She is a good woman.

—Yes, I say.

Her mobile phone is in her hand. She holds it up.

—I can make a call, she says. —That's all I'd need.

—No, I say. —Thank you.

She shrugs again.

—You know best. I suppose.

—Yes, I say.

She steps aside. He doesn't move. She walks behind me. He doesn't move. She walks away. He doesn't move. He stays in the alley. I am in the department-store corridor. The door begins to close. I stop it.

He speaks.

—Come on out here till we have a chat.

I step out. I let go of the door. I hear it close behind me; I hear it click, shut, locked. I do not look back.

—So, he says. —What's the story?

It is not a question. It is not a real question. An answer does not interest him. I see men to my right. They have entered the alley; they were there already. Two men. I have seen them before. They were with him the night he forced me into his Honda jeep. I do not look at these men. I concentrate on the important man.

—So, he says, again.

Still, it still rains.

—You're a bit of a messer, he says. —Aren't you?

—No, I say. —I am not.

He looks at me.

Carefully. For the first time.

Too late.

—Right, he says.

It is as if he shakes himself, as if he has just now woken up.

He must take control.

But I will not be controlled.

I walk away.

I walk. Past his colleagues. They move, prepared to grab, to hit—unsure. I walk. I do not look back.

I will walk away from here. Because I have decided to.

If he shouts I will hear but I will not listen.

If they grab my shoulders I will feel their hands but I will ignore them.

I will feel their blows but I will not stop or turn around. I will fall forward and refuse to look.

If he shoots me I will die. I will be gone. He will gain nothing. He knows this. Now.

He understands.

—Hey! Hey!

I walk away.


CHAPTER NINE

I walk out of the alley. To a narrow street that is always dark. I do not look behind. I do not hurry. I hear no one behind me. I do not think that I am followed.

I am now on Grafton Street. I am not a fool. I do not think that the crowds will bring me safety. If the man wishes to injure me, if he thinks that he must, he will.

I walk.

If he decides to hurt me, or kill me, because I have humiliated him in front of his colleagues, he will wait. He will not do it here. There are too many people, and too many security cameras. If he wants to teach me, and others, a lesson, he might do it here: Nowhere is safe—*do as we say*.

I do not think that he will attack me here. Perhaps he knows: he can teach me nothing.

I am a fit man and I enjoy walking. Just as well—as they say here. I must walk all day.

Fuck that.

I know that I am smiling. It is strange. I did not know that I was going to. It is good. To find the smile, to feel it.

I pass a man who is standing on a crate. He is painted blue and staying very still. When somebody puts money into the bucket in front of him, he moves suddenly. Perhaps I will do that. I will paint myself blue. I will disappear.

—Fuck that.

A man looks at me, and looks away.

I am the blue man who says Fuck that.

I must walk. All this day.

I cannot sit. I cannot stop. I cannot go home. I must be free. I must keep walking.

I walk. I walk all day. Through Temple Bar. Along the river, past tourists and heroin addicts, strangely sitting together. Past the Halfpenny Bridge and O'Connell Bridge. Past the Custom House and the statues of the starving Irish people. I walk to the Point Depot. Across the bridge—the rain has stopped, the clouds are low—I walk past the toll booths, to Sandymount. No cars slow down, no car door slams behind me. I am alone.

I walk on the wet sand. I see men in the distance, digging holes in the sand. They dig for worms, I think. They look as if they stand on the sea. It is very beautiful here. The ocean, the low mountains, the wind.

It is becoming dark when I cross the tracks at the station called Sydney Parade.

I will go to work. I will not let them stop me. I will go to work. I will buy a bicycle. I will buy a mobile phone. I am staying. I will not paint myself blue. I will not disappear.

It is dark now. It is dangerous. Cars approach, and pass.

I walk the distance to Temple Bar. I walk through crowds and along parts of the streets that are empty. I pass men alone and women in laughing groups.

I am, again, on Grafton Street, where my wandering started this morning. I walk past the blue man. It seems that he has not moved.

I arrive at Temple Bar. A drunk man steps into my way. His friends are behind him. His shoulder brushes mine.

—Sorry, bud.

I make sure that there is no strong contact. I walk through his friends. I do not step off the pavement. I do not increase my pace.

I reach the restaurant at the same time as Kevin. I wait, as he locks his bicycle.

—Did you get a good night's sleep last night? he says.

I understand. This is called slagging.

—Yes, I say. —Thank you.

—Does she snore? he asks.

I surprise myself.

—Only time will tell, I say.

He laughs. I also laugh. I know now what I must do, where I must go. But, first, there is something that I must know.

—Please, I say. —Kevin.

It is later. The restaurant is closed. I cycle Kevin's bicycle; it is mine for tonight.

I remember her corner. I remember her house.

I ring the bell. I wait.

I look behind me. No jeep, no waiting men.

I hear the door. I turn. She is there.

—Well, she says.

—Good evening.

—So, she says. —Do you remember my name?

—Yes, I say.

Kevin told me. I wrote it on my sleeve.

—Yes, I say. —Your name is Ailbhe.

—Ten out of ten, she says. —Enter.

—Please, I say.

I look at the street. I look at her.

—I might be in danger, I say.

—I like the sound of that, she says. —Come in.

# A CHILD'S BOOK OF
# SICKNESS AND DEATH

*by* CHRIS ADRIAN

**M**Y ROOM, 616, is always waiting for me when I get back, unless it is the dead of winter, rotavirus season, when the floor is crowded with gray-faced toddlers rocketing down the halls on fantails of liquid shit. They are only transiently ill, and not distinguished. You earn something in a lifetime of hospitalizations that the rotavirus babies, the RSV wheezers, the accidental ingestions, the rare tonsillectomy, that these sub-sub-sickees could never touch or have. The least of it is the sign that the nurses have hung on my door, silver glitter on yellow poster board: CHEZ CINDY.

My father settles me in before he leaves. He likes to turn down the bed, to tear off the paper strap from across the toilet, and to unpack my clothes and put them in the little dresser. "You only brought halter tops and hot pants," he tells me.

"And pajamas," I say. "Halter tops make for good access. To my veins." He says he'll bring me a robe when he comes back, though he'll likely not be back. If you are the sort of child who only comes into the hospital once every ten years, then the whole world comes to visit, and your room is filled with flowers and chocolates and aluminum balloons. After the tenth or fifteenth admission the people and the flowers stop coming. Now I get flowers only if I'm septic, but my Uncle Ned makes a donation to the Short Gut Foundation of America every time I come in.

"Sorry I can't stay for the H and P," my father says. He would usually stay to answer all the questions the intern du jour will ask, but during this admission we are moving. The new house is only two miles from the old house, but it is bigger, and has views. I don't care much for views. This side of the hospital looks out over the park and beyond that to the Golden Gate. On the nights my father stays he'll sit for an hour watching the bridge lights blinking while I watch television. Now he opens the curtains and puts his face to the glass, taking a single deep look before turning away, kissing me goodbye, and walking out.

After he's gone, I change into a lime-green top and bright white pants, then head down the hall. I like to peep into the other rooms as I walk. Most of the doors are open, but I see no one I know. There are some orthopedic-looking kids in traction; a couple wheezers smoking their albuterol bongs; a tall thin blonde girl sitting up very straight in bed and reading one of those fucking Narnia books. She has CF written all over her. She notices me looking and says hello. I walk on, past two big-headed syndromes and a nasty rash. Then I'm at the nurse's station, and the welcoming cry goes up, "Cindy! Cindy! Cindy!" Welcome back, they say, and where have you *been*, and Nancy, who always took care of me when I was little, makes a booby-squeezing motion at me and says, "My little baby is becoming a woman!"

"Hi everybody," I say.

*See the cat? The cat has feline leukemic indecisiveness. He is losing his fur, and his cheeks are hurting him terribly, and he bleeds from out of his nose and his ears. His eyes are bad. He can hardly see you. He has put his face in his litter box because sometimes that makes his cheeks feel better, but now his paws are hurting and his bladder is getting nervous and there is the feeling at the tip of his tail that comes every day at noon. It's like someone's put it in their mouth and they're chewing and chewing.*

*Suffer, cat, suffer!*

I am a former twenty-six-week miracle preemie. These days you have to be a twenty-four-weeker to be a miracle preemie, but when I was born you were still pretty much dead if you emerged at twenty-six weeks. I did well except for a belly infection that took about a foot of my gut—nothing a big person would miss but it was a lot to one-kilo me. So I've got difficult bowels. I don't absorb well, and get this hideous pain, and barf like mad, and need tube feeds, and beyond that sometimes have to go on the sauce, TPN—total parenteral nutrition, where they skip my wimpy little gut and feed me through my veins. And I've never gotten a pony despite asking for one every birthday for the last eight years.

I am waiting for my PICC—you must have central access to go back on the sauce—when a Child Life person comes rapping at my door. You can always tell when it's them because they knock so politely, and because they call out so politely, "May I come in?" I am watching the meditation channel (twenty-four hours a day of string ensembles and trippy footage of waving flowers or shaking leaves, except late, late at night, when between two and three a.m. they show a bright field of stars and play a howling theremin) when she simpers into the room. Her name is Margaret. When I was much younger I thought the Child Life people were great because they brought me toys and took me to the playroom to sniff Play-Doh, but time has sapped their glamour and their fun. Now they are mostly annoying, but I am never cruel to them, because I know that being mean to a Child Life specialist is like kicking a puppy.

"We are collaborating with the children," she says, "in a collaboration of color, and shapes, and words! A collaboration of poetry and prose!" I want to say, people like you wear me out, honey. If you don't go away soon I know my heart will stop beating from weariness, but I let her go on. When she asks if I will make a submission to their hospital literary magazine I say, "Sure!" I won't, though. I am working on my own project, a child's book of sickness and death, and cannot spare thoughts or words for Margaret.

Ava, the IV nurse, comes while Margaret is paraphrasing a submission—the story of a talking IV pump written by a seven-year-old with only half a brain—and bringing herself nearly to tears at the recollection of it.

"And if he can do that with half a brain," I say, "imagine what I could do with my whole one!"

"Sweetie, you can do anything you want," she says, so kind and so encouraging. She offers to stay while I get my PICC but it would be more comforting to have my three-hundred-pound Aunt Mary sit on my face during the procedure than to have this lady at my side, so I say no thank you, and she finally leaves. "I will return for your submission," she says. It sounds much darker than she means it.

The PICC is the smoothest sailing. I get my morphine and a little Versed, and I float through the fields of the meditation channel while Ava threads the catheter into the crook of my arm. I am in the flowers but also riding the tip of the catheter, à la fantastic voyage, as it sneaks up into my heart. I don't like views, but I like looking down through the cataract of blood into the first chamber. The great valve opens. I fall through and land in daisies.

I am still happy-groggy from Ava's sedatives when I think I hear the cat, moaning and suffering, calling out my name. But it's the intern calling me. I wake in a darkening room with a tickle in my arm and look at Ava's handiwork before I look at him. A slim PICC disappears into me just below the antecubital fossa, and my whole lower arm is wrapped in a white mesh glove that looks almost like lace, and would have been cool back in 1983, when I was negative two.

"Sorry to wake you," he says. "Do you have a moment to talk?" He is a tired-looking fellow. At first I think he must be fifty, but when he steps closer to the bed I can see he's just an ill-preserved younger man. He is thin, with strange hair that is not so much wild as just wrong somehow, beady eyes and big ears, and a little beard, the sort you scrawl on a face, along with devil horns, for purposes of denigration.

"Well, I'm late for cotillion," I say. He blinks at me and rubs at his throat.

"I'm Dr. Chandra," he says. I peer at his name tag: Sirius Chandra, MD.

"You don't look like a Chandra," I say, because he is as white as me.

"I'm adopted," he says simply.

"Me too," I say, lying. I sit up and pat the bed next to me, but he leans against the wall and takes out a notepad and pen from his pocket. He proceeds to flip the pen in the air with one hand, launching it off the tips of his fingers and catching it again with finger and thumb, but he never writes down a single thing that I say.

\*     \*     \*

*See the pony? She has dreadful hoof dismay. She gets a terrible pain every time she tries to walk, and yet she is very restless and can hardly stand to sit still. Late at night her hooves whisper to her, asking, "Please, please, just make us into glue," or they strike at her as cruelly as anyone who ever hated her. She hardly knows how she feels about them anymore, her hooves, because they hurt her so much, yet they are still so very pretty—her best feature, everyone says—and biting them very hard is the only thing that makes her feel any better at all. There she is, walking over the hill, on her way to the horse fair, where she'll not get to ride on the Prairie Wind, or play in the Haunted Barn, or eat hot buttered morsels of cowboy from a stand, because wise carnival horses know better than to let in somebody with highly contagious dismay. She stands at the gate watching the fun, and she looks like she is dancing but she is not dancing.*

*Suffer, pony, suffer!*


"What do you know about Dr. Chandra?" I ask Nancy, who is curling my hair at the nursing station. She has tremendous sausage curls and a variety of distinctive eyewear that she doesn't really need. I am wearing her rhinestone-encrusted granny glasses and can see Ella Thims, another short-gut girl, in all her glorious, gruesome detail where she sits in her little red wagon by the clerk's desk. Ella had some trouble finishing up her nether parts, and so was born without an anus, or vagina, or a colon, or most of her small intestine, and her kidneys are shaped like spirals. She's only two, but she is on the sauce, also. I've known her all her life.

"He hasn't rotated here much. He's pretty quiet. And pretty nice. I've never had a problem with him."

"Have you ever thought someone was interesting? Someone you barely knew, just interesting, in a way?"

"Do you like him? You like him, don't you?"

"Just interesting. Like a homeless person with really great shoes. Or a dog without a collar appearing in the middle of a graveyard."

"Sweetie, you're not his type. I know that much about him." She puts her hand out, flexing it swiftly at the wrist. I look blankly at her, so she does it again, and sort of sashays in place for a moment.

"Oh."

"Welcome to San Francisco." She sighs. "Anyway, you can do better than that. He's funny-looking, and he needs to pull his pants up. Somebody should tell him that. His mother should tell him that."

"Write this down under 'chief complaint,'" I had told him. "I am *sick* of love." He'd flipped his pen and looked at the floor. When we came to the social history I said my birth mother was a nun who committed indiscretions with the parish deaf-mute. And I told him about my book—the cat and the bunny and the peacock and the pony, each delightful creature afflicted with a uniquely horrible disease.

"Do you think anyone would buy that?" he asked.

"There's a book that's just about shit," I said. "Why not one that's just about sickness and death? Everybody poops. Everybody suffers. Everybody dies." I even read the pony page for him, and showed him the picture.

"It sounds a little scary," he said, after a long moment of pen-tossing and silence. "And you've drawn the intestines on the outside of the body."

"Clowns are scary," I told him. "And everybody loves them. And hoof dismay isn't pretty. I'm just telling it how it is."

"There," Nancy says. "You are *curled!*" She says it like, you are *healed.* Ella Thims has a mirror on her playset. I look at my hair and press the big purple button underneath the mirror. The playset honks, and Ella claps her hands. "Good luck," Nancy adds, as I scoot off on my IV pole, because I've got a date tonight.

One of the bad things about not absorbing very well and being chronically malnourished your whole life long is that you turn out to be four and a half feet tall when your father is six-four, your mother is five-ten, and your sister is six feet even. But one of the good things about being four and a half feet tall is that you are light enough to ride your own IV pole, and this is a blessing when you are chained to the sauce.

When I was five I could only ride in a straight line, and only at the pokiest speeds. Over the years I mastered the trick of steering with my feet, of turning and stopping, of moderating my speed by dragging a foot, and of spinning in tight spirals or wide loops. I take only short trips during the day, but at night I cruise as far as the research building that's attached to, but not part of, the hospital. At three a.m. even the eggiest heads are at home asleep, and I can fly down the long halls with no one to see me or stop me except the occasional security guard, always too fat and too slow to catch me, even if they understand what I am.

My date is with a CFer named Wayne. He is the best-fed CF kid

I have ever laid eyes on. Usually they are blond, and thin, and pale, and look like they might cough blood on you as soon as smile at you. Wayne is tan, with dark brown hair and blue eyes, and big, with a high wide chest and arms I could not wrap my two hands around. He is pretty hairy for sixteen. I caught a glimpse of his big hairy belly as I scooted past his room. On my fourth pass (I slowed each time and looked back over my shoulder at him) he called me in. We played a karate video game. I kicked his ass, then I showed him the meditation channel.

He is here for a tune-up—every so often the cystic fibrosis kids will get more tired than usual, or cough more, or cough differently, or a routine test of their lung function will be precipitously sucky, and they will come in for two weeks of IV antibiotics and aggressive chest physiotherapy. He is halfway through his course of tobramycin, and bored to death. We go down to the cafeteria and I watch him eat three stale donuts. I have some water and a sip of his tea. I'm never hungry when I'm on the sauce, and I am absorbing so poorly now that if I ate a steak tonight a whole cow would come leaping from my ass in the morning.

I do a little history on him, not certain why I am asking the questions, and less afraid as we talk that he'll catch on that I'm playing intern. He doesn't notice, and fesses up to the particulars without protest or reservation as we review his systems.

"My snot is green," he says. "Green like that." He points to my green toenails. He tells me that he has twin cousins who also have CF, and when they are together at family gatherings he is required to wear a mask so as not to pass on his highly resistant mucoid strain of Pseudomonas. "That's why there's no camp for CF," he says. "Camps for diabetes, for HIV, for kidney failure, for liver failure, but no CF camp. Because we'd infect each other." He wiggles his eyebrows then, perhaps not intentionally. "Is there a camp for people like you?" he asks.

"Probably," I say, though I know that there is, and would have gone this past summer if I had not been banned the year before for organizing a game where we rolled a couple of syndromic kids down a hill into a soccer goal. Almost everybody loved it, and nobody got hurt.

Over Wayne's shoulder I see Dr. Chandra sit down two tables away. At the same time that Wayne lifts his last donut to his mouth, Dr. Chandra lifts a slice of pizza to his, but where Wayne nibbles like an invalid at his food, Dr. Chandra stuffs. He just pushes and pushes the pizza into his mouth. In less than a minute he's finished it. Then he gets up and shuffles past us, sucking on a bottle of water, with bits of cheese in his beard. He doesn't even notice me.

When Wayne has finished his donut I take him upstairs, past the sixth floor to the seventh. "I've never been up here," he says.

"Heme-Onc," I say.

"Are we going to visit someone?"

"I know a place." It's a call room. A couple of years back an intern left his code cards in my room, and there was a list of useful door combinations on one of them. Combinations change slowly in hospitals. "The intern's never here," I tell him as I open the door. "Heme-Onc kids have a lot of problems at night."

Inside are a single bed, a telephone, and a poster of a kitten in distress coupled with an encouraging motto. I think of my dream cat, moaning and crying.

"I've never been in a call room before," Wayne says nervously.

"Relax," I say, pushing him toward the bed. There's barely room for both our IV poles, but after some doing we get arranged on the bed. He lies on his side at the head with his feet propped on the nightstand. I am curled up at the foot. There's dim light from a little lamp on the bed stand, enough to make out the curve of his big lips and to read the sign above the door to the hall: LASCIATE OGNE SPERANZA, VOI CH'INTRATE.

"Can you read that?" he asks.

"It says, 'I believe that children are our future.'"

"That's pretty. It'd be nice if we had some candles." He scoots a little closer toward me. I stretch and yawn. "Are you sleepy?"

"No."

He's quiet for a moment. He looks down at the floor, across the thin, torn bedspread. My IV starts to beep. I reprogram it. "Air in the line," I say.

"Oh." I have shifted a little closer to him in the bed while fixing the IVs. "Do you want to do something?" he asks, staring into his lap.

"Maybe," I say. I walk my hand around the bed, like a five-legged spider, in a circle, over my own arm, across my thighs, up my belly, up to the top of my head to leap off back onto the blanket. He watches, smiling less and less as it walks up the bed, up his leg, and down his pants.

\*   \*   \*

*See the zebra? She has atrocious pancreas oh! Her belly hurts her terribly—sometimes it's like frogs are crawling in her belly, and sometimes it's like snakes are biting her inside just below her belly button, and sometimes it's like centipedes dancing with cleats on every one of their little feet, and sometimes it's a pain she can't even describe, even though all she can do, on those days, is sit around and try to think of ways to describe the pain. She must rub her belly on very particular sorts of trees to make it feel better, though it never feels very much better. Big round scabs are growing on her tongue, and every time she sneezes another big piece of her mane falls out. Her stripes have begun to go all the wrong way, and sometimes her own poop follows her, crawling on the ground or floating in the air, and calls her cruel names.*

*Suffer, zebra, suffer!*


Asleep in my own bed, I'm dreaming of the cat when I hear the team; the cat's moan frays and splits, and the tones unravel from each other and become their voices. I am fully awake with my eyes closed. He lifts a mangy paw, saying goodbye.

"Dr. Chandra," says a voice. I know it must belong to Dr. Fell, the GI attending. "Tell me the three classic findings on X-ray in necrotizing enterocolitis." They are rounding outside my room, six or seven of them, the whole GI team: Dr. Fell and my intern and the fellow and the nurse practitioners and the poor little med students. Soon they'll all come in and want to poke on my belly. Dr. Fell will talk for five minutes about shit: mine, and other people's, and sometimes just the idea of shit, a Platonic ideal not extant on this earth. I know he dreams of gorgeous, perfect shit the way I dream of the cat.

Chandra speaks. He answers *free peritoneal air* and *pneumatosis* in a snap but then he is silent. I can see him perfectly with my eyes still closed: his hair all ahoo; his beady eyes staring intently at his shoes; his stethoscope twisted crooked around his neck, crushing his collar. His feet turn in, so his toes are almost touching. Upstairs with Wayne I thought of him.

Dr. Fell, too supreme a fussbudget to settle for two out of three, begins to castigate him: a doctor at your level of training should know these things; children's lives are in your two hands; you couldn't diagnose your way out of a wet paper bag; your ignorance is deadly, your ignorance can *kill.* I get out of bed, propelled by rage, angry at haughty Dr. Fell and at hapless Dr. Chandra, and angry at myself for being this angry. Clutching my IV pole like a staff I kick open the door and scream, scaring every one of them: "Portal fucking air! Portal fucking air!" They are all silent, and some of them are white-faced. I am panting, hanging now on my IV pole. I look over at Dr. Chandra. He is not panting, but his mouth has fallen open. Our eyes meet for three eternal seconds and then he looks away.

Later I take Ella Thims down to the playroom. The going is slow, because her sauce is running and my sauce is running, so it takes some coordination to push my pole and pull her wagon while keeping her own pole, which trails behind her wagon like a dinghy, from drifting too far left or right. She lies on her back with her legs in the air, grabbing and releasing her feet, and turning her head to say hello to everyone she sees. In the hall we pass nurses and med students and visitors and every species of doctor, attendings and fellows and residents and interns, but not my intern. Everyone smiles and waves at Ella, or stoops or squats to pet her or smile closer to her face. They nod at me, and don't look at all at my face. I look back at her, knowing her fate. "Enjoy it while you have it, honey," I say to her, because I know how quickly one exhausts one's cuteness in a place like this. Our cuteness has to work very hard here. It must extend itself to cover horrors—ostomies and scars and flipper-hands and harelips and agenesis of the eyeballs—and it rises to every miserable occasion of the sick body. Ella's strange puffy face is covered, her yellow eyes are covered, her bald spot is covered, her extra fingers are covered, her ostomies are covered, and the bitter, nose-tickling odor of urine that rises from her always is covered by the tremendous faculty of cuteness generated from some organ deep within her. Watching faces I can see how it's working for her, and how it's stopped working for me. Your organ fails, at some point—it fails for everybody, but for people like us it fails faster, having more to cover than just the natural ugliness of body and soul. One day you are more repulsive than attractive, and the good will of strangers is lost forever.

It's a small loss. Still, I miss it sometimes, like now, walking down the hall and remembering riding down this same hall ten years ago on my Big Wheel. Strangers would stop me for speeding and cite me with a hug. I can remember their faces, earnest and open and unassuming, and I wonder now if I ever met someone like that where I could go with them, after such a blank beginning. Something in the way that Dr. Chandra looks at me has that. And the Child Life people look at you that way, too. But they have all been trained in graduate school not to notice the extra head, or the smell, or the missing nose, or to love these things, professionally.

In the playroom I turn Ella over to Margaret and go sit on the floor in a patch of sun near the door to the deck. The morning activity, for those of us old enough or coordinated enough to manage it, is the weaving of gods' eyes. At home I have a trunkful of gods' eyes and potholders and terra-cotta sculptures the size of your hand, such a collection of crafts that you might think I'd spent my whole life in camp. I wind and unwind the yarn, making and then unmaking, because I don't want to add anything new to the collection. I watch Ella playing at a water trough, dipping a little red bucket and pouring it over the paddles of a waterwheel. It's a new toy. There are always new toys, every time I come, and the room is kept pretty and inviting, repainted and recarpeted in less time than some people wait to get a haircut, because some new wealthy person has taken an interest in it. The whole floor is like that, except where there are pockets of plain beige hospital nastiness here and there, places that have escaped the attentions of the rich. The nicest rooms are those that once were occupied by a privileged child with a fatal syndrome.

I pass almost a whole hour like this. Boredom can be a problem for anybody here, but I am never bored watching my gaunt yellow peers splashing in water or stacking blocks or singing along with Miss Margaret. Two wholesome Down's syndrome twins—Dolores and Delilah Cutty, who both have leukemia and are often in for chemo at the same time I am in for the sauce—are having a somersault race across the carpet. A boy named Arthur who has Crouzon's syndrome—the bones of his skull have fused together too early—is playing Chutes and Ladders with a girl afflicted with Panda syndrome. Every time he gets to make a move, he cackles wildly. It makes his eyes bulge out of his head. Sometimes they pop out—then you're supposed to catch them with a piece of sterile gauze and push them back in.

Margaret comes over, after three or four glances in my direction, noticing that my hands have been idle. Child Life specialists abhor idle hands, though there was one here a few years ago, named Eldora, who encouraged meditation and tried to teach us Yoga poses. She did not last long. Margaret crouches down—they are great crouchers, having learned that children like to be addressed at eye level—and, seeing my gods' eye half-finished and my yarn tangled and trailing, asks if I have any questions about the process.

In fact I do. How do your guts turn against you, and your insides become your enemy? How can Arthur have such a big head and not be a super-genius? How can he laugh so loud when tomorrow he'll go back to surgery again to have his face artfully broken by the clever hands of well-intentioned sadists? How can someone so unattractive, so unavailable, so shlumpy, so low-panted, so pitiable, keep rising up, a giant in my thoughts? All these questions and others run through my head, so it takes me a while to answer, but she is patient. Finally a question comes that seems safe to ask. "How do you make someone not gay?"

*See the peacock? He has crispy lung surprise. He has got an aching in his chest, and every time he tries to say something nice to someone, he only coughs. His breath stinks so much it makes everyone run away, and he tries to run away from it himself, but of course no matter where he goes, he can still smell it. Sometimes he holds his breath, just to escape it, until he passes out, but he always wakes up, even when he would rather not, and there it is, like rotten chicken, or old, old crab, or hippopotamus butt. He only feels ashamed now when he spreads out his feathers, and the only thing that gives him any relief is licking a moving tire—a very difficult thing to do.*

*Suffer, peacock, suffer!*

It's not safe to confide in people here. Even when they aren't prying—and they do pry—it's better to be silent or to lie than to confide. They'll ask when you had your first period, or your first sex, if you are happy at home, what drugs you've done, if you wish you were thinner and prettier, or that your hair was shiny. And you may tell them about your terrible cramps, or your distressing habit of having compulsive sex with homeless men and women in Golden Gate Park, or how you can't help but sniff a little bleach every morning when you wake up, or complain that you are fat and your hair always looks as if it had just been rinsed with drool. And they'll say, I'll help you with that bleach habit that has debilitated you separately but equally from your physical illness, that dreadful habit that's keeping you from becoming more perfectly who you are. Or they may offer to teach you how the homeless are to be shunned and not fellated, or promise to wash your hair with the very shampoo of the gods. But they come and go, these interns and residents and attendings, nurses and Child Life specialists and social workers and itinerant tamale-ladies—only you and the hospital and the illness are constant. The interns change every month, and if you gave yourself to each of them they'd use you up as surely as an entire high-school football team would use up their dreamiest cheerleading slut, and you'd be left like her, compelled by your history to lie down under the next moron to come along.

Accidental confidences, or accidentally fabricated secrets, are no safer. Margaret misunderstands; she thinks I am fishing for validation. She is a professional validator, with skills honed by a thousand hours of role playing—she has been both the querulous young lesbian and the supportive adult. "But there's no reason to change," she tells me. "You don't have to be ashamed of who you are."

This is a lesson I learned long ago, from my mother, who really was a lesbian, after she was a nun but before she was a wife. "I did not give it up because it was inferior to anything," she told me seriously, the same morning she found me in the arms of Shelley Woo, my neighbor and one of the few girls I was ever able to lure into a sleepover. We had not, like my mother assumed, spent the night practicing tender, heated frottage. We were hugging as innocently as two stuffed animals. "But it's all *right*," she kept saying against my protests. So I know not to argue with Margaret's assumption, either.

It makes me pensive, having become a perceived lesbian. I wander the ward thinking, "Hello, nurse!" at every one of them I see. I sit at the station, watching them come and go, spinning the big lazy Susan of misfortune that holds all the charts. I can imagine sliding my hands under their stylish scrubs—not toothpaste-green like Dr. Chandra's scrubs, but hot pink or canary yellow or deep-sea blue, printed with daisies or sun faces or clouds or even embroidered with dancing hula girls—and pressing my fingers in the hollows of their ribs. I can imagine taking off Nancy's rhinestone granny-glasses with my teeth, or biting so gently on the ridge of her collarbone. The charge nurse—a woman from the Philippines named Jory—sees me opening and closing my mouth silently, and asks if there is something wrong with my jaw. I shake my head. There's nothing wrong. It's only that I am trying to open wide enough for an imaginary mouthful of her soft brown boob.

If it's this easy for me to do, to imagine the new thing, then is he somewhere wondering what it would feel like to press a cheek against my scarred belly, or to gather my hair in his fists? When I was little my pediatrician, Dr. Sawyer, used to look in my pants every year and say, "Just checking to make sure everything is *normal*." I imagine an exam, and imagine him imagining it with me. He listens with his ear on my chest and back, and when it is time to look in my pants he stares long and long and says, "It's not just *normal*, it's *extraordinary!*"

A glowing radiance has just burst from between my legs, and is bathing him in converting rays of glory, when he comes hurrying out of the doctor's room across from the station. He drops his clipboard and apologizes to no one in particular, and glances at me as he straightens up. I want him to smile and look away, to duck his head in an aw-shucks gesture, but he just nods stiffly, then walks away. I watch him pass around the corner, then give the lazy Susan a hard spin. If my own chart comes to rest before my eyes, it will mean that he loves me.

*See the monkey? He has chronic kidney doom. His kidneys are always yearning toward things—other monkeys and trees and people and different varieties of fruit. He feels them stirring in him and pressing against his flank whenever he gets near to something that he likes. When he tells a girl monkey or a boy monkey that his kidneys want to hug them, they slap him or punch him or kick him in the eye. At night his kidneys ache wildly. He is always swollen and moist-looking. He smells like a toilet because he can only pee when he doesn't want to, and every night he asks himself, how many pairs of crisp white slacks can one monkey ruin?*

*Suffer, monkey, suffer!*

Every fourth night he is on call. He stays in the hospital from six in the morning until six the following evening, awake all night on account of various intern-sized crises. I see him walking in and out of rooms, or peering at the two-foot-long flow sheets that lean on giant clipboards on the walls by every door, or looking solemnly at the nurses as they castigate him for slights against their patients or their honor—an unsigned order, an incorrectly dosed medication, the improper washing of his hands. I catch him in the corridor in what I think is a posture of despair, sunk down outside Wayne's door with his face in his knees, and I think that he has heard about me and Wayne, and it's broken his heart. But I have already dismissed Wayne days ago. We were like two IV poles passing in the night, I told him.

Dr. Chandra is sleeping, not despairing, not snoring but breathing loud through his mouth. I step a little closer to him, close enough to smell him—coffee and hair gel and something like pickles. A flow sheet lies discarded beside him, so from where I stand I can see how much Wayne has peed in the last twelve hours. I stoop next to him and consider sitting down and falling asleep myself, because I know it would constitute a sort of intimacy to mimic his posture and let my shoulder touch his shoulder, to close my eyes and maybe share a dream with him. But before I can sit Nancy comes creeping down the hall in her socks, a barf basin half full of warm water in her hands. A phalanx of nurses appears in the hall behind her, each of them holding a finger to her lips as Nancy kneels next to Dr. Chandra, puts the bucket on the floor, and takes his hand away from his leg so gently I think she is going to kiss it before she puts it in the water. I just stand there, afraid that he'll wake up as I'm walking away, and think I'm responsible for the joke. Nancy and the nurses all disappear around the corner to the station, so it's just me and him again in the hall. I drum my fingers against my head, trying to think of a way to get us both out of this, and realize it's just a step or two to the dietary cart. I take a straw and kneel down next to him. It's a lot of volume, and I imagine, as I drink, that it's flavored by his hand. When I throw it up later it seems like the best barf I've ever done, because it is for him, and as Nancy holds my hair back for me and asks me what possessed me to drink so much water at once I think at him, It was for you, baby, and feel both pathetic and exalted.

I follow him around for a couple call nights, not saving him again from any more mean-spirited jokes, but catching him scratching or picking when he thinks no one is looking, and wanting, like a fool, to be the hand that scratches or the finger that picks, because it would be so interesting and gratifying to touch him like that, or touch him in any way, and I wonder and wonder what I'm doing as I creep around with increasingly practiced nonchalance, looking bored while I sit across from him, listening to him cajole the radiologist on the phone at one in the morning, when I could be sleeping, or riding my pole, when he is strange-looking, and cannot like me, and talks funny, and is rumored to be an intern of small brains. But I see him stand in the hall for five minutes staring at an abandoned tricycle, and he puts his palm against a window and bows his head at the blinking lights on the bridge in a way that makes me want very much to know what he is thinking, and I see him, from a hiding place behind a bin full of dirty sheets, hopping up and down in a hall he thinks is empty save for him, and I am sure he is trying to fly away.

Hiding on his fourth call night in the dirty utility room while he putters with a flow sheet at the door to the room across the hall, I realize that it could be easier than this, and so when he's moved on, I go back to my room and watch the meditation channel for a little while, then practice a few moans, sounding at first too distressed, then not distressed enough, then finally getting it just right before I push the button for the nurse. Nancy is off tonight. It's Jory who comes, and finds me moaning and clutching at my belly. I get Tylenol and a touch of morphine, but am careful to moan only a little less, so Jory calls Dr. Chandra to come evaluate me.

It's romantic, in its way. The lights are low, and he puts his warm, freshly washed hands on my belly to push in every quadrant, a round of light palpation, a round of deep. He speaks very softly, asking me if it hurts more here, or here, or here. "I'm going to press in on your stomach and hold my hand there for a second, and I want you to tell me if it makes it feel better or worse when I let go." He listens to my belly, then takes me by the ankle, extending and flexing my hip.

"I don't know," I say, when he asks me if that made the pain better or worse. "Do it again."


*See the bunny? She has high colonic ruin, a very fancy disease. Only bunnies from the very best families get it, but when she cries bloody tears and the terrible spiders come crawling out of her bottom, she would rather be poor, and not even her fancy robot bed can comfort her, or even distract her. When her electric pillow feeds her dreams of happy bunnies playing in the snow, she only feels jealous and sad, and she bites her tongue while she sleeps, and bleeds all night while the bed dabs at her lips with cotton balls on long steel fingers. In the morning a servant drives her to the Potty Club, where she sits with other wealthy bunny girls on a row of crystal toilets. They are supposed to be her friends, but she doesn't like them at all.*

*Suffer, bunny, suffer!*


When he visits I straighten up, carefully hiding the books that Margaret brought me, biographies of Sappho and Billie Jean King and HD. She entered quietly into my room, closed the door, and drew the blinds before producing them from out of her pants and repeating that my secret was safe with her, though there was no need for it to be secret, and nothing to be ashamed of, and she would support me as fully in proclaiming my homosexuality as she did in the hiding of it. She has already conceived of a banner to put over my bed, a rainbow hung with stars, on the day that I put away all shame and dark feelings. I hide the books because I know all would really be lost if he saw them and assumed the assumption. I do not want to be just his young lesbian friend. I lay out refreshments, spare cookies and juices and puddings from the meal trays that come, though I get all the food I can stand from the sauce.

I don't have many dates, on the outside. Rumors of my scarred belly or my gastrostomy tube drive most boys away before anything can develop, and the only boys that pay persistent attention to me are the creepy ones looking for a freak. I have better luck in here, with boys like Wayne, but those dates are still outside the usual progressions, the talking more and more until you are convinced they actually know you, and the touching more and more until you are pregnant and wondering if this guy ever even liked you. There is nothing normal about my midnight trysts with Dr. Chandra, but there's an order about them, and a progression. I summon him and he puts his hands on me, and he orders an intervention, and he comes back to see if it worked or didn't. For three nights he stands there, watching me for a few moments, leaning on one foot and then the other, before he asks me if I need anything else. All the things I need flash through my mind, but I say no, and he leaves, promising to come back and check on me later, but never doing it. Then, on the fourth night, he does his little dance and asks, "What do you want to do when you grow up? I mean, when you're bigger. When you're out of school, and all that."

"Medicine," I say. "Pediatrics. What else?"

"Aren't you sick of it?" he asks. He is backing toward the door, but I have this feeling like he's stepping closer to the bed.

"Maybe. But I have to do it."

"You could do anything you want," he says, not sounding like he means it.

"What else could Tarzan become, except lord of the jungle?"

"He could have been a dancer, if he wanted. Or an ice-cream man. Whatever he wanted."

"Did you ever want to do anything else, besides this?"

"Never. Not ever."

"How about now?"

"Oh," he says. "Oh, no. I don't think so. No, I don't think so." He startles when his pager vibrates. He looks down at it. "I've got to go. Just tell Jory if the pain comes back again."

"Come over here for a second," I say. "I've got to tell you something."

"Later," he says.

"No, now. It'll just take a second." I expect him to leave, but he walks over and stands near the bed.

"What?"

"Would you like some juice?" I ask him, though what I really meant to do was to accuse him, ever so sweetly, of being the same as me, of knowing the same indescribable thing about this place and about the world. "Or a cookie?"

"No thanks," he says. As he passes through the door I call out for him to wait, and to come back. "What?" he says again, and I think I am just about to know how to say it when the code bell begins to chime. It sounds like an ice-cream truck, but it means someone on the floor is trying to die. He jumps in the air like he's been goosed, then takes a step one way in the hall, stops, starts the other way, then goes back, so it looks like he's trying to decide whether to run toward the emergency or away from it.

I get up and follow him down the hall, just in time to see him run into Ella Thims's room. From the back of the crowd at the door I can see him standing at the head of the bed, looking depressed and indecisive, a bag mask held up in his hand. He asks someone to page the senior resident, then puts the mask over Ella's face. She's bleeding from her nose and mouth, and from her ostomy sites. The blood shoots around inside the mask when he squeezes the bag, and he can't seem to get a tight seal over Ella's chin. The mask keeps slipping while the nurses ask him what he wants to do.

"Well," he says. "Um. How about some oxygen?" Nancy finishes getting Ella hooked up to the monitor and points out that she's in a bad rhythm. "Let's get her some fluid," he says. Nancy asks if he wouldn't like to shock her, instead. "Well," he says. "Maybe!" Then I get pushed aside by the PICU team, called from the other side of the hospital by the chiming of the ice-cream bell. The attending asks Dr. Chandra what's going on, and he turns even redder, and says something I can't hear, because I am being pushed farther and farther from the door as more people squeeze past me to cluster around the bed, ring after ring of saviors and spectators. Pushed back to the nursing station, I am standing in front of Jory, who is sitting by the telephone reading a magazine.

"Hey, honey," she says, not looking at me. "Are you doing okay?"


*See the cat? He has died. Feline leukemic indecisiveness is always terminal. Now he just lies there. You can pick him up. Go ahead. Bring him home and put him under your pillow and pray to your parents or your stuffed plush Jesus to bring him back, and say to him, "Come back, come back." He will be smellier in the morning, but no more alive. Maybe he is in a better place, maybe his illness could not follow him where he went, or maybe everything is the same, the same pain in a different place. Maybe there is nothing all, where he is. I don't know, and neither do you.*

*Goodbye, cat, goodbye!*


Ella Thims died in the PICU, killed, it was discovered, by too much potassium in her sauce. It put her heart in that bad rhythm they couldn't get her out of, though they worked over her till dawn. She'd been in it for at least a while before she was discovered, so it was already too late when they put her on the bypass machine. It made her dead alive—her blood was moving in her, but by midmorning of the next day she was rotting inside. Dr. Chandra, it was determined, was the chief architect of the fuck-up, assisted by a newly graduated nurse who meticulously verified the poisonous contents of the solution and delivered them without protest. Was there any deadlier combination, people asked each other all morning, than an idiot intern and a clueless nurse?

I spend the morning on my IV pole, riding the big circle around the ward. It's strange, to be out here in the daylight, and in the busy morning crowd—less busy today, and a little hushed because of the death. I go slower than usual, riding like my grandma would, stepping and pushing leisurely with my left foot, and stopping often to let a team go by. They pass like a family of ducks, the attending followed by the fellow, resident, and students, all in a row, with the lollygagging nutritionist bringing up the rear. Pulmonary, Renal, Neurosurgery, even the Hypoglycemia team are about in the halls, but I don't see the GI team anywhere.

The rest of the night I lay awake in bed, waiting for them to come round on me. I could see it already: everybody getting a turn to kick Dr. Chandra outside my door, or Dr. Fell standing casually with his foot on Dr. Chandra's neck as the team discussed my latest ins and outs. Or maybe he wouldn't even be there. Maybe they send you home early when you kill somebody. Or maybe he would just run and hide somewhere. Not sleeping, I still dreamed about him, huddled in a linen closet, sucking on the corner of a blanket, or sprawled on the bathroom floor, knocking his head softly against the toilet, or kneeling naked in the medication room, shooting up with Benadryl and morphine. I went to him in every place, and put my hands on him with great tenderness, never saying a thing, just nodding at him, like I knew how horrible everything was. A couple rumors float around in the late morning—he's jumped from the bridge; he's thrown himself under a trolley; Ella's parents, finally come to visit, have killed him; he's retired back home to Virginia in disgrace. I add and subtract details—he took off his clothes and folded them neatly on the sidewalk before he jumped; the trolley was full of German choir boys; Ella's father choked while her mother stabbed; his feet hang over the end of his childhood bed.

I don't stop even to get my meds—Nancy trots beside me and pushes them on the fly. Just after that, around one o'clock, I understand that I am following after something, and that I had better speed up if I am going to catch it. It seems to me, who should really know better, that all the late, new sadness of the past twenty-four hours ought to count for something, ought to do something, ought to change something, inside of me or out-side in the world. But I don't know what it is that might change, and I expect that nothing will change—children have died here before, and hap-less idiots have come and gone, and always the next day the sick still come to languish and be poked, and they will lie in bed hoping, not for healing, a thing which the wise have all long given up on, but for something to make them feel better, just for a little while, and sometimes they get this thing, and often they don't. I think of my animals and hear them all, not just the cat but the whole bloated menagerie, crying and crying, *Make it stop.*

Faster and faster and faster—not even a grieving short-gut girl can be forgiven for speed like this. People are thinking, *She loved that little girl* but I am thinking, *I will never see him again.* Still, I almost forget I am chasing something and not just flying along for the exhilaration it brings. Nurses and students and even the proudest attendings try to leap out of the way but only arrange themselves into a slalom course. It's my skill, not theirs, that keeps them from being struck. Nancy tries to stand in my way, to stop me, but she wimps away to the side long before I get anywhere near her. Doctors and visiting parents and a few other kids, and finally a couple security guards, one almost fat enough to block the entire hall, try to arrest me, but they all fail, and I can hardly even hear what they are shout-ing. I am concentrating on the window. It's off the course of the circle, at the end of a hundred-foot hall that runs past the playroom and the PICU. It's a portrait frame of the near tower of the bridge, which looks very orange today against the bright blue sky. It is part of the answer when I understand that I am running the circle to rev up for a run down to the window that right now seems like the only way out of this place. The fat guard and Nancy and a parent have made themselves into a roadblock just beyond the turn into the hall. They are stretched like a Red-Rover line from one wall to the other, and two of them close their eyes, but don't break, as I come near them. I make the fastest turn of my life and head away down the hall.

It's Miss Margaret who stops me. She steps out of the playroom with a crate of blocks in her arms, sees me, looks down the hall toward the window, and shrieks "Motherfucker!" I withstand the uncharacteristic obscenity, though it makes me stumble, but the blocks she casts in my path form an obstacle I cannot pass. There are twenty of them or more. As I try to avoid them I am reading the letters, thinking they'll spell out the name of the thing I am chasing, but I am too slow to read any of them except the far-thest one, an R, and the red Q that catches under my wheel. I fall off the pole as it goes flying forward, skidding toward the window after I come to a stop on my belly outside the PICU, my central line coming out in a pull as swift and clean as a tooth pulled out with a string and a door. The end of the catheter sails in an arc through the air, scattering drops of blood against the ceiling, and I think how neat it would look if my heart had come out, still attached to the tip, and what a distinct, once-in-a-lifetime noise it would have made when it hit the floor.

# HOT PINK

*by* ADAM LEVIN

**M**Y FRIEND JOE COJOTEJK and myself were on our way to Nancy and Tina Christamesta's, to see if they could drive to Sensei Mike's housewarming barbecue in Glen Ellyn. Cojo's cousin Niles was supposed to take us, but last-minute he got in his head it was better to drink and use fireworks with his girlfriend. He called to back out while we were in the basement with the heavy bag. We'd just finished drawing targets on the canvas with marker. I wanted small red bull's-eyes, but Joe thought it would be better to represent the targets like the things they stood for. He'd covered a shift for me at the lot that week, so I let him have his way; a triangle for a nose, a circle for an Adam's apple, a space for the solar plexus, and for the sack a saggy-looking shape. The bag didn't hang low enough to have realistic knees.

When my mom yelled down the stairs that Niles was on the phone, I was deep into roundhouse kicks—I wanted to land one on each target, consecutively, without pausing to look at them, or breathing, and I was getting there: I was up to three out of four (I kept missing the circle)—so I told Cojo take the call, and it was a mistake. Cojo won't argue with his family. Everyone else, but not them. He gets guilty with them. When he came back down the basement and told me Niles was ditching out, I bolted upstairs to call him myself, but all I got was his machine with the dumbass message:

"You've reached Niles Cojotejk, NC-17. Do you love me? Are you a very sexy lady? Speak post-beep, baby."

I hung up.

My mom coughed.

I said, "Eat a vitamin." I took two zincs from the jar on the tray and lobbed one to her. She caught it in her lap by pushing her legs together. It was the opposite of what a woman does, according to the old lady in *Huckleberry Finn* who throws the apple in Huck's lap to blow his fake-out. Maybe it was Tom Sawyer and a pear, or a matchbox. Either way, he was cross-dressed.

The other zinc I swallowed myself. For immunity. The pill trailed grit down my throat and I put my tongue under the faucet.

"What happened to cups?" my mom said. That's how she accuses people. With questions.

I shut the tap. I said, "Did something happen to cups?"

"Baloney," she said.

Then I got an inspiration. I asked her, "Can you make your voice low and slutty?"

"Like this?" she said, in a low, slutty voice.

"Will you leave a message on Niles's machine?"

"No," she said.

"Then I'm going away forever," I said. "Picture all you got left is bingo and that fat-ass Doberman chewing dead things in the gangway. Plus I'll give you a dollar if you do it." I said, "You can smoke two cigarettes on that dollar. Or else I'll murder you, violently." I picked up the nearest thing. It was a mortar or a pestle. It was the empty part. I waved it in the air at her. "I'll murder you with *this*."

"Gimme a kiss!" she sang. That's how she is. A pushover. All she wants is to share a performance. To riff with you. It's one kind of person. Makes noise when there's noise, and the more noise the better. The other kind's a soloist, who only starts up when it's quiet, then holds his turn like it'll never come again. Cojo's that kind. I don't know who's better to have around. Some noise gets wrecked by quiet and some quiet gets wrecked by noise. So sometimes you want a riffer and other times a soloist and I can't decide which kind I am.

I dialed the number. For the message, I had my mother say, "You're rated G for Gypsy, baby." Niles is very sensitive about getting called a Gypsy. I don't know what inspired me with the idea to have my mom say it to him in a low, slutty voice, but then I got a clearer idea.

I dialed the number again and got her to say the same thing in her regular voice. Then I called four more times, myself, and I said it in four different voices: I did a G, a homo, a Paki, and a Dago. I'm good at those. I thought I was done, but I wasn't. I did it once more in my own voice, so Niles would know it was me telling people he's a Gypsy.

My mom said, "You're a real goof-off, Jack."

Cojo came upstairs, panting. "Tina and Nancy," he said.

I thought: Nancy, if only.

Cojo said, "They might have a car."

It was a good idea. I called. They didn't know for sure about a car, but said come over and drink. I kissed my mom's head and she gave me money to buy her a carton of Ultralights. I dropped the money in her lap and pulled a jersey over my T. Cojo said it was too hot out for both. It was too hot out for naked, though, so it wouldn't matter anyway. Except then I noticed Joe was also wearing a jersey and a T, and I didn't want to look like a couple who planned it, which Joe didn't want either, which is what he meant by too hot out, so I dumped the jersey for a Mexican wedding shirt and we split.

Five minutes later, Cojo and myself were feared, and soon after that, I learned something new about talking and how to use it to intimidate people.


How I knew we were feared was a full-grown man walking the other way on the other side of the street looked at us and nodded. It's a small thing to do but it meant a lot. My lungs tickled at the sight of it. I got this tightness down the center of my body, like during a core-strength workout. Or trying to first-kiss someone and you can't remember where to put your hands. Even thinking about it, I get this feeling. This stranger, nodding at you from all the way across the street.

It was late in the afternoon by then, and tropical hot, but overcast with small black clouds. And the wind—it was flapping the branches. Wing-shaped seed-pods rattled over the pavement and the clouds blew across the sun so fast the sky was blinking. It opened my nose up. The street got narrow compared to me. The cars looked like Hot Wheels. And in my head, my first thing was that I felt sorry for this guy who nods. It's like a salute, this kind of nod.

But then my second thing is: you better salute me, Clyde. And I get this picture of holding his ears while I slowly push his face into his brains with my forehead. I got massive neck muscles. I got this grill like a chimney and an ugly thing inside me to match it. I feel sorry for a person, it makes me want to hurt him. Cojo's the same way as me, but crueler-looking. It's mostly because of the way we're built. We're each around a buck-seventy, but I barrel in the trunk. Joe's lean and even, like a long Bruce Lee. He comes to all kinds of points. And plus his eyes. They're a pair of slits in shadow. I got comic-strip eyes, a couple black dimes. My eyes should be looking in opposite directions.

I ran my hands back over my skull. It's a ritual from grade school, when we used to do battle royales at the pool with our friends. We got it from a cartoon I can't remember, or a video game. You do a special gesture to flip your switch; for me it's I run my hands back over my skull and, when I get to the bottom, I tap my thumb knuckles, once, on the highest-up button of my spine. You flip your switch and you've got a code name. We were supposed to keep our code names secret, so no one could deplete their power by speaking them, but me and Cojo told each other. Cojo's special gesture was wiping his mouth crosswise, from his elbow to the backs of his fingertips. Almost all the other special gestures had saliva in them. This one kid Winthrop would spit in his palms and fling it with karate chops. Voitek Moitek chewed grape gum, and he'd hock a sticky puddle in his elbow crooks, then flex and relax till the spit strung out between his forearms and biceps. Nick Rataczeck licked the middle of his shirt and moaned like a deaf person. I can't remember the gestures of the rest of the battle-royale guys. By high school, we stopped socializing with those guys and after we dropped out we hardly ever saw them. I don't know if they told each other their code names. They didn't tell me.

Cojo's was War, though. Mine was Smith. It's embarrassing.

I coughed the tickle from my lungs and Joe stopped walking, performed his gesture, and was War.

He said to the guy, "What," and the guy shuddered a little. The guy was swinging a net-sack filled with grapefruits and I hated how it bounced against his knee. I hated he had them. It made everything complicated. My thoughts were too far in the background to figure out why. Something about peeling them or slicing them in halves or eighths and what someone else might prefer to do. I always liked mine in halves. A little sugar. And that jagged spoon. It's so specific.

The guy kept moving forward, like he didn't know Joe was talking to him, but he was walking slower than before. It was just like the nod. The slowness meant the exact opposite of what it looked like it meant. I'm scared of something? I don't look at it. I think: If I don't see it, it won't see me. Like how a little kid thinks. You smack its head while it's hiding in a peek-a-boo and now it believes in God, not your hand. But everyone thinks like that sometimes. I'm scared my mom's gonna die from smoking, the way her lungs whistle when she breathes fast, but if I don't think about it, I think, cancer won't think about her. It's stupid. I know this. Still: me, everyone. Joe says "What," to a guy who's scared of him, the guy pretends Joe's not talking to him. The guy pretends so hard he slows down when what he wants is to get as far the hell away from us and as fast as he can.

Joe says, "I said, 'What.'"

"I'm sorry," the guy says.

"Sorry for what?" Joe says, and now he's crossing the street and I'm following him.

I say, "Easy, Cojo," and this is when I learn something new about how to intimidate people. Because even though I say "Easy, Cojo," I'm not telling Cojo to take it easy. I'm not even talking to Cojo. I'm talking to the guy. When I say "Easy, Cojo," I'm telling the guy he's right to be scared of my friend. And I'm also telling him that I got influence with my friend, and that means the guy should be scared of me, too. What's peculiar is when I open my mouth to say "Easy, Cojo," I *think* I'm about to talk to Cojo, and then it turns out I'm not. And so I have to wonder how many times I've done things like that without noticing. Like when I told my mom I'd kill her and waved the empty thing at her, I wasn't really threatening her, it was more like I was saying, "Look, I'll say a stupid thing that makes me look stupid if you'll help me out." But that was different, too, from this, because my mom knew what I meant when I said I'd kill her, but this guy here doesn't know what I mean when I say "Easy, Cojo." He gets even more scared of Joe and me, but he gets that way because he thinks I really *am* talking to Joe.

I say it again. I say, "Easy, Cojo."

And Cojo says, "Easy what?"

And now the guy's stopped walking. He's standing there. "I'm sorry," he says.

"'Cause why?" Cojo says. "Why're you sorry? Are you sorry you nodded at me like I was your son? Like I was your boy to nod at like that? I don't know you."

"I'm sorry," the guy says. The guy's smiling like the situation is very lighthearted, but it's like yawning after tapping gloves on your way back to the corner. A lie you tell yourself. And I'm thinking there's nothing that's itself. I'm thinking everything is like something else that's like other something elses and it's all because I said "Easy, Cojo" and didn't mean it, or because this guy nodded.

I think like this too long, I get a headache and pissed off.

I put my arm around Cojo. I say, "Easy, Cojo."

"Fuck easy," Cojo says to me. And when Cojo says that, it's like the same thing as when I said "Easy, Cojo." I know Cojo isn't really saying "Fuck easy" to me. He wouldn't say that to me. He's saying "Fear us" to the guy. But I don't know if Cojo knows that that's what he's doing with "Fuck easy." That's the problem with everything.

"Give us your fruit," I tell the guy.

"My—"

"What did you say?" Joe says.

"Easy, Cojo," I tell him.

Then the guy hands his grapefruits to me.

I say to him, "Yawn."

He can't. Cojo yawns, though. And then I do.

Then I tell the guy to get out of my sight and he does it because he's been intimidated.


Nancy Christamesta is no whore at all. And I'm no Jesus, but still I want to wash her feet. Nancy's so beautiful, my mind doesn't think about fucking her unless I'm drunk, and even then it's just an idea: I don't run the movie through my head. Usually, I imagine her saying, "Yes," in my ear. That's all it takes. Maybe we're on a rooftop, or the sixty-ninth floor of the Hancock with the restaurant that spins, but the "Yes" part is what counts. It's a little hammy. I've known her since grade school, but I've only had it for her since she was fourteen. It happened suddenly, and that's hammy too. I was eighteen, and it started at the beach—sunny day and ice cream and everything. Our families went to swim at Oak Street on a church outing and I saw her sneak away to smoke a cigarette in the tunnel under the Drive. There's hypes and winos who live in there, so I followed her, but didn't let her know. I waited at the mouth, where I could hear if anything happened, and when she came back through, she was hugging herself around the middle for warmth. A couple steps out of the tunnel, her left shoulder strap fell down and, when she moved to put it back, a bone-chill shot her posture straight and a sound came from her throat that sounded like "Hi." I didn't know if it was "Hi" or just a pretty noise her throat made after a bone-chill. I didn't think it was "Hi," because I was behind her and I didn't think she'd seen me. I wanted it to be "Hi," though. I stood there a minute after she walked away, thinking it wasn't "Hi" and wishing it was. That was that. That's how I knew what I felt.

Now she's seventeen, and it's old enough, I think. But she's got this innocence, still. It's not she's stupid—she's on the honor roll, she wants to be a writer—but Joe and I were over there a couple months earlier, at the beginning of summer, right when him and Tina were starting up. They went off to buy some beer and Nancy and I waited in her room. Nancy was sitting in this shiny beanbag. She had cutoff short-shorts on, and every time she moved, her thighs made the sticking sound that you know it's leg-on-vinyl but you imagine leg-on-leg. I had it in my head it was time to finally do something. I laid down on the carpet, next to her, listening, and after a little while, I said, "What kind of name is Nancy for you, anyway?"

Nancy said, "Actually, I think Nancy's a pretty peculiar name for me. But I always thought that was because it's mine."

See, I was flirting. I was teasing her. It was my voice she was supposed to hear, not the words it said. But it was the words she heard, and not my voice. It was an innocent way to respond. And I didn't know what to do, so I told her she was nuts.

She said, "No. Listen: Jack... Jack... Jack... Does it sound like your name, still?"

It completely sounded like my name, but I didn't say that because hearing it was as good as "Yes" in my ear and I wanted her to keep going. I wanted to tell her I loved her. Instead, I said "it." I said, "I love it." She said, "Jack… Jack… Jack. I'm glad, Jack Jack."

If she didn't have innocence, she'd have heard what my voice meant and either shut me down or flirted back at me.

When we got to their house on the day of the nodding guy, she was sitting on the stoop with a notebook, wearing flip-flops, which made it easy to admire the shape of her toes. Most people's toes look like extra things to me, like earrings or beards. Nancy's look necessary. They work for her.

Joe went inside to find Tina.

Nancy said, "What's with the grapefruits?"

I said, "We intimidated a man. It's all words."

"I don't like that spoon," she said. "I clink my teeth. It chills me up." She was still talking about grapefruits.

"They're not for you," I said. "They're for your parents."

"What's all words?" she said.

I said, "You don't say what you mean. You pretend like you're talking about something else. It works."

"A dowry goes to the groom, not the other way around," she said.

I said, "What does that have to do with anything?"

She said, "Implications. Indirectness. And suggestion."

Was she fucking with me? I don't even know if she was fucking with me. She's a wiseass, sometimes, but she's much smarter than me, too. And plus she was high. I would've taken a half-step forward and kissed her mouth right then, except I wasn't also high, and that's not kosher. Plus I probably wouldn't have stepped forward and it's just something I tell myself.

"Come inside with me," she said.

She kicked off her sandals and I followed her to the kitchen. It's a walk through a long hallway and Nancy stopped every couple steps for a second so that I kept almost bumping her. She said, "You should take your shoes off, Jack. And your socks. The floor's nice and cold."

That was a pretty thought, but getting barefoot to feel the coldness of a floor is not something I do, so I told her, "You're a strange one." Nancy likes people to think she's strange, but she doesn't like people thinking that she likes them to think that, so it was better for me to say than it sounds, even though she spun around and smacked me on the arm when I said it, which also worked out fine because I was flexed. I was expecting a smack. I know that girl.

In the kitchen, Cojo was drinking beer with Tina and Mr. Christamesta. Mr. Christamesta was standing. He's no sitter. He's 6'5" and two guys wide. I can't imagine a chair that would hold him. He could wring your throat one-handed. If there was a black-market scientist who sold clones derived from hairs, he'd go straight for the clog in Mr. Christamesta's drain whenever the customer wanted a bouncer. That's what he looks like: the father of a thousand bouncers. Or a bookie with a sandwich-shop front, which is what he is. But it's a conundrum after you talk to him, because you don't think of him like that. You talk to him, you think: He's a sandwich-shop owner who takes a few bets on the side. Still, he's the last guy in Chicago whose daughter you'd want to date. Him or Daley. But a father-in-law is a different story.

He said to me, "Jack Krakow! What's with the grapefruits?"

I didn't want to think about the grapefruits. The grapefruits made me sad.

I said, "They're for you, Sir, and Mrs. Christamesta."

"You're so formal, Jack. You trying to impress me or something? Why you trying to impress me, now? You want to marry my daughter? Is that it? My Nancy? You want to take my Nancy away from her papa? You want to run away with her to someplace better? Like that song from my youth? If. it's. the. last. thing. you ev-er do? You want to be an absconder, Jack? With my daughter? So you bring me grapefruits? Citrus for a daughter? What kind of substitute is that? It's pearls for swine, grapefruits for Nancy. Irrespectively. It's swine for steak and beef for venison. You like venison? I love venison. But I also love deer, Jack. I love to watch deer frolic in the woods. Do you see what I mean? The world's complicated. It's okay, though. I am impressed with your grapefruits. You have a good heart. You're golden. I like you. Just calm down. We're standing in a kitchen. It's air-conditioned. Slouch a little. Have a beer."

He handed me a bottle. I handed him the grapefruits. He's got thumbs like ping-pong paddles, that guy. He could slap your face from across the country.

What sucked was, grapefruits or no, I *was* trying to impress him, and I *did* come for his daughter, and he wouldn't be so jolly about it if he knew that, so I knew there was no way he knew it. And since he didn't know it, I knew Nancy didn't know it, because those two are close. So I was like one of these smart guys like Clark Kent that the girl thinks of like an older brother. Except I'm not smart. And my alter ego isn't Superman, who she loves. At best I'm Smith, who no one knows his name but Cojo.

The one good thing about Mr. Christamesta going off on those tangents was it got Nancy laughing so hard she was shaking. She pushed her head against my shoulder and hugged around me to hold my other shoulder with her hands. For balance. And I could smell her hair, and her hair smelled like apples and girl, which is exactly what I would've imagined it smelled like in my daydreams of "Yes," if I was smart enough to imagine smell in the first place. I don't think I have the ability to imagine smell. I never tried, but I bet I can only do sound and sight.

An unfortunate thing about Nancy's laughing was how it drew her mom in from the living room. She's real serious, Mrs. Christamesta. So serious it messes with her physically. She's an attractive woman, like Nancy twenty years later and shorter-haired—see her through a window or drive by her in the car, it's easy to tell. If you're eating dinner with her, though, or at church, and she knows she's being looked at, the seriousness covers up the beauty. It's like she doesn't have a face; just her eyebrows like a V and all the decisions she made about her hairstyle. My whole life, I've seen Mrs. Christamesta laugh at three or two jokes, and I've never heard her crack a one.

"You, young lady," she said, "and you, too," to Tina, "have to quit smoking those drugs."

That got Nancy so hysterical that I had to force myself to think about the grapefruits again, about that guy coming home with no grapefruits and acting like he just forgot or, even worse, him going back to the store and getting more grapefruits and then, when he got home, making this big ceremony around cutting them or peeling them, whatever his family did with them. I had to think about that so I wouldn't start laughing with Nancy. If I laughed, it would look like I was laughing at Mrs. Christamesta. And maybe I would be.

"It's because you give them beer," she said to her husband.

"Is it you want a beer, honey?" he said to her.

She bit her lip, but took a seat.

He got up real close to her and said it again. "Is all you want is a beer?" He crouched down in front of her chair so his shirt rode up and I saw his lower back. His lower back was white as tits, and not hairy at all, which surprised me. He held her neck, and touched those paddles to her ears. "Is it you want a grapefruit?" he said. "I'll cut you a grapefruit. I'll peel you a grapefruit. I'll pulp it in the juicer. I'll juice it in the pulper. Grapefruit in segments, in slices, or liquefied. And beer. All or any. Any combination. All for you. Am I not your husband? Am I not a good husband? Am I not a husband to prepare you citrus on a sunny weekend in the windy city? Have I ever denied you love in any form? Have I ever let your gorgeous face go too long unkissed? How could I? What a brute," he said. "What a drunken misanthrope. What a cruel, cruel man," he said. "I'll zest the peel with the zester and cook salmon on the grill for you. I'll sprinkle pinches of zest for you. On top of the salmon." Then he kissed her face. Thirty, twenty times.

That was the fourth time I ever saw Mrs. Christamesta laugh. Or the third. And thank God because I was done feeling sorry for that nodding guy. I lost it so hard that when the laughter was finished with me I was holding Nancy's hand and she was tugging on the front of my shirt and I didn't remember how we got that way.

I made a violent face at her, all teeth and nostrils. For comedy. Then she pinched me on my side and I jumped back fast, squealing like a little girl.

"Fucken girl," Cojo whispered. But he didn't mean it how it sounded. It was nice of him to say to me. Brotherly.

Mr. Christamesta threw a key at me. "You okay to drive?" he said. "You're okay," he said. He kissed his wife's neck and we went out the back door. To the garage.

The Christamestas have two cars. Both of them are Lincolns and both Lincolns are blue. I tried the key on the one on the left. It was the right choice.

Cojo called shotgun, but he was kidding. I held the shotgun door open for Nancy, and Cojo tackled Tina into the back seat.

We stopped at the Jewel for some patties and nacho chips, and then we were on our way.

* * *

I forgot to mention it was furniture day. Two Sundays a year, Chicago's got furniture day. You put your old furniture in the alley, in the morning, and scavengers in vans take it to their houses and junk shops. If no one wants it, the garbage trucks come in the afternoon and they bring it to the dump. That's what makes it furniture day—how the garbage trucks come. That's why there were garbage trucks on a Sunday.

One of them had balloons tied to its grill with ribbon. We got stopped at a light facing it. Grand and Oakley. We were going south on Oakley. That light takes forever. Grand's a main artery. It's dominant. Grand vs. Oakley? Oakley gets stomped.

There were white balloons and blue ones and some yellows. I don't know what color the ribbon was, but I knew it wasn't string because it shined.

Nancy said, "Do you think it's a desperate form of graffiti, Jack?"

Jack. I checked the rearview. Tina had her feet in Joe's lap. Joe was pretending to look out his window, but what he was doing was looking *at* the window. It was tinted, and he was looking at Tina's legs, reflected. Tina has good legs. You notice them. You feel elderly.

I said to Nancy, "It's probably the driver had a baby."

She said, "I think maybe some tagger got his markers and his spray-cans taken, and he was sitting on the curb out front of his house, watching all the trucks making pickups and feeling worthless because he couldn't do anything about it. He didn't want to write 'wash me' with his finger in the dirt along the body since there's nothing original about that, and he didn't want to brick the windshield because he wasn't someone who wanted to harm things, but still he found himself reaching down into the weeds of the alley to grasp something heavy. He needed to let the world know he existed, and without paint or markers, bricking a windshield was the only way he could think to do it. Except then, right then, right when he gets hold of the brick—and it's the perfect brick, a cement quarter-cinderblock with gripping holes for his fingers, it fits right in his hand—he hears his little sister, inside the house. She's singing through the open window of her bedroom, above him. She's happy because yesterday was her birthday and she got all the toys she wanted, and it reminds the boy of the party they had for her, how he decorated the house all morning and his sister didn't even care because all she really wanted was to unwrap her presents—the party meant nothing to her, not even the cake, much less the decorations—and so this boy races inside, to the hallway in his mom's house, and tears a balloon cluster from the banister he tied it to, then races back out front, decorates the grill of the garbage truck."

Finally, the light turned green. If you're Oakley, you get about seven seconds before Grand starts kicking your ass again.

I said, "It could be the driver got married."

Nancy said, "And maybe it wasn't even today. Maybe it was sometime last week. Maybe those balloons have been there for nine, ten days because the driver thinks it's pretty. Because he understands what it means, you know? Or maybe because he doesn't understand what it means, because it's a conundrum, but it's a nice conundrum, something he wants to figure out."

"It could be his son," I said. "It could be it was his son got married or had a baby," I said.

Nancy said, "Oh." And I knew I shouldn't have said what I said. She was trying to start something with me and I kept ending it. She wanted me to tell her a fantasy story. I'm a meathead. A misinterpreter. Like hot pink? For years I thought it was regular pink that looked sexy on whoever was wearing it. And that Bob Marley song? I thought he was saying that as long as you stayed away from women, you wouldn't cry. Even after I figured it out, it's still the first thing I think when it comes on the radio. It's like when I'm wrong for long enough, I can't get right. I had a fantasy story in my head, but I didn't say it. And why not?

We were merging onto the Eisenhower when this guy in a Miata blew by us on the ramp and I had to hit the brakes a little. Everyone cussed except Nancy, who was spaced out, or pretending to be. Then we got quiet and Joe said, "What kind of fag drives a Miata?"

And Tina said, "Don't." Tina goes to college at UIC. She was a junior, like I would have been. "Don't say fag," she said.

"Fag faggot fag," Cojo said. "It's just words. It's got nothing to do with who anyone wants to fuck." He took out a cigarette. He said, "This is a fag in England." He lit the cigarette. He said, "I know fags who've screwed hundreds of women. I know fags who screw no one. Have a fag," he said. He gave the cigarette to Tina and lit a second one for himself. He said, "That rapist Mike Tyson's a fag. And my cousin Niles. He's screwing his girlfriend even as we speak to each other here in this very car. There's fags who like windmills and fags on skinny bicycles. I know fags who fix cars and fags who pour concrete. Regis Philbin's a fag. Kurt Loder and that fag John Norris. Lots of TV and movie guys. Rock stars. Pretty much all of them. So what? It's a word. It means asshole, but it's quicker to say and more offensive cause it's only fags who say asshole like it's any kind of insult. Even jerk's better than asshole. Asshole's a fagged-out word, and fag's offensive. And it should be offensive. I want it to be offensive. Someone calls me a Polack? I'm offended. But I'm a fucken Ukrainian, you know? I don't give a shit about the Polish people. No offense, Krakow, but I don't give a fuck for your people. Someone calls me Polack, though, I'll tear his jaws off at the hinge. And 'cause why? 'Cause he's saying I'm Polish? No. 'Cause he's saying Polish people are lowlifes? No. He's trying to offend me is why. When he's calling me Polack, he's calling me fag. He's calling me asshole. So fine. You're pretty. Okay. You smell good. You say smart things to me when you're not telling me the right way to talk. Good news. I like you. I want to spend all my money on you. I want to take you on vacation to an island where there's coconuts and diving. Miatas are for assholes if it makes you more comfortable. But the asshole in that Miata's got fagged-out taste is what I'm telling you."

Tina said, "You've thought about this a lot, Cojo."

"I got a gay cousin," he said. "A homosexual. Lenny. He fucks men, and that's not right and it makes me sick, but that's not why he's a fag. He's a fag because whenever someone calls him fag, it's me who ends up in a fight, not him. He's a fag because he won't stand up for himself. Imagine: your own cousin a fag like that. That's how it is to be me. Not just one but two fags in the family—Lenny the homofag and don't forget about Niles the regular fag who all he does is chase girls—but I'm the only one can say it, right? About how my family's got some fags in it, I mean. Don't you ever bring it up to me. It's like a big secret, and tell the truth it makes me uncomfortable to talk about, so let's just stop talking about it, okay?"

Joe was always talking to girls about Lenny. Sometimes Lenny had cancer and sometimes he was a retard. In 1999, he was usually Albanian. But there wasn't any Lenny. I know all Joe's cousins. So do the Christamestas. Lenny was fiction. But I didn't say. If he did have a cousin Lenny, and this Lenny was a gay, Cojo would defend his cousin Lenny against people who called Lenny fag. So Cojo was telling a certain kind of truth. And it never really mattered to Tina, anyway. She'd just wanted to know Joe cared what she thought of him, and the effort it took him to come up with that bullshit about fags and assholes—that made it obvious he cared. And Joe is definitely crazy for Tina. He discusses it with me. All the things he wants to buy her. Vacations on islands with sailboats and mangos, fucking her on a hammock. They'd still never fucked, but they mashed pretty often. So often it was comfortable. So comfortable they started in the back seat of the car, which was not comfortable for me, sitting next to Nancy, who's staring at the carton of patties in her lap while the sister gets mauled. I hit as many potholes as I could. The Ike's got thousands.

Finally we arrived at the wrong barbecue. We were supposed to go to 514 Greenway and we went to 415. It was my fault. I wrote it down wrong when Sensei Mike told us at the dojo on Friday.

But 415 was raging. Fifty, forty people. Mostly middle-aged guys, wearing Oxfords and sandals. Some of them had wives, but there weren't any babies, which always spooks me a little, a barbecue without babies. It's like if you ever had a father who shaved off his mustache.

It took us a few minutes of looking around for Sensei Mike before we noticed this banner hanging off the fence. It said, "HAPPY TENURE, PROFESSOR SCHINKL!" By then, we all had bottles of beer in our hands. The beers tasted yeasty. They were from Belgium. That's what set the whole thing off.

The four of us were half-sitting along the edge of the patio table, trying to decide if it was more polite to finish the beers there or take them with us to look for Sensei Mike's house when this guy came up and made a show of adjusting his sunglasses. First he just lowered them down the bridge of his nose so we could see one of his eyebrows raise up. But then he was squinting at us over the frames and he had a hand on his hip. He stayed that way for a couple of wheezy breaths, then tore the sunglasses off his face with the other hand and held them up in the air behind his ear like he was gonna swat us. Instead, he let the shades dangle and he said, "Hmmmmmm." The sound of that got the attention of some other people. They weren't crowding up or anything, but they were looking at us.

The guy said, "Hmmmmmm," again, but with more irritation than the first time. Like a whining, almost.

"How ya doin'?" Cojo said to him. Nancy leaned into me, but it was instinct, nothing to make a big deal of. Tina held her beer close. Cojo was smiling, which is not a good thing for him to do around people who don't know him. His smile looks like he's asking you to stop making him smile. It's got no joy. It's because of his smile that I retrieve the cars when we work the lot together. If customers tip, it's usually on the way out.

Real slow and loud, the guy said, "How's. Your Belgian. Beer?"

So the beer was his and he was attached to it in some sick way. Like fathers and the end-piece of the roast beef. He wasn't anyone's father, though, this guy. He was being a real prick about the beer is what he was, but it was the wrong barbecue and he was harmless so far. He was tofu in khakis. About as rough as a high-school drama teacher. Still, he could've been Schinkl for all we knew, so he didn't get hit.

"You want one?" Cojo said. He said, "I think there's one left in the cooler by the grill."

The guy stared at Joe, just to let him know that he'd heard what Joe said, but was ignoring him. Then he spun on Nancy. He said, "Is that *ground chuck* in your lap, young lady? Do you mean to wash down those patties of *ground chuck* with my imported. Belgian. Beer?" He poked the meat.

I said, "Hey."

"Hay's for horses," he said, the fucken creep.

A woman in the crowd—they were crowding up, now—said, "Calm down, Byron."

He poked the meat again, hard. Busted a hole in the plastic wrap. Nancy flinched and I had that fucker in an arm-lock before the meat hit the ground. Joe dumped his beer in the lawn and broke the bottle on the table edge. We moved in front of the Christamestas, like shields. I had Byron bent in front of me, huffing and puffing.

I didn't want the girls to see us get beat down, but I thought about afterward, about Nancy holding my hands at my chest and wiping the blood from my face with disinfected cottonballs, how I could accidentally confess my love and not be held responsible since I'd have a serious concussion.

Byron said, "Let go."

"You got a thin voice," I told him.

I pulled his wrist back a couple degrees. His fingers danced around.

Every guy in that yard was creeping toward us, saying "Hey" and "Hey, now." There were too many of them, broken bottle or no. All we had left was wiseass tough-guy shit. "Hey," they said. And Joe said, "Hay's for horses," and I forced a laugh through my teeth like I was supposed to. They kept creeping. Little baby steps. Tina whispered to Nancy, "Can we go? Let's just go."

"Just let go of me!" Byron said. "Let go of me!"

I said, "What!"

He shut his mouth and the crowd stopped moving. They stopped right behind where the patio met the grass. That's when it occurred to me the reason they weren't pummeling us was Byron. They didn't want me to damage him. And that meant that I controlled them. I thought: We got a hostage. I thought: All we have to do is take him out the gate on the side of the house, get him to the car, then drop him in the street and drive off. I was gonna tell Joe, but then Nancy started talking.

"Do you guys know Sensei Mike?" she said.

This chubby drunk guy was wobbling at the front of the crowd. He said, "What?" But it sounded like "Whud?" That's how I knew he was a lisper, even before he started lisping. Because he had adenoid problems. The first lisper I ever knew in grade school had adenoid problems. Brett Novak. He said his own name "Bred Novag." Mine he said "Jag Gragow." When people called him a lisper, I didn't know what a lisper was, so I decided he was a lisper not just because of what he did to *s* sounds, but because of what he did to *t* sounds and *k* sounds, too. So I thought this chubby drunk guy was a lisper, because I used to be wrong about what a lisper was and so "lisper" is the first thing I think when I hear adenoid problems. But since the chubby guy turned out to be a lisper after all, my old wrongness made it so I was right. It was like if Nancy wore hot pink. The color would look sexy on her, and because it would look sexy on her, I'd say it was "hot pink," and I'd be right, even though I didn't know what I was saying. I'd be right because of an old misunderstanding.

"Sensei Mike?" said Nancy. "We came for Sensei Mike." Her voice was trembling. I could've killed everybody.

The guy said, "Thenthaimigue? Ith that thome thort of thibboleth?"

This got laughs. The crowd thought it was very clever for the lisper to say a word like *shibboleth* to us.

But fuck them for thinking I don't know *shibboleth*. Some people don't, but I do. It's from the Old Testament. In CCD they told us we shouldn't read the Old Testament till we were older because it was violent and confusing and totally Christless, so I read some of it (I skipped Leviticus and quit at Kings). The part with *shibboleth* is in Judges: there were the Ephrathites who were these people who couldn't make the sound *sh*. They were at war with the Gileadites. The Gileadites controlled all the crossings on the Jordan River, and the main thing they didn't want was for the Ephrathites to get across the river. The problem was the Ephrathites looked exactly like the Gileadites and spoke the same language, too; so if an Ephrathite came to one of the crossings, the Gileadites had almost no way of telling that he was an Ephrathite. Not until Jephthah, who was the leader of the Gileadites, remembered how Ephrathites couldn't make the *sh* sound—that's when he came up with the idea to make everyone who wanted to cross the river say the word *shibboleth*. If they could say *shibboleth*, they could pass, but if they couldn't say it, it meant they were an enemy and they got slain. So *shibboleth* was this code word, but it didn't work like a normal code word. A normal code word is a secret—you have to prove you know what it is. *Shibboleth*, though—it wasn't any secret. Jephthah would tell you what it was. What mattered was how you said it. How you said it is what saved your life, or ended it.

I said to the lisper, "I know what's a shibboleth, and Sensei Mike's no shibboleth. And you're no Jephthah, either." It came out wormy and know-it-all sounding. I sounded like I cared what they thought of me. Maybe I did. I don't think so, though.

"Are you jogueing?" he said. "Whud gind of brude are you? Do you *offden* find yourthelf engaging in meda-converthathions?" He pronounced the *t* in *often*, the prick, and on top of it, he turned it into a fucken *d*.

All those guys laughed anyway. It was funnier to them than the shibboleth joke. It was the funniest thing they'd ever heard.

And I was sick of getting laughed at. And I was sick of people asking me questions that weren't questions.

I pulled on Byron's arm and he moaned. Cojo slapped him on the chops and the lisper stepped back into the crowd, to hide.

The crowd started shifting. But not forward. Not in any direction really, not for too long. It swelled in one place and thinned in another, like a water balloon in a fist. It was in my fist.

I saw the lisper's head craned up over the shoulder of a guy who'd snuck to the front, and that's when I knew.

They didn't stop creeping up at the patio because they were scared of what I'd do to their friend and his arm. They stopped at the patio to give us space. They stopped at the patio so I could do whatever I'd do to Byron and they could watch.

I said to Nancy, "You and Tina go get the car, okay?"

Nancy reached in my pocket for the keys and whispered, "Be careful." Then Tina kissed Joe. The girls ran off. It could've been a war movie. It could've been Joe and I going to the front in some high-drama war movie. It was a little hammy, but that didn't bother me.

As soon as I was sure the girls were clear, I asked Joe, with my eyes and eyebrows, if he thought we should run for it.

He told me with his shoulders and his chin that he thought it was a good idea.

Then I got an inspiration. I started yelling at the top of my lungs: "AHHHHHH!"

The whole crowd went pop-eyed and stepped back and stepped back and stepped back. I got a huge lung capacity. I think I yelled for about a minute. I yelled till my throat bled and I couldn't yell anymore. Then I dropped Byron, and we took off.

Nancy was just pulling out of the parking spot when we got to the car. Some of the sickos from the barbecue ran out onto the street, and one of them was shouting, "We'll call the police!"


We still didn't know Sensei Mike's right address and the girls decided it was probably better to get out of Glen Ellyn, so we headed back to Chicago. When we got to the Christamesta house, Tina and Joe went inside and I followed Nancy around the neighborhood on foot, not saying anything. I don't know how long that lasted. It was dark, though. We ended up at the park at Iowa and Rockwell, under the tornado slide, sitting in pebbles, our backs against the ladder. Nancy opened her purse and pulled out a Belgian beer.

I popped it with my lighter and gave it to her. She sipped and gave it back. I sipped and gave it back.

I've told a lot of girls I was in love with them. There's some crack-ass wisdom about it being easier to say when you don't mean it, but that's not why I didn't say it to Nancy. I didn't say it because every time I've said it, I meant it. If I said it again, it would be like all those other times, and all those other times—it went away. And silence wasn't any holier than saying it. Just more drama for its own sake. All of it's been done before. It's been in TV shows and comic books and it's how your parents met. And there's nothing wrong with drama, I don't think. And there's nothing wrong with drama for its own sake, either. What's wrong is drama that doesn't know it's drama. And what's wrong is doing the same thing everyone else does and thinking you're original, thinking you're unpredictable.

I said, "Maybe it's 'cause he wanted racing stri—" and the sound cut off. My throat was killing me from the yelling and it closed up.

Nancy said, "Your voice is broken."

And that was an unexpected way to put it, drama or no.

I swigged the beer again and told her, all raspy, "Maybe it's racing stripes. The guy wanted racing stripes."

"What?" she said.

"Don't what me," I said. I gulped more beer. I said, "He wanted to paint racing stripes and the city wouldn't let him. There's a code against painting stripes on city vehicles. So every day he ties the balloons on the grill. And maybe that's a half-ass way to have racing stripes, but then maybe he figures stripes on a garbage truck aren't really racing stripes to begin with, so he doesn't mind using balloons. Or maybe he does mind, but he keeps it to himself because he's not a complainer. Maybe he just keeps tying balloons on the grill, telling himself they're as good as racing stripes, and maybe one day they will be."

"That's a sad story," Nancy said. She carved SAD! in the pebbles with the bottle of beer.

"How's it *sad*?" I said.

Under SAD! she carved a circle with an upside-down smile.

"It's not sad," I said.

She said, "I don't believe that."

"But I'm telling you," I said.

She said, "Then I don't believe you, Jack."

And did I kiss her then? Did Nancy Christamesta close her eyes and tilt her head back, away from the moon? Did she open her mouth? Did she open it just a little, just enough so I could feel her breath on my chin before she would kiss me and then did I finally kiss her?

Fuck you.

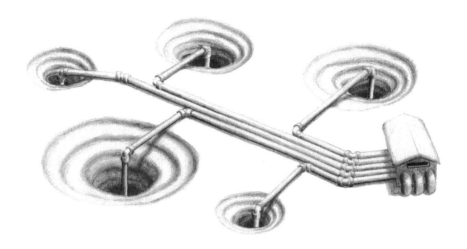

# THE SPECIALIST

*by* ALISON SMITH

THE FIRST ONE said it was incurable. The next agreed. "Incurable," he sighed. The third one looked and looked and found nothing. He tapped her temple. "It's all in your head," he said. The fourth one put his hand in and cried, "Mother! Mother!" The fifth never saw anything like it. "I never saw anything like it," he gasped as he draped his fingers over his stethoscope. The sixth agreed with the first and the seventh agreed with the third. He parted her legs and said, "There's nothing wrong with you."

Alice sat up. The paper gown crinkled. Her feet gripped the metal stirrups. "But it hurts," she said and she pointed.

"Maybe it's a rash," Number Seven said and he gave her some small white pills. They did not help. "Maybe it's spores," he said and he gave her a tube of gel. This made it worse. "Maybe it's a virus." He gave her a bottle of yellow pills. When Alice returned for the fourth time and told Number Seven it was not better, he slumped against the examining table, his white coat trailing. "There's nothing left," he said.

"Nothing?" Alice asked. "What am I going to do?"

He put his finger to her lips and shook his head. "Not here," he said.

That evening, Number Seven took Alice out to dinner. He leaned in over the herb-encrusted salmon croquettes. "Do you mind if I call you Alice?" he asked.

Alice frowned. "What's wrong with me?"

Number Seven pushed the fish around his plate. "I don't know," he said and then he started to cry.

"It's okay," Alice murmured. "At least you tried."

He touched her hand. She held her napkin. She could not eat. Everything tasted incurable. The rice, the saffron asparagus soufflé, the flaming liquor in the dessert—all of it, incurable.

The eighth told her it was the feminine bleeding wound. "All women have it," he said. The ninth told her she didn't use it enough. "It's atrophied," he said as he peeled off his latex gloves with a little shiver.

"But," said Alice as she sat up on her elbows, "it hurts."

The tenth said, "Call me Bob, why don't you?" He looked inside and shook his head. He sat next to her. Alice held on to the edge of the metal table. "I've been thinking," he whispered. She could smell the Scope on his breath. "I've got something that could fix this."

"Oh?" said Alice and she brightened. She felt the hair on his arm brush against her thigh.

"Yes," said Bob. He nodded his head up and down. It was then that she caught sight of the bulge inside Number Ten's slacks.

Alice decided to try a new town, a larger one. Back east, she thought, where the civilized people live. This town had underground tunnels with trains inside. On her first day, Alice descended the cement stairs, walked onto a waiting car and sat down. The orange plastic seat cupped her thighs. The doors sighed shut. The rails rushed along beneath her. She liked the dark, jerking movement of it, the idea of the ground flying by, right beside her. When the car stopped and the doors flew open, Alice emerged. She walked up another cement staircase and found herself in an entirely different part of the city.

"Brilliant," Alice thought.

She rode the underground trains for days.

Then Alice discovered take-out. As she did not have a phone in her one-room walk-up, she had to call from the payphone on the corner when she wanted to place an order. But she did not mind. Alice liked everything about take-out. She liked the warm white boxes with their fold-away lids, the plastic utensils, the stiff paper bags that held in the gooey warmth. She believed that a city which could deliver such delicacies right to your door was a city of great promise. Alice stayed up late, ate Indian lentil soup from a box and said, out loud, "This is it. This is where I'll find it."

She found a job stocking shelves in a bookstore.

The eleventh told her try something different.

"I've seen this before. There's nothing for it," he said and he gave her a card with a number on it. "Try this anyway." Under the number were printed the words, "Psychic Healer."

This card led Alice to Number Twelve. She was alternative. "Find a piece of gold," Number Twelve said, "real gold. Boil it for three days and keep the water. Store it in a cool place. Drink this water every day for a month."

Number Twelve nodded. Alice nodded. "It aches," she said.

A pinched smile lighted across Number Twelve's face. She clasped her hands together. Gold bangles tripped down her arms and she nodded some more.

Alice did not have any gold. No ring, no brooch, not even a pendant. So she bought a set of gold-rimmed plates at the Salvation Army and boiled them for three days. The painted flowers dissolved into the water, turning it pink, then green and then, finally, the color of mud. Alice slurped at her box of green lentil soup and stared into the murky liquid.

The thirteenth was also alternative. He said, "Imagine a white light entering your body. Its energy fills you. Imagine this white light healing your internal wound."

"A wound?" Alice thought. "Is that what I have?"

Alice ordered more take-out.

The fourteenth was recommended by the thirteenth. This one did not even have a card. Instead, he had fountains, dozens of them. In the waiting room tiny gurgling pumps sprouted out of copper bowls. Held in place with river stones, they bubbled and chattered all around her.

Number Fourteen was a mumbler. He swallowed his words, half-spoken. He talked into the collar of his shirt. Alice leaned in. She could not hear him over the sound of running water. "I beg your pardon?" she asked.

"Become one with the water," Number Fourteen mumbled, "and you will find your cure."

"How?" asked Alice.

Number Fourteen spread his arms. He smiled. He closed his eyes. Alice leaned in and waited. He said nothing. She thought perhaps he had fallen asleep. "Sir," she whispered. "Sir?"

But Number Fourteen did not answer.

Alice found an indoor lap pool. After her morning shift at the bookstore, she swam up and down between the ropes. The water soothed her— the buoyancy of it, the soft fingers of cold. That winter, Alice swam and swam. She swam so many laps that her fingers pruned and her shoulders grew broad and taut. Every day, when she had completed her laps, Alice would linger in the pool. She held on to the side, gasping for breath, and floated. She spread her arms, tilted her head back and let the water surround her like a shapeless, soft eraser. But every time she stepped out of the pool, the ache returned.

Alice waited. She thought perhaps what she needed was rest. Perhaps what the ache wanted was to be left alone. So for an entire year she tried to ignore it. She did not see a single doctor. She swam up and down between the ropes. She shelved books. She rode the subway. Closing her eyes, she leaned her head against the plastic seat and waited for her life to change. Every night, she called for take-out from the pay phone on the corner. Every day, she gazed down at the neat lines of bills in the bookstore cash register.

Through it all, the ache zinged and popped. It burned and festered. And the pain of it began to eat away at her. At times, Alice felt certain there must be little left inside her. And that year, the-year-of-not-trying, something cold and hard slipped inside Alice and her heart became like a knife drawer. Sharp and shining, she kept it closed.

Then Alice met the Specialist.

"The best in the city," her coworker whispered, handing her a card as she adjusted the sale sign by the overstock books. "He's a specialist."

Alice shook her head. "I'm done with doctors," she whispered back.

"Just try," her coworker said. "Try this one."

Alice had to wait a month for an appointment and when she did finally see him, when at last she climbed up onto his metal table and leaned back, the Specialist said she was empty.

"Empty!" he shrieked, his head popping up from behind the paper sheet. "There's nothing there!" He probed deeper. "It's cold," he cried. "It's so cold!" And then something strange happened, something entirely new.

Alice heard a muffled shrieking and a great sucking sound. The room filled with a gust of cold air and then—silence. The Specialist was gone.

Alice sat up on her elbows and looked around her. "Where is he?" she asked the nurse.

"In there!" the nurse cried as she pointed between Alice's legs. "And he's caught!"

Alice plucked at the sheet, looking beneath it. Nothing. She leaned over and peered under the table. Still nothing. The Specialist was nowhere. Alice sat back on the metal table, her feet suspended in the stirrups. She lay very still and listened. She could hear a distant sound. The Specialist's voice, frantic and screaming, echoed somewhere below her. Alice looked over at the nurse. The nurse shook her head. Alice crossed her arms and waited.

After twenty minutes Alice shifted her weight and moved to rise. As she did, the distant echo grew louder. Then, with a terrible rush of cold air, The Specialist reemerged. His head rising above the paper sheet, his teeth chattering, a single icicle hung from the end of his nose.

"This is unbelievable," cried the Specialist. He pressed a red button. "Code Blue," he screamed into a mesh speaker in the wall. "I need a second opinion!" He paced. The icicle at the end of his nose began to melt. "I've got to get documentation," he said. "I need pictures. I need verification." He pressed the red button again and called into the mesh speaker. "Please, can I get some help in here!" His icicle dripped on the paper sheet.

"I'll help," the nurse said. She set down her clipboard.

"No," said the Specialist. "I need a doctor. This is, is…" he looked down at Alice and shook his head, "unprecedented."

"I don't know about that," said the nurse and she ducked her head below the paper sheet. "How deep did you get?" she asked.

"Deep enough," the Specialist said.

"Hmm," said the nurse.

"Oh!" said the Specialist, "If you don't believe me, I'll prove it."

The Specialist rushed out of the room. He returned moments later with a snowsuit, a pith helmet, and a flashlight. He suited up. "I'm going in," he said. "Do you need anything?" he asked Alice.

Alice shrugged.

"Why don't you order Chinese," he said. "I may be a while."

"Take-out," thought Alice, and she warmed to the Specialist. "Even if he did say I was empty and cold inside."

The Specialist put his hand inside Alice, then his arm. Before he could say another word, there was a great sucking sound, the room filled with a gust of cold air and, for the second time that day, the Specialist fell inside Alice.

The hours passed. The take-out arrived. Alice slurped her noodles. She asked for a pillow, but the Nurse was busy peering into the pages of an enormous black book. She wondered where the Specialist had gone. She stretched her arms up over her head, sat back, and picked up her box of noodles.

An hour later, the Specialist emerged. When she saw him rise up from between her legs, covered in icicles and shivering, Alice set down her chopsticks.

"My God, there's nothing in there!" the Specialist cried, his face shining with cold. "Nothing! Miles of it! I could not even find the edges of her."

Alice gazed at the Specialist's chapped hands. She had to admit that they did look quite frostbitten. Alice reached for her sweater. The Specialist set down his flashlight and rushed away to record his findings. The nurse followed, waving a clipboard. Alice was alone.

One at a time, she removed her feet from the stirrups. She stretched out. She pulled the paper gown tight against herself. She looked around the room. On one wall hung a print of a field of poppies, red and bursting. On the other, a picture of a snowy tundra. After waiting on the table for quite a while, Alice sighed. "They must have forgotten about me," she thought. She looked at her watch. If she didn't leave now, she would be late for her shift at the bookstore. She stood up, found her slacks and blouse, and began to dress.

Just as she was stepping into the second pant leg, the Specialist burst into the room holding a camera. "I must have you for my new research project," he cried. "You must stay with me and work." He grasped her shoulders. Alice held on to the waist of her slacks. "A woman with nothing inside but a cold, hard breeze!" he gazed out beyond her, at the field of poppies. Then he looked down at Alice, as if he were seeing her for the first time. "I've never found anything like you," he smiled. "Come with me! We'll travel the world. We'll meet all the great doctors. We'll stay in the best hotels. Separate rooms, of course."

Alice thought for a moment. She knew it could not be true. She knew that there was something inside her, something more than a cold, hard breeze. But no one had made this much of a fuss over her before. No one had ever seemed to care like he did. This Specialist may not have understood her, but something about her thrilled him.

"Maybe that's more important than understanding," Alice thought. She looked into the Specialist's eyes. They were green, the color of shallow ocean water. She felt a little pull in her chest, a soft tug, as if the drawer of her heart were opening. She saw the roped lane at the swimming pool and the beige mouth of the bookstore cash register, gaping, and she realized that she was lonely.

"Will you help me, then?" she asked. "If I go with you, will we find a cure for the constant ache? The pain of it, it tires me so."

"Pain?" The Specialist tilted his head to one side. No one had told him this. "You have pain?" He paused a moment, then he shrugged and embraced Alice. He picked her up and swung her around twice.

The rush of air past her face, the whirl of the white, sanitary room as it flew by, it startled Alice. A new feeling, a feeling she could not quite describe, flooded her veins. It was not happiness, but it was close. The closest she had been in a long time.


In Atlantic City they praised her, treated her like royalty. "The Queen of Emptiness!" they said. In Hershey they offered her a complimentary sun-suit with a picture of the arctic printed on it, and a sash that read: "Miss Iceberg," its pink letters marching across the white satin.

The Specialist developed a slide show to accompany his demonstration. "Dim the lights," he said. Alice liked this part best. She hated it when he called her up on stage, when he poked and prodded with his cold, clammy hands. Alice sunk back in her seat and watched the photographs glow and shimmer against the white screen. She never tired of looking at them. "A distant landscape," the Specialist barked, his hand on the remote. "Cold, empty, devoid of life as we know it." Alice watched as the mysterious vistas appeared before her: a blue wash of glaciers, a white seamless line of snow. "The Interior of Alice N. is like a frozen tundra. Nothing can live there!" the Specialist bellowed across the darkened room.

This is where Alice always lost track. It never failed. Every time the Specialist started in on the part about the cold and the snow stuck up inside her, Alice felt the room begin to spin. Her vision tunneled. She watched the Specialist's mouth move and she knew that he was talking, that he was explaining to the crowd of doctors behind her what it was like to be her, what it was like to be inside of her. But she could not make out what he said.

In Gainesville she could smell the ocean, but it was too far to reach. She wanted to swim. The Specialist said, "We have no time for recreation." And so she lay on the bed while he rifled through his papers. She imagined herself in the water, the salt shine rising up, coating her white arms.

In Louisville they laughed her off stage and the Specialist after her. "There's no such thing," the doctors said. "No such thing as a woman with nothing inside but a cold, hard breeze!"

"You don't believe me?" the Specialist said. He pointed at Alice, "Then why don't you look for yourself?"

The room fell silent. The doctors blanched. They stepped away from the stage. Someone dropped a clipboard. It skittered across the concrete floor.

The Specialist nodded. He stepped up to the podium once again. "I thought so," he said. "I thought that would stop you." He put his arm around Alice. "When you're ready to do some real research, you'll know where to find us." He guided her off.

They headed west. Later, years later, long after the National Guard had captured him, the Specialist would say that it was Los Angeles where it all started to go wrong. For it was there, swept along by the bright lights and the promise of fame, that he decided to put Alice on the talk-show circuit. "To broaden your audience," the Specialist said and he spread his arms wide to make his point.

The Specialist bought her a new suit. He said it was a present for their success. "Now we've hit the big time!" he beamed at her.

Alice met the talk-show host in the dressing room moments before she was to go on air.

"It is a pleasure to meet you, Miss Empty," he said and he kissed her cheek.

His mustache made her sneeze. Alice wiped her nose and asked for a glass of water. The host smiled at Alice. His white teeth shimmered under the green room lights. He leaned in close to Alice and looked at her, into her face, closely. It had been so long since someone had looked at her like that. Alice tipped her head down. She blushed. She placed the rim of the glass against her lips and sipped.

"She's going to need make-up!" the Host bellowed.

After her make-up session, the host guided her on stage. Under the bright lights, the makeup felt like a thick, gooey mask.

"Here's the little lady with the big empty!" the Host said.

An applause sign popped up. The Host turned toward the Specialist. He wanted to see all the comparative charts. He wanted the entire history of his research. "Start from the beginning," the host said, leaning forward in his over-stuffed chair, "and don't leave out a thing."

The Specialist was happy to oblige. He pulled out statistics on the discrepancy between the size of Alice's outside and her inside. "The circumference of her torso," he said and he pointed at one chart, "as opposed to the circumference of her interior." He pointed to a second chart. "Alice defies logic!" This is where he always got excited. "She's an impossibility!" he cried. "And here she sits before you."

The Host smiled. "A woman who laughs in the face of science!"

The camera cut to a psychiatrist who spoke about the physical-manifestation-of-a-mental-state-brought-on-by-extreme-stress. He ended with, "It's remarkable. Quite remarkable."

The Host opened the discussion up to the audience. Alice was asked questions about her personal life that puzzled her. "How much do you eat?" "Do you like cold weather?" "Do you have a boyfriend?" Alice squirmed in her seat. The Host broke in. "Don't worry," he patted Alice's hand. "We'll find you a boyfriend," he said. "No doubt about that!" The audience cheered. Then a woman from the back row stood up, tapped the mike, and asked, "Does it ever hurt? I mean, does it ache?"

Alice felt her face flush and tingle. Finally, a question that she wanted to answer. She cleared her throat. "As a matter of fact," Alice began and then she lost the thread of her thought. She faltered.

The Host tapped his fingers together and waited. The Specialist shifted in his seat. "Go on," he nodded.

"As a matter of fact," she tried again, but the words would not come.

The Host put his hand on Alice's shoulder. "Hold that thought," he smiled. He turned and spoke to the camera lens. "We'll be right back."

"We're going back to Gainesville," the Specialist said the following morning while they were in a cab on the way to the airport. "You're not ready for the big time. We need to rehearse."

As they handed in their boarding passes and headed for the gate, they were intercepted by a man in a black suit with an ear prompt. "Excuse me," he said. "I've been sent by the talk show. They want you back."

The Specialist blinked. "Really? They want us?"

The man held his ear prompt and nodded. It turned out that Alice was a hit. Alice and her frozen tundra were the topic-of-the-day on every major morning newscast.

So Alice and the Specialist returned to the studio. Alice submitted to the creams and cover-up, the blush and shadow of the make-up artist. Once again, Alice and the Specialist found themselves under the hot studio lights, awaiting further instruction. The host beamed at them. The second interview went better than the first. The Specialist showed more slides.

Alice was relieved when they dimmed the lights. The monitor flooded with the bright grays and whites of the frozen tundra. A distant sun bounced off all that glacial terrain. Before she knew it, the show was over and Alice found herself in her new suit in the green room once again, scraping make-up off her face.

By the end of the week Alice and the Specialist were regulars on the talk show. "It seems like everybody wants a piece of the little girl with the big empty," the host smiled. He winked at Alice.

Reporters hounded them. Hotel staff hovered. Crowds formed around them wherever they went. And then, one day, the tide turned. The skeptics arrived—researchers and doctors, lab technicians and the geologists—all of whom did not believe in the cold-and-empty theory. They sat in the studio audience, crossed their arms and waited. "For some solid evidence," they whispered. "For one verifiable fact," they sneered.

The skeptics stared dubiously at the Specialist's charts. They recalculated his measurements. They scratched their heads. They lifted their chins. "Impossible," they said. "There's no such thing."

The Specialist was right there, his hand on Alice's shoulder, starting in with his challenge. "If you don't believe me," he began, "then why don't you see for yourself?"

Again, the room fell silent. Someone dropped a pen. They all stepped back.

"I thought so," the Specialist said.

But he spoke too soon. From the back, a white-coated lab technician with a shock of bright red hair, stepped out of the crowds and raised his hand. "I'll go," he said. "I'd like to see."

And then another stepped forward. And another. And another. They all wanted to see this empty landscape, firsthand. Soon there was a line forming at the edge of the stage.

"We'll go," they cried. "We want to see this cold hard breeze for ourselves."

"But," the Specialist stammered, waving his arms above his head, "it's too dangerous! It's not for the faint of heart!"

They would not listen to reason.

In the end, four men suited up and approached Alice. Each one ducked below the paper sheet. Each one slipped in, slowly at first, and then, with a rush of cold air, they disappeared.

Only three came back. Snow-crusted and shivering, one by one they climbed out of her, a gust of wind sweeping through the studio as they stepped onto solid ground. They brushed the snow off their shoulders. They straightened their wool caps. They rubbed their chapped hands together. They clapped each other on the back and nodded.

"It's true," they said. "It's huge and empty."

They nodded. They smiled. They looked around and counted. One. Two. Three. Their smiles faded. The fourth man was not among them. The three men turned around and stared at Alice. They gazed at the modesty sheet draped over her knees. They peeked under it. Nothing. So they sat down and waited.

"I'm sure he's just late," said the first man. "He stopped to take some photos," said the second. The third shifted in his seat, brushed the snow off his mittens and said nothing.

And so they waited, all of them, the three men, the Specialist and the studio audience. The Host paced. "This is highly irregular," he muttered. Then the network offered him round-the-clock coverage till the fourth man returned and the Host brightened.

The hours turned into days and still they waited. A vigil formed around the examination table. Doctors trickled in throughout the day, journalists clamored at the studio doors. The three men sat up front, right next to Alice. They called for him, the lost man, alone and wandering up inside Alice.

"I told you," the Specialist cried. "I warned you all!"

But no one was listening to him. The three men talked of extreme temperatures, the endless landscape, and lost provisions.

"Did he bring any food?" an audience member asked. "Did he pack his canteen?" asked another. "Did he wear his long johns?" his mother cried over the television satellite. Then someone suggested forming a search party. The three men who had survived to tell the story of Alice's insides shook their heads. "Why?" the people asked.

"Because it's cold in there," the three who came back said. "It's damn cold." They held their arms and shivered.

The Specialist nodded. "That's true," he mumbled as he sidled toward the door.

Someone grabbed his arm. "Where are you going?"

"I forgot my lunch," he said. "I'll be right back."

The doctors all shook their heads. "You'll stay right here," they said, "until you return the Fourth Man."

The Specialist threw up his hands. "Don't look at me! I didn't take him." He pointed at Alice. "She did."

Alice lay on the studio's examination table. By the third day, her back was in knots. Bedsores formed on Alice's skin. They grew weepy with infection. She asked if she could get up and try shaking him out. The doctors huddled in the corner and discussed the possibility. They nodded at each other. One of them stepped forward. "It might work."

Slowly, very slowly, Alice removed her feet from the stirrups, first the right and then the left. She slid her body to the edge of the examination table and placed one foot on the ground.

Alice shook and shook. She stomped her feet. She jumped up and down. She walked up the center aisle of the auditorium. She walked down the side aisle. She held on to the edge of the stage and stomped until her feet burned and her breath came hard. But it did not work. The fourth man did not emerge.

The three men who made it back alive helped her up onto the examination table. They tried calling his name. They tried playing his favorite music, pressing the speaker against Alice's exposed abdomen. They tried baking his favorite foods. They called in a diviner with his forked stick. They called in a meteorologist. He lined his instruments up and down her body, and shook his head. "Storm's coming," he said.

The doctors leaned in. "Storm's coming?" they asked. "Where?"

The meteorologist pointed at Alice. "In there."

They called in an Eskimo. "There are 437 words for snow," he whispered.

"But how do we get him out?" the doctors asked.

The Eskimo nodded, his fur cap shining under the examination lamp. "437 words," he said.

By then, it was day six. The doctors shook their heads. "There's no way," they whispered, "what with the exposure and the lack of food, there's no way he's still alive."

On the seventh day of the vigil, they sent for the lost man's wife. She spread Alice's legs, bent down and shivered. "What do I do?" she trembled. "What do I do down here?"

"Call to him," the doctors urged. "Call his name."

She called. "Honey?" she crooned. "Come out, come home!"

There was no answer. The wife began to sob. She clung to Alice. Her arms wrapped around Alice's bent legs, "Give him back," she pleaded. "Give him back!"


For a while, the story of the girl with nothing but a cold, hard breeze inside her swept through all the news stations. When the drama heightened with the missing fourth man, the networks' ratings went through the roof. It was all anybody could talk about: "What does it mean that she is cold and empty inside?" they asked. "Where did the fourth man go?" When Alice and the Specialist disappeared, the story made international news.

They had slipped out one night, three weeks into the vigil for the fourth man. It was not a well-planned escape, but somehow it worked. They tiptoed right past the studio security guards, cut the wire that led to the exit alarm and crawled out onto the highway. They flagged down a passing car. The driver took them all the way to the Nevada border. Desert rain washed across the stranger's windshield as Alice huddled close to the Specialist. They were on the lam together. For once, they were running in the same direction, with the same goal in mind—to get away from the doctors. A week later, he left her.

It was an eerily still day. They were holed up in an Econo Lodge outside Las Vegas. "We're going to split up," he had whispered, his hands grasping her shoulders as they had on their first meeting. "I'll go north. You go west."

"Why?" she asked.

He let go of her, walked over to the motel window. Parting the curtain an inch with his index finger, he stared out at the parking lot. "If you don't know that by now, I'm not going to be the one to tell you."

Alice gazed at him. There he stood in his rumpled seersucker suit, pigeon-toed and balding, a slice of desert sunlight cutting across his stricken face. Despite his odd theories, Alice had grown fond of the Specialist. She stood up, smoothed her skirt, and crossed to him. He held a photo in his hand. In it, the Specialist stands in full gear, his bright blue parka shining in the winter sunlight, surrounded by vast fields of snow, miles of it mounding up, soft and seamless and white. He smiles into the camera. Alice took his shaking hand in hers. "That's not really me," she said. She looked into his eyes—warm and moist, green as the sea.

"But I have evidence," he whispered back. "I have irrefutable evidence." He looked away again, out at the cactus shivering in the hot wind, just beyond the motel parking lot.

He left the next morning, before dawn, with one blue Samsonite carry-on and a hotel face cloth shielding his balding head from the hot Nevada sun. Alice feigned sleep throughout this long departure. As he folded his three dress shirts and zipped up his utility bag, as he combed the last few strands of hair over the crown of his head and trimmed his beard, Alice watched. Through half-closed eyes she saw him place a single envelope on the bedside table, cross to the motel door, unbolt the lock and slip away into the rising heat. After he left, she opened the envelope. There was no note, no instructions, no forwarding address, nothing, but a single photograph of a man standing in a field of snow.

That afternoon, Alice dyed her hair. She slipped into the motel laundry facility and quietly removed a pair of jeans and a new T-shirt from one of the dryers. Alice had never stolen anything before and the thrill of it, the getting-away-with-it feeling flooded her veins. Flushing with pleasure, she shimmied into the jeans. She sold her one good suit and bought a bus ticket back to California where she found work at a bakery on a strip right near the boardwalk. From her station behind the kneading tables, she could smell the ocean.

Back at the studio the Host was shocked by their disappearance. "How could you let this happen?" he asked his staff. "Right out from under my nose." But the two were gone. Not a single trace of them remained. A search party was formed, the Host leading the effort. "In the name of science," he blustered. "In the name of justice!" The camera recorded it all.

Following an anonymous tip, they headed north. They hired dogsleds and glided through the Yukon. They assumed that Alice and the Specialist, partners in this absurd crime, would always be together. The Fourth Man's wife came along. She rode just behind the dogs, a fur-lined parka framing her face. She called his name. Her voice echoed across the frozen landscape.

And for a while, that was all Alice saw. Every night before she fell asleep in her little apartment above the bakery, Alice turned on the evening news and there she was, the fourth man's wife. Chilblains had swollen her fingers. Her nose and cheeks were rubbed raw from exposure. She blinked into the camera. "Wherever you are, if you can hear me, call this number," the wife pleaded. "We don't want to hurt you. I just want my husband back."

The heat from the large ovens burned the hair off Alice's arms. It opened her pores and sweat ran down her back, formed half moons under her shirtsleeves. She reveled in the sloppy warmth of the bakery, in the easy camaraderie with her coworkers. Evenings, after the baking was done, her coworkers unfolded lawn chairs on the boardwalk and watched the red ball of the sun slide lower in the sky till it sat on the edge of the ocean. When it broke open and began to sink, the colors bled across the water. Alice often joined them. She liked the feel of the ocean breeze on her arms and neck. The wind lifted her hair and fluttered across her cheeks. She closed her eyes, leaned back and listened to the bakery girls talk about their boyfriends.

In the mornings, when the other bakers wandered outside for a smoke break, Alice would slip into the back room. Nestled into the tiered rising racks lay warm mounds of dough, resting like sleeping bodies, between the sheets of metal shelving. She gazed at the pastries. The raw, white buns, dusted in a layer of flour, slowly expanded as the yeast pulled in the surrounding air and the soft bodies of dough rose. One morning, when the owner was late and the other girls lingered over their cigarettes, taking one last pull, wandering further away from the back door out toward the beach, Alice slipped her hand in between the rising racks and caressed the new, white flesh.

All the while, miles away, deep in the north country, a search party combed Alaska and the Northern Territory. They found nothing. No sign of Alice. No trace of the fourth man. For eleven months they rode up and down over the snow-packed ground, the dogs barking in the cold, the fourth man's wife crying into the wilderness.

Then, a year later, the Host got a new tip and this one was solid. It led them right to the Specialist. He had taken refuge in a tiny Inuit community, trading his gold watch for the price of a safe haven for twelve months. But, at the end of the year, when he started conducting research, running experiments on the local girls, looking for another Alice, the villagers turned him in.

The morning the authorities went out and found him, Alice was in the middle of cutting dough for hot-crosse buns. The girl who ran the cash register rushed in, calling, "They caught him!"

"Who?" asked Alice, sliding a baker's knife through the dough.

"The Specialist! They caught the Specialist."

Alice let her hands fall to her sides. The girl turned on the TV. Once again Alice found herself gazing into the frozen tundra. The dogs barked outside the igloo. The snow was so cold it had turned icy and blue. They had the igloo surrounded and still, The Specialist would not give himself up. In the end, they smoked him out. Alice watched as the Specialist ran, half-naked, across the fields of snow. They shot him with a stun gun and he fell like a wild deer, his body sliding across the ice.

Alice stepped out onto the beach. The sign above the bakery switched on. Neon flooded the glass tubes, hovering and jumping to life in the crystalline air, calling to her, calling out OPEN. She remembered the poppies, bright and red on the wall in the examination room, and the Specialist's shallow-water eyes. She remembered the hotel in the desert, the stillness of the morning air, the cactus shuddering outside her window and the moment—before he left her, before he was gone—when she held his hands, still and cold, in her own. It had been years of waiting and holding herself, of trying to find the answer, the end, the other side of the mysterious pain, and how it had changed her, carved out her insides.

Alice walked toward the shore, stepping closer to the ocean than she had allowed herself to go in a long time. At the edge, she bent down and placed her fingers in the water. Her hands and arms were coated with pastry flour, rendering her whiter than usual, white as a ghost. The flour dissolved off her skin. It shimmered and flickered, falling away from her, toward the sand below. She let her wrists slip into the water, then her forearms, and her elbows. Waves crawled up her skin, licking the clouds of flour until the whiteness shifted. It moved off of Alice and into the water. The air around her grew solid and soft, as if it were made of pillows. And the ocean, which for hundreds of thousands of years had been whining outside the door, falling over and over itself, reaching for the shore, the ocean stopped. The white foaming crests of the waves stilled. The green water, shallow and undulating below her, grew viscous; it grew hard as fine crystal. Slowly, what lived inside Alice—the bright, soft, swelling snow, the cold, hard breeze, all of it—slipped out, and the ocean became a field, and the field became a tundra and it rolled out, like a door opening up, swinging loose on its hinges.

As Alice gazed out on the tundra she noticed beyond the last snowy hill, something bright and shining, something calling to her, crying, "Alice, Alice, I'm here." She stepped forward, away from the huddle of shops by the boardwalk and the flickering light of the neon sign and onto the white glaciers. She walked toward the tiny speck and as she walked the speck divided into a shock of red hair and a white lab coat and there before her in the distance stood the fourth man. His hand floated above his head as he waved and he called to her, his voice bugling out, a reveille, calling her name, calling out across the frozen fields of snow.

# THE MEDICINE MAN

*by* KEVIN MOFFETT

WHEN I'M LOW, I go to Bel-Air Plaza to look for the medicine man, Broom. He's not a medicine man in the exact sense, the ordained-by-his-fellow-tribesmen sense, but a generally wizened hard-looking Seminole Indian who works crushing boxes and sweeping. People call him Broom, which I figure is more nasty than honorary, like the old Russians in the building where I live call me Florida Power because sometimes I wear a hat that says Florida Power. Crushing boxes and sweeping is no proper vocation for a medicine man, even nonordained from a tribe that isn't officially recognized as a tribe. Early in school you're taught that Seminole is the only tribe never to officially surrender to the U.S. government and the only to help runaway slaves escape from crackers, which is whites with whips. My sister's husband says I'm manic depressant because sometimes I feel low and sometimes, like currently, high, and I think Indians are party to powerful secret forces even if they themselves aren't aware of it, like Broom isn't aware of it.

I didn't used to be so low-high. As a kid I played all the made-up games with my sister, Sally, games I can't recall now though I recall learning the rules, which varied from game to game, and now just to think about them, the rules, causes me, like it never used to, a certain quickness. Sally remembers the games and the rules to the games. Sally was a nice kid and is still nice. Maybe it's the games we played that made me low-high, or the rules to the games, which continued when the games ended, and often *became* the games, and continue now. Does anyone else feel a little pride to hear sirens and pull over to the roadside to let an ambulance or a police car pass by? It calms me.

Walking does too, especially mornings before the recycling truck comes, the blue bins curbed and filled with beer bottles, wine bottles, soup cans, leaflets, newspapers, antennas, half-and-half cartons, test tubes, magazines, cereal boxes, toothpastes. All this out in the open, this suggestion, to me it's like looking into people's secrets.

And visiting Sally, my sister, who lives in a condo at the beach with her husband, Steve, who teaches study skills at Flagler College. They're getting ready to have a baby, and what I really want to tell you about is the earphones and Sally's stomach, but I need to tell you first about Broom the medicine man, which I started to. He's who I was looking for before going to Sally's condo and seeing her with the conductant jelly on her stomach and the earphones which I put on while Steve said, *Do either of you have a goddamn*—but not yet, not yet.

Broom. Everyone knows you're supposed to bring a gift when you consult a medicine man, something valuable to you but not him so he can throw it away without regret. When I went to see Broom I had been low for almost six days. A thing happened at Indigo Pines, where I live with old people who're Russian Jews, escaped communists or escaped from the communists, they won't tell me which. These escaped Russians are old, old. I used to say I love all people, before these Russians, but now I can't. Now I love only most people and I've started to suspect that once you start decreasing a thing it's easy to keep going. I'm allowed to live at Indigo Pines even though I'm not old or Russian or sick or ready to be.

Indigo Pines prints the menus in both Russian and English and they're set in two stacks on a table in front of the cafeteria before it opens for dinner. I was early. I could smell it was zucchini latkes, that mossy smell zucchini latkes have, and I sat down and read the menu next to three Russians who are always sitting on the purple loveseat in front of the cafeteria, talking Russian or playing a Russian game with wooden pegs in a triangle, which is what they were doing tonight. The dinner menu said zucchini latkes with Provençal sauce, which is spaghetti sauce, and at the bottom of the menu inside the Dinner Events box I read, Tonight Is Indigo Pines Poetry Night! Between dinner and dessert, we will be passing out words and you will surprise us with your creativity! Should be fun!

When I read that, why didn't I leave and go to Hogan's Heros for an eight-inch number seven, no mustard, no lettuce, pressed, and watch them playing shuffleboard on that long tabletop with sawdust and spinny silver pucks, and eat alone but not lonesome with the noisy TV noise and eager-people-standing-around-the-shuffleboard-table noise? Hogan's serves mugs of beer and sandwiches called heros, which you order by number. I once overheard a woman there say she wanted no hot peckers on her hero and she meant, I've thought about it, hot peppers. Number seven means ham.

Being low-high causes bad decisions. I stayed at Indigo Pines for zucchini latkes with the thirty or so Russians who sat at the white-nylon-tableclothed tables in the same groups of five and six I'm familiar with and ate and talked Russian while I ate my latkes alone, and lonesome. Two Russians across the table from me gestured like weightlifters and laughed. I was wondering about *passing out words* by repeating it to myself while eating my latkes. The more I repeated *passing out words* the more it sounded like something I might want to stay around for and I started to get excited, high. Plus, dessert was fruit blintzes, which is like pancakes and good.

*Passing out words* meant being given a plastic Ziploc filled with white pieces of paper with words typed on them. The Russians in charge of Poetry Night were young Russians. They cleared away my plate, leaving a fork for the blintzes, and then handed me a Ziploc. One of them said, Take a few minutes and make a poem. Remember, one sentence is all it takes to surprise us with your creativity! And so on. The young Russians who work at Indigo Pines are pale and have bright blue eyes like huskies. They're a little nicer than the old Russians but still not nice.

My Ziploc was stapled shut and I opened it and put all my words on the white tablecloth in front of me with a few flower-formed stains from the Provençal sauce. My words were: On Some For Time The What And Mister Blew If. I was trying to figure out the rules of the game, what was expected of me to make this poem out of these words, who I would surprise with what, and why. I raised my hand to try to get the attention of one of the young Russians in charge of Poetry Night to tell them I wanted a new

Ziploc of words, these are poor words I was going to tell them, but they, the Russians, the young Russians—all these Russians in Florida!—were gone. The quickness. Like being sped up and slowed down at the same time. These *words*.

I tried to piece together a poem out of On Some For Time The What And Mister Blew If, moving the words around on the white tablecloth, but I couldn't come up with anything that made sense. The two Russians across from me had pieced theirs together, and were gesturing and laughing again. I wanted to spill something steaming on them. The first cafeteria poem was read by a short old Russian who wears his silver apartment key, or some silver key, on a shoestring necklace around his neck. He stood up, two tables away from my table, cleared his throat, and read, Trees whine circles in thirsty eve-ninks, my dear only.

It sounded more Russiany than that, but I especially remember eve-ninks, which is evenings, thirsty eve-ninks, and I can understand cold eve-ninks and stormy eve-ninks and windy and happy eve-ninks, but *thirsty* eve-ninks? All the other Russians clapped for the thirsty eve-ninks and I clapped as well only because after the Russian read the poem he bowed to each side of the cafeteria and smiled and sat down. If this didn't entirely seem like a thing a Russian would do who wasn't nice, I asked myself while I clapped, why not? I didn't know and don't know.

The next few cafeteria poems were a lot like the trees whining in thirsty eve-ninks. Snakes rolling teeth and similar jigsawed poems spoken slow and formal like Russians speak. In front of and behind me, at the cafeteria's long picnic tables covered with white tablecloths, the Russians read their poems and clapped for other poems, and I started to panic. I was no closer to having a poem than when I took the words out of the bag, these poor words, and I decided to stand up. Actually, I didn't decide, I just stood up and when I did, decided it was a good idea. I left behind my fruit blintzes and walked toward the exit and before I could open the thick metal door with its square window trapping a grid of strings like tennis-racket strings, where you can't see outside until you're right against it, I heard one of the Russians say, Exit Florida Power.

I was starting to feel the quickness from the poem rules and thinking about rules from the made-up games I played with Sally and can't recall, and my poor Ziploc of words, then the thirsty eve-ninks, the Russians clapping,

*Exit Florida Power.* By the time I climbed the eight sets of stairs to my apartment, which I do when I remember for exercise, I was, I knew, low. I knew because I went straight to the stove and put on water for hot tea. I had started shivering on the last few stairs, nothing seeming more true than the feeling of being trapped quick inside your body quick inside your body quick inside your body, which is the only way I know to say it.

And five days later—you don't want a sum-up of the five days which… the worst thing about low-highness is when you're high and most suitored by the unpredicted joys, you don't want anything to do with them, but when you're low, you beg for the unpredicted joys, and then where are they, you going through the old Tupperware of family photographs again like a punishment, and I can't call Sally because of Steve, alone and lonesome with nothing but time, nothing but time, and where are they?—I finally had my cafeteria poem:

*Mister, and if some blew on, for the time what?*

I was still low so I went to look for the medicine man.

Indigo Pines and Sally and the medicine man and I are all in Flagler, Florida, named after the man who built hotels a hundred years ago, and railroad bridges across the Keys. You learn this early in school in Florida along with De Soto and De Leon, who are Spaniard explorers, and the correct spelling of Florida cities with Indian names like Kissimmee, Sarasota, Palatka, Pensacola, and about the Seminoles helping runaway slaves escape from crackers (whites with whips). They don't teach you the railroad bridges aren't there anymore. You have to go see for yourself.

Everyone knows you should bring a gift when you consult a medicine man, so I looked around my apartment for something valuable to me and not him so he can throw it away without regret when I give it to him. I've been to the medicine man about a half-dozen times now, and I'm running out of gifts and the best I could do this time was my only pair of long underwear which you probably don't think you would need in Florida, the Sunshine State, but trust me.

Flagler is Old Florida, which means few tourists. Bel-Air Plaza is shaped like an opened-up box with the top off to the left side and the box opened up to the ocean right across Atlantic Avenue. Nobody much shops at Bel-Air Plaza, which used to have a magic shop when I was a kid, where you could look at tricks and bins full of fake vomits and fake poohs, but now it has a Super Dollar store, Mister Video, and a wig store called An Affair For Hair. Broom is usually behind Super Dollar, which spans the whole bottom of Bel-Air Plaza's box shape and faces the beach, so that's where I looked for him, and where I found him, smoking a cigarette on the edge of the loading dock behind Super Dollar, where he works crushing boxes and sweeping. When he saw me approaching with the long underwear, Broom dropped his cigarette and hopped off the loading dock, pivoted the cigarette out, looked at me sideways like people do for effect not real study, and said, Is there a reason you're carrying around a pair of dirty britches, my man?

I saw that he had two oval bright-orange stickers stuck to his white Super Dollar apron, one that said BONELESS and beneath it one that said SKINLESS, like on packages of chicken.

It's a gift for you, I said. The medicine man.

He looked at me sideways a little more. This is just to unnerve you if someone ever tries it on you. The medicine man said, real slowly, A gift. For me. The medicine man. (He laughed, again for effect. Only when I'm low would I know this.) He said, Look, man, I told you: I'm just tan. I live with my grandparents across the street and cain't go anywhere because I cain't drive a car. (*Cain't*, the medicine man said, which means poor and Georgia. Only when I'm low.) He said, I'm no medicine man; I'm no Indian. I'm Dominican, Mexican, Hawaiian, I don't know what. My grandparents won't tell me. I been throwing away all that junk you give me.

We, Broom and I, do this routine every time I come to him. I don't care if he lives with his grandparents, cain't (Georgia) drive a car, and isn't full-on Seminole, which nearly no Seminoles are anymore. I said, I *know* you throw it away. It's what medicine men are supposed to do.

There's plenty of people in Flagler like Broom, people you meet who come off at first as mean and unagreeable but who are mostly, I think, afraid, and probably I'm talking about me, too. Looking for the medicine man doesn't make sense to anyone but me and it doesn't need to and I've been in Flagler all my life and I don't want to leave. This isn't sad or heroic, really, but I think it's important. Broom wants to drive and cain't, my sister wanted to leave Flagler and cain't. We all have our illusions, I wanted to say to the medicine man, you thought you were telling me something I didn't know. Instead I said, I need some rest.

And as if he had already read my mind, as if he were keyed into my frequency, the medicine man was showing me pills.

Two of these, he said, and you'll sleep like a baby.

I looked at the pills, two liver-colored capsules in a roughened palm, roughened like oak bark or like he'd been messing with car engines. I don't want to sleep like a baby, I said.

The medicine man's hand closed quick on the pills, which he then shoved into the pocket of his light-green Super Dollar slacks, pressed neat with a sharp crease down the side, and I don't think I want to say much more about the medicine man. Think of me, in back of Super Dollar with him and his pills waiting for me to leave like I was at his front door and had handed him a package not addressed to him. I said *thanks* like a question and left, disappointed, like you, maybe.


What's wrong with me? Why aren't I normal? Walking toward Sally's condo from Bel-Air Plaza, I watched one of those single-person planes that fly over the beach towing a banner with an advertisement on it: BOOTHILL TAVERN: YOU'RE BETTER OFF HERE THAN ACROSS THE STREET and I frowned because across the street from the Boothill Tavern is an old cemetery. I frowned even though I'd seen the advertisement before.

We all have our illusions. When I'm low it's hard to think of anything except how I'm low, anything except me me me, which is like thinking of the rules to those made-up games instead of the game itself, being so concerned with how you are doing, or how you are supposed to be doing, that the *how* overwhelms the *you*, and the thinking about how I'm low becomes the reason I'm low. But often enough I find some unpredicted joy that calms me. Pulling over to let ambulances or police cars pass by, or walking around near the beach houses, especially mornings before the recycling truck comes, calms me. Walking to my sister's condo, I noticed a single blue recycling bin, likely left out too late for the recycling truck, curbed and open and filled entirely with about two dozen Mama and Papa Gus whipping-cream cartons. Secrets.

By the time I got to Sally's condo, I was feeling sluggish but anxious, like, have you seen the slowed-down footage of hummingbirds feeding over flowers, with the fastness of the hummingbirds residing in the slowness of the footage? The slower the footage the faster the hummingbird feeds. I felt poised for disappointment. I dialed Sally's condo and someone answered and buzzed me in by pushing seven on the other end of the line. They didn't even say hello. Sally would've said hello. There's a camera fixed above the phone in front of the condo which you can watch if you live at the Admiralty Club, seeing who comes and goes on channel 32. Steve (Sally would've said hello) must have been watching channel 32 and answered the phone and pushed seven on the telephone, which releases the lock on the front door to the condo, without saying hello, and this probably sounds paranoid, but it's true.

I walked the twelve flights to Sally's condo, which I do when I remember for exercise. She lives on the sixth floor, the top floor. I knocked on the front door with a brass knocker I'd never noticed before, and heard Sally yell, Back here. It didn't sound at the front door like a yell and she meant, I knew, back patio.

I went down the front hallway, through the dining room to the living room, where the television was turned to channel 32, and I watched the black-and-white footage of the phone in front of the condo, where I just was, no one coming or going right now, and the bare light above the phone turned on, which the mailman does when he comes so people in the building can turn to channel 32 to see if their mail has arrived, and I was dreading Steve, whose voice I could hear from where I stood, arguing with Sally about something. He is always arguing with Sally about something.

I know why I don't like Steve but that doesn't make me feel any better. On the back patio he was saying, Well, let's take it back then.

Sally says, I'm worried. Aren't you supposed to hear something?

Steve: It must be broken. Goddamnit. Where are the batteries? Let's take it back.

Sally: Aren't you worried?

Steve: Of course I'm not worried.

On channel 32 a man has picked up the phone in front of the condo and is dialing, looking at the camera, he must know the camera's there, and smiling and waving, whoever he's calling must be watching channel 32, and he hangs up the phone and goes inside.

Well, Charlie, Steve says. He has opened the patio door, a sliding screen door and is standing on the track, smiling with his teeth clenched. He says, What you got there?

The underwear. I forgot to give it to Broom and it's been gripped in my hand so long I've forgotten it's there, balled up and useless-feeling, who needs long underwear in Florida, but you do sometimes, trust me, and I say, They were for Broom.

Steve says, I see. The medicine man?

Me: That's him. He isn't official.

Steve: Of course. Listen, Sally's out back, but now's probably not a good time. You understand, I'm sure.

Sally says, Don't listen to him, Charlie. Come back here.

Steve walks past me, real close so I have to step forward out of his way so he can pass, and I walk out to the back patio and close the screen door, tossing the underwear behind a potted flower, a white potted flower that looks like an oleander, which are poisonous. Sally is sitting in one of the reclining beach chairs with the white plastic straps and her shirt is pulled high over her stomach, which by now is swelled like a spider stomach and the sight of it, with clear jelly rubbed on her stomach so it shines, surprises me.

Please tell me what you're doing, I say.

She says, Where have you been, Charlie? I've been worried, I've been calling, I left messages with Mr. Sharova. (Mr. Sharova's the superintendent of Indigo Pines.)

I feel terrible, I say. There was poetry in the cafeteria and my words were like On Some If Blew What, Jesus. What's that box? What were those games we used to play? When's the baby coming?

Not for a while, she says. Relax, sit down.

I sit in one of the reclining beach chairs, which always makes me feel silly, and look at the ocean for the first time. I had forgotten there was such a pretty view from the back porch of Sally's condo, the sun going down and the sky is peach and clear, the ocean shining, shivering. I look at Sally who's looking at me, and I know I'm going to have a difficult time describing Sally. I've tried and it's like trying to pinpoint why certain smells are pleasing, or colors. She's tan, she wears wire-rimmed glasses, when she's not around she's a sensation I can't separate from the sensing. Here's Steve.

He says, Ginger ale for the mother-to-be, a beer for the uncle-to-be, and a g-and-t for the father-to-be.

G-and-t means gin-and-tonic. I say, I don't want beer, I don't drink beer. (This isn't true.)

Sally says, Do you think we should call the doctor?

Steve: Jesus, no. Calm down, it's Saturday.

Me: What doctor? What's wrong?

Steve: The earphones are broken and now Sally's panicking for no reason. Where'd your underwear go, Charlie?

Sally says something right after this, but I want to tell you the reason Steve keeps asking me about the underwear is not because he cares about the underwear but because he's an asshole.

Sally: I don't feel anything. My stomach's numb.

Steve: The earphones are broken.

Me: What earphones? What's wrong?

Sally pulls out a pair of earphones from the box next to her chair, which look like normal earphones but they're attached by a cord to a white plastic microphone, and says, We're listening for the baby's heartbeat.

Steve says, They're broken.

Sally puts the earphones back into the box and looks at Steve with a sort of relaxed anger I recognize from a long time ago, her looking at our parents that way, but too nice or something to yell at them and him, Steve, like I would, like I want to. Steve. I know he isn't doing anything particularly terrible, just asking about my underwear, which is annoying and not terrible, and saying the earphones are broken, which Sally doesn't seem to think is true, and drinking his g-and-t (gin-and-tonic), and saying things like *g-and-t for the father-to-be*, annoying not terrible, but trust me.

Sally says, So where have you been?

I say, Mostly in my apartment, going through old pictures.

Though it sounds like all this is happening right now, currently, it, this conversation, the earphones, already happened a few days ago and the reason I'm telling you about it is I feel high right now, and I think what did it was being with Sally on the back patio of her condo. Sally has brown hair which used to be curly and is still curly.

I say, Do you remember any of the games we used to play?

Sally laughs like letting a brief hiss out of a tire and says, Is it the games again, Charlie?

I guess it is, I think but don't say, and I remember I've asked her this before, gone through the old pictures before, but it feels good to ask it, to do it, like going to see the medicine man, and next time I'll probably ask it again. It feels good to have someone to ask questions you need the answers to. It feels good to give Broom a gift knowing he'll throw it away.

Sally says, He used to be such a good artist. (She's talking to Steve but to me really, if that makes sense.) I remember him going to the beach and coming home with like twenty drawings, birds, tourists, dunes. We used to have them hanging all over the house.

Sketches, I say.

They were *good*, Sally says.

Steve clink-clinks the g-and-t ice cubes in the glass, and I take a sip of the beer I've been holding, which I don't mean to do, but once I do, I take another.

I say, Where'd everybody we used to know go?

Sally says, It's okay.

I want to tell her about the Russians, Poetry Night, my poor words, Broom, talking to Sally always makes me feel better, not what's said but the saying it, the game not the rules. But there's Steve again, or still, clink-clinking his g-and-t, too lazy to get another one, maybe, leaning against the patio rail, waiting to stomp out anything I say.

I say, What's it like to have something alive inside you?

This sounds more philosophical than I intend it to, and I'm glad when Sally doesn't answer. Maybe I didn't ask it out loud. Sally wants a family. She used to have long conversations with her stuffed animals, which she collected, inventing personalities for each one of them, and feuds and marriages, and once she walked into the kitchen with a Ziggy doll and held it up to me where I was sitting. I remember the confused expression on Ziggy's face, and Sally said, she was maybe ten years old, she said, Ziggy's dead. Ziggy looked normal enough to me, maybe a little confused like wondering why nothing good ever happens to him, but we dug a hole and buried him anyway and that was that. I hope Sally didn't stay in Flagler to take care of me, but I suspect she did. If so, she married Steve because of me, she's unhappy because of me, my being attached to her is like an anchor being attached to her.

Steve looks like he's going to laugh. He says: So tell us, Charlie, can a medicine man marry you?

A medicine man is allowed to marry whoever he wants, I say, though I don't know if this is true.

Steve says, No, I mean, can a medicine man preside over a wedding, like a priest, or the captain of a cruise ship?

Sally looks at Steve with more relaxed anger, and when someone like Sally is angry at you, you should feel awful, awful. I say, Nothing funny about medicine men, Steve. They *help* people.

Steve says, So do I. He clink-clinks the g-and-t ice cubes again and I take another sip of beer, and I know why Steve thinks I'm manic depressant. It's because when I'm around Sally, who's the only person I'm not uncomfortable around—when I said before that I used to say I love all people until the Russians, that was a lie, not that I used to say it, I did, but that I meant it, I didn't. When Steve sees me around Sally he thinks I act around Sally like I act all the time, and me hating Steve probably has little to do with him and a lot to do with Sally, whose stomach I've been looking at, the clear jelly shining sort of reddish in the peach light, and it surprises me again, once I realize what I'm looking at. Sally says, Conductant. It's for the sound. She saw me looking.

I say, I would like to listen to the baby's heartbeat.

I don't want to think I said this from meanness, knowing it would make Steve angry, though I might have. After saying it the idea seems like a decent-enough one. I'm the baby's uncle-to-be, why shouldn't I want to listen to its heartbeat?

Steve says, The earphones are broken.

Sally pulls the earphones out of the box again and unwraps the cord because it's tangled around itself and hands me the earphones while Steve repeats, They're broken.

One of the games we used to play involved running around and hiding, but it wasn't hide-and-go-seek. You had to switch hiding places every so often—this was outside at night—in the dark, and you counted to fifty, or a hundred, and switched hiding places, or yelled when you were yelled at, teasing the person who had to find you. It was called chase something-something. Sally hands me the earphones and I put them on as Steve's talking, saying, Do either of you have a goddamn—

Then they're on, the earphones, no more Steve, and when Sally turns on the machine, which I see says BabyBeat on the side and looks like a plastic microphone, a child's toy, I know right away that Steve's wrong, the earphones are not broken. He's still talking but I'm watching Sally who watches her stomach, the clear shiny reddish jelly, conductant, and I can hear a dead-space sound on the earphones like the static sound in-between space transmissions, after an astronaut says *over*, that dead watery static sound, and I'm thinking there's something wrong with Sally, something terrible, and she's moving the microphone over the conductant, over her stomach which she's still watching, and I'm watching her, she looks so sad, and Steve's talking *rah-rah-rah-rah*, probably still clink-clinking his g-and-t, though I can't hear it over the dead-space sound, unchanging as she moves the microphone over the conductant, and as I'm getting ready to take off the earphones, which are heavy and tight on my head, Sally moves the microphone under her belly button, pushed out of its socket, the belly button is, her stomach is so huge, and right before I take off the earphones, I hear a faint *buh-buh-buh-buh-buh*, faster than a normal heartbeat, but definitely a heartbeat, *buh-buh-buh-buh-buh*, fast and faint then louder as Sally slowly moves the microphone higher along her stomach, and I say, Hold it right there.

Sally stops and looks up from her stomach, at me, and Steve stops his *rah-rah-rah*, probably stops clink-clinking his g-and-t, though I can't hear anything but the *buh-buh-buh-buh-buh*, faster than a normal heartbeat and loud with the dead watery sound beneath it, but now something alive in the water. Sally is looking at me with obvious expectation holding the microphone on the conductant below her belly button, and there are wide tracks in the conductant from the microphone, and I don't want to say anything because of Steve. I want Sally to know by looking at me. I nod neutrally at Sally and Sally smiles, which means she knows and I know and Steve, who is moving toward me to take the earphones, doesn't know, and I'll end here after I tell you what Sally told Steve when he moved toward me to take the earphones and I held the earphones tight to my head, looked at Steve, and Sally said, loud enough for me to hear over the *buh-buh-buh-buh-buh* and the dead watery sound, Sally said, Don't move. I held the earphones tight to my head, already feeling better, and Sally said to Steve, Don't move a single goddamn muscle.

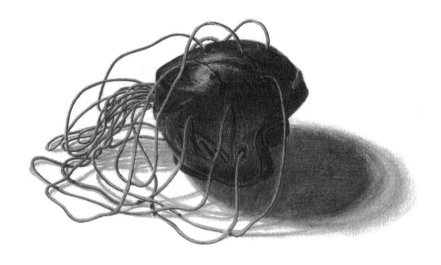

# MUDDER TONGUE

*by* BRIAN EVENSON

I

THERE CAME A certain point, in his speech, in his confrontation with others, in his smattering with the world, when Hecker realized something was wrong. Language was starting to slip in his mouth, words substituting themselves for one another, and while his own thoughts remained lucid as ever, sometimes they could only be made manifest on his tongue if they were wrung out or twisted or set with false eyes. False eyes? Something like that. His sense of language had always been slightly fluid; it had always been easy for him, when distracted, to substitute one word for another based on sound or rhythm or association or analogy, which was why people thought him absentminded. But this was different. Then, when distracted, he hadn't known when he misspoke, had only been cued by the expression on the faces of those around him to backtrack and correct. Now, he *heard* himself say the wrong word, knew it to be wrong even while he was saying it, but was powerless to correct it. There was something seriously wrong with him, something broken. He could grasp that, but could not understand where it was taking him.

The first time it happened, the look on his face had been one of appalled wonder—or so he guessed from the look of glee his daughter offered in return.

"Oh, Daddy," she said, for even though she was mostly grown she still called him Daddy for reasons he neither understood nor encouraged. "It's not gravy you mean, but fishing."

Gravy? he thought. Fishing? There was too far a gap between the two terms to leap from one to the other by any logic available to him. He had heard his voice say *gravy* while his mind was busy transmitting *fishing* to his tongue. He was amazed by what he heard coming out of his mouth, didn't understand why it didn't have some relation to his thoughts. But to his daughter he was merely the same old father: absentminded, distracted.

"Oh," he said. "Of course. Termite." And was amazed again. But to his daughter he was only playing a game, taunting her. And then, a moment later, he was fine. He could say *fishing* again when he meant fishing. He alone knew something was seriously wrong. When would his daughter realize? he wondered. What, he wondered, was happening?


There were days. They kept coming and going. He opened his mouth and he closed his mouth. Mostly what he heard form on his tongue made sense, but sometimes not. When not, he entered into an elaborate and oblique process of trying to convey what he had in fact intended. In the best of circumstances the person or persons came up with the words themselves and offered them to him. Nodding, not speaking, he accepted them, hoping that when he next opened his mouth his brain and tongue would have realigned.

He quickly acquired a dread of meetings, of speaking in front of his colleagues. Once, his language collapsed in the middle of articulating a complaint against his chair, colleagues touching their glasses or faces and staring at him and waiting for him to go on. Fear-stricken enough to improvise, he stood, speechless and shaking his head, and walked out. Some of them later congratulated him on his courageous gesture, but others shied away.

His daughter began to notice a tentativeness to him, though that was not how she would have phrased it. But he could see her watching him, slightly puzzled. His past personal behavior had been eccentric enough, he discovered, that she was willing to give him an alibi for almost anything. And yet, she still sensed something was wrong. At night, after she claimed to have gone to bed, he would sometimes hear her sliding through the halls. He would shift in his cushion on the sofa to find her behind, in the doorway, staring at the back of his head.

"Why do you melba?" he said to her. "Pronto."

She looked at him seriously, as if she understood, and then, nodding, returned to bed.


The dog began acting strangely, panting heavily around him, keeping a distance when he tried to approach, creeping slowly off with its tail flattened out. *Am I the same person?* he wondered. Perhaps that was it, he thought, perhaps he was not. Or perhaps he was only part of himself, and whoever else he also was had never learned to speak properly.

He tried to make friends with the dog again, offering it treats, which sometimes it took gingerly with its teeth, careful not to touch his hand.


In the classroom, where before he had been sure of himself, aggressive even, he became jittery, always waiting for the moment when the smooth surface of his language would be perforated. He took to dividing his students into small groups, speaking to them as little as possible. He tried, mornings before a class, to practice what he was going to say to propel them into their groups as quickly as possible, how to deflect or quickly answer any potential questions. But however many times he uttered his spiel perfectly beforehand, the actual moment of recitation was always up for grabs.

He instead began practicing alternatives for each sentence: on the first moment of collapse he would switch, attempting to get the same thing across with a different sentence pattern, entirely different words. But if a sentence crumbled, which it did once or twice per class—often enough in any case that the students, like his dog, like his daughter, like his colleagues, seemed now always to be looking at him oddly—the alternative usually crumbled away as well. But if a third variant did not hold, the fourth usually did, if there had to be a fourth, for by that time his mind had cycled around to a track that allowed it direct contact with his tongue again.

And thus it took a number of weeks before he found himself standing at the front of the class with all his options exhausted in the gravest misspeakings, each more outrageous than the last, so much so that he was afraid to say another word. The class, a carefully wrapped part of him noted, was more uniformly attentive than they had been at any other time in the semester, peculiarly primed to receive knowledge. But he had nothing to offer them. So instead he turned, wrote something banal on the board. *Nature of evil. Consider and discuss.* And then, suddenly, he could speak again.

For a time it seemed that writing would be his salvation. In the classroom, whenever his words started to come out maddened or stippled or gargled he would turn to the board and write what he had actually meant. This worked fine up to a point, though he had to admit it sometimes looked odd when he suddenly stopped speaking and began to write. But still it could be dismissed by students as mere eccentricity, or as an attempt to avoid having to repeat something twice.

At home, such a strategy was more fraught, fraughter. Any time he tried it with his daughter he found her turning away before he could find a pen, she perhaps believing that he had decided to ignore her. Elsewhere too, it didn't seem to work. At a restaurant, one could point at an item on the menu but this wasn't well received, and the one time he tried this in a social situation it was thought he was making fun of the deaf.

But there were other places it did work. He could talk to his colleagues by note or by email as long as he wasn't physically present. He also tried leaving his daughter scrawled messages, but she chose to ignore them or pretended she hadn't seen them. Once, when he asked her about one, whether she had seen it, she looked at him fixedly for some time before finally rolling her eyes and saying, "Yes, Daddy."

"Well?" he said.

"Well, what?"

"What's your answer?"

She shook her head. "No answer."

"But," he said. "Corfu?"

"Corfu?" she said. "In Greece? What are you talking about? Don't play games with me, Daddy."

"Sandwich," he said and covered his mouth.

"Here I am, Daddy," she said, angry. "Right here. I'm usually right here. I'm not going to let you mess with me. If you want to ask me something you can just open your mouth and ask me."

But he couldn't just open his mouth, he realized. He didn't dare. *Sandwich?* he thought. He sat staring at her, hand over mouth, trying to gather the courage to speak, to misspeak, until, fuming, she gave a little cry and marched out of the room.

II

As his condition worsened, he stayed silent for hours. His daughter rallied, sometimes referring to him railingly as "the recluse," as in *How's the old recluse this morning?*, at other times merely accusing him of becoming *pensive in his dotage*. Where, he wondered, had she picked up the word *dotage*? The frequency of his misspeakings grew until finally he felt he could no longer meet his class; the last few weeks of the term he phoned in sick nearly every day, or rather had his daughter phone in for him. He sent his lesson plans in by email, got a colleague to fill in for him, finally wrote a letter to the department chair requesting early retirement.

"You're lonely," his daughter said to him one evening. "You need to get out more."

He shook his head no.

"You need to date," she said. "Do you want me to set you up with someone?"

He shook his head emphatically no.

"All right," she said. "A date it is. I'll see what I can do."

She began to bring home brochures from dating services, and left the *women seeking men* page of the city's weekly out with a few choice ads circled. Was he *adventuresome*? No, he thought, reading the ads, he was not. Did he like long walks and a romantic dinner for two on the beach? No, he did not care for sand in his food. *Bookish*? Well, yes, but this woman's idea of high lit, as it turned out later in the ad, was John Irving. Unless the Irving referred to was Washington Irving of *Sleepy Hollow* fame. Was that any better?

And what would he put in his own ad? *SWM, well past prime, losing ability to speak, looks for special companionship that goes beyond words?* He groaned and arranged everything in a neat little stack at the back of his desk.

A few days later, email messages began showing up addressed to "Silver Fox" or "the silver fox" or, in one case, "Mr. F. Silver." They were all from women who claimed to have seen his "posting" and who were "interested." They wanted, they all said in different but equally banal ways, to *get to know him better.*

He dragged his daughter in and pointed at the screen. "Already?" she said.

He nodded. He had begun to write something admonitory down for her to read but she was ignoring him, had taken over his chair, was scrolling through each woman's message.

"No," he said. "I don't—"

"And this one," she was saying, "what's wrong with this one?"

"But I don't," he said. "Any of them, no."

"No?" she said. "But why not? Daddy, you *said* you wanted to go on a date. I asked you, *Daddy*, and *you* said yes."

No, he thought, that was not what he had said. He had said nothing. He opened his mouth. "Doctorate," he said.

"Doctor?" she said, and looked at him sharply, her eyes narrowing. "Are you all right?"

That was not what he had meant his mouth to say, not that at all.

"You prefer the one that's a doctor?" his daughter said, clicking open each message in turn as she talked. "But I don't think any of them are."

But what was he to do? he wondered. First of all nobody would listen, and second of all, even if they did listen, he himself did not know, from moment to moment, what, if anything, he was actually going to say.

She was there, chattering away in front of him, hardly even hearing what she herself was saying. Why not tell her, he wondered, that something was seriously wrong with him? What was there to be afraid of?

But no, he thought, the way people looked at him already, it was almost more than he could bear, and if it came tinged with pity he would no longer feel human. Better to keep it to himself, hold it to himself as long as possible. And then he would still be, at least in part, human.

\* \* \*

In the end he took her by the shoulders and, while she protested, silently pushed her out of the room. His head had started to ache, the pain pooling in his right eye. He closed his door and then returned to the computer, deleting the messages one after another. They were all, he saw, carefully constructed, with each woman trying to present herself as unique or original or witty but each doing so by employing the same syntactical gestures, the same rhetorical strategies, sometimes even the exact same phrase, as the others. *This is what it means to be immersed in language*, he thought, *to lose one's ability to think. To speak other people's words. But the only alternative is not to speak at all. Or was it? Nature of evil*, he thought. *Define and discuss.*

Depressed, he glanced through the last three messages. God, his head hurt. The first message was addressed to "silver fox" with three exclamation points following fox. It was from someone who had adopted the moniker "2hot2handel." Music lover or bad speller? he wondered. He deleted it. The second to the last one was to "F. Silver," from "OldiebutGoodie." Oh, God, he thought, and deleted it. The pain made his eye feel like a knife was being pushed through it. The eye was beginning to water. He clenched it shut as tight as he could and covered it with his hand. He stood, tipping his chair over, and stumbled about the room, knocking into what must have been walls.

Someone was knocking on the door. "Daddy," someone was calling, "are you all right?" Somewhere a dog was growling. He looked up through his good eye and saw, framed in the doorway, a girl.

"Tights," he said, "cardboard boxes," and collapsed.

### III

He awoke to a buzzing noise, saw it was coming from an electric light, fluorescent, inset in the ceiling directly above his head. His daughter was there beside him, looking at his face.

He opened his mouth, then closed it again.

"No," she said. "Just rest."

He nodded. He was in a bed, he saw, not his bed. There was a rail to either side of him, to hold him in.

"I'm going to get the doctor," she claimed. "Don't move."

Then she was gone. He closed his eyes, swallowed. The pain in his head was still there, but subdued now and no longer sharpened into a hard point. He rolled his head to one side and back again, pleased that he could still do so.

His daughter returned, the doctor beside her, a smallish tanned man hardly bigger than her.

"Mr. Hecker?" the doctor said, setting down a folder and snapping on latex gloves. "How are we feeling?"

"Groin," he said. *Goddamn*, he thought.

"Your groin hurts? It's your head we're concerned about, but I'll look at the groin too if you'd like."

Hecker shook his head. "No? Well, then," said the doctor. "No to the groin, then." He clicked on a penlight, peered into first one eye then the other. "Any headaches, Mr. Hecker?"

He hesitated, nodded.

"Head operations in your youth? Surgeries of the head? Cortisone treatments? Bad motorcycle wrecks? Untreated skull injuries?"

Hecker shook his head.

"And how are we feeling now?" he asked.

Hecker nodded. *Good*, he thought, *good enough.* He opened his mouth. The word *good* came out.

The doctor nodded. He stripped the gloves off his hands and dropped them into the trash. He came back and sat on the bed.

"I've looked at your X-rays," he said.

Hecker nodded.

"We should chat," the doctor said. "Would you like your daughter to stay for this?"

"Of course I can be here for this," his daughter said. "I'm legally an adult. Be here for what?" she asked.

Hecker shook his head.

"No?" said the doctor. He turned to Hecker's daughter. "Please wait in the hall," he said.

His daughter looked at the doctor and then opened her mouth to speak, and then gave a little inarticulate cry and went out. The doctor came closer and sat on the edge of the bed.

"Your X-rays," said the doctor. "I don't mean to frighten you but, well, I'd like to run some tests." He took the folder from the bedside table and took the X-rays out, held them above Hecker, in the light. "This cloudiness," he said. "Do you see it? I'm concerned."

Hecker looked. The dark area, as far as he could tell, ran all the way from one side of his skull to the other.

"We'll have to run some tests," said the doctor. "Do you want to let your daughter know?"

Hecker hesitated. Did he want to tell her? No, he thought, but he wasn't certain why. Did he want to shield her or simply shield himself from her reaction? Or was it simply he didn't trust words anymore, at least not when they came out of his own mouth? Maybe someone else could tell her. Maybe he would figure out what to do when he had to.

"Perhaps no need to frighten her until the results are back," said the doctor, watching him closely. "There's no reason to panic yet," he said. He turned and began to write on his chart. "Any difficulties? Loss of motor skills? Speech problems? Anything out of the ordinary?"

Hecker hesitated. Was there any point trying to explain? "Speech," he finally tried to say, but nothing came out. Why nothing? he wondered. Before, there had at least always been something, even if it was the wrong thing. Frustrated, he shook his head.

The doctor took it to mean something. He smiled. "That's good, then," he said. "Very good indeed."

A few days later, waiting for the results of the tests, he began to panic. *First*, he thought, *I will lose all language, then I will lose control of my body, then I will die.*

He tried to push them out of his head, such thoughts, with little success. Now, having resigned from teaching, he didn't know what to do with himself. He sat around the house, read, watched his daughter out of the corner of his eye. He had a hard time getting himself to do anything productive. He felt more and more useless, furtive. She was oblivious, he thought, she had no idea that she would watch him first lose the remainder of his speech, then slowly fall apart, wasting away. Having to live through that, she would probably pray for his death long before it actually arrived.

*And so will I*, he thought.

*Better to die quickly*, he told himself, *smoothly, and save both yourself and those close to you. More dignified.*

He pushed the thought down. It kept rising.

His daughter was trying to hand him the telephone. It was the doctor calling with the test results. "Standish," Hecker said into the receiver. But the doctor was too worried about what he had to say, about saying it right, in the kindest way possible, in the most neutral words imaginable, to notice.

The tests, the doctor claimed, had *amplified his concern.* What he wanted to do was to recommend a specialist to Hecker, a brain surgeon, a good one, one of the best. He would open Mr. Hecker's skull at a certain optimal spot, take a look at what was really going on in there, and make an assessment of whether it could be cut out, if there was any point in—

"I didn't mean that," said the doctor nervously. "There's always a point. I'm saying it wrong." The proper terminology to describe this was *exploratory surgery*. Did he understand?

"Yes," Hecker managed. "Was fish guillotine sedentary?"

"Hmmm? Necessary? I'm afraid so, Mr. Hecker."

How soon, he wanted to know, could Mr. Hecker put his affairs in order? Not that there was any serious immediate risk, but better safe than sorry. When, he wanted to know, was Mr. Hecker able to schedule the exploratory surgery? Did he have any concerns? Were there any questions that remained to be answered?

Hecker opened his mouth to speak but felt already that anything he said would be wrong, perhaps in several ways at once. So he hung up the telephone.

"What did he say?" his daughter was asking him.

"Nobody," he said. "Wrong finger."

IV

*First*, he thought over and over, *I will lose all language, then I will not be able to control my body. Then I will die.*

All he could clearly picture when he thought about this was his daughter, her life crippled for months, perhaps years, by his slow, gradual death. He owed it to her to die quickly. But perhaps, he thought, his daughter's suffering was all he could think about because his own was harder to face. Even as he was now, stripped only partly of language, life was nearly unbearable.

*First*, he thought. *And then. And then.*

He remembered, he hadn't thought about it for years, his own father's death, a gradual move into paralysis, until the man was little more than a rattling windpipe in a hospital bed and a pair of eyes that were seldom open and, when they were, were thick with fear.

*Like father, like son*, he thought.

*First*, he thought. *Then. Then.*

He lay in bed staring up at the ceiling. When it was very late and his daughter was asleep, he got up out of bed and climbed up to the attic and took his shotgun out of its case and cleaned it and loaded it. He carried it back downstairs and slid it under his bed.

*No*, he thought, *No first, no thens.*


He was in bed again, staring, thinking. The character of the room seemed to have changed. He could not bear to kill himself with his daughter in the house, he realized. That would be terrible for her, much more terrible than watching him die slowly. And too horrible for him to think about. No, that wouldn't do. He had to get her out.


But ever since he had been to the hospital, she had been sticking near him, never far away, observing him. She kept asking him what exactly was wrong with him, what had the doctor told him, why hadn't she been allowed to hear? And then, what had the doctor said on the telephone? She was always giving him cups of soup, which he took a few sips from and then left to scum over on the bookshelves, the fireplace mantle, the windowsills. It wasn't fair, she said, she had only him, they only had each other, but the way he was acting now she didn't even feel like she had him. What had the doctor said? What exactly was wrong with him? Why wouldn't he tell her? Why wouldn't he speak? All he had to do, she told him, was to open his mouth.

But no, that wasn't all. No, it wasn't as simple as that. And yes, he knew he should tell her but he didn't know what to say or if he *could* say it. And he didn't want her pity—he wanted only to be what he had always been for her, her father, not an old dying man.

But she wouldn't let up. She was making him insane. If she wanted a fight, he would fight. He turned on her and said, utterly fluent, "Don't you have someplace to be?"

"Yes," she said fiercely. "Here."

"Fat cats," he misspoke, and, suddenly helpless again, turned away.

He made a grocery list, a long one, and offered it to her. She glanced at it.

"Groceries, Daddy?" she said. "Since when did you have anything to do with groceries?"

He shrugged.

"Besides," she said, "we have half this stuff already. Did you even open the cupboards?"

He was beginning to have trouble with one of his fingers. It kept curling and uncurling of its own accord, as if no longer part of his body. He hid it from his daughter under his thigh when he was seated, felt it wriggling there like a half-dead worm. He and his daughter glared at each other from sofa and armchair respectively, she continuing to hector him with her questions, he remaining silent, sullen.

He ate holding his utensils awkwardly, to hide the rogue finger from her. She took this as an act of provocation, accused him of acting like a child.

It went on for three or four days, both of them at an impasse, until finally she screamed at him and, when he refused to scream back, left the house. He watched the door clack shut behind her. How long would she be gone? Long enough, he hoped.

He got the shotgun out from under the bed and leaned it against the sofa. He dialed 911.

"What's your emergency?" a woman's voice responded.

"I've just killed myself," he told her. "Hurry, please. Cover the body before my daughter gets home."

But it didn't come out like that. It was only what his mind was saying, his tongue uttering something else entirely.

"Excuse me?" said the operator.

He tried again, his voice straining with urgency.

"Is this a prank call?" the operator said. "This isn't funny."

He fell silent, tried to gather himself.

"Sir?" said the operator. "Hello?"

He looked desperately around the room. The dog was now regarding him intently, ears perked. He picked up the shotgun, held it one-handed near the receiver, and fired it into the wall behind the sofa. The kickback hurt his wrist and made him drop the weapon. The dog skittered out of the room, yelping.

He put the receiver to his ear again. The operator was talking more urgently now. He hung up the telephone.

Picking up the gun again, he sat down on the sofa. He hoped they would come soon, and that it would be soon enough, before his daughter's return. He leaned back and closed his eyes, trying to gather himself.

When he was calm again, he braced the shotgun's stock between the insoles of his feet and brought the barrels to his face. Carefully, he slipped the ends of the barrels into his mouth.

It was then that his daughter chose to return. He heard her open the front door and then she came into the room, her face pale. It was clear she had been crying. She came in and saw him and stopped dead, then stood there, her face draining of blood. They stayed there like that, staring, neither caring to be the first to look away.

He waited, wondering what words he could use, what he could possibly say to her. How could he ever talk his way out of this one?

"Daddy?" she said finally. "What are you doing?"

And then the words came to him.

He lifted his mouth off the barrels and licked his lips. "Insect," he explained as tenderly as he possibly could. "Grunion. Tentpole motioning."

# GOD LIVES IN
# ST. PETERSBURG

*by* TOM BISSELL

G OD, IN TIME, takes everything from everyone. Timothy Silverstone believed that those whose love for God was a vast, bor-
derless frontier were expected to surrender everything to Him,
gladly and without question, and that those who did so would live to see
everything and more returned to them. After college he had shed America
like a husk and journeyed to the far side of the planet, all to spread God's
word. Now he was coming apart. Anyone with love for God knows that
when you give up everything for Him, He has no choice but to destroy
you. God destroyed Moses; destroyed the heart of Abraham by revealing
the deep, lunatic fathom at which his faith ran; took everything from Job,
saw it did not destroy him, then returned it, which did. Timothy recon-
ciled God's need to destroy with God's opulent love by deciding that, when
He destroyed you, it was done out of the truest love, the deepest, most
divine respect. God could not allow perfection—it was simply too close to
Him. His love for the sad, the fallen, and the sinful was an easy, uncompli-
cated love, but those who lived along the argent brink of perfection had to
be watched and tested and tried.

Timothy Silverstone was a missionary, though on the orders of his or-
ganization, the Central Asian Relief Agency, he was not allowed to admit
this. Instead, when asked (which he was, often and by everyone), he was

to say he was an English teacher. This was to be the pry he would use to widen the sorrowful, light-starved breach that, according to CARA, lay flush across the heart of every last person in the world, especially those Central Asians who had been cocooned within the suffocating atheism of Soviet theology. "The gears of history have turned," the opening pages of Timothy's CARA handbook read, "and the hearts of 120 million people have been pushed from night into day, and all of them are calling out for the love of Jesus Christ."

As his students cheated on their exams, Timothy drifted through the empty canals between their desks. His classroom was as plain as a monk's sleeping quarters; its wood floors groaned with each of his steps. Since he had begun to come apart, he stopped caring whether his students cheated. He had accepted that they did not understand what cheating was and never would, for just as there is no Russian word which connotes the full meaning of *privacy*, there is no unambiguously pejorative word for *cheat*. Timothy had also stopped trying to teach them about Jesus because, to his shock, they already knew of a thoroughly discredited man who in Russian was called *Hristos*.

Timothy's attempts to create in their minds the person he knew as Jesus did nothing but trigger nervous, uncomfortable laughter Timothy simply could not bear to hear. Timothy could teach them about Jesus and His works and His love, but *Hristos* grayed and tired his heart. He felt nothing for this impostor, not even outrage. Lately, in order to keep from coming apart, he had decided to try to teach his students English instead.

"Meester Timothy," cried Rustam, an Uzbek boy with a long, thin face. His trembling arm was held up, his mouth a lipless dash.

"Yes, Rustam, what is it?" he answered in Russian. Skull-clutching hours of memorizing rows of vocabulary words was another broadsword Timothy used to beat back coming apart. He was proud of his progress with the language because it was so difficult. This was counterbalanced by his Russian acquaintances, who asked him why his Russian was not better, seeing that it was so simple.

After Timothy spoke, Rustam went slack with disappointment. Nine months ago, moments after Timothy had first stepped into this classroom, Rustam had approached him and demanded (actually using the verb *demand*) that Timothy address him in nothing but English. Since then his memorized command of English had deepened, and he had become by spans and cubits Timothy's best student. Timothy complied, asking Rustam "What is it?" again, in English.

"It is Susanna," Rustam said, jerking his head toward the small blonde girl who shared his desk. Most of Timothy's students were black-haired, sloe-eyed Uzbeks like Rustam—the ethnic Russians able to do so had fled Central Asia as the first statues of Lenin toppled—and Susanna's blonde, round-eyed presence in the room was both a vague ethnic reassurance and, somehow, deeply startling. Rustam looked back at Timothy. "She is looking at my test and bringing me distraction. Meester Timothy, this girl cheats on me." Rustam, Timothy knew, had branded onto his brain this concept of cheating, and viewed his classmates with an ire typical of the freshly enlightened.

Susanna's glossy eyes were fixed upon the scarred wooden slab of her desktop. Timothy stared at this girl he did not know what to do with, who had become all the children he did not know what to do with. She was thirteen, fourteen, and sat there, pink and startled, while Rustam spoke his determined English. Susanna's hair held a buttery yellow glow in the long plinths of sunlight shining in through the windows; her small smooth hands grabbed at each other in her lap. All around her, little heads bowed above the clean white rectangles on their desks, the classroom filled with the soft scratching of pencils. Timothy took a breath, looking back to Rustam, unable to concentrate on what he was saying because Timothy could not keep from looking up at the row of pictures along the back wall of his classroom, where Ernest Hemingway, John Reed, Paul Robeson, and Jack London stared out at him from plain wooden frames. An identical suite of portraits—the Soviet ideal of good Americans—was found in every English classroom from here to Tbilisi. Timothy knew that none of these men had found peace with God. He had wanted to give that peace to these children. When he came to Central Asia he felt that peace as a great glowing cylinder inside of him, but the cylinder had grown dim. He could barely even feel God anymore, though he could still hear Him, floating and distant, broadcasting a surf-like static. There was a message woven into this dense noise, Timothy was sure, but no matter how hard he tried he couldn't decipher it. He looked again at Rustam. He had stopped talking now and was waiting for Timothy's answer. Every student in the classroom had looked up from their tests, pinioning Timothy with their small impassive eyes.

"Susanna's fine, Rustam," Timothy said finally, turning to erase the nothing on his blackboard. "She's okay. It's okay."

Rustam's forehead creased darkly but he nodded and returned to his test. Timothy knew that, to Rustam, the world and his place in it would not properly compute if Americans were not always right, always good, always funny and smart and rich and beautiful. Never mind that Timothy had the mashed nose of a Roman pugilist and a pimply face; never mind that Timothy's baggy, runneled clothing had not been washed for months; never mind that once, after Rustam had asked about the precise function of "do" in the sentence "I do not like to swim," Timothy stood at the head of the class for close to two minutes and silently fingered his chalk. Meester Timothy was right, even when he was wrong, because he came from America. The other students went back to their exams. Timothy imagined he could hear the wet click of their eyes moving from test to test, neighbor to neighbor, soaking up one another's answers.

Susanna, though, did not stir. Timothy walked over to her and placed his hand on her back. She was as warm to his touch as a radiator through a blanket, and she looked up at him with starved and searching panic in her eyes. Timothy smiled at her, uselessly. She swallowed, picked up her pencil and, as if helpless not to, looked over at Rustam's test, a fierce indentation between her yellow eyebrows. Rustam sat there, writing, pushing out through his nose hot gusts of air, until finally he whirled around in his seat and hissed something at Susanna in his native language, which he knew she did not understand. Again, Susanna froze. Rustam pulled her pencil from her hands—she did not resist—snapped it in half, and threw the pieces in her face. From somewhere in Susanna's throat came a half-swallowed sound of grief, and she burst into tears.

Suddenly Timothy was standing there, dazed, rubbing his hand. He recalled something mentally blindsiding him, some sort of brainflash, and thus could not yet understand why his palm was buzzing. Nor did he understand why every student had heads bowed even lower to their tests, why the sound of scratching pencils seemed suddenly, horribly frenzied and loud. But when Rustam—who merely sat in his chair, looking up at Timothy, his long face devoid of expression—lifted his hand to his left cheek, Timothy noticed it reddening, tightening, his eye squashing shut, his skin lashing itself to his cheekbone. And Timothy Silverstone heard the sound of God recede even more, retreat back even farther, while Susanna, between sobs, gulped for breath.

Naturally, Sasha was waiting for Timothy in the doorway of the teahouse across the street from the Registan, a suite of three madrasas whose sparkling minarets rose up into a haze of metallic, blue-gray smog. Today was especially bad, a poison petroleum mist lurking along the streets and sidewalks and curbs. And then there was the heat—a belligerent heat; to move through it felt like breathing hot tea.

Timothy walked past the tall, bullet-shaped teahouse doorway, Sasha falling in alongside him. They did not talk—they rarely talked—even though the walk to Timothy's apartment in the Third Microregion took longer than twenty minutes. Sasha was Russian, tall and slender with hair the color of new mud. Each of Sasha's ears was as large and ornate as a tankard handle, and his eyes were as blue as the dark margin of atmosphere where the sky became outer space. He walked next to Timothy with a lanky, boneless grace, and wore blue jeans and imitation-leather cowboy boots that clomped emptily on the sidewalk. Sasha's mother was a history teacher from Timothy's school.

When his drab building came into sight Timothy felt the headachy swell of God's static rushing into his head. It was pure sound, shapeless and impalpable, and as always he sensed some egg of sense or insight held deep within it. Then it was gone, silent, and in that moment Timothy could feel his spirit split from his flesh. *For I know*, Timothy thought, these words of Paul's to the Romans so bright in the glare of his memory they seemed almost indistinct from his own thoughts, *that nothing good dwells within me, that is, in my flesh. I can will what is right, but I cannot do it.*

As they climbed the stairs to Timothy's fifth-floor apartment, Sasha reached underneath Timothy's crotch and cupped him. He squeezed and laughed, and Timothy felt a wet heat spread through him, animate him, flow to the hard, stony lump growing in his pants. Sasha squeezed again, absurdly tender. As Timothy fished for the keys to his apartment door Sasha walked up close behind him, breathing on Timothy's neck, his clothes smelling—-as everyone's clothes here did—as though they had been cured in sweat.

They stumbled inside. Sasha closed the door as Timothy's hands shot to his belt, which he tore off like a rip-cord. He'd lost so much weight his pants dropped with a sad puff around his feet. Sasha shook his head at this—he complained, sometimes, that Timothy was getting too skinny—and he stepped out of his own pants. Into his palm Sasha spit a foamy coin of drool, stepped toward Timothy and with the hand he spit into grabbed his penis. He pulled it toward him sexlessly, as if it were a grapple he was making sure was secure. Sasha laughed again and he threw himself over the arm of Timothy's plush red sofa. Sasha reached back and with medical indelicacy pulled himself apart. He looked over his shoulder at Timothy, waiting.

The actual penetration was always beyond the bend of Timothy's recollection. As if some part of himself refused to acknowledge it. One moment Sasha was hurling himself over the couch's arm, the next Timothy was inside him. *I can will what is right, but I cannot do it.* It began slowly, Sasha breathing through his mouth, Timothy pushing further into him, eyes smashed shut. What he felt was not desire, not lust; it was worse than lust. It was worse than what drove a soulless animal. It was some hot tongue of fire inside Timothy that he could not douse—not by satisfying it, not by ignoring it. Sometimes it was barely more than a flicker, and then Timothy could live with it, nullify it as his weakness, as his flaw. But without warning, in whatever dark, smoldering interior shrine, the flame would grow and flash outward, melting whatever core of Timothy he believed good and steadfast into soft, pliable sin.

Timothy's body shook as if withstanding invisible blows, and Sasha began to moan with a carefree sinless joy Timothy could only despise, pity, and envy. It was always, oddly, this time, when perched on the edge of exploding into Sasha, that Timothy's mind turned, again, with noble and dislocated grace, to Paul. *Do not be deceived!* he wrote. *Fornicators, idolaters, adulterers, male prostitutes, sodomites—none of these will inherit the kingdom of God. And this is what some of you used to be. But you were washed, you were sanctified, you were justified in the name of Lord Jesus Christ and in the Spirit of our God.* It was a passage Timothy could only read and reflect upon and pray to give him the strength he knew he did not have. He prayed to be washed, to be sanctified in the name of Jesus, but now he had come apart and God was so far from him. His light had been eclipsed, and in the cold darkness that followed, he wondered if his greatest sin was not that he was pushing himself into non-vaginal warmth but that his worship was now for man and not man's maker. But such taxonomies were of little value. God's world was one of cruel mathematics, of right and wrong. It was a world that those who had let God fall from their hearts condemned as repressive and awash in dogma—an accurate but vacant condemnation, Timothy knew, since God did not anywhere claim that His world was otherwise.

A roiling spasm began in Timothy's groin and burst throughout the rest of his body, and in that ecstatic flooded moment nothing was wrong, nothing, with anyone, and he emptied himself into Sasha without guilt, only with appreciation and happiness and bliss. But then it was over, and he had to pull himself from the boy and wonder, once again, if what he had done had ruined him forever, if he had driven himself so deeply into darkness that the darkness had become both affliction and reward. Quickly Timothy wiped himself with one of the throw pillows from his couch and sat on the floor, sick and dizzy with shame. Sasha, still bent over the couch, looked back at Timothy, smirking, a cloudy satiation frosting his eyes. "*Shto?*" he asked Timothy. *What?*

Timothy could not—could never—answer him.


The next morning Timothy entered his classroom to find Susanna seated at her desk. Class was not for another twenty minutes, and Susanna was a student whose arrival, on most days, could be counted on to explore the temporal condition between late and absent. Timothy was about to wish her a surprised "Good morning" when he realized that she was not alone.

A woman sat perched on the edge of his chair, wagging her finger and admonishing Susanna in juicy, top-heavy Russian. Her accent was unknown to Timothy, filled with dropped Gs and a strange, diphthongal imprecision. Whole sentence fragments arced past him like softballs. Susanna merely sat there, her hands on her desktop in a small bundle. Timothy turned to leave but the woman looked over to see him caught in mid-pirouette in the doorjamb. She leapt up from his chair, a startled gasp rushing out of her.

They looked at each other, the woman breathing, her meaty shoulders bobbing up and down, her mouth pulled into a rictal grin. "*Zdravstvuite,*" she said stiffly.

"*Zdravstvuite,*" Timothy said, stepping back into the room. He tried to smile and the woman returned the attempt with a melancholy but respectful nod. She was like a lot of women Timothy saw here—bull-necked, jowled, of indeterminate age, as sexless as an oval. Atop her head was a lumpen yellow-white mass of hairspray and bobby pins, and her lips looked as sticky and red as the picnic tables Timothy remembered painting, with his Christian youth group, in the parks of Green Bay, Wisconsin.

"Timothy Silverstone," she said. *Teemosee Seelverstun.* Her hands met below her breasts and locked.

"Yes," Timothy said, glancing at Susanna. She wore a bright, bubblegum-colored dress he had not seen before, some frilly, ribboned thing. As if aware of Timothy's eyes on her, Susanna bowed over in her chair even more, a path of spinal knobs surfacing along her back.

"I am Irina Dupkova," the woman said. "Susanna told me what happened yesterday—how you reacted to her... problem." Her joined hands lifted to her chin in gentle imploration. "I have come to ask you, this is true, yes?"

Her accent delayed the words from falling into their proper translated slots. When they did, a mental deadbolt unlocked, opening a door somewhere inside Timothy and allowing the memory of Rustam's eye swelling shut to come tumbling out. A fist of guilt clenched in his belly. *He had struck a child.* He had hit a boy as hard as he could, and there was no place he could hide this from himself, as he hid what he did with Sasha. Timothy felt faint and humidified, his face pinkening. "Yes, Irina Dupkova," he said, "it is. And I want to tell you I'm sorry. I, I—" He searched for words, some delicate, spiraled idiom to communicate his remorse. He could think of nothing, entire vocabularies lifting away from him like startled birds. "I'm sorry. What happened made me... very unhappy."

She shot Timothy a strange look, eyes squinched, her red lips kissed out in perplexion. "You do not understand me," she said. This was not a question. Timothy glanced over at Susanna, who had not moved, perhaps not even breathed. When he looked back to Irina Dupkova she was smiling at him, her mouthful of gold teeth holding no gleam, no sparkle, only the metallic dullness of a handful of old pennies. She shook her head, clapping once in delight. "Oh, your Russian, Mister Timothy, I think it is not so good. You do not *vladeyete* Russian very well, yes?"

"*Vladeyete*," Timothy said. It was a word he was sure he knew. "*Vladeyete*," he said again, casting mental nets. The word lay beyond his reach somewhere, veiled.

Irina Dupkova exhaled in mystification, then looked around the room. "You do not know this word," she said in a hard tone, one that nudged the question mark off the end of the sentence.

"Possess," Susanna said, before Timothy could lie. Both Timothy and Irina Dupkova looked over at her. Her back was still to them, but Timothy could see that she was consulting her CARA-supplied Russian-English dictionary. "*Vladeyete*," she said again, her finger thrust onto the page. "Possess."

Timothy blinked. "*Da*," he said. "*Vladeyete*. Possess." For the benefit of Irina Dupkova he smacked himself on the forehead with the butt of his palm.

"Possess," Irina Dupkova said, as if it had been equally obvious to her. She paused, her face regaining its bluntness. "Well, nevertheless, I have come here this morning to thank you."

Timothy made a vague sound of dissent. "There is no need to thank me, Irina Dupkova."

"You have made my daughter feel very good, Timothy. Protected. Special. You understand, yes?"

"Your daughter is a fine girl," Timothy said. "A fine student."

With that Irina Dupkova's face palled, and she stepped closer to him, putting her square back to the doorway. "These filthy people think they can spit on Russians now, you know. They think independence has made them a nation. They are animals, barbarians." Her eyes were small and bright with anger.

Timothy Silverstone looked at his scuffed classroom floor. There was activity in the hallway—shuffling feet, children's voices—and Timothy looked at his watch. His first class, Susanna's class, began in ten minutes. He moved to the door and closed it.

Irina Dupkova responded to this by intensifying her tone, her hands moving in little emphatic circles. "You understand, Timothy, that Russians did not come here willingly, yes? I am here because my father was exiled after the Great Patriotic War Against Fascism. Like Solzhenitsyn, and his careless letters. A dark time, but this is where my family has made its home. You understand. We have no other place but this, but things are very bad for us now." She flung her arm toward the windows and looked outside, her jaw set. "There is no future for Russians here, I think. No future. None."

"I understand, Irina Dupkova," Timothy said, "and I am sorry, but you must excuse me, I have my morning lessons now and I—"

She seized Timothy's wrist, the ball of her thumb pressing harshly between his radius and ulna. "And this little hooligan Uzbek thinks he can touch my Susanna. You understand that they are animals, Timothy, yes? *Animals.* Susanna," Irina Dupkova said, her dark eyes not leaving Timothy's, "come here now, please. Come let Mister Timothy see you."

In one smooth movement Susanna rose from her desk and turned to them. Her hair was pulled back into a taut blonde ponytail and lay tightly against her skull, as fine and grained as sandalwood. She walked over to them in small, noiseless steps, and Timothy, because of his shame for striking Rustam before her eyes, could not bear to look at her face. Instead he studied her shoes—black and shiny, like little hoofs—and the thin legs that lay beneath the wonder of her white leggings. Irina Dupkova hooked Susanna close to her and kissed the top of her yellow head. Susanna looked up at Timothy, but he could not hold the girl's gaze. He went back to the huge face of her mother, a battlefield of a face, white as paraffin.

"My daughter," Irina Dupkova said, nose tilting downward into the loose wires of Susanna's hair.

"Yes," Timothy said.

Irina Dupkova looked over at him, smiling, eyebrows aloft. "She is very beautiful, yes?"

"She is a very pretty girl," Timothy agreed.

Irina Dupkova bowed in what Timothy took to be grateful acknowledgment. "My daughter likes you very much," she said, looking down. "You understand this. You are her favorite teacher. My daughter loves English."

"Yes," Timothy said. At some point Irina Dupkova had, unnervingly, begun to address him in the second-person familiar. Timothy flinched as a knock on the door sounded throughout the classroom, followed by a peal of girlish giggling.

"My daughter loves America," Irina Dupkova said, ignoring the knock, her voice soft and insistent.

"Yes," Timothy said, looking back at her.

"I have no husband."

Timothy willed the response from his face. "I'm very sorry to hear that."

"He was killed in Afghanistan."

"I'm very sorry to hear that."

"I live alone with my daughter, Timothy, in this nation in which Russians have no future."

Lord, please, Timothy thought, make her stop. "Irina Dupkova," Timothy said softly, "there is nothing I can do about any of this. I am going home in three months. I cannot—I am not able to help you in that way."

"I have not come here for that," she said. "Not for me. Again you do not understand me." Irina Dupkova's eyes closed with the faint, amused resignation of one who had been failed her whole life. "I have come here for Susanna. I want you to have her. I want you to take her back to America."

*Struck dumb* had always been a homely, opaque expression to Timothy, but he understood, at that moment, the deepest implications of its meaning. He had nothing to say, *nothing*, and the silence seemed hysterical.

She stepped closer. "I want you to take my daughter, Timothy. To America. As your wife. I will give her to you."

Timothy stared her in the face, still too surprised for emotion. "Your daughter, Irina Dupkova," he said, "is too young for such a thing. *Much too young.*" He made the mistake of looking down at Susanna. There was something in the girl Timothy had always mistaken for a cowlike dullness, but he could see now, in her pale eyes, savage determination. The sudden understanding that Susanna's instigation lay behind Irina Dupkova's broke through Timothy's sternum.

"She is fourteen," Irina Dupkova said, moving her hand, over and over again, along the polished sheen of Susanna's hair. "She will be fifteen in four months. This is not so young, I think."

"*She is too young*," Timothy said with a fresh anger. Again he looked down at Susanna. She had not removed her eyes from his.

"She will do for you whatever you ask, Timothy," Irina Dupkova was saying. "Whatever you ask. You understand."

Timothy nodded distantly, a nod that both understood but did not understand. In Susanna's expression of inert and perpetual unfeeling, he could see that what Irina Dupkova said was right—she would do whatever he asked of her. And Timothy Silverstone felt the glisten of desire at this thought, felt the bright glint of a lechery buried deep in the shale of his mind. *My God,* he thought. *I will not do this.* He was startled to realize he had no idea how old Sasha was. Could that be? He was tall, and his scrotum dangled between his legs with the heft of post-adolescence, but he was also lightly and delicately haired, and had never, as far as Timothy could tell, shaved or needed to shave. Sasha could have been twenty-two, two years younger than Timothy; he could have been sixteen. Timothy shook the idea from his head.

"I have a brother," Irina Dupkova was saying, "who can arrange for papers that will make Susanna older. Old enough for you, in your nation. It has already been discussed. Do you understand?"

"Irina Dupkova," Timothy said, stepping backward, both hands thrust up, palms on display, "I cannot marry your daughter."

Irina Dupkova nearly smiled. "You say you cannot. You do not say you do not want to."

"Irina Dupkova, *I cannot do this for you.*"

Irina Dupkova sighed, chin lifting, head tilting backward. "I know why you are here. You understand. I know why you have come. You have come to give us your Christ. But he is useless." Something flexed behind her Slavic faceplate, her features suddenly sharpening. *"This* would help us. *This* would save."

Timothy spun around, swung open his classroom door, poked his head into the hallway and scattered the knot of chattering children there with a hiss. He turned back toward Irina Dupkova, pulling the door shut behind him with a bang. They both stared at him, Irina Dupkova's arm holding Susanna close to her thick and formless body. "You understand, Timothy," she began, "how difficult it is for us to leave this nation. They do not allow it. And so you can escape, or you can marry." She looked down at herself. "Look at me. This is what Susanna will become if she remains here. Old and ugly, a ruin." In Irina Dupkova's face was a desperation so needy and exposed Timothy could find quick solace only in God, a mental oxbow that took him to imagining the soul within Susanna, the soul being held out for him to take away from here, to sanctify and to save. That was God's law, His imperative: *Go therefore and make disciples of all nations.* Then God's distant broadcast filled his mind, and with two fingers placed stethescopically to his forehead Timothy turned away from Irina Dupkova and Susanna and listened so hard a dull red ache spread behind his eyes. The sound disappeared.

"Well," Irina Dupkova said with a sigh, after it had become clear that Timothy was not going to speak, "you must begin your lesson now." Susanna stepped away from her mother and like a ghost drifted over to her desk. Irina Dupkova walked past Timothy and stopped at his classroom door. "You will think about it," she said, turning to him, her face in profile, her enormous back draped with a tattered white shawl, "you will consider it." Timothy said nothing and she nodded, turned back to the door, and opened it.

Students streamed into the room on both sides of Irina Dupkova like water coming to a delta. Their flow hemmed her in, and Irina Dupkova's angry hands fluttered and slapped at the black-haired heads rushing past her. Only Rustam stepped aside to let her out, which was why he was the last student into the room. As Rustam closed the door after Irina Dupkova, Timothy quickly spun to his blackboard and stared at the piece of chalk in his hand. He thought of what to write. He thought of writing something from Paul, something sagacious and unproblematic like *We who are strong ought to put up with the failings of the weak*. He felt Rustam standing behind him, but Timothy could not turn around. He wrote the date on the board, then watched chalkdust drift down into the long and sulcated tray at the board's base.

"Meester Timothy?" Rustam said finally, his artificial American accent tuned to a tone of high contrition.

Timothy turned. A bruise like a red-brown crescent lay along the ridge of Rustam's cheekbone, the skin there taut and shiny. It was barely noticeable, really. It was nothing. It looked like the kind of thing any child was liable to get, anywhere, doing anything. Rustam was smiling at him, a bead of wet light fixed in each eye. "Good morning, Rustam," Timothy said.

Rustam reached into his book bag, then deposited into Timothy's hand something Timothy remembered telling his class about months and months ago, back before he had come apart; something that, in America, he had said, students brought their favorite teachers. It got quite a laugh from these students, who knew of a different standard of extravagance needed to sway one's teachers. Timothy stared at the object in his hand. An apple. Rustam had given him an apple. "For you," Rustam said softly, turned and sat down.

Timothy looked up at his classroom to see five rows of smiles. Meester Timothy will be wonderful and American again, these smiles said. Meester Timothy will not hit us, not like our teachers hit us. Meester Timothy will always be good.

Woolen gray clouds floated above the Registan's minarets, the backlight of a high, hidden sun outlining them gold. Some glow leaked through, filling the sky with hazy beams of diffracted light.

Timothy walked home, head down, into the small breeze coming out of the Himalayan foothills to the east. It was the first day in weeks that the temperature had dipped below 38° C, the first day in which walking two blocks did not soak his body in sweat.

Sasha stood in the tall doorway of the teahouse, holding a bottle of orange Fanta in one hand and a cigarette in the other. Around his waist Sasha had knotted the arms of Timothy's gray-and-red St. Thomas Seminary sweatshirt (Timothy didn't recall allowing Sasha to borrow it), the rest trailing down behind him in a square maroon cape. He slouched in the doorway, one shoulder up against the frame, his eyes filled with an alert, dancing slyness. Sasha let the half-smoked cigarette drop from his fingers and it hit the teahouse floor in a burst of sparks and gray ash. He was grinding it out with his cowboy-boot tip when Timothy's eyes pounced upon his. "*Nyet*," Timothy said, still walking, feeling on his face the light spume of rain. "*Ne sevodnya*, Sasha." *Not today, Sasha.* Timothy eddied through the molded white plastic chairs and tables of an empty outdoor café, reached the end of the block and glanced behind him.

Sasha stood there, his arms laced tight across his chest, his face a twist of sour incomprehension. Behind him a herd of Pakistani tourists was rushing toward the Registan to snap pictures before the rain began.

Timothy turned at the block's corner even though he did not need to. In the sky a murmur of thunder heralded the arrival of a darker bank of clouds. Timothy looked up. A raindrop exploded on his eye.

Timothy sat behind his workdesk in his bedroom, a room so small and diorama-like it seemed frustrated with itself, before the single window that looked out on the over-planned Soviet chaos of the Third Microregion: flat roofs, gouged roads that wended industriously but went nowhere, the domino of faceless apartment buildings just like his own. The night was impenetrable with thick curtains of rain, and lightning split the sky with electrified blue fissures. It was the first time in months it had rained long enough to create the conditions Timothy associated with rain: puddles on the streets, overflowing gutters, mist-cooled air. The letter he had started had sputtered out halfway into its first sentence, though a wet de facto period had formed after the last word he had written ("here") from having left his felt-tip pen pressed against the paper too long. He had been trying to write about Susanna, about what had happened today. The letter was not intended for anyone in particular, and a broken chain of words lay scattered throughout his mind and Timothy knew that if only he could pick them up and put them in their proper order, God's message might at last become clear to him. Perhaps, he thought, his letter was to God.

Knuckles against his door. He turned away from his notebook and wrenched around in his chair, knowing it was Sasha from the lightness of his three knocks, illicit knocks that seemed composed equally of warning and temptation. Timothy snapped shut his notebook, pinning his letter between its flimsy boards, and winged it onto his bed. As he walked across his living room, desire came charging up in him like a stampede of fetlocked horses, and just before Timothy's hand gripped the doorknob he felt himself through his Green Bay Packers sweatpants. A sleepy, squishy hardness there. He opened the door. Standing in the mildewy darkness of his hallway was not Sasha but Susanna, her small nose wrinkled and her soaked hair a tangle of spirals molded to her head. "I have come," she said, "to ask if you have had enough time to consider."

Timothy could only stare down at her. It occurred that he had managed to let another day go by without eating. He closed his eyes. "Susanna, you must go home. Right now."

She nodded, then stepped past him into his open, empty living room. Surprise rooted Timothy to the floorboards. "Susanna—" he said, half reaching for her.

After slipping by she twirled once in the room's center, her eyes hard and appraising. This was a living room that seemed to invite a museum's velvet rope and small engraved plaque: SOVIET LIFE, CIRCA 1955. There was nothing but the red sofa, a tall black lamp which stood beside nothing, and a worn red rug that did not occupy half the floor. Susanna seemed satisfied, though, and with both hands she grabbed a thick bundle of her hair and twisted it, water pattering onto the floor. "We can fuck," she said in

English, not looking at him, still twisting the water from her hair. She pronounced it *Ve con foke*. She took off her jacket and draped it over the couch. It was a cheap white plastic jacket, something Timothy saw hanging in the bazaars by the thousand. Beneath it she was still wearing the bubble-gum dress, aflutter with useless ribbonry. Her face was wet and cold, her skin bloodless in the relentless wattage of the lightbulb glowing naked above her. She was shivering.

Timothy heard no divine static to assist him with Susanna's words, only the awful silent vacuum in which the laws of the world were cast and acted upon.

"We can fuck," Susanna said again.

"Stop it," Timothy said.

"We can," she said in Russian. "I will do this for you and we will go to America."

"No," Timothy said, closing his eyes.

She took a small step back and looked at the floor. "You do not want to do this with me?"

Timothy opened his eyes and stared at the lamp that stood next to nothing. He thought that if he stared at it long enough, Susanna might disappear.

"I have done this before with men."

"You have," Timothy said—it was a statement—his throat feeling dry and paved.

She shrugged. "Sometimes." She looked away. "I know what you think. You think I am bad."

"I am very sad for you, Susanna, but I don't think that."

"You will tell me this is wrong."

Now both of Timothy's hands were on his face, and he pushed them against his cheeks and eyes as if he were applying a compress. "All of us do wrong, Susanna. All of us are bad. In the eyes of God," he said with listless conviction, "we are all sinners."

A knowing sound tumbled out of Susanna. "My mother told me you would tell me these things, because you believe in *Hristos*." She said nothing for a moment. "Will you tell me about this man?"

Timothy split two of his fingers apart and peered at her. "Would you like me to?" he asked.

She nodded, scratching at the back of her hand, her fingernails leaving a crosshatching of chalky white lines. "It is very interesting to me," Susanna said, "this story. That one man can die and save the whole world. My mother told me not to believe it. She told me this was something only an American would believe."

"That's not true, Susanna. Many Russians also believe."

"God lives for Russians only in St. Petersburg. God does not live here. He has abandoned us."

"God lives everywhere. God never abandons you."

"My mother told me you would say that, too." From her tone, he knew, she had no allegiance to her mother. She could leave this place so easily. If not with him, she would wait for someone else. She shook her head at him. "You have not thought about marrying me at all."

"Susanna, it would be impossible. I have a family in America, friends, my church... they would see you, and they would know. You are not old enough to trick anyone with papers."

"Then we will live somewhere else until I do." She looked around, her wet hair whipping back and forth. "Where is your bed? We will fuck there."

"*Susanna*—"

"Let me show you what a good wife I can be." With a shoddy fabric hiss her dress lifted over her head and she was naked. For all her fearlessness, Susanna could not anymore meet Timothy's eye, her xylophonic ribcage heaving, the concave swoop of her stomach breathing in and out like that of a panicked, wounded animal. She hugged herself, each hand gripping an elbow. She was smooth and hairless but for the blonde puff at the junction of her tiny legs. She was a thin, shivering fourteen-year-old girl standing naked in the middle of Timothy's living room. Lightning flashed outside— a stroboscope of white light—the room's single bright light bulb buzzing briefly, going dark, and glowing back to strength.

His bedroom was not dark enough to keep him from seeing, with awful clarity, Susanna's face tighten with pain as he floated above her. Nothing could ease the mistaken feeling of the small tight shape of her body against his. After it was over, he knew the part of himself he had lost with Sasha was not salvaged, and never would be. *I can will what is right, but I cannot do it.* He was longing for God to return to him when His faraway stirrings opened Timothy's eyes. Susanna lay beside him, in fragile, uneasy sleep. He was drawn from bed, pulled toward the window. The beaded glass was cool against his palms. While Timothy waited—God felt very close now—he imagined himself with Susanna, freed from the world and the tragedy of its limitations, stepping with her soul into the house of the True and Everlasting God, a mansion filled with rooms and rooms of a great and motionless light. Even when Susanna began to cry, Timothy could not turn around, afraid of missing what God would unveil for him, while outside, beyond the window, it began to rain again.

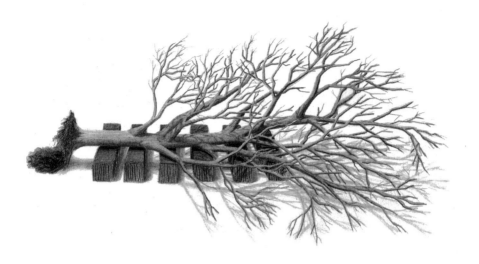

# IN A BEAR'S EYE

*by* YANNICK MURPHY

S HE HEARD THE BEAR. It hooted like an owl, only lower, sounding like an owl far down in a well or in a cave. She looked out the window. There it was, in the field above the pond on its hind legs. It shook the apples from the apple tree. Her boy did not look up at the bear in the field. He was by the pond. The bear was not so close but neither was he far away. If the bear had wanted to, the bear could run to the boy and the bear could be on her boy in no time at all, in the time it took an apple to fall from the branch and onto the field.

She ran outside with her gun.

Her boy had brown hair that over summer had turned almost blond. In the light of the setting sun she imagined how her boy's hair would look golden, how when he moved about, as he never kept still, how the color of his hair would surely catch anyone's eye, even a bear's.

When she was a girl she wanted her hair to turn that color. She cut lemon wedges and folded them around the strands of hair and pulled down on the lemon wedges, all the way to the ends. She would then lie down and bathe in the sun. She spread her hair out behind her on the towel. The strands were sticky. There was lemon pulp clinging to them in places. Bees flew close to her hair. The color stayed a light brown.

The gun was heavier than she had remembered. There was probably some muscle in her arm that was once stronger when she had carried the gun with her husband through the woods. They had hunted grouse every season. Now the muscle was weak. To get to her boy she knew that she would have to first crouch behind the rock wall and then, like a soldier, she would have to run and hide behind trees. She would have to be in some way like a snake. Serpentine, her pattern. Isn't that what a soldier would say? Serpentine, she would have to run down the line of trees that bordered the field for a few hundred feet. She did not think she could do it. She would eventually be seen. The bear would stop shaking the apple tree and look around, sniffing the air. The bear might come at her.

Her husband was the one who always shot the grouse. He was a good shot. She always aimed too high. Her husband, while she was aiming, would put his hand on top of her gun, to lower it down, but still she never shot a grouse.

The boy took some small rocks from the pond's shoreline. He stood up and threw them into the water.

"Sit down," she said out loud in a whisper that didn't sound to her like her own voice.

The boy was not doing well in school. He liked to read during class. Beneath the desk he would hold an open book. A book about beavers or silk moths or spiders. The teacher sent him home with notes for his mother. The notes said the boy must pay attention. Her boy would sometimes read to her from his books while they ate dinner. There were things she had never learned as a girl. A silkworm female moth is born without a mouth. It does not live long enough to eat. It only lives long enough to mate and lay its eggs before it dies. Her boy would stop and show her the pictures. She would shake her head. She was amazed at how much she had never learned as a girl her boy's age. Had she just been too busy squeezing lemon wedges onto her hair? Her boy never said he was sad that his father, her husband, had died. But she knew he was sad. Her husband was like a book that could talk. At the dinner table he would tell their boy about science and math. He talked about zero. "Zero scared the ancients," her husband said. "No one wanted to believe that there could be nothing."

He walked into the ocean one day and he did not stop walking. She liked to think he was still walking under the water. Skates stirred up sand and rose to the surface as he walked by them. Water entered his shirt cuffs and his shirt back ballooned. She and her boy sometimes talked about it. Her boy said how the hair on his head must be floating up and wavering like the long leaves of sea plants. Her boy said how his father must be reaching out to the puffer fish, wanting to see them change into prickly balls. His father must be touching everything as he walks, the craggy sides of mouths of caves where groupers lurk and roll their eyes, the white gilled undersides of manta rays casting shadow clouds above him. "My father must be in China by now," the boy said to his mother.

China because after he had died and the boy and the mother cleared out the father's drawers, they found a travel brochure for China. They had no idea the father was interested in going to China, but the words SEE THE WALL were written on the outside of the brochure.

The mother now saw how the sun was going behind the hillside. Its last rays hit the black steel of her gun and it hit the very top of her boy's hair before it sunk down. The bear was finished. It had knocked almost all the apples to the ground. He began to eat them. The mother thought how the boy would be safe now, the bear would eat and then leave and she would not have to run closer to the bear, going from tree to tree, looking for a shot she would probably miss because her husband was not there to put his hand on her gun, pushing down, keeping her from aiming too high.

Not long ago the boy's teacher had come to see her. She held open the screen door for the teacher and told her to come in. They sat in the kitchen and the teacher asked the boy if she could speak with his mother alone. The boy nodded and slid a book off the kitchen table and left the room. The mother could hear the boy walk up the stairs and close the door to his room.

"Your boy is a smart boy," the teacher said. "The death of his father must have come as a shock. But still," the teacher said, "there is school."

She looked into her refrigerator to offer the teacher something. There wasn't much. She hadn't been to the store in days. She opened the bottom bin and found two lemons. She took them out and put them on the table where they rolled for a moment. The mother got her wooden chopping board and placed the lemons on it and cut each lemon in four. She pushed the chopping board toward the teacher. "Please, have some."

The teacher did not say anything. After a while the teacher said, "I'm sorry. I'll come back another day to talk about your son." When the teacher left, the mother went upstairs to her boy. He was reading a book about spiders. Together they laid on his bed and looked at the pictures.

She would take her boy on a trip. They would go to China. They would see the wall. They would look for signs of him. She had yet to tell the teacher how her boy would miss days of school, even weeks.

Now, at the pond, the boy thought he would try it. He walked in slowly. The brown water filled his tennis shoes. It was cold. The boy knew from his books that beavers had flaps of skin behind their front teeth. They could shut the flaps when underwater, sealing the water out of their mouths and lungs. When the water came above the boy's eyes and finally over his head, the boy imagined he had these flaps. He opened his eyes underwater. The darkness was like four walls all around him. Maybe he could reach out and touch them.

The bear stopped eating. It sniffed the air and lifted its head. It went toward the pond. When it walked it looked like a man who was sauntering. She did not know before how bears hooted like owls, how they sauntered like men. She followed it. She did not run from tree to tree. She ran in a straight line. "No, no, you'll never shoot anything running at it like that," she could hear her husband say. Where was her boy? Where was her husband?

She saw ripples in the pond where her boy had gone in and then she noticed that the bear was looking at her. Its upper lip was curled. It had white on its chest, the shape of a diamond, but not perfect, a diamond being stretched, a diamond melting. She let the gun drop. She ran fast through the milkweed. The butterflies flew ahead of her. She ran past the bear. She dove into the water on top of the ripples made by her boy. She wanted to save him. She wanted to tell him he did not have to drown. She swam down, wishing she could call to him underwater, wishing she could see through the black silt. She had not taken a breath before she went down and she could not believe she did not need one. She thought for a moment how everyone must be wrong, there was no need to hold your breath underwater. She now knew it. She thought her boy knew it too. They had both found out a secret. She could stop thrashing about in the water now, looking for her boy. He would come up and out when he was ready. When she came to the surface she realized the pond was shallow. She was standing with the water only coming to her hip.

Her boy was on the other side of the pond. He was sitting on a large flat rock on the shore. He was holding something in his hand. The bear was watching them, his lip no longer curled. She walked to her boy while still in the water. It dragged her shirtsleeves and her pantlegs behind her. She moved her hair away from her eyes.

The boy had mud in his hand that he had scooped from the bottom of the pond.

"What's that?" she said.

"Maybe some gold," the boy said, moving the mud around and poking at it in his palm.

"Look over there," the mother said, pointing to the bear. The bear turned and sauntered away.

"Yes," said her boy. "I saw him ages ago. He likes the apples from our apple tree."

That night she told the boy that maybe they had better not go on their trip to China after all. There was school to think about. The boy nodded. "All right," he said.

She thought how she missed her husband. She thought how she would now miss him the way other women must miss their dead husbands. She would wear his shirts. Isn't that what other women did? They took long walks and thought about their husbands and when they sweat the smell that came up to them was not the smell of themselves but the smell of their dead men?

# AFTER THE DISASTER

### A LOVE STORY

*by* BEN EHRENREICH

1

AFTER THE DISASTER no one went to the Natural History Museum anymore. Crowds still pushed their way into the Met and the Modern for the first few weeks till every last painting, sculpture, mobile, and video installation was stolen, slashed, smashed, or shat upon. Across the park, though, things were quiet. People had been there. They had left signs, traces, trash. Graffiti stretched improbably over the domed ceiling of the planetarium. The gift shop and cafeteria had been looted. Kaleidoscopes and maps of the solar system and plush stuffed hyenas lay strewn about the floor. Not a crumb of food remained. The big blue whale had been cut down and sprawled broken on the floor of the cafeteria. Squatters apparently had at some point taken up residence in its cavernous fiberglass belly, leaving behind beer cans, ashes, and a shit-stained bedroll. Like Jonah, though, they were nowhere to be found. Whoever had been there had not been particularly ambitious, or rapacious, or mad. For when Bruno returned one last time to wander the museum's marbled halls in search of Mildred and the giant squid, his heart aflutter with lust and longing, he found that the now-dusty glass-encased displays of silverbacks and okapis, bison and antelope, lions and emu, each arranged in perfect nuclear family units, were entirely undisturbed. Who had time for nature anymore?

He first encountered the squid by accident, weeks before the world as he had known it so effortlessly dissolved. He'd had no idea what he would find. He wandered into the museum to avoid a storm that, in the middle of a peaceful walk through the park, had broken without warning or apology. He stayed only because he knew that, despite the posted $9.50 "suggested contribution," the kind-eyed folks behind the admission desk would let you in for a quarter, a penny, or a dime. Bruno's pocket contained two nickels, a dime, three pennies, and two crumpled dollar bills. Not without some pride, he paid with a dime.

Still soaked, his hair sticking to his forehead and his shirt clinging to his sunken chest, Bruno dragged himself up a flight of wide marble stairs. He found himself in the Hall of Biodiversity, where he marveled at the many forms of life, large and small, furred and smooth, striped and spotted, every one of them irrevocably dead. A herd of stiffened pachyderms, feet raised, tusks lowered, tentlike ears eternally at attention, stood in the middle of the room, frozen in mid-stomp. Stuffed sharks swam suspended from the ceiling. Along the walls formaldehyde-bleached lobsters sulked in oversized Mason jars beside legions of fluorescent blue beetles, dried fungi, glass-eyed rodents, and lacquered frogs. CARTILAGINOUS FISH, announced a placard.

At the end of the hall stood a single uniformed guard, his hands clasped loosely behind his back. A dim blue light shined sullenly forth from the corner behind him. Its source, Bruno saw, was a low tank, about twelve feet long and three high. Inside it was the giant squid. Four Korean children in bright rain slickers walked by, paused long enough to observe the squid, and, screeching in exaggerated disgust, scurried off.

Around the tank on all sides were blocks of italicized text in white letters on a navy background. Before even glancing at the tank's contents, Bruno read, "The giant squid has never been seen alive in its natural habitat." The squid, he saw, lay in an ethanol-filled casket, its white, papery flesh peeling as if sunburnt, flecks of its skin littering the blue bottom of the tank. It was surely dead, and very far from home.

"The giant squid is the largest of the invertebrates," he read on. "Females can reach seventy feet in length." This squid, however, was male and only twenty-five feet in length, though it looked much smaller. In truth, only the two tentacles were that long, and they had been folded back to rest upon the squid's lifeless head. Its white and pulpy arms were tangled atop one another, an orgy of chalk-white eels. Each one was lined with round, once-lethal suckers, now arrayed haphazardly, comically even, a drunken chorus line of pupilless eyeballs. The creature's dead eye was enormous and terribly sad, a grey and faded lump of useless meat, loose in its tattered socket.

Bruno did not notice Mildred at first. But she lingered on beside him as others came, took a quick look, tittered for a moment, perhaps flashed a snapshot or two, and moved on. Despite the closeness of the air in the museum, she wore a thick, black, woolen overcoat, which hung baggily over her wiry, almost brittle frame. After staring wordlessly at the squid for a spell, she turned to Bruno and spoke. "Amazing, isn't it?" she asked, letting a smile race across her lips and swiftly disappear, leaving her face awaiting Bruno's response with blank expectancy. A long white hand emerged from the wide sleeve of her coat and shook a strand of hair from her eyes.

Bruno was not accustomed to speaking with strangers, especially those of the female sort. Truth be told, he was not lately accustomed to speaking with anyone at all. Nonetheless, he grinned with as much warmth as he could muster and nodded his assent. Mildred's face relaxed. There was a softness to her eyes that spread into the harsh lines of her cheekbones and chin, almost blurring them when she smiled, which she did once more. Breaking her gaze, Bruno turned again to the squid's cadaver, its flesh heavy and wrinkled, bloodless and white.

"Did you know that they're bright red when they're alive?" Mildred asked. "A deep scarlet." Her green eyes widened as she said it.

"I had no idea."

Mildred pointed to the long tentacle that stretched limply to the end of the tank before doubling back again. "The males carry sperm in there," she said. "I read this. In a magazine. They shoot it through the tentacle—the penis is somewhere else, I don't know where—but they shoot it through the tentacle when they meet a female. And the females can hold it there, in their tentacle, until they're ready to fertilize themselves."

Bruno watched Mildred closely. Was this a come-on? Her eyes gave nothing away, staring as they were at the squid and not at him. "How do they know when they're ready?" he asked.

Mildred considered this for a moment, then shrugged. "I suppose they just know. The article said they probably travel alone, giant squids. It can be so long that they won't see another squid that whenever they see one they mate, because it might be the only squid of the opposite sex they'll ever see. I guess you'd call it mating. They know this because they found a female once with sperm still in her tentacle. She'd never used it."

"I wonder if they enjoy it," Bruno said, and was embarrassed to find himself blushing.

Mildred at last looked up. "Squids?"

"Yeah."

She shook her head. "I don't know. I hope so."

The guard standing next to the tank shifted his weight from one foot to the other, brushed at his mustache, and glanced nervously from Mildred to Bruno.

Mildred wrapped her fingers lightly around Bruno's upper arm. He tensed it involuntarily. Her nails, he noticed, were painted blue. "What do you like about the giant squid?" she asked.

Bruno felt his cheeks redden once again. "I didn't know anything about them until today. I guess just that, that no one knows anything about them."

Mildred pursed her lips and nodded. "The mystery," she said. She let her hand fall from his arm. His bicep was warm where her fingers had been. "What about you?" he asked her. But Mildred's only answer was to flash a tight smile and ask him the time. He told her it was four fifteen and she said she had to run.

"Nice to meet you," Bruno said.

"Nice to meet you," said Mildred, and turned to go.


Bruno waited for the storm to clear before leaving the museum. It was dark when he at last shuffled down the steps and gazed up at Teddy Roosevelt in bronze, mounted high on his horse, one hand on his gun, flanked on both sides by loyal, naked, and manifestly noble savages, Indian to his left, African on his right, facing down an invisible enemy floating above the trees of the park. Inside, Bruno knew, was the squid, slowly disintegrating in its long blue tank. And somewhere, perhaps not far, was Mildred.

He circled the block twice, peeking into each cafe and corner deli, then extended the radius of his search by one block and then by two blocks, until a cab sped through a puddle on the corner of 77th and Broadway, coating him with inky muck. He gave up and commenced the long trek home to save on subway fare. Bruno slogged through the park, which smelled of rain and rotting leaves. He walked all the way down and across town, through streets that smelled of rain and garbage and of good hot food he couldn't afford, over the bridge which smelled of rust and urine and through one last piss- and trash-stinking mile to his home, cursing himself all the while for not at least asking her to join him for a cup of coffee in the cafeteria, right there under the ridged white belly of the big blue whale. How often do you meet someone, he asked himself, someone you can really talk to?

That night Bruno dreamed of the ocean. He dreamed of infinite blackness and cold. He breathed the frigid water as if it were air. With each breath the cold filled him to his very center, which was darker and colder than even the depths of the sea. There was no above and no below, no light anywhere. None of the fish had eyes. They were white and bloated and the shadows beneath their scales were blue. They didn't swim but drifted, directionless. His legs and arms were tangled in long belts of rubbery kelp. Ice-white shrimp nibbled at his fingertips, his nipples, his shrunken prick. And he heard a sweet sad song, the moaning of the waves, and the water turned scarlet, warm and thick. He saw Mildred swimming past him, her limbs, like his, trailing kelp. She smiled at him. Between the strands of seaweed he could make out her small and purple nipples, the sharp shadows of her ribs and her jutting hip bones, black tendrils of pubic hair floating across her thighs. As she kicked her legs he spied her labia, scarlet in the scarlet sea, the hollows of her knees, and the sole of one arched foot.

When Bruno awoke his face was wet with tears.

There was no hot water that morning. In the shower Bruno stood far from the stream, and as far as he could from the mildewed shower curtain. Shivering, he looked down at his pale body, at his knobby knees, his shriveled, bouncing cock, at the small black hairs on his wrists. He thought of the giant squid, of its tangled legs, dead in its casket, not red but white and trapped forever. He thought of the white flesh of Mildred's wrists peeking out from under her baggy coat, of her long white neck beneath her straight black hair. He rinsed the soap from his body and dried himself.

That afternoon Bruno returned to the museum. He paid his dime, walked upstairs to the Hall of Biodiversity, past the pack of pachyderms, the lacquered frogs and bottled lobsters. Mildred was not there, but the giant squid remained. It had not shifted so much as a tentacle.

Bruno lingered by the squid for an hour. He paced in front of its case. He looked for her in the cafeteria, by the great mammals of Africa and the mammals of the Americas, by the dinosaur skeletons and by the Indian canoe, but he did not find her. He left the museum. He bought a hot dog with everything and ate it on the damp marble steps, following Teddy Roosevelt's cold imperial gaze above the treeline and across the park.

Five days went by before Bruno returned to the museum. It was again a Tuesday, as it had been when he had first seen the squid and first met Mildred. From the very end of the Hall of Biodiversity he saw her, still wearing her baggy coat despite the weather, her head slightly bowed, her face hidden beneath her hair. He quickened his pace, wanting to run, but not wanting to be out of breath when he arrived at her side. Soon the pachyderms, with all their ancient bulk, blocked his line of vision. He passed the father, his proud tusks raised in challenge, the mother just beside and a little behind him, and between the sturdy legs of their long-dead offspring he could see Mildred's feet—her pale ankles bare, sockless in red sneakers—as they swiveled around and she walked away. When Bruno emerged from behind the wrinkled posterior of the last juvenile pachyderm, she was gone. He hurried past the squid, which he almost expected to acknowledge him, to point with one of its eight legs or two tentacles and let him know which way she'd gone. But it did not, and he did not see her in the hallway behind its long case. He didn't see her on the stairs, or in the gift shop on the landing, or in the great muralled hall below. He loitered outside the ladies' room, left the museum and circled the block not once but three times, all to no avail.

So Bruno walked back up the stairs to await her return to the squid.

Its white eye lolled in its socket like a rotting scallop, pupilless, unwinking and dead. Giant squids have larger eyes, Bruno read, than any other animal. The eye of the giant squid can grow to fifteen inches in diameter. There was an image of such an eye beside the text on the display case, perfectly round, the size of a dinner plate, its pupil still intact but without an iris, colorless. It looked nothing like the flaccid white eye of the squid preserved beside it, an eye which communicated nothing, not even death.

It would be wrong to say, in retrospect, that the disaster came without warning. There were rumblings and there were whispers. For those who look for such things, there were signs. The moon did not always complete its full circuit; more and more gunshots, screams, and screeching tires could be heard in the night; the sun rose an hour late one morning, then two hours early the next; everyone had the same mild flu; bond prices fluctuated wildly; pigeons and squirrels were more skittish than usual. But Bruno noticed none of this.

He sat in his kitchen on a bentwood chair he had found on the street and opened a can of squid. The chair's wicker seat had been torn out, so he sat as lightly as he could on its wooden frame. He dumped the can's contents—six squid, each about five inches in length, floating in brine dyed purple with ink—into a bowl. They smelled like a shallow tide pool on a hot and windless day. In death, their skin was scarlet once more, if only because their own ink had stained it so. They had been cooked prior to canning until their flesh was so brittle that they broke when he handled them. Their bodies tore into neat, papery rings, exposing a grey substance that the can's label described as "viscera." Inside the squid, surrounded by this viscera, was a transparent shard of cartilage, like an elongated arrowhead, called a quill. It was the closest thing to a skeleton the squid had. He brought the bowl of squid to the table and carefully sat down on the broken chair. The squids, he noticed, still had eyes, with tiny black pupils intact.

Bruno returned to the museum each of the two following Tuesdays and once on a Saturday, but he did not see Mildred again. He continued to dream of her, sometimes in the awful solitude of the deep, as on that first night. Sometimes she would take his arm in her hand on the street or in the halls of the museum and kiss him or whisper something incomprehensible in his ear, then run away. She was always barefoot in his dreams. In the mornings he remembered her feet, long and white. One night he dreamed she came to his apartment. They stood in his kitchen, by the sink. She was fully clothed, in her coat as always, but Bruno was naked. Her eyes were red and inflamed. She caressed his penis with her right hand, which was very cold, and scolded him for not having been gentler with the canned squids, for breaking them right there by the sink. The quill he had removed from one was still on the counter, pointing at him accusingly. As he felt himself approaching climax, he saw that the skin of his cock was beginning to peel in her grip, like the dead flesh of the giant squid.

The disaster fell that Monday, and Bruno stayed indoors for the next two weeks. At night the western sky was bright with distant fires. Tremors shook the windows in their panes. With each muffled boom Bruno's furniture leapt about the floor. The winds didn't let up till the weekend, and Bruno couldn't sleep for their howling through the streets. He lay on his lumpy mattress watching the sheetrock glow again red and yellow as another blast gripped the city. And as the cracks in the plaster once more cast their shadows stark above his head, he wondered about Mildred, if she was warm enough, if she was safe, if she'd gotten sick, if she had enough food to eat and clean water to drink, if she'd been hurt, if wherever she was she ever thought of him.

Bruno paced and counted the linoleum tiles on the kitchen floor. There were nineteen of them, and, he was fairly sure, 461 ceramic tiles in the bathroom. Bruno read old newspapers, even the ads. He did all the crosswords. He did push-ups and sit-ups and jumping jacks. He used an extension cord as a jump rope until the downstairs neighbors fired a shot through the floor. It left a small hole, which he patched with a rag. He wrote a letter to his father who died when he was four, then thought better of it and tore it to shreds. He sat on the edge of the bathtub and wept and slapped himself in the face. He counted the tiles again. There were 456. He filled the margins of the phone book with sketches of Mildred and of the giant squid and of Mildred and himself together wrapped in the squid's eight legs and two tentacles until all his pens ran out of ink. He took the back off a transistor radio and tried to figure out how it worked. He pulled the motor out of his deceased refrigerator and later reinstalled it, none the wiser for his efforts. He masturbated repeatedly into the same dirty sock, imagining Mildred's breath on his navel, her long hair in his eyes, her blue-painted nails pulling on his scrotum.

Bruno trapped cockroaches in empty tin cans, thinking he might need them one day. He soaked stale bread in water and ate it with salt. He opened his last can of corned beef on Thursday and ran out of sardines on Sunday morning. He ate a few spoonfuls of cold beans from the can with crackers twice a day after that and cut back on the push-ups and masturbation.

The morning after the night that Bruno took his final swallow of beans, shook the last cracker crumbs from the bottom of the bag and licked them from his palm, the water gave out. The faucets spun round and round, but not a trickle poured forth. It was time, Bruno knew, to venture out into the world.

2

He left his apartment without giving much thought to his destination. He would follow his stomach, he decided. But in the end it was something else that led Bruno on his wanderings, and he found himself, to his surprise, once again on the wide marble steps of the museum. Teddy Roosevelt had been removed from his high post and lay on his side in the middle of the street, still mounted on his now horizontal horse, contemplating the well-clogged gutters. The stone base of the statue had been shattered and Teddy's once faithful savage companions had apparently abandoned him.

Bruno climbed the stairs and pushed through the great wooden doors. The lobby was empty. Its floor was strewn with brochures and crumpled floorplans, which leapt about like tumbleweeds in the breeze that blew through the deserted streets and in through the open door. Before he got to the top of the first flight of stairs, Bruno heard it, a series of dull thumps unconnected by any discernible rhythm. As he rushed past the landing and down the darkened Hall of Biodiversity, he mistook the banging for the unsteady murmurs of his own agitated heart. But he found its source at the very end of the hall. There was Mildred, hacking away at the squid's tank with a crowbar. She had made no mark at all in the thick glass. Bruno was nearly at her side before she noticed his presence. She stopped in midswing and let the crowbar fall to her side. Her black coat had been thrown on the floor behind her and her T-shirt was dark with sweat. Her bony shoulders shook with exhaustion. "Will you help me?" she asked.

Bruno took the crowbar from her, swung it back above his head and let it fall with all his weight on the glass. The shock of the blow rang through his joints and the bones of his fingers, wrists, and elbows. It was all he could do to keep the crowbar from flying from his grip, but he had dislodged only the tiniest chip of glass. Another swing bore the same result. Bruno motioned to Mildred to follow him to the other end of the hall. Once there, he lifted her up, then jumped himself, and they swung from the end of the great ivory tusk of the largest of the pachyderms. It broke free with a crack and a moan and clattered to the marble floor. Straw spilled from the cavity they'd opened in the dead elephant's face. Its glass eyes did not blink.

They charged the display case with the broad end of the tusk. On their eighth or ninth try, their battering ram crashed through the glass. A wave of rank ethanol burst through, soaking them, and the giant squid, stiff and white, rolled with a thud to the floor. Mildred dropped the tusk, leapt into Bruno's arms, and kissed him noisily on the lips. Before he could respond, she was on her knees, carefully picking shards of glass from the squid's tangled arms. She looked up at him and pushed a knot of wet hair from her eyes. Two of the squid's arms were cradled in her lap. "You'll help me, won't you?" she asked. "I can't carry him home alone."

Bruno nodded.

"I live nearby," she said. "It won't take long."

The squid was heavier than it looked. Soft and fleshy as it appeared, death had hardened its body and stiffened its legs. It stank of ammonia and brine. They heaved the mantle and head onto Bruno's back. Mildred did her best to carry the extended legs and tentacles, but one or another of them kept slipping from her grasp. Before they reached the stairs at the end of the hall, Bruno stumbled and fell. The squid pinned him to the floor. Mildred rolled it off of him and helped him up. She lifted his chin and inspected his face for bruises. "Are you all right?" she asked.

Bruno took her hand from his face and held it in his. "I've been looking for you," he said.

Mildred gave his hand a squeeze and turned away. Something in her face seemed to dim. "This isn't going to work," she said, and Bruno felt a sharp, tight pain encircling his ribs.

Mildred looked around the long, dim hall. "Maybe if we wrapped him in my coat," she said, "we could just pull him."

The pain dispersed and warmth returned to Bruno's limbs and he pulled Mildred to him and kissed her. She smiled tightly, pecked him on the lips, then turned and ran for her coat, which she had forgotten by the broken window. "We have to hurry," she yelled over her shoulder. "He won't last long unless he's in alcohol and we don't want to be out after dark."

They rolled the squid onto the jacket, its legs and tentacles trailing off behind it. They buttoned it in, then each took one woolen arm and pulled. The squid, like a monstrous scarecrow, slid along the smooth floors to the top of the staircase. Bruno supported its body from below. The alcohol had quickly soaked through the coat and he could feel the animal's cold and surprisingly brittle form inside it. He backed it slowly down the stairs while Mildred guided its arms and tentacles. With each step, the bundled squid gave out a soft and squishy thud. "Be careful," Mildred said.

They pulled the squid across the wide lobby and down the stairs to the street. The air had chilled. The old stone apartment buildings and the tall glass office towers across the park glowed pink in the light of the setting sun. Above them hung the moon, pink too and abnormally large, a shade less than full. The sidewalk was trickier. The cement was not as smooth as the marble floors of the museum and they were forced to stop every few yards to disengage a corner of Mildred's jacket, or the slender tip of one of the squid's eight legs, from a hidden crack in the pavement. Three loud pops rang through the air, gunshots a few blocks to the south. Bruno froze for a moment, his eyes wide with uncertainty, until Mildred motioned him on.

A young boy, barefoot in shorts and a T-shirt, sprinted out of the park and into the street a half block ahead of them. Three older boys ran after him. One caught him by his shirt, which tore loudly as he was thrown to the asphalt. The others raced in and commenced kicking him in the ribs and face. They dragged him screaming back into the park by his ankles. Bruno stopped again and dropped the squid. "There's nothing you can do," Mildred said, and kept pulling.

They had made it almost to 83rd Street when a man dressed in camouflage fatigues scurried into the middle of Central Park West behind them. He stopped, spun around, and emptied an automatic pistol at his pursuers, who were still invisible around the corner. As he turned to run again, Bruno and Mildred heard another shot. They pulled the squid into the shelter of a doorway and huddled together, crouching. The man's head was thrown forward and his body crumpled to the asphalt. Bruno could not see any blood. Three overweight men in tattered police uniforms approached the body with their guns drawn. They prodded it with their feet, then, satisfied that the man was dead, took his gun, boots, and jacket before returning in the direction from which they'd come.

Bruno and Mildred held each other tightly, each with one arm wrapped around the squid. She stood up first and tried to pull him up, but Bruno just looked at her. "Come on," she said. "Get up."

He tried to laugh, but what came out was more of a stifled retch. "It's not like this in Brooklyn," he managed. "I had no idea."

"Two more blocks and we're home."

At the corner of 85th Street, Mildred told Bruno it would be just two blocks more. The muscles in his back and thighs were cramping. His clothes reeked of ammonia and decay. They stayed close to the buildings and ran when they had to cross the street. As they crossed 89th, Bruno felt the squid suddenly grow heavier. He gave it a sharp tug and, just as Mildred screamed "Wait!", commenced pulling. His burden felt surprisingly lighter. Bruno kept moving until he heard her voice again. "Wait," she repeated, her voice firmer this time. He stopped and looked back. The squid's head, arms and tentacles had broken off from its body in a single clump and lay limply alone on the sidewalk. Only the mantle was still wrapped in Mildred's coat. A tentacle had gotten caught in a storm grate and wrapped itself around the steel grillwork. She pried it loose, then sat, crouching with the tentacle in her hand, shaking her head. "I'm sorry," Bruno said.

A burst of shots from an automatic weapon rang out nearby—Bruno couldn't tell from which direction. He pulled the squid's head under the overcoat, shoving it into the detached mantle as best as he could. Another shot echoed across the avenue and Mildred sprang up and began pulling. "We're almost there," she said.

On the next block Mildred stopped in front of a short, brass-railed staircase. They lugged the squid to the top of the stairs and through a varnished mahogany door. It was harder now that the squid was no longer in one piece. Mildred rushed them through an elegant, wood-paneled entryway and up three more flights of stairs. She had to stop every few feet to unravel the squid's tentacles from the carved wooden pillars supporting the banister and to reinsert its head into its body. "The door at the end of the hall," she said, and produced a ring of keys from the pocket of her jeans.

The apartment was dark, but Bruno could make out tall bookshelves along a distant wall as he and Mildred stumbled in. The carpet was soft beneath his feet. He let himself fall against the wall and slid into a slump on the floor. "Not yet," Mildred said. "Just help me get him into the bathroom. Then you can rest all you want. Please."

But Bruno did not stir. "What's going on out there?" he asked.

"I want to put him in the tub. It'll only take one more minute."

Bruno looked up at her. Her arms were wrapped around the squid's eight legs, which she supported from below with one raised knee. She was shaking with fatigue. The squid's arms shimmied soggily in hers. "Is it always like that?" Bruno asked.

Mildred at last let the squid drop to her knee, and from there, carefully, to the ground in front of her. "Didn't you know?" she said. "Where have you been?"

Bruno shrugged helplessly. "It's quiet in Brooklyn at night."

Mildred unbuttoned the coat which the squid, in two pieces now, was just barely wearing. She stared at the half foot of empty space separating the squid's head from its body, then closed her eyes and leaned her head against the wall. "At night it's bad," she said, "like you saw. At first it was like that in the daytime too, only much worse."

"What were they going to do to that kid?"

Mildred abruptly stood and wiped her palms on her jeans. "I don't know," she said.

She took Bruno's hand and helped him up. The squid's flesh glowed blue in the dark. Its white eye rested limply on the carpet. The smell of ammonia had gotten stronger. They wrapped it again in the coat and each grabbed an end. Mildred led the way around the corner and the squid slid heavily between them.

The apartment was bigger than it had at first seemed. They passed through three large rooms before Mildred opened the door to the bathroom. She produced a cigarette lighter from a shirt pocket and lit a wide red candle sitting on the sink. Mirrors on two walls reflected the flame about the room and Bruno could see all three of them, Mildred, himself, and their ghostly companion, all the same shade of pale orange. In one corner of the room was a low black porcelain tub, the fancy kind with jets set into its sides. They heaved the squid's tail in first, propping it up against the edge of the tub and letting it drop noisily over. The head, arms, and tentacles remained on the floor. Mildred shook her head. "I can't believe you fucking broke him."

Bruno lifted the giant squid's head into the tub and maneuvered it back inside the mantle as Mildred struggled with the arms and tentacles. Barely the first yard of them fit in the bathtub. The bulk of the stiff and tortured mass stuck straight out above the bathroom floor and rested on the lid of the toilet across the room.

From a cabinet beneath the sink, Mildred pulled a cardboard box filled with blue-labeled plastic bottles of rubbing alcohol. She handed a bottle to Bruno and opened one herself, pouring its contents into the tub. They emptied all twenty-four bottles, but the resulting puddle was barely an inch and a half deep. "Shit," Mildred said.

She sat on the edge of the tub, bit her lip, and absentmindedly caressed the squid's extended arms. "We'll have to use water," she announced.

"You still have water?" Bruno asked, but before the last word had escaped his lips, Mildred had twisted the taps and the tub had begun to fill.

"There's no hot water," she said, "but there's plenty of cold."

"Do you have any salt?"

"What for?"

"Add it to the water, like brine. Maybe it'll keep longer."

Mildred hustled off to the kitchen and came back with a can of Morton's salt and another candle. She emptied the can into the tub. "Help me stir it."

Bruno pushed the sleeve of his shirt up to his elbow. He got on his knees beside her and pushed the cold liquid around the tub. "Is it supposed to smell like that?" he asked.

"Like ammonia?"

Bruno nodded.

"To keep them buoyant, giant squids have these little pockets of ammonium chloride solution in their muscles, like balloons. It's lighter than water, so they float. They don't have air bladders like fish. Otherwise they would have to keep moving all the time to keep from sinking."

"Like sharks."

"I guess," Mildred shrugged. "I don't know about sharks. If you want to clean up, there are clean towels in the closet behind you. I'll give you some privacy."

Once she had closed the door behind her, Bruno stripped off his clothes and splashed his face with cold water. He rubbed soap onto a washcloth and scrubbed the dried sweat and the stink of ammonia and pickled rot from his body. He bent to wash his face again and, for an instant as he straightened, in the mirror behind him he saw the squid's arms and tentacles rise from the tub and toward him. When he turned, the squid had not moved. He laughed to himself and wagged a finger at it. "Stay," he said.

The door opened suddenly and Bruno scrambled to cover himself. He dangled the washcloth over his crotch. Mildred laughed and threw him a towel. "Sorry," she said. "I thought you were done. It's my turn."

She held the door open for him. As he bent to grab his wet clothes from the floor, she told him to leave them, that she had dry ones he could wear. She handed him a candle. "I'll be out in a minute."

In the first room he came to, Bruno almost tripped on a low, glass-topped coffee table. Beside it was a plush velvet couch. He put the candle on the table and sat to wait for Mildred, listening to the rush of water running behind the bathroom door. He let himself sink into the couch and imagined Mildred standing naked in front of the sink, the giant squid in the tub behind her. He imagined her bare neck and the harsh curve of her spine glowing orange in the candlelight. He imagined the broken squid beckoning to her from behind with a single raised tentacle.

When Bruno awoke the next morning, he found himself in an unfamiliar room. The walls and ceiling were paneled with a warm, dark wood and carved into intricate geometrical moldings. In one corner stood an antique wooden desk with dozens of very small drawers. There were two well-stuffed chairs upholstered in velvet, and a glass-topped coffee table on which sat a single unlit candle. He lay on a deep, soft couch made of the same fabric as the chairs. Under his head was a pillow and he was wrapped in a duvet, beneath which he wore only a damp towel.

On one of the chairs, Bruno found a neatly folded stack of clothes. There was a pair of men's worsted dress pants and a white cotton shirt, white boxer shorts, an undershirt, and a pair of black silk socks rolled tidily into a ball. The boxers were two or three inches too wide at the waist, as were the pants, which barely fell below his ankles. The shirt's sleeves didn't reach his wrists, though the neck was a good inch wider than his. On each cuff were embroidered the initials *RG* in tight silken script.

Holding his pants and underwear up with one hand to keep them from slipping down his hips, Bruno inspected the rest of the apartment. The floors of each room were covered with Oriental carpets and the walls with ornately framed paintings and prints. Bruno recognized one of the paintings from books he'd had to study in school. The next room over was apparently a study. Its walls were lined with bookshelves filled with sturdy old leather-bound volumes. The room itself was dominated by a heavy oak desk, atop which sat an open laptop computer, its screen lifeless, its keys coated with dust. The study adjoined a dining room, furnished with a long, linen-covered table and twelve tall-backed chairs, which opened on one side to a kitchen and on the other to the living room, high-ceilinged and sparsely furnished, one wall giving way to a huge bay window with, largely hidden by heavy drapes, a view of the park. The moon, nearly full, still hung pale and low in the morning sky. Save the shimmering of the leaves in the wind, nothing moved in the park or in the streets.

Bruno was standing by the window, the drapes pulled back, gazing out over the city, when he felt a hand on his shoulder. He spun around to find Mildred, her hair still tousled with the night's odd angles. Her eyes were ringed with dark circles, but she had pulled her face into a smile that was by all appearances genuine. "Good morning," she said.

"Good morning."

"Do you want some coffee?"

"You have coffee?"

"Only a couple pounds are left," Mildred said, "but this counts as a special occasion."

"How do you mean?" asked Bruno, who was not altogether certain that his feelings for Mildred were reciprocated. Was it the squid's presence she wanted to celebrate, or his own?

Mildred did not answer, but asked again if he wanted coffee. "Sure, of course," Bruno replied. "But how are you going to make it?"

He followed Mildred into the kitchen where she produced a small camping stove and gestured to a cabinet filled with propane canisters. "There's enough for at least a year if I'm careful," she said. "Plenty of food, too."

She opened a door beside the refrigerator that led into a long and spacious pantry, its shelves stocked with food. There were heavy bags of rice, dried beans of every size and color, boxes and boxes of pasta and crackers, shelf after shelf of canned goods—no Vienna sausages or sardines here, but pâté de foie gras and spring lamb stew, vichyssoise and Alaskan crabmeat. There were tins of truffles, jugs of deep green olive oil, boxes of chocolates, bags and bags of venison jerky, salted cod, mixed nuts and dried apricots and cherries. One corner was filled with five-gallon jugs of water stacked to the ceiling. Beside them were piled cases of wine, a few boxes of scotch and a few of cognac, even a case of champagne.

In his astonishment Bruno could form no words at all. Mildred smiled slyly, twisted the valve on the stove, lit a match, and then watched the burner leap into flame. "This apartment belonged to a man who was privy to information that almost no one else had access to. He was able to begin preparing long before anyone knew there was anything to prepare for."

"Where is he now?"

"The day after it happened I ran out to the museum but I couldn't get in. They were fighting in the street right out front. When I came back I saw them leading him away at gunpoint. There were six of them, in real uniforms, new ones. They'd pulled a pillowcase over his head, but I knew it was him from his walk, the shape of him. They put him in a jeep and drove off."

"Are these his clothes?"

"Yes," Mildred looked at him and raised one playful eyebrow. "I'll find you a belt." She stared at the blue flame of the camp stove and said, almost forgetfully, "I was his secretary."

"And he let you stay here?"

Mildred did not answer, but lifted the coffeepot from the burner and took two mugs from a cupboard above the sink. "There's no milk," she finally said. "Do you take sugar?"

"Yeah," said Bruno. "Two."


When he'd finished his coffee, Bruno felt a rumbling in his lower intestines and excused himself. There was no window in the bathroom, so he lit the candle on the sink with a book of matches Mildred had left there for that purpose. It was with a shock of remembrance that, as the light splashed about the mirrored room, Bruno saw once again the fractured squid lolling in the bottom of the bathtub, its arms shooting out over the end of the tub like the branches of a stunted and terrible tree. In his awe of the apartment's riches and his anxiety for Mildred's affection, he had forgotten the silent companion that had brought them together. But there it was. Its limbs swayed in the flickering candle light; its head and tail bobbed in the brine. The ammoniac stench had not faded. Bruno pushed the beast's stiffened legs from the toilet seat, dried it with crumpled toilet paper, let his pants fall to his knees without unbuttoning them, and sat. He had not eaten enough in recent days for his bowels to be very fruitful. He sat on the toilet and groaned, his thighs shuddering and in the process occasionally brushing a cold, slime-slicked tentacle. When he was finished, he washed his hands and dabbed with moistened toilet tissue at the spots where his legs had made contact with the creature's corpse.

Emerging from the bathroom, Bruno found Mildred sitting on the couch on which he had slept, her elbows on her knees and her head in her hands. The pillow and duvet were gone. Mildred looked up and, seeing him, brightened. "Try this belt on," she said. "We may have to poke an extra hole in it. Richard was a little thicker than you."

"No, this is okay. How do I look?"

She covered her mouth with her hand. Cinched tight at the waist, the slacks bulged out above the belt but barely reached his ankles. "You look good," she said. "A bit like Huck Finn, but good."

Bruno tried to laugh. He couldn't think of anything to say. He rolled up his sleeves and pushed a stray shirttail into his pants. He crossed his arms and combed at his hair with his fingers. He uncrossed his arms. "Are my clothes dry yet?"

"I don't know. I haven't checked. You don't like these ones?" she laughed.

"No, it's not that. They're fine. It's only, I just thought that when the other ones dry I could go."

"Where will you go?"

"I don't know."

"Back to Brooklyn?"

"I guess."

"Do you have any water left there?"

"No."

"What about food?"

"No. Not anymore."

"So why go?"

"I just thought…"

"What did you think?"

"Well I didn't know if you…"

Something hard and bright shined in Mildred's eyes. Seeing it, Bruno found himself unable to finish his sentence.

"You know, after all this you still haven't told me your name," Mildred said.

"It's Bruno."

"Bruno," Mildred repeated. "My name is Mildred. Would you like to sit down?"

"Sure," said Bruno. He lowered himself into an armchair.

"Not there." She patted the couch beside her. "Here."


In the daytime they pulled open the heavy drapes and let the cloud-occluded sun fill the rooms with light as best it could. They walked through the apartment naked, or nearly so, lounging in unbuttoned shirts, french cuffs flapping at their wrists, with cashmere socks to warm their feet as they shuffled across cold parquet floors. They rarely spoke, but napped and read to themselves from the heavy, leather-bound books they found in the study and on oak shelves in the bedrooms.

And when Mildred would shake her hair from her eyes, put her book down on the carpet, and gesture to Bruno with a crooked finger, he would cross the room and join her on the couch and their hands would find each other under their unbuttoned shirts. Their lovemaking was gentle and leisurely, filled with fluttering kisses and the lightest of caresses. At times they barely moved, but held each other, stroking one another with an eyelash, a lock of hair. Bruno learned to love every corner of Mildred's body, each hair under her arms or between her thighs, the scars on her elbows and knees from girlhood tumbles, the sad, lost look in her eyes when he put himself inside her. Even when he was not holding her, the glow of her touch remained on his limbs and on his face, a quiet, quivering joy.

The bliss of Bruno's days was interrupted only by trips to the bathroom, which he took as infrequently as possible. The twisted squid in the tub chilled him. The fascination he had felt for it, locked away, unchanging in a museum display case, had turned to revulsion under such close quarters. The cloying scent of its slow decay, which had begun to creep in beneath the ever-present stench of ammonia, sickened him. He felt its legs writhing and reaching for him every time he turned his back on it to pee. The odors of the giant squid lingered in his nostrils for an hour after he left the room, and for the length of that hour he could not help closing his heart to Mildred, regarding even her smiles with suspicion, finding in the traces of warmth her hands left on his body, no matter how tenderly, only disgust.

Bruno and Mildred did not share a bed. She assigned him a bedroom, its walls painted green, and took another for herself. They retired each night to their own rooms after watching the rays of the sun fade out the window, over the park, across the face of the motionless moon. Bruno never questioned the arrangement.

When she came to him at night, though, she came on like a fury. He would wake, startled, with her hands and mouth on him, her hair warm and wet and slick, her fingertips wrinkled, haunted by the smell of ammonia. She did not kiss his lips or his face, but pulled with her teeth at his nipples, at the flesh of his stomach and thighs, at his bony shoulders. The moonlight cast dense black shadows beneath each of her ribs and below her jutting hips. She seemed to move in fragments, like a filmstrip slowed. She took him into her mouth almost brutally, she shoved a brusque finger into his ass, she pulled him quickly into her. Their bodies slapped together, all bone and collision, and the sheets whispered in protest beneath them. But no sooner had Mildred's back arched and a long broken gasp escaped her, than she slid out of the room in silence, leaving Bruno, shaken and drained, to contemplate the slow movement of shadows on the ceiling as the damp sheets grew cold beneath him.

Bruno could never get back to sleep on the nights she came to him, and could barely drag himself through what little activity was required by the following day, speaking rarely to Mildred, longing for solitude and wide open spaces. But some nights he slept peacefully, uninterrupted by nocturnal visitors, and awoke with a smile on his lips that only grew wider when he rose and first cast eyes on Mildred. And then there were the nights Bruno feared most of all, when he was visited only by dreams of drowning, of Mildred diving, pulling him into the depths of the sea. He would dream of walking the streets at night, stumbling in the dark and falling backward into a puddle, long white tentacles holding him down, sputtering for air as the black water filled his lungs, and would wake, gasping, his hair wet and tangled, the sheets soaked and twisted. He would lean out the window to suck in the night air, but he could not escape the stench of ammonia and rot, which had sunk not only into his pores and nostrils, but deeper still.


On the fourteenth evening after their reunion, Bruno and Mildred opened a bottle of champagne to celebrate their first two weeks together. They ate a full tin of pâté de foie gras, spread on hard and salty crackers, and washed it down with Veuve Cliquot, warm and from the bottle. They lit far more candles than necessity required, piled cushions on an aging Oriental carpet, and made love on the floor, as if in slow motion, swallowing each other's smallest movements like the last drops of sweet fresh water on earth.

Afterward they lay sprawled on the floor, a tangle of limbs, and opened a bottle of brandy. They passed it back and forth, licking from each other's chest and chin whatever spilled from the bottle's neck. "How much," Bruno asked, "would this have cost us before?"

"You mean the cognac?"

"Yeah."

"I don't know. In a restaurant, maybe twenty dollars a glass, or a snifter, they call them—something like that."

"For one glass?" Bruno laughed. "I always thought it was a bum's drink. That's what they drank on the corner, by the liquor store where I lived. E&J from the bottle. No snifters."

Mildred kissed him and took the bottle from his hand. "This is not E&J."

"Did you ever," he asked her, tracing with one finger the line of her jaw, her neck, her bony shoulder, "order a twenty dollar glass of brandy?"

She shook her head. "No, but I served them."

Three muffled blasts sounded in the distance, and Bruno and Mildred were silent. They stood, naked, arm in arm, and looked out the window. Fires glowed on the horizon to the north. Smaller ones burned here and there in the park beneath them, the scattered camps of squatters or soldiers or bums. Two strange white stars arced soundlessly above the squatting moon and on across the sky, then a third. They hit the earth and the distant fires flared white, a premature and insufficient dawn. A few seconds later the sounds of the explosions followed, three faraway thuds, hollow and deep.

"They're mortars, I think," Mildred said. "Maybe something heavier. I don't really know. In the Bronx, it looks like." She turned to retrieve the bottle of cognac. Bruno took it from her hand and drank.

A tear fell from his eye. "Why?" he said, gesturing to the world outside. "Why all this? What happened?"

Mildred smiled weakly and wiped the tear from his cheek. "Politics, I guess." She pulled Bruno to her and hugged him. "It's late," she said. "Let's go to sleep."

"Wait," Bruno said. "First tell me, why the squid?"

She stiffened slightly in his arms and stepped away. "What do you mean?"

"Why is it here? Why did you take it?"

"*We* took it, remember. Because it wouldn't have lasted in the museum. It was only a matter of time before vandals got to it."

"But why did you want it?"

Mildred shrugged and smiled sadly. She turned her back on Bruno and pulled a shirt from under the cushions piled on the floor. She buttoned it slowly. "I'm too tired for this, Bruno, and a little too drunk. Tomorrow."

She kissed his brow and walked away.

Bruno did not sleep that night. He lay in bed and tried without success to impose some order on the thoughts chasing each other furiously about his mind. He got up and stumbled to the bathroom, intending just to pee, but the rising stench of the putrefying squid turned his booze-uneasy stomach and he found himself on his knees before the toilet, brandy and sharp undigested bits of cracker burning his throat. He rose too quickly, felt the cold touch of the squid's rot-slicked tentacles on his naked back, and fell to his knees to vomit once more.

He did not go back to bed, but returned to the window. He stood for hours, shivering, warming himself only with brandy, watching bright shells scar the sky before bursting silently aflame in unseen streets. A skirmish broke out in the park. Screams and gunshots rose in the thin night air. The fighting spread into the street just a block away. Shadowy figures ran and dodged, taking cover behind cars long abandoned. The clatter of boots four stories below, muzzle flashes and groans. A bullet ricocheted off the bricks a few yards from the window. Bruno threw himself to the floor, hid his head under a pillow, and wept.

He didn't fall asleep until dawn and awoke shortly thereafter on the rug, still naked, his head throbbing. The apartment, save Bruno and the giant squid, was empty. Mildred's bed had been made. Bruno washed himself without lighting the candle above the sink to avoid seeing what he knew lurked behind him in the tub. He held his breath until he left the room. No sooner had he dressed than he lay down again, reclining on the living room couch. Picking up an open volume of Melville from the floor, he began reading where Mildred had left off: "…curling and twisting like a nest of anacondas, as if blindly to clutch at any hapless object within reach. No perceptible face or front did it have; no conceivable token of either sensation or instinct…"

The words fell through Bruno's eyes but stuck to nothing. He read them again and again found his mind drifting off between clauses. He put the book down and closed his eyes. Would Mildred return? Bruno paced from room to room, twisting the untucked tail of his shirt in his fist. The smell of the rotting squid, sharp and thick, had spread throughout the apartment. Bruno pulled the bathroom door shut and opened all the windows. The curtains billowed in the cross breeze. Cloudlets of dust and hair tumbled across the table tops and the parquet floors. Slipping a cashmere sweater over his shirt and a tweed jacket over the sweater, Bruno leaned out the window.

The park was quiet, the streets abandoned. A greasy snake of smoke stretched above the trees on the other side of the reservoir. Bruno yelled Mildred's name into the empty city, but heard not even an echo in response, only the thin whimpering of the wind. He collapsed onto the sofa, hugging himself and rocking slowly, certain she would not be back.

It was the jiggling of the lock that roused him. He scanned the room for a weapon and, finding none, scurried into the kitchen. He met Mildred in the hallway, a carving knife in one hand, a hefty tin of vichyssoise held high above his head in the other. Mildred, looking out from under the two cardboard boxes she had clutched to her chest, did not flinch. She smiled, amused, and said, "Put those down and help me."

Bruno happily complied, taking the boxes from her hands, putting them both on the floor and hugging her tightly as she tried to wriggle out of her coat.

"Where did you go?" he demanded, and before she could answer added, "I was so worried. I didn't think you were coming back."

"You thought I would leave you?"

"I didn't know."

"Where would I go?"

"Where did you go?"

"I had to get more—"

Bruno interrupted, "How could you go out alone like that? You know how it is out there."

Mildred waited. "Do you want to know where I went?"

Bruno nodded. "I'm sorry," he said. "I've just been worried."

She picked up one box and asked Bruno to get the other. He followed her to the bathroom, where she put the box on the toilet and lit the candle. "I can't believe how lucky I was," she said, her eyes glowing in the flickering crimson light. "It didn't take long at all." She opened the box and pulled from it a plastic bottle of rubbing alcohol.

"You got two cases?" Bruno asked.

"For a pound of coffee and a box of chocolates," Mildred gloated, smiling broadly. She emptied the bottle into the milky fluid, clotted and rank, that obscured the lower half of the giant squid, then opened another.

Bruno tried not to look at the broken corpse, which was now covered in a mucilaginous layer of rot. "Where?" he asked.

"In that little triangular park over at Broadway and 72nd. People meet every day to trade what they can. You just have to pray you don't get robbed coming or going, and that the militias or the cops don't show."

When they had shaken the last drop of ethanol from the last bottle, Mildred blew out the candle and, grinning mischievously, pushed Bruno into the hallway. She unbuttoned his shirt, let his trousers fall to the ground, and, tugging gently at his penis, which was already hard in her hand, pulled him to the floor.

After fifteen minutes, the knots of Bruno's spine ached from grinding into the hard wood floor. Mildred rose and fell above him, her hands pushing against his chest, her body shiny with sweat, but Bruno lay still, no longer rising to meet her thrusts. "I'm getting sore," she said, slowing her pace.

He lifted her off of him. "I can't do this with that thing in there."

Mildred reached behind her and swung the bathroom door shut. "Do you want to go in the other room?"

Bruno sat up, leaning his back against the wall. "I want to know what it's doing here."

Mildred stood and pulled Bruno's shirt over her pale back, which was covered, like her neck and face, with red splotches from the pressure of Bruno's fingers. Shaking her head with irritation, she walked off down the hall, buttoning the shirt as she went. Bruno followed and found her lying on the sofa, her legs crossed, angrily staring into the book open in her lap, tapping its cover with blue-painted nails. "Why did you bring it here?" he asked.

She closed the book. "You wanted it too. Don't pretend you didn't. You kept going back to the museum. What brought *you* back? And don't give me any shit about 'the unknown,'" she sneered.

"I wanted you. I was looking for you."

"Well, you found me." She picked up the book again, her jaw clenched, and began to read. They did not speak for the rest of the day.


Before the hollow evening light had fled the city entirely, Mildred retired to her bedroom and closed the door. Bruno, who had for hours been sitting on the bare floor in the corner of the living room, his head sagging between his knees, fetched the brandy from the kitchen pantry. The bottle was still half full despite the previous night's efforts. He sat on the velvet couch and drank, watching the shadows lengthen and mingle until they had invaded every last inch of the room. He watched the stars appear one by one, leisurely, like guests to an all-night party. He watched the moon brighten, its rays hardening and chasing the shadows from a slowly shifting trapezoidal patch of carpet, from a table top, from the sole of his bare foot.

All was still. No shells arced through the moonlit sky, no blasts shook Bruno's jaw. Not even a gunshot rang out above the park. Bruno tilted the brandy into his mouth. He could smell, from two rooms away, the heavy, acrid stench of the squid. It was time, he decided, to leave.

In his bedroom, Bruno removed the worsted trousers, tailored shirt, and V-neck sweater, and donned again the threadbare corduroys, T-shirt, and windbreaker he had worn the day he left his home in Brooklyn. He kept only the cashmere socks, pulling his sneakers on over them, knotting one lace where it threatened to tear. He thought of leaving a note, but could think of nothing to write, and left, pulling the door closed quietly behind him.

It was colder in the street than Bruno had imagined. He had not been outside in weeks, and opening the windows occasionally had made him only vaguely aware of seasonal change. The wind rattled the few dry leaves still clinging to the trees in the park. Bruno buttoned his jacket, pulled up its collar, and headed downtown. Better to avoid the park, he decided.

It would rain, Bruno was sure of it. Every once in a while it would rain. He would go back to his old place and collect rainwater in pots and pans on the fire escape. He would trap pigeons and squirrels and catch fish in the river with a bent safety pin and a ball of twine. He would twist chain-link fences into crab traps. He had been fine before Mildred, and would be fine after her. He would bathe in the river. He would shit in a bag and save it for fertilizer for the garden he would grow, if only he could find the seeds.

Two men stepped from the park into the street a half block ahead of him. They were walking downtown. One wore a dented policeman's cap and what remained of a blue dress uniform. A pistol hung low on his hip. The other wore what appeared in the moonlight to be a pinstripe suit, topped with a motorcycle helmet. A shotgun, its stock and barrel sawn off, swung from his hand.

Bruno kept tight to the side of the building, taking shelter in its shadow, and slowed his pace, stepping as softly as he could. He would be fine in Brooklyn. He had never had much—what would really change? Winter was coming, but he could sew a coat from the hides of squirrels and rats, use their sinews and tendons as thread. He had grown flabby these last weeks, but he knew his body and mind would soon be leaner, stronger. He could defend himself if he had to, but who would bother him? What did he have that anyone would want to steal?

Three more men appeared a block or so ahead, heading uptown. Two of them wore dark blue shirts adorned with epaulettes and badges, tattered jodhpurs tucked into soiled boots. Bruno could not see the third for the shadows, only the silhouette of the rifle slung over his shoulder, an absurdly long ammunition clip protruding from its breach.

Bruno ducked into a shallow doorway, then peeked his head out. The two groups had stopped to confer. They turned to walk together uptown. In a few seconds, they would be at Bruno's doorway. He tried the door, but it was locked. He was ten yards from the corner of 92nd. If he ran away from them, he would have to run straight for nearly a full block before he could turn onto 93rd. He breathed in deeply, stepped out of the doorway and turned to his right, walking directly toward the five policeman, trying once again to stick to the shadows. Before he had walked two paces, one of the men put his arm in the air, and all five stopped. The first raised his rifle to his shoulder. Bruno crouched and sprinted for the corner. As he flung himself around the bend he heard a bullet shatter the bricks of the building beside him, then another.

Bruno ran, zigzagging, avoiding the moonlight, his heart pounding faster than his feet. Another shot rang out and the air beside his ear was suddenly warm, then cold again. He dove behind a stoop. His pursuers stood in the middle of the intersection, guns drawn. Bruno edged himself out, keeping low, hoping the shadows would conceal him. He had only taken a half dozen steps when the bullets began to swim again through the air around him, crashing into the sidewalk, spraying his calves with pebbled cement. He dove behind the next stoop, heard three more shots, then a voice, "Save it."

Bruno crouched in the dark, shivering. His pants, he noticed, were wet in the crotch, and warm. They soon grew cold in the night air. The moment he was sure the men had gone and was certain his legs would hold him, Bruno stood, walked around the block, and headed back uptown.

Without looking first for Mildred, hoping instead that she was sleeping and would not notice he had been gone, Bruno went straight to the bathroom, stripped off his soiled cords and underpants, and threw them in a corner. He breathed through his mouth and kept his back to the tub. He lit the candle and found a washcloth hanging beside the sink. Soaping it, he felt something touch his thigh. A chill rose through his body as he imagined the squid rearing in the tub behind him, reborn. But he saw nothing in the mirror save his own reflection, the flickering candlelight reflected orange in his panicked eyes. And whatever it was that brushed again across his legs was firm, and, though cold and wet, not slicked with slime. Bruno turned.

Propped up in the tub, crowded by the squid, lay Mildred, one pale arm intertwined with the squid's twisted limbs, her flesh wrinkled from soaking and almost indistinguishable in the dim light from the creature's own, except for one dark nipple floating above the foul alcoholic brine. Her other arm hung over the edge of the tub, grasping now at Bruno's knee. Her head lolled, hair woven into pillow of stiffened tentacles. Her eyes were half open, and less than half awake. "Bruno," she moaned. "I dreamed you left me."

Bruno knelt beside the tub and kissed Mildred's fluttering eyelids closed. He cradled her head in his arms, watched his tears splash in the hollows of her cheeks, and, for a moment at least, did not even notice the cold and oozing corpse on which his forearms rested.

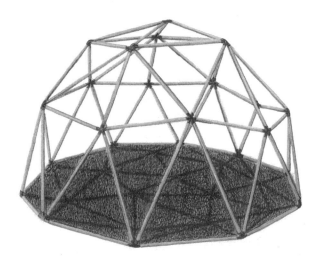

# TO SIT, UNMOVING

*by* SUSAN STEINBERG

A MAN GRABBED MY FATHER by his shirt. Then he punched my father's face.

My father fell backward into the street.

The man stooped in the street to my father. He pushed his fingers into my father's pants pocket. He fished out my father's wallet. Then he ran.

This was on the island. Puerto Rico. In the city. San Juan. On a street in the city. I don't know which. But the street was a low-lit street. And nothing was open on the low-lit streets that late at night but bars.

My father couldn't tell much of the man. There was a ski cap he said. A dark coat he said.

The fist before it reached his face.

What else, I said.

I mean I would have said.

I mean you would have said had you been sitting at the table in my father's office the following morning.

What I mean is had he been your father.

But there was nothing else.

My father fell backward into the street, his hands moving up to his eyes.

\*   \*   \*

In the city were wild kids shooting up. Hookers poking from doorways.

This we heard from the man with the mustache who stood at the desk in the lobby.

The concierge, said my father to me and my brother, and he said it slow, like *con-ci-erge*.

The hotel limo wouldn't take us to the city. It would only take us to my father's factory and to other hotels that looked like ours. But my father said that this was stupid, that we were from a city and big deal this one he said.

I'll rent a sports car, he said. A red one, he said winking at my brother who lay on his side on the lobby floor.

In the city were wild dogs. Low-lit streets.

The concierge pulled his mustache in a way that looked like it should have hurt. But his mustache looked fake and I knew my brother would piss his pants if I said this.

You'll get stabbed in the city, the concierge said, looking at me. He pulled on his mustache, and to my brother I said, Look, and pulled on the skin above my lip so it looked like it hurt. My brother laughed and rolled onto his back.

My father said, Stabbings. Big deal.

Stabbings, he said. We've got stabbings at home.

We had shootings as well. My brother and I heard shots at night from the park.

People walked over my brother and my brother tried to grab their legs.

My father said, We're from Bal-ti-more, and made his hand like he was holding a knife, ready to stab.

The concierge said, There are private restaurants here. In the good parts, he said. Keep to the private beaches, he said.

There was a Chinese restaurant in the hotel lobby and the inside looked like China. The Mexican one looked like Mexico and the music in each was different.

The lobby stores sold watches and gold chains and suntan oil. They sold American papers and American drinks. We liked the American drinks. We were Americans, and in America, or the States as my father told me and my brother to say, we drank regular drinks. We did everything regular in the States. We weren't stuck in the States in a dull hotel. We could walk after school to the city park. We could walk home alone at night.

My father threw some dollars onto the desk. He said, Sports car. Red. My brother thought this was funny. This, because my brother's brain was wired wrong. He wasn't retarded. But his brain told him to do things other ways. Like sometimes it told him to laugh a lot. Sometimes it said to be silent. There were days we could poke and poke him in the ribs and he still wouldn't say one word. Those days he wore his headphones. He listened to metal and my father said, You'll rot your brain.

My father nudged my brother with his foot. He said, Get up, son, and my brother grabbed my father's leg.

The concierge spoke Spanish on the phone. We knew he was talking shit about us. We were white, as if you didn't know this. We were stupid white fuckers. We were rich white fucks.

This is not anger. I am not angry.


We sat nights, my father on dates, in the hotel room. There was nowhere else to go. We could play on the sidewalk outside the hotel just until it got dark. Just until the concierge shooed us back inside. At nights the lobby stores were closed. And we were not allowed on the beach. Dangerous kids hung out on the beach after dark. The concierge said, Do you want to get killed, and my brother made a gun with his hand and said, Pow. Nights we ordered room service and charged it to the room. There was American food on all the menus. We ordered from the American side. But it all tasted weird and Puerto Rican. The hamburgers came on regular bread. The potatoes were bananas. The TV shows were all in Spanish. Only some words were English. Chevrolet. Golden Skillet. My brother laughed at the cartoon commercials. There was one for chicken, one for something else. A drink.


To say my father was an inventor would be to lie. He mostly invented things that didn't work. In fact, only one thing worked, and you couldn't call someone an inventor when he invented only one thing that worked.

It would be to say I was a killer because I had one murderous moment one night with some kids in the park.

It would be to say my brother was a genius because he had one good idea, just one, once, slamming into the soft walls of his rotted brain.

The things my father built that didn't work were kept in boxes in a room in our house in the States. I never knew what these things were supposed to do, but there were wires and powders and pieces of foam in boxes, always, in this room in the house.

When he invented the one thing that worked, some filter that clicked into some kind of mask that factory workers would strap to their faces in order to breathe, he took me and my brother to California. A celebration. My mother was dying and couldn't go. I mean she was literally dying. My father said, You could use the air, but she said, Go, to my father and went back to sleep.

My father took us to a restaurant that overlooked a city. Los Angeles, I think, but we were so far up on the top of a hill it didn't matter what city it was.

My father called the waitress darling. He held her by her wrist. He ordered a bottle of wine. Three glasses, he said and winked at my brother. He talked about things we didn't understand. He said his filter could take dust from the air. It could crush the dust to smaller bits. The waitress laughed and said, I don't get it. She walked away.

People want to breathe, my father said. I'm an inventor, for the love of God.

My brother drank his wine like it was water, and my father said, Easy, son.

He smacked the table. Do you hear me, he said.

My brother looked up.

Not you, said my father. Your sister, he said. She never listens.

Below us the city's white lights blinked. It could have been home, how it looked. It could have been me and my brother dusted in sand, high up in the city park.

My father said the waitress was a dog.

My brother looked about to laugh.

A toast, said my father.

We raised our glasses.

To dust, he said.

Dust was mostly human skin. I learned this in school.

My brother barked at the waitress.

My father touched our glasses with his glass.

*　*　*

When the man in the coat and cap ran off my father rose to his knees. He must have looked like he was praying. Or like he was drunk. Motionless, touching his bloody face. Struggling to stand while holding his nose. Then the blood between his fingers. Dirt on the knees of his pants.

No big deal, he said.

He could wash the pants.

And he had nothing in the wallet.

A couple bills, he said.

And the wallet was a cheap one bought on the island.

His license. No big deal.

You can replace a license, my father said. They give anyone a license on this backward island.

Even the ladies, said my father.

He was with some lady, a date, in the city. She worked in my father's factory.

He said, She's the best-looking one. Her hair. It's danger.

Hot to fucking trot, he said.

Before the date, he took me and my brother for a ride in the sports car around the hotels. The tires squealed. My brother screamed when the car went faster.

My father said, That's right, son. He said, This is the life.

He stopped the car outside the hotel. He said, This is your stop. He said, I've got a date. He said, Hot to trot. He slapped my brother on the back. Be good, he said.

We were in his office the following morning. My father had spent the night in the office. He had called us before he went to sleep. He said, I'm working late. Go to sleep, he said. But we watched TV instead.

In the morning the concierge knocked on the door. He said, Let's go. We would ride in the limo to my father's factory. The limo was better than the sports car. We could see out the windows of the limo, but no one could see us in it. People always tried to see inside. Kids pushing their bikes up the street. Ladies in cars beside us. When I gave them the finger my brother laughed.

There were plates of eggs and fruit on a table in my father's office, but we didn't eat. My father had two black eyes, a blood-crusted nose. His words sounded thick and slurred.

He said, I was barely out of the car and this guy he grabbed me. He punched me. I fell backward to the street. And my nose was bleeding like hell.

He and the date were getting some drinks in the city.

I'm allowed, he said.

He said, Isn't that right, son. He looked at my brother, who looked at the silver pitcher on the table. The pitcher curved inward then out. On the inward, things looked upside-down. My brother and I liked to look at ourselves in the pitcher. We looked wild and snake-haired and monstrous.

It wasn't a pitcher you put things in.

My father said, Don't touch the pitcher.

He said, Touch it and die.

He was looking at me.

Five hundred dollars, he said, it cost me.

Keep off it, he said.

I didn't touch it, I said.

You were about to, he said.

My brother couldn't look at my father's face. I had to look.

My father said, A knuckle sandwich. Pow, he said.

He nudged my brother and said, Pow.

My father said, She liked the car. Of course she liked the car, he said. They all like the car. She turned everything on. The radio. Click. The heater. Click. He said, Click click click, and looked at my brother to make him laugh. Click, he said and poked my brother in the gut.

My brother got up from the table and sat on the floor.

My father said, A son of a gun.


When the filters filled with dust they were trashed. Then the trash was poured into landfills. And landfills were full of rats. My father should have known this. He went to school. He should have known about landfills. And about rats. How these rats had very sharp teeth. How they could find the filters in the landfills. How they could chew straight through the filters.

You're crazy, said my father.

He said to my brother, Your sister's crazy.
My brother laughed.
But I knew dangerous dust was released by rats.
It became a part of the air again.


My brother wasn't retarded. He just couldn't learn right. His brain made things backward. Like his right and left. And telling time. And he couldn't tie shoes. He wore slip-on sneakers. The kind with the Velcro. They always looked crooked, too big for his feet.

It's a phase, said my father.

He's a genius, he said.

But my brother and I knew better. His brain was our secret. Only he and I knew how truly fucked-up it was.

My father said, It's because of your mother.

She was sick, then dead.

But that wasn't it.


The masks were sewn in a factory on the island. The factory was small and made only masks. Bigger factories made the filters. These were in Baltimore and I had been to these factories with my brother. They were big and full of workers working big machines. The workers were men who smoked while they worked. No one talked. They didn't like me and my brother running around. We tried to push buttons on the machines when the men weren't looking, and my brother would squeal like a fucking retard and the men would say to my father, Get these kids out, and come walking at us in a slow monster way that made my brother squeal even harder, and I was the one to tell the workers to get back to work, and they laughed at me, like, Who the fuck does she think she is, but they knew who I was.

At some point they would be working for me.

We all liked the island factory better. The workers on the island were ladies who spoke Spanish and played with my brother's hair. My father went to the island over the summers. It used to be he went alone. But now he had to take us.

Weekends we stood in the ocean. We collected snails in a bucket and raced them on the sand. My father slept on a chair. We put snails on my father's feet to make him jump. He said, What the hell. He didn't shave on the weekends. The ladies around him laughed when he jumped.

There were crazy kids who climbed the palms. They picked coconuts and split them up with a knife. They sold them one for a dollar to me and my brother. They told us we were stupid fucks. They said, They're free if you climb the tree. Neither of us could climb a tree with no branches. They said we were rich white fucks. We already knew this. The boys didn't wear shoes or shirts. They're free, they said. But we gave them the dollars.

My father called the kids the Coco Locos.

He said, Keep away from those dirty kids.

We went weekdays to my father's office. It had a glass door. On the other side of the door was the factory. We could see the ladies hunched over their table sewing masks. The ladies couldn't see us in the office though. The door was like the limo windows. I liked to be on the unmirrored side. Though sometimes I couldn't help it. Sometimes there were limos with other people in them. And I was with my brother on the mirrored side. We were playing on the hotel sidewalk. And I wanted to look in the mirror. But I knew better than to look too hard. Even my brother knew someone could be giving the finger.

When the ladies used the mirror to fix their lipstick, my father stood on our side and said, Stupid estupidos. Sometimes he opened the door into the ladies. Sometimes he said something funny like, Working hard I see.

The ladies took breaks from sewing masks. There was pan de agua and coffee. They prayed before eating by closing their eyes and moving their lips.

They're devout, said my father. De-vout. Good ones, he said.

I had heard my father ask the ladies to dinners. Lucky you darling, my father would say. Good food darling. Buena comida.

I'm allowed, he would say to me and my brother.

I had seen my father touch the ladies. I had seen him touch their asses.

My father's coffee was blacker than theirs, made in his own pot. The ladies spooned him sugar.

Some ladies wore masks after eating their pan de agua. The factory air was dusty.

Once I said, Funny.

My father said, What.

Dust, I said. Here.

He said, You don't know funny.


In Baltimore was the park on the hill where under the sand was wet.

China, I said, if you dig deep enough.

My brother's sneakers never looked right.

There were days I could barely look at him.

In the park were monkey bars. Rusted swing sets.

There was a slide where we slid into sand.

My brother and I went to the park after school. The monkey bars at the park were higher than the ones in the schoolyard. We perched on the monkey bars and watched the sunset. The sky turned orange. Then back to blue. We could see the whole city lit up below. We never talked. We sometimes heard gunshots. We mostly listened to traffic.


There was a time my father would say to me, One day it's yours.

All of it, he would say.

He would gesture to what. A hotel room. A factory. A view. The leather inside of a rented car.

And I would say, I don't want it.

And he would say, You don't know what you want.

And I would say, I know what I don't want.

And he would say, You don't know shit.

And my brother would put his headphones on and turn up the metal and rock his head in a retard way.

And my father would look at me.

And the feeling in my gut.


When my father called England and France he waved us away and mouthed, England, or, France. He said, Go.

Outside goats ate the parking lot weeds. My brother and I threw sticks to the goats. They were so stupid, these island goats. Sometimes they ate the sticks. And sometimes they came running at us like dogs.

The ladies' husbands pulled into the lot. They waited in their cars in cotton shirts. They smoked cigarettes down to the filters and flicked their filters to the lot. All of the goats would go after the filters. The husbands never laughed at the goats. Their windows were open even in rain. Fast-speed island music played. When the husbands waved we looked at the ground.


On the low-lit street the date ran off.

Sure she ran, my father said. She was scared, he said. She's young.

He wore a ski cap, he said. Imagine. A coat.

On an island for God's sake, said my father.

He said, Who wears a coat on an island.

Then pow, said my father.

Sure she ran.

Brass knuckles, he said.

Lousy island, he said.

He pulled my nose.

Eat your eggs, he said.


Maryland. Shaped like a gun. The city not far from the trigger. A house in the city. A bedroom in the house. A bed in the bedroom pushed to the wall. Under the blanket. Morning in winter. A streak of light piercing the curtain. Dust forming in the streak of light. A single dot of dust. Its flight across the room.


On a ride in the sports car, it was me and my father's date in the back.

The best-looking one in the factory, he said. Boy look at that body. Out to here.

Look at her body boy, said my father. You won't see that in the States.

My brother sat in the front. He read a comic and listened through headphones.

The spitting image, said my father, slapping his back. A son of a gun.

This was a Friday. He drove us to a dinner in the city. We took the highway. We were speeding to get there. The lady drivers were the worst, said my father. The ladies shouldn't even have a license, he said. Watch this, he said as he cut one off. Watch this.

They swore in Spanish at my father.

He said, That'll show them to mess with a genius.

A man in San Juan grabbed my father's shirt. He punched my father's face. My father fell.

So this was my father lying in the street. My father with a bloody nose. Blood on his best cotton shirt. My rich white American father, an inventor of something that let people breathe.

This wasn't your father.

I wish it had been yours.

Then I could say the right things to you and we could have a drink and maybe laugh at the thought of your father all fucked-up in the street.

But your father would never have been lying on some low-lit street in San Juan.

Your father would never have been bleeding like that, like some stupid fucker, just bleeding like that.

I asked my father about the dust.

I said, Where does it go.

He said, It goes in the filter.

It gets crushed, he said.

Then what, I said.

He said, It stays in the filter.

But what if it gets out, I said.

He said, It won't get out.

I said, But what if rats in the landfills chew through the filters.

He said, Rats cannot chew through the filters.

I said, Yes they can.

He said, No they can't.

I said, Yes they can.

He said, Do you want to be poor.

*    *    *

There was a day my brother and I were looking through my father's failed inventions for no good reason other than my mother would die and she wanted the house clean, and we were cleaning the room where he kept his failed inventions, his assembled bits of wire and foam and string and metal, and we laughed pretty hard when my brother picked up some crazy-looking object, an object that looked like a robot built by retard kids, and I remember saying, What the fuck, and my brother said, Look, and put the object on a table and pushed a small red button on its front, and the whole thing shook, then split in two.

When my brother and I perched on the monkey bars no one could see us. It was too dark. And we were too high up. Not even the kids who stood below us could see us up there.

The kids were drunk. Sometimes they threw bottles at each other. Sometimes we got sprayed from the crashing bottles.

Sometimes the kids pissed into the sand. They were crazy kids. Girls and boys. And they couldn't see us where we perched.

It was hard not to laugh. We knew we could have scared them. We knew we could have jumped onto their backs. It scared us to think how we could scare them. We could have made them piss their pants.

But we liked the park.

So we held our breath.

We sat, silent, unmoving.

Some masks didn't work. These came back to the island in dirty boxes. Some of the boxes were very small and crammed with masks. The boxes were piled in the factory.

My father would blame the ladies.

You're not sewing them tight, he would say.

Peru would call. And Mexico.

Those days my father slammed his fist to the desk.

He stared at the pile of boxes.

He screamed for hours into the phone.

He would say, You're just not using them right.

Those days my brother watched the ladies work. I sat in the lot with the goats. I waited for the husbands to wait for the ladies.


Mornings in Baltimore. Winter mornings. The curtain pierced by a streak of light. And dust rode on the streak of light. And if I waved my pillow the dust would scatter. I would choose a single dot of dust. It would travel upward like a leaf in a storm. Like a single snowflake in a gust of air. It would pass forever through space and time. This speck of ancient human skin. The air was always full of dust. And nothing could crush it.


On the ride to our dinner in the city my father said, Listen.

He talked of factories in foreign countries.

You don't want to know, he said.

But he at least made a filter to help.

He looked at me in the rearview mirror.

Sweatshops, he said. Now they can breathe.

He said, That's my job.

I looked out at the wilted highway palms.

He said, Listen.

In the rearview mirror he was eyes and eyebrows. A piece of forehead.

He said, There's dangerous dust all around us.

He said, My filter can crush the dust.

It's a killer, he said pointing his hand like a gun at my brother's head.

The date picked dirt out from under her nails. Her nails were red and very long.

He said, Do me a favor.

He said, Please don't talk.

I'm not talking, I said.

He said, Shut your face.

He said, Don't even start.

Other drivers looked at us. Some were men. Their windows were open, their arms out the windows. Our windows were up.

My father said, What do you know about landfills.

But I wasn't thinking about the rats. About their sharp teeth chewing straight through the filters. The dangerous dust released.

I was watching a kid in the car next to ours. He was in the backseat like I was. He was watching me through the window too, but then he was gone.

My brother said nothing, reading his comic. We could hear his music.

My father said, What does she know. He looked at my brother. He said, Your sister's crazy. He laughed. He nudged my brother's arm.

My brother was off in his own crazy world. Who knew what he thought. His brain was made of dirt. Or shells. Or rotten fruit.

My father's forehead was sweating. The back of his neck was sweating. He said, You don't know shit. He smacked the wheel. He said, You just don't know.

There was dried grass all along the roadside. Signs for things. Drinks. Chickens, live and cooked.

He smacked the wheel. He said, What do you know.

Empanadas. Succulent ribs. Lemon-lime drink.

You know nothing, he said.

Homestyle empanadas. Like your mother's empanadas.

My mother made no empanadas.

We had regular food. American food.

Fried chicken in a bucket. Buttered rolls in a bucket. Regular drinks.

He said, Listen to me.

He said, You don't listen.

Then he slowly stopped the car in a lane on the highway. The date said something sad in Spanish. Cars screeched to a stop behind us. My father put the car into park. He got out of the car and walked into traffic.


In California my father rented a car and took us to theme parks. My brother and I rode the rides while my father sat on a bench drinking coffee from a paper cup.

At one park we could pan for gold. We left the park with vials of dirt. There were specks of gold in the dirt. It was hard to see the specks.

Hold that dirt, said my father.

You'll be rich, he said.

He took us to a restaurant, and the city blinked below us.

The wine made me feel like I could laugh. My brother's face was red.

My father said, This is the life.

I said, What do you mean.

I mean the life, he said.

Big deal, I said. And I knew that if I laughed my brother would start laughing too. And I knew that if my brother started that every person in the restaurant would turn and stare because my brother sounded like a retard, and now he was drunk, as well.

So I held my breath and thought of my mother dying.


There was a time my father would say to me, One day it's yours.

I would take over. The men would work for me. The ladies too.

But the rats, I would say.

So my brother could take over instead. My brother the genius who couldn't tie a shoe.


The kids who came to the park at night were drunk. They were the wild kind of kids. They threw bottles, and hard. They were looking for a fight. They could have killed us you know.


I imagine your father lying there on that street and how I would think what a fuckup, your father, and I would tell you this, and maybe we would laugh together over a drink and I would confess to you that my father, too, was a fuckup.

But it was my father lying in the street like that, and so I'm kind of alone here, you see, because your father, though maybe a fuckup in his own fucked-up way, is not the fuckup mine is.

Your father would never have been there, and you know it, and we will never have a drink and laugh it up.

\*     \*     \*

We were sitting the three of us in a lane on the highway. On a Friday of all days. Car horns blaring. Cars swerving around us. It was me and the date in the backseat. My brother's music went all the way up. My father was walking along the shoulder. Then he shrunk out of sight. A goat was walking along the shoulder. My brother saw the goat and laughed. Cars were nearly hitting us. I don't have to tell you how fast they were going. Our car shook when the others passed. It occurred to me to drive the car. But I didn't know how to drive yet. My father's date was crying. I wasn't old enough to drive. I said to the date, Drive the car. I wasn't nice in how I said it. Her shoulders were shaking. She looked so stupid. Like a stupid kid. Her shoulders shook from crying. I said, Drive-o the fucking car-o. I pointed to the steering wheel. I made my hands like I was driving. I yanked on her arm. I screamed, Drive-o drive-o! She climbed over into the driver's seat. I looked at her ass when she climbed over. Her pants were tight and pink. My brother moved his head to his music. He laughed but he couldn't hear himself laugh. He couldn't hear how stupid he sounded, how fucking retarded, and I can't even tell you what it did to me when he laughed like this. What it did to me in my gut. I said, Stop it you retard. Stop it you retard fucker. Look, he couldn't hear me. And he wasn't retarded. He was wired wrong. And we were about to be killed and it wasn't by our own choosing. The date drove slow and found my father walking. The goat was walking with him. Minutes we crept beside the two. My father walking rigid. His face and neck were red. The goat bounced beside him. The cars behind us nearly slammed us. I screamed at my brother to roll down his window. I took his headphones off his ears. I screamed again. Then my brother was crying. I screamed at my father to get in the car. I said to the date, Stop that crying el stupid-o bitch-o. The cars behind us nearly killed us. The goat ran into brown weeds off the highway.

I imagine my father laughs at some point, lying there on his back, facing nothing, the sky, and who knows what it looked like, the sky, that night, and, really, who cares.

I imagine, too, he had a bit too much to drink, and suddenly the whole thing seems very funny to my father, lying there, a fucking genius, an inventor for fuck's sake, his back pressed to the street.

Then he tries to move his arms to get himself up and the pain moves in faster than he can lift his body from the ground and he starts thinking it's not really so funny anymore, this life, the utter absurdity of it all, this life, I mean, really, the minute by minute tedious choice between pain and death.

Is this too much.


On the low-lit street the date ran like hell. She didn't come in to work the next morning.

She left me there, my father said.

My father and I sat at the table. No one was eating. My brother sat on the floor.

Pow, said my father.

Brass knuckles, he said.

And, he said, he has my wallet.

And he really socked me good.

My brother laughed.

My father looked over at my brother.

My father said, Is something funny.

My brother was laughing on the floor.

My father got up and walked toward my brother. My brother's sneakers were cockeyed, the Velcro undone.

My father was staring, noticing something.

I said, Don't stare.

He said, Tie your shoes, son.

But there were no ties.

He said, Did you hear me, son.

He walked closer to my brother.

My brother back-crept to a corner.

My father said, You think this is funny.

He said, You think it's funny that your father got socked.

My brother laughed. I knew he was laughing at the word socked. I knew he would think this word was funny. And my father said it thick and slurred. It sounded more like thocked. And that was funny.

My father said, What's funny, son.

I said, Did you thock him back.

My father turned to look at me. His eyelids were swollen.

Who do you think you are, he said.

You should have thocked him, I said.

My father's nose was bleeding again.

My brother was laughing his head off.

My father turned to my brother.

I picked up the pitcher.

You should have thocked him, I said.

My father turned. He said, You know nothing.

He said, Do yourself a favor. He said, Put that pitcher down.

You should have crushed him, I said.

I was standing by the table.

Then I was standing on a chair.

He said, Get off that chair.

My brother put his headphones on. He turned his music up. I could hear his music. Some metal song I had heard before. And I heard the ocean. Or was it the air. Something whistled. My brother's head rocked. Light came from the window. There were millions of dust specks in the light. I said, This place is fucking dusty. I laughed at this. My father did not. He lifted his plate. He raised it higher. I threw the pitcher. He threw the plate.


As my father was getting back into the car he said to me, You don't know shit.

The date climbed into the back.

Drivers swore at us. My father drove. We ate somewhere in the city. Rice and beans. Plantains. Everything was soft and wet.

My brother read his comic. He wore his headphones.

The date looked at her lap. She was devout. A good one. But her pants were pink and up her crack. In the States she would have been another kind of lady. My brother and I saw this kind of lady when we took the long way home from the park. Some of the ladies were men. They called my brother Sugar. This made my brother laugh.

*   *   *

I should say, before I forget, that I liked the city. San Juan. Music came from every doorway. There were dogs on the sidewalks. Hookers on the sidewalks. Smells like the smell of burning meat.

On the ride home from dinner no one spoke. I sat as far from the date as I could. I pressed my face to the window and thought of my face pressed to the window. I thought of what it looked like from the other side. I thought of some kid in another backseat. How he would look at me with my face pressed tight. He would know I was stupid and from the States. He would know I couldn't climb a palm. I couldn't split a coconut. I liked American coconut shredded in a bag. Hamburgers on rolls. Kentucky Fried. And I thought of the goat who ran into weeds. And I thought of how to find the goat. And if I found the goat of what I would do. I would treat it like it was a dog.

I don't believe there was a man in a ski cap. I think the date punched my father in the face. I think the date's husband punched my father in the face. I think a hooker punched my father in the face. I think a wild kid stabbed my father in the face. I think a lady driver ran over my father's face. I think a Coco Loco split open my father's face. I think the concierge shot my father in the face. I think the goats bit my father's face. I think the rats chewed my father's face. I think the ghost of my mother punched my father in the face. I think my brother laughed in my father's face. I think I threw a pitcher at my father's face. I threw a pitcher at my father's face. I was aiming for my father's face. My father ducked. I threw a pitcher at the wall behind my father.

My brother was the one called retarded in school, and I was the one to punch the kids who called him retarded.

And my brother could say the alphabet backward and he could count backward and he could do other things that I couldn't do.

And I wasn't retarded.

\*     \*     \*

There was a night, late, my father out, my brother and I sneaked to the beach. We saw kids on the beach and a fire burning. The Coco Locos and their friends around a fire.

When they saw us they screamed out, America!

They said, Stupid fucks.

But they laughed so we walked even closer.

A radio on the sand played fast-speed music. Some kids danced in the sand by the fire. Sparks from the fire scared my brother. He looked like he was about to cry. He started to back-creep to the hotel. I felt that weirdness in my gut. But before I could call him a fucking retard, and before someone else could call him a retard, and before I could punch that person in the face, someone, a girl, held my brother's arm. Next thing, my brother was walking toward the fire. Next he was dancing on the sand. I have to say he danced like a retard. It wasn't his kind of music.

And there was a night my brother and I walked home from the city park. The street was unlit and we were the only ones. A car slowed beside us. We kept on walking. It was Baltimore and we knew how to get home. The car crept along and we walked a bit faster. The window went down. The man said, Get in, and we ran.

And I always wondered, years after the man slowed his car and said, Get in, where we might have gone had we gotten in.

There was bread on the floor. Fruit on the floor. Splinters of glass and broken dishes. Egg yolk stuck to the walls. To my arms.

I was still standing on the chair.

The silver pitcher had rolled back and back and back then stopped.

My brother went to the factory. The ladies would give him pan de agua. They would call him Sweetie and play with his hair.

I don't know how long we stood like that.

My father picked up the pitcher.

I don't need to say how fucked-up it was.

My father said, Who do you think you are.

I was taller on the chair. I was crazy, monstrous, on the chair.

I said, Who do you think *you* are.

The pitcher had hit the wall behind him. It was all fucked-up. I don't need to say how dented.

My father said, I know who I am.

I wanted to see myself on the pitcher. It was all dented now. I wanted to see what the pitcher could do.

My father said, You know who I am.

I could have jumped him from the chair. I could have made him piss his pants.

I'm a genius, he said.

I could have crushed him to bits.

I'm your father, he said.


My brother could hang upside-down on the monkey bars and the blood never rushed to his head.

He could jump off the monkey bars and land on his knees or his face or his back and not cry.

So he was the one to jump off the monkey bars that one time, that last time we went to the park. He was the one to land on those kids and I was the one laughing my ass off.


And on the monkey bars that last time, I remember thinking, Don't do it, because I could feel what he was about to do.

And I remember thinking, Do it already, because who knows why. I just did.

My mother had already died. My father was moving around the house. He was putting things into boxes and bags. He was trashing his failed inventions. None worked the way they should have worked. We were leaving for the summer for the island.

So that one time, the last time we went to the park, my brother jumped onto those kids.

And I can't tell you how scared those kids were. I mean they nearly died. They never saw it coming. I just laughed my ass off. And at that moment I felt very alive. And I knew that I was very alive. And I knew that the moment would pass. And that's how I knew I was very alive and that living was the step before not living. I mean that living was the step before dust. And dust was some crazy kind of eternal. And the whole world felt crazy, and I was laughing too hard. And before I fell from laughing so hard I was yanked down from my perch. And we both got punched and punched and punched. And it was worth it.


But every time before that time we sat there silent, unmoving.

At home my mother drifted in and out of what was next.

My father, the TV blue on his face, half-slept on the edge of a chair.

Below the kids pissed onto the swings.

The kids made out in the sand.

The city blinked like stars.

And when the sky was blackest and the kids left the park, my brother and I jumped down from our perch and walked the long way home.

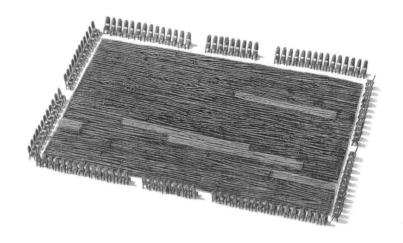

# A PRECURSOR
# OF THE CINEMA

*by* STEVEN MILLHAUSER

E VERY GREAT INVENTION is preceded by a rich history of error. Those
false paths, wrong turns, and dead ends, those branchings and veer-
ings, those wild swerves and delirious wanderings—how can they fail
to entice the attention of the historian, who sees in error itself a promise of
revelation? We need a taxonomy of the precursor, an esthetics of the not-
quite-yet. Before the cinema, that inevitable invention of the mid-1890s,
the nineteenth century gave birth to a host of brilliant toys, spectacles, and
entertainments, all of which produced vivid and startling illusions of motion. It's a seductive pre-history, which divides into two lines of descent. The
true line is said to be the series of rapidly presented sequential drawings that
create an illusion of motion based on the optical phenomenon known as per-
sistence of vision (Plateau's Phenakistoscope, Horner's Zoetrope, Reynaud's
Praxinoscope); the false line produces effects of motion based on visual illusions of another kind (Daguerre's Diorama, with its semitransparent painted
screens and shifting lights; sophisticated magic-lantern shows with double
projectors and overlapping views). But here and there we find experiments in
motion that are less readily explained, ambiguous experiments that invite the
historian to follow obscure, questionable, and at times heretical paths. It is in
this twilit realm that the work of Harlan Crane (1844–1888?) leads its enig-
matic life, before sinking into a neglect from which it has never recovered.

Harlan Crane has been called a minor illustrator, an inventor, a genius, a charlatan. He is perhaps all and none of these things. So little is known of his first twenty-nine years that he seems almost to have been born at the age of thirty, a tall, reserved man in a porkpie hat, sucking on a pipe with a meerschaum bowl. We know that he was born in Brooklyn, in the commercial district near the Fulton Ferry; many years later he told W. C. Curtis that from his bedroom window he had a distant view of the church steeples and waterfront buildings of Manhattan, which seemed to him a picture that he might step into one day. His father was a haberdasher who liked to spend Sundays in the country with oil paints and an easel. When Harlan was thirteen or fourteen, the Cranes moved across the river to Manhattan. Nothing more is known of his adolescence.

We do know, from records discovered in 1954, that Crane studied drawing in his early twenties at Cooper Union and the National Academy of Design (1866–1868). His first illustrations for *Harper's Weekly*—"Selling Hot Corn," "The Street Sweeper," "Fire Engine at the Bowery Theater," "Unloading Flour at Coenties Slip"—date from 1869; the engravings are entirely conventional, without any hint of what was to come. It is of course possible that the original drawings (since lost) contained subtleties of line and tone not captured by the crude wood engravings of the day, but unfortunately nothing remains except the hastily executed and poorly printed woodcuts themselves. There is evidence, in the correspondence of friends, to suggest that Crane became interested in photography at this time. In the summer of 1870 or 1871 he set up against one wall of his walk-up studio a long table that became a kind of laboratory, where he is known to have conducted experiments on the properties of paint. During this period he also worked on a number of small inventions: a doll with a mechanical beating heart; an adaptation of the kaleidoscope that he called the Phantasmatrope, in which the turning cylinder contained a strip of colored sequential drawings that gave the illusion of a ceaselessly repeated motion (a boy tossing up and catching a blue ball, a girl in a red dress skipping rope); and a machine that he called the Vivograph, intended to help amateurs draw perfect still lifes every time by the simple manipulation of fourteen knobs and levers. As it turned out, the Vivograph produced drawings that resembled the scrawls of an angry child, the Phantasmatrope, though patented, was never put on the market because of a defect in the shutter mechanism that was essential for masking each phase of motion, and the beating hearts of his dolls kept suddenly dying. At about this time he began to paint in oils and to take up with several artists who later became part of the Verisimilist movement. In 1873 he is known to have worked on a group of paintings clearly influenced by his photographic studies: the Photographic Print series, which consisted of several blank canvases that were said to fill gradually with painted scenes. By the age of thirty, Harlan Crane seems to have settled into the career of a diligent and negligible magazine illustrator, while in his spare time he painted in oils, printed photographs on albumen paper, and performed chemical experiments on his laboratory table, but the overwhelming impression he gives is one of restlessness, of not knowing what it is, exactly, that he wants to do with his life.

Crane first drew attention in 1874, when he showed four paintings at the Verisimilist Exhibition held in an abandoned warehouse on the East River. The Verisimilists (Linton Burgis, Thomas E. Avery, Walter Henry Hart, W. C. Curtis, Octavius Ward, and Arthur Romney Ropes) were a group of young painters who celebrated the precision of photography and rejected all effects of a dreamy, suggestive, or symbolic kind. In this there was nothing new; what set them apart from other realist schools was their fanatically meticulous concern for minuscule detail. In a Verisimilist canvas it was possible to distinguish every chain stitch on an embroidered satin fan, every curling grain in an open package of Caporal tobacco, every colored kernel and strand of silk on an ear of Indian corn hanging from a slanted nail on the cracked and weather-worn door of a barn. But their special delight was in details so marvelously minute that they could be seen only with the aid of a magnifying glass. Through the lens the viewer would discover hidden minutiae—the legs of a tiny white spider half hidden in the velvet folds of a curtain, a few breadcrumbs lying in the shadow cast by a china plate's rim. Arthur Romney Ropes claimed that his work could not be appreciated without such a glass, which he distributed free of charge to visitors at his studio. Although the Verisimilists tended to favor the still life (a briarwood pipe lying on its side next to three burnt matches, one of which was broken, and a folded newspaper with readable print; a slightly uneven stack of lovingly rendered silver coins rising up beside a wad of folded five-dollar bills and a pair of reading glasses lying on three loose playing cards), they ventured occasionally into the realm of the portrait and the landscape, where they painstakingly painted every individual hair on a gentleman's beard or a lady's muff, every lobe and branching vein on every leaf of every sycamore and oak. The newspaper reviews of the exhibition commended the paintings for illusionistic effects of a remarkable kind, while agreeing that as works of art they had been harmed by the baleful influence of photography, but the four works (no longer extant) of Harlan Crane seemed to interest or irritate them in a new way.

From half a dozen newspaper reports, from a letter by Linton Burgis to his sister, and from a handful of scattered entries in journals and diaries, we can reconstruct the paintings sufficiently to understand the perplexing impressions they caused, though many details remain unrecoverable.

*Still Life with Fly* appears to have been a conventional painting of a dish of fruit on a table: three apples, a yellow pear, and a bunch of red grapes in a bronze dish with repoussé rim, beside which lay a woman's slender tan-colored kid glove with one slightly curling fingertip and a scattering of envelopes with sharply rendered stamps and postmarks. On the side of one of the red-and-green apples rested a beautifully precise fly. Again and again we hear of the shimmering greenish wings, the six legs with distinct femurs, tibias, and tarsi, each with its prickly hairs, the brick-red compound eyes. Viewers agreed that the lifelike fly, with its licorice-colored abdomen showing through the silken transparence of the wings, was the triumph of the composition; what bewildered several observers was the moment when the fly darted suddenly through the paint and landed on an apple two inches away. The entire flight was said to have lasted no more than half a second. Two newspapers denied any movement whatever, and it remains uncertain whether the fly returned to its original apple during visiting hours, but the movement of the painted fly from apple to apple was witnessed by more than one viewer over the course of the next three weeks and is described tantalizingly in a letter of Linton Burgis to his sister Emily as "a very pretty simulacrum of flight."

*Waves* appears to have been a conventional seascape, probably sketched during a brief trip to the southern shore of Long Island in the autumn of 1873. It showed a long line of waves breaking unevenly on a sandy shore beneath a melancholy sky. What drew the attention of viewers was an unusual effect: the waves could be clearly seen to fall, move up along the shore, and withdraw—an eerily silent, living image of relentlessly falling waves, under a cheerless evening sky.

The third painting, *Pygmalion*, showed the sculptor in Greek costume standing back with an expression of wonderment as he clutched his chisel and stared at the beautiful marble statue. Observers reported that, as they looked at the painting, the statue turned her head slowly to one side, moved her wrists, and breathed in a way that caused her naked breasts to rise and fall, before she returned to the immobility of paint.

*The Séance* showed eight people and a medium seated in a circle of wooden chairs, in a darkened room illuminated only by candles. The medium was a stern woman with heavy-lidded eyes, a fringed shawl covering her upper arms, and tendrils of dark hair on her forehead. Rings glittered on her plump fingers. As the viewer observed the painting, the eight faces gradually turned upward, and a dim form could be seen hovering in the darkness of the room, above or behind the head of the medium.

What are we to make of these striking effects, which seem to anticipate, in a limited way, the illusions of motion perfected by Edison and the Lumière brothers in the mid-1890s? Such motions were observed in no other of the more than three hundred Verisimilist paintings, and they inspired a number of curious explanations. The "trick" paintings, as they came to be called, were said to depend on carefully planned lighting arrangements, as in the old Diorama invented by Daguerre and in more recent magic-lantern shows, where a wagon might seem to move across a landscape (though its wheels did not turn). What this explanation failed to explain was where the lights were concealed, why no one mentioned any change in light, and how, precisely, the complex motions were produced. Another theory claimed that behind the paintings lay concealed systems of springs and gears, which caused parts of the picture to move. Such reasoning might explain how a mechanical fly, attached to the surface of a painting, could be made to move from one location to another, but we have the testimony of several viewers that the fly in Crane's still life was smooth to the touch, and in any case the clockwork theory cannot explain phenomena such as the falling and retreating waves or the suddenly appearing ghostly form. It is true that Daguerre, in a late version of his Diorama, created an illusion of moving water by the turning of a piece of silver lace on a wheel, but Daguerre's effects were created in a darkened theater, with a long distance between seated viewers and a painted semitransparent screen measuring some seventy by fifty feet, and cannot be compared with a small canvas hanging six inches from a viewer's eyes in a well-lit room.

A more compelling theory for the historian of the cinema is that Harlan Crane might have been making use of a concealed magic lantern (or a projector of his own invention) adapted to display a swift series of sequential drawings, each one illuminated for an instant and then abolished before being replaced by the next. Unfortunately there is no evidence whatever of beams of light, no one saw a tell-tale flicker, and we have no way of knowing whether the motions repeated themselves in exactly the same way each time.

The entire issue is further obscured by Crane's own bizarre claim to a reporter, at the time of the exhibition, that he had invented what he called "animate paint"—a paint chemically treated in such a way that individual particles were capable of small motions. This claim—the first sign of the future showman—led to a number of experiments performed by chemists hired by the Society for the Advancement of the Arts, where at the end of the year an exhibition of third-rate paintings took place. As visitors passed from picture to picture, the oils suddenly began to drip down onto the frames, leaving behind melting avenues, wobbly violinists, and dissolving plums. The grotesque story does not end here. In 1875 a manufacturer of children's toys placed on the market a product called Animate Paint, which consisted of a flat wooden box containing a box of brightly colored metal tubes, half a dozen slender brushes, a manual of instruction, and twenty-five sheets of specially prepared paper. On the advice of a friend, Crane filed suit; the case was decided against him, but the product was withdrawn after the parents of children with Animate Paint sets discovered that a simple stroke of chrome yellow or crimson lake suddenly took on a life of its own, streaking across the page and dripping brightly onto eiderdown comforters, English-weave rugs, and polished mahogany tables.

An immediate result of the controversy surrounding Crane's four paintings was his expulsion from the Verisimilist group, which claimed that his optical experiments detracted from the aim of the movement: to reveal the world with ultra-photographic precision. We may be forgiven for wondering whether the expulsion served a more practical purpose, namely, to remove from the group a member who was receiving far too much attention. In any case, it may be argued that Crane's four paintings, far from betraying the aim of the Verisimilists, carried that aim to its logical conclusion. For if the intention of verisimilism was to go beyond the photograph in its attempt to "reveal" the world, isn't the leap into motion a further step in the same direction? The conventional Verisimilist wave distorts the real wave by its lack of motion; Crane's breaking wave is the true Verisimilist wave, released from the falsifying rigidity of paint.

Little is known of Crane's life during the three years following the Exhibition of 1874. We know from W. C. Curtis, the one Verisimilist who remained a friend, that Crane shut himself up all day in his studio, with its glimpse of the distant roof of the Fulton Fish Market and a thicket of masts on the East River, and refused to show his work to anyone. Once, stopping by in the evening, Curtis noticed an empty easel and several large canvases turned against the wall. "It struck me forcibly," Curtis recorded in his diary, "that I was not permitted to witness his struggles." Exactly what those struggles were, we have no way of knowing. We do know that a diminishing number of his undistinguished woodcut engravings continued to appear in *Harper's Weekly*, as well as in *Appleton's Journal* and several other publications, and that for a time he earned a small income by tinting portrait photographs. "On a long table at one side of the studio," Curtis noted on one occasion, "I observed a wet cell, a number of beakers, several tubes of paint, and two vessels filled with powders." It remains unclear what kinds of experiment Crane was conducting, although the theme of chemical experimentation raises the old question of paint with unusual properties.

In 1875 or 1876 he began to frequent the studio of Robert Allen Lowe, a leading member of a loose-knit group of painters who called themselves Transgressives and welcomed Crane as an offender of Verisimilist pieties. Crane began taking his evening meals at the Black Rose, an ale house patronized by members of the group. According to Lowe, in a letter to Samuel Hope (a painter of still lifes who later joined the Transgressives), Crane ate quickly, without seeming to notice what was on his plate, spoke very little, and smoked a big-bowled meerschaum pipe with a richly stained rim, a cherrywood stem, and a black rubber bit as he tilted back precariously in his chair and hooked one foot around a table leg. He wore a soft porkpie hat far back on his head and followed the conversation intently behind thick clouds of smoke.

The Transgressive movement began with a handful of disaffected Verisimilists who felt that the realist program of verisimilism did not go far enough. Led by Robert Allen Lowe, a painter known for his spectacularly detailed paintings of dead pheasants, bunches of asparagus, and gleaming magnifying glasses lying on top of newspapers with suddenly magnified print, the Transgressives argued that Verisimilist painting was hampered by its craven obedience to the picture frame, which did nothing but draw attention to the artifice of the painted world it enclosed. Instead of calling for the abolishment of the frame, in the manner of trompe l'oeil art, Lowe insisted that the frame be treated as a transition or "threshold" between the painting proper and the world outside the painting. Thus in a work of 1875, *Three Pears*, a meticulous still life showing three green pears on a wooden table sharply lit by sunlight streaming through a window, the long shadows of the pears stretch across the tabletop and onto the vine-carved picture frame itself. This modest painting led to an outburst of violations and disruptions by Lowe and other members of the group, and their work made its way into the Brewery Show of 1877.

The Transgressive Exhibition—better known as the Brewery Show, since the paintings were housed in an abandoned brewery on Twelfth Avenue near the meat-packing district—received a good deal of unfavorable critical attention, although it proved quite popular with the general public, who were attracted by the novelty and playfulness of the paintings. One well-known work, *The Window*, showed a life-sized casement window in a country house. Real ivy grew on the picture frame. *The Writing Desk*, by Robert Allen Lowe, showed part of a roll-top desk in close-up detail: two rows of pigeonholes and a small, partly open door with a wooden knob. In the pigeonholes one saw carefully painted envelopes, a large brass key, folded letters, a pince-nez, and a coil of string, part of which hung carelessly down over the frame. Viewers discovered that one of the pigeonholes was a real space containing a real envelope addressed to Robert Allen Lowe, while the small door, composed of actual wood, protruded from the picture surface and opened to reveal a stoneware ink bottle from which a quill pen emerged at a slant. Several people reached for the string, which proved to be a painted image. *Grapes*, a large canvas by Samuel Hope, showed an exquisitely painted bunch of purple grapes from which real grapes emerged to rest in a silver bowl on a table beneath the painting. After the first day, a number of paintings had to be roped off, to prevent the public from pawing them to pieces.

In this atmosphere of playfulness, extravagance, and illusionist wit, the paintings of Harlan Crane attracted no unusual attention, although we sometimes hear of a "disturbing" or "uncanny" effect. He displayed three paintings. *Still Life with Fly #2* showed an orange from which the rind had been partially peeled away in a long spiral, half a sliced peach with the gleaming pit rising above the flat plane of its sliced flesh, the hollow, jaggedly broken shell of an almond beside half an almond and some crumbs, and an ivory-handled fruit knife. To the side of the peach clung a vertical fly, its wings depicted against the peach-skin, its head and front legs rising above the exposed flesh of the peach. An iridescent drop of water, which seemed about to fall, clung to the peach-skin beside the fly. A number of viewers claimed that the fly suddenly left the canvas, circled above their heads, and landed on the upper right-hand corner of the frame before returning to the peach beside the glistening, motionless drop. Several viewers apparently swatted at the fly as it flew beside them, but felt nothing.

A second painting, *Young Woman*, is the only known instance of a portrait in the oeuvre of Harlan Crane. The painting showed a girl of eighteen or nineteen, wearing a white dress and a straw bonnet with a cream-colored ostrich plume, standing in a bower of white and red roses with sun and leaf-shadow stippling her face. In one hand she held a partly open letter; a torn envelope lay at her feet. She stood facing the viewer, with an expression of troubled yearning. Her free hand reached forward as if to grasp at something or someone. Despite its Verisimilist attention to detail—the intricate straw weave of the bonnet, the individual thorns on the trellis of roses—the painting looked back to the dreary conventions of narrative art deplored by Verisimilists and Transgressives alike; but what struck more than one viewer was the experience of stepping up close to the painting, in order to study the lifelike details, and feeling the unmistakable sensation of a hand touching a cheek.

The third painting, *The Escape*, hung alone in a small dusky niche or alcove. It depicted a gaunt man slumped in the shadows of a stone cell. From an unseen window a ray of dusty light fell slantwise through the gloom. Viewers reported that, as they examined the dark painting, in the twilit niche, the prisoner stirred and looked about. After a while he began to crawl forward, moving slowly over the hard floor, staring with haunted eyes. Several viewers spoke of a sudden tension in the air; they saw or felt something before or beside them, like a ghost or a wind. In the painting, the man had vanished. One journalist, who returned to observe the painting three days in succession, reported that the "escape" took place three or four times a day, at different hours, and that, if you watched the empty painting closely, you could see the figure gradually reappearing in the paint, in the manner of a photographic image appearing on albumen paper coated with silver nitrate and exposed to sunlight beneath a glass negative.

Although a number of newspapers do not even mention the Crane paintings, others offer familiar and bogus explanations for the motions, while still others take issue with descriptions published in rival papers. Whatever one may think of the matter, it is clear that we are no longer dealing with paintings as works of art, but rather with paintings as *performances*. In this sense the Brewery Show represents the first clear step in Harlan Crane's career as an inventor-showman, situated in a questionable realm between the old world of painting and the new world of moving images.

It is also worth noting that, with the exception of Lowe's *Writing Desk*, Transgressive paintings are not trompe l'oeil. The trompe l'oeil painting means to deceive, and only then to undeceive; but the real ivy and the real grapes immediately present themselves as actual objects disruptively continuing the painted representation. Harlan Crane's animate paintings are more unsettling still, for they move back and forth deliberately between representation and deception, and have the general effect of radically destabilizing the painting—for if a painted fly may at any moment suddenly enter the room, might not the painted knife slip from the painted table and cut the viewer's hand?

After their brief moment of notoriety in 1877, the Transgressives went their separate ways. Samuel Hope, Winthrop White, and C. W. E. Palmer returned to the painting of conventional still lifes; Robert Allen Lowe ventured with great success into the world of children's-book illustration; and John Frederick Hill devoted his remaining years to large, profitable paintings of very white nudes on very red sofas, destined to be hung above rows of darkly glistening bottles in smoky saloons.

Crane now entered a long period of reclusion, which only in retrospect appears the inevitable preparation for his transformation into the showman of 1883. It is more reasonable to imagine these years as ones of restlessness, of dissatisfaction, of doubt and questioning and a sense of impediment. Such a view is supported by the few glimpses we have of him, in the correspondence of acquaintances and in the diary of W. C. Curtis. We know that in the summer of 1878 he took a series of photographs of picnickers on the Hudson River, from which he made half a dozen charcoal sketches that he later destroyed. Not long afterward, he attempted and abandoned several small inventions, including a self-cleaning brush: through its hollow core ran a thin rubber tube filled with a turpentine-based solvent released by pressing a button. For a brief time he took up with Eliphalet Hale and the Sons of Truth, a band of painters who were opposed to the sentimental and falsely noble in art and insisted on portraying subjects of a deliberately vile or repellent kind, such as steaming horse droppings, dead rats torn open by crows, blood-soaked sheets, scrupulously detailed pools of vomit, rotting vegetables, and suppurating sores. Crane was indifferent to the paintings, but he liked Hale, a soft-spoken God-fearing man who believed fervently in the beauty of all created things.

Meanwhile Crane continued to take photographs, switching in the early 1880s from wet-collodion plates to the new dry-gelatin process in order to achieve sharper definition of detail. He also began trying his hand at serial photography. At one period he took scores of photographs of an unknown woman in a chemise with a fallen shoulder strap as she turned her face and body very slightly each time. He tested many kinds of printing paper, which he coated with varying proportions of egg white, potassium iodide, and potassium bromide, before sensitizing the prepared paper in a solution of silver nitrate. He told W. C. Curtis that he hated the "horrible fixity" of the photographic image and wished to disrupt it from within. In 1881 or 1882 we find him experimenting with a crude form of projector: to an old magic lantern he attached a large, revolving glass disk of his own invention on which transparent positives were arranged in phase. One evening, to the astonishment of Curtis, he displayed for several seconds on a wall of his studio the Third Avenue El with a train moving jerkily across.

But Crane did not pursue this method of bringing photographs to life, which others would carry to completion. Despite his interest in photography, he considered it inferior to painting. After attending a photographic exhibition with W. C. Curtis, he declared: "Painting is dead," but a week later at an oyster bar he remarked that photography was a "disappointment" and couldn't compare with paint when it came to capturing the textures of things. What is striking in the career of Harlan Crane is that more than once he seemed to be in the direct line of invention and experimentation that led to the cinema of Edison and the Lumières, and that each time he turned deliberately away. It was as if he were following a parallel line of discovery, searching for an illusion of motion based not on serial photographs and perforated strips of celluloid, but on different principles altogether.

The Phantoptic Theater opened on October 4, 1883. People purchased tickets at the door, passed through a foyer illuminated by brass gas-lamps on the walls, and made their way toward an arched opening half-concealed by a thick crimson curtain hung on gold rings. The curtain, the arch, and the rings turned out to be images painted on the wall; the actual entrance was through a second, less convincing curtain that opened into a small theater with a high ceiling, worn red-plush seats for some three hundred people, a cut-glass chandelier, and a raised stage with a black velvet curtain. Between the audience and the stage stood a piano. Newspaper reports differ in certain details, but the performance appears to have begun by the emergence from a side door of a man in evening dress and gleaming black shoes who strode to the piano bench, flung out his tails, sat grandly down, threw back his head, and began to play a waltz described variously as "lively" and "melancholy." The hissing gas-jets in the chandelier grew quiet and faint as the footlights were turned up. Slowly the black curtain rose. It revealed an immense oil painting that took up the entire rear wall of the stage and was framed on three sides by a polished dark wood carved with vine leaves and bunches of grapes.

The painting showed a ballroom filled with dancers: women with roses and ropes of pearls in their high-piled hair, heavily flounced ball-gowns that swept along the floor, and tight-corseted bosoms pressing against low-cut necklines trimmed with lace; men with beards and monocles, tight-waisted tailcoats, and very straight backs. A hearth with a fire was visible in one wall, high windows hung with dark-blue velvet curtains in another. As the audience watched and the pianist played his lively, melancholy waltz, the figures in the painting began to dance. Here the newspaper accounts differ. Some say the figures began to waltz suddenly, others report that first one pair of dancers began to move and then another—but it is clear to everyone that the figures are moving in a lifelike manner, made all the more convincing by the waltz music welling up from the piano. Other movements were also observed: the flames in the fireplace leaped and fell, a man leaning his elbow on the mantelpiece removed his monocle and replaced it in his eye, and a woman with yellow and pink roses in her hair fanned herself with a black silk fan.

The audience, exhilarated by the spectacle of the waltzing figures, soon began to notice a second phenomenon. Some of the dancers appeared to emerge from the ballroom onto the stage, where they continued waltzing. The stage, separated from the first row of seats by the piano and a narrow passageway, gradually seemed to become an extension of the ballroom. But the optical effect was unsettling because the dancers on the stage were seen against a ballroom that was itself perceived as a flat perspective painting—a painted surface with laws of its own. After no more than a minute or two the dancers returned to the painting, where for several minutes they continued to turn in the picture until the last notes of the waltz died away. Gradually—or suddenly, according to one journalist—the figures became immobile. In the auditorium, the gaslights in the chandelier were turned up.

From a door at stage-left emerged Harlan Crane, dressed in black evening clothes and a silk top hat that glistened as if wet in the glare of the gas-jets. He stepped to the front of the stage and bowed once to enthusiastic applause, sweeping his hat across his body. He rose to wait out the shouts and cheers. Holding up a hand, he invited the audience onto the stage to examine his painting, asking only that they refrain from touching it. He then turned on his heel and strode out of sight.

An assistant came onto the stage, carrying a long red-velvet rope. He suspended the rope between two wooden posts at both ends of the painting, some three feet from its surface.

Members of the audience climbed both sets of side steps onto the stage, where they gathered behind the velvet rope and examined the vast canvas. Sometimes they bent forward over the rope to study the painting more closely through a lorgnette or monocle. In this second phase of the show, the theater may be said to have withdrawn certain of its features and transformed itself into an art museum—one that contained a single painting. The evidence we have suggests that it was in fact an oil painting, with visible brushstrokes, rather than a screen or other surface onto which an image had been cast.

There were three showings daily: at two o'clock, four o'clock, and eight o'clock. Crane, who was present at every performance, never varied his routine, so that one wit said it wasn't Harlan Crane at all, but a mechanical figure, like Kempelen's Chess Player, fitted out with one of Edison's talking machines.

Contemporary accounts speculate lavishly about the secret of the motions, some seeing the Phantoptic Theater as a development of the old Diorama, others arguing that it was done with a specially adapted magic lantern that projected serial images of dancers onto a motionless background. But the motions of the Diorama were nothing like those of the Phantoptic Theater, for Daguerre's effects, produced by artful manipulation of light, were limited to extremely simple illusions, such as lava or masses of snow rushing down the side of a mountain; and the theory of serial projection, while anticipating later advances in the development of the cinema, cannot explain the emergence of the dancers onto the stage. For their part, the dancers on stage were variously explained as real actors appearing from behind a curtain, as images projected onto "invisible" screens, and as optical illusions produced by "hidden lenses" that the writer does not bother to describe. In truth, the riddle of Crane's *Ballroom* illusions has never been solved. What strikes the student of cinema is the peculiar position assumed by Crane and his theater with respect to the history of the illusion of motion. For if in one respect the Phantoptic Theater shares the late-nineteenth-century fascination with the science of moving images, in another it looks back, far back, to a dim, primitive world in which painted images are magical visions infused with the breath of life. Crane's refusal to abandon painting and embrace the new technology of serial photographs, his insistence on creating illusions of motion that cannot be accounted for in the new way, make him a minor, quirky, exasperating, and finally puzzling figure in the pre-history of the cinema, who seizes our attention precisely because he created a riddling world of motion entirely his own.

For a while the daily shows of the Phantoptic Theater continued to draw enthusiastic audiences, even as the press turned its gaze in other directions. By the end of the year, attendance had begun to decline; and by the middle of January the theater rarely held more than a few dozen people, crowded expectantly into the front rows.

We have several glimpses of Crane during this period. In the diary of W. C. Curtis we hear that Crane is hard at work on a new painting for his theater, though he refuses to reveal anything about it; sometimes he complains of "difficulties." One evening in December, Curtis notes with surprise the presence of a youngish woman at the studio, with auburn hair and a "plain, intelligent" face, whom he recognizes as the woman in the chemise. Crane introduced her first as Annie, then as Miss Merrow; she lowered her eyes and quickly disappeared behind a folding screen that stood in one corner of the studio. After this, Curtis saw her now and then on evening visits, when she invariably retreated behind the screen. Crane never spoke of her. Curtis remarks on his friend's "secretive" nature, speculates that she is his mistress, and drops the subject.

One evening at an ale house, Crane suddenly began to speak of his admiration for Thomas Edison. Unfolding a newspaper, he pointed to an interview in which the inventor insisted on the importance of "chance" in his discoveries. Crane read several passages aloud, then folded the paper and looked up at Curtis. "A methodical man who believes in chance. Now what does that sound like to you, Curtis?" Curtis thought for a moment before replying: "A gambler." Crane, looking startled and then pleased, gave a laugh and a shake of the head. "I hadn't thought of that. Yes, a gambler." "And you were thinking—" "Oh, nothing, nothing—do you have any matches, Curtis, I never seem to—but a methodical man, who believes in chance—tell me, Curtis, have you ever heard a better definition of an artist?"

Not until March of 1884 was a new piece announced. The opening took place at eight o'clock in the evening. The black velvet curtain rose to reveal *Picnic on the Hudson*, a monumental painting that showed groups of picnickers sitting in sun-checked green shade between high trees. Sunlight glowed in sudden bursts: on the corner of a white cloth spread on the grass, on a bunch of red grapes in a silver dish, on the lace sleeve of a lavender dress, on the blue-green river in the background, where sunlit portions of a two-stacked steamer were visible through the trees. As the pianist played a medley of American melodies ("Aura Lee," "Sweet Genevieve," "Carry Me Back to Old Virginny," "I'll Take You Home Again, Kathleen"), *Picnic on the Hudson* began to show signs of life: the second of the steamer's smokestacks emerged fully from behind the trunk of an oak, a squirrel moved along a branch, the hand of a picnicker held out a glistening crystal glass, into which, from the mouth of a wine bottle, poured a ruby-colored liquid. A small boy in boots and breeches and a feathered hat strolled into view, holding in one hand a red rubber ball. A young woman, wearing a straw poke bonnet trimmed with purple and gold pansies, slowly smiled. The several groups of men and women seated on the grass seemed to feel a great sense of peacefulness, in the warm shade, under the trees, on a summer afternoon beside the Hudson. A number of viewers later said that the painting created in them a feeling of deep repose.

As the picnickers relaxed on the riverbank, one of them, a mustached young man in a bowler hat who had been gazing toward the river, turned his head lazily in the direction of the audience and abruptly stopped. The woman in the straw bonnet, following his gaze, turned and stared. And now all the faces of the people in the painting turned to look toward the viewers, many of whom later spoke of feeling, at that moment, a sensation of desire or yearning. Someone in the audience rose and slowly climbed the steps to the stage; others soon followed. Once on the stage, they walked up and down along the painting, admiring its Verisimilist accuracy of detail—the brown silk stitching on the back of a woman's white kid glove, the webbed feet and overlapping feather-tips of a tiny seagull sitting on the railing of the steamer, the minuscule fibers visible in the torn corner of a folded news-paper on the grass. Contemporary reports are unclear about what happened next, but it appears that a man, reaching out to feel the canvas, experienced in his fingertips a sensation of melting or dissolving, before he stepped into the painting. Those who entered the painting later reported a "dreamlike feeling" or "a sense of great happiness," but were less clear about the physi-cal act of entry. Most spoke of some kind of barrier that immediately gave way; several felt hard canvas and paint. One woman, a Mrs. Amelia Hart-man, said that it reminded her of immersing herself in the ocean, but an ocean whose water was dry. Inside the painting, the figures watched them but did not speak. The mingling seems to have lasted from about ten min-utes to half an hour, before the visitors experienced what one described as a "darkening" and another as "stepping into deep shade." The deep shade soon revealed itself to be a corridor lit by dimmed gas-jets, which led to a door that opened into the side of the auditorium.

When all the members of the audience had returned to their seats, the pianist drove his music to a crescendo, threw back his head with a great agitation of hair, struck three ringing chords, and stopped. The figures in the painting resumed their original poses. Slowly the curtain came down. Harlan Crane walked briskly out onto the apron, bowed once, and strode off. The showing was over.

Newspaper reviews outdid themselves in their attempts to explain the new range of effects produced by Crane in *Picnic on the Hudson*. The *New York News* proposed a hollow space behind the painting, with actors and a stage set; the picture, an ingenious deception, was nothing but a diaphanous screen that separated the actors from the stage. The proposed solution fails to mention the hardness of the canvas, as reported by many members of the audience, and in any case it cannot explain why no one ever detected anything resembling a "diaphanous screen," or how the mysterious screen vanished to permit entry. Other explanations are equally unsatisfactory: one columnist described the barrier as an artificially produced "mist" or "vapor" onto which magic lantern slides were projected, and another suggested that the audience, once it reached the stage, had inhaled an opiate sprayed into the atmosphere and had experienced a shared hallucination.

These explanations, far from revealing the secret of Crane's art, obscured it behind translucent, fluttering veils of language, which themselves were seductive and served only to sharpen the public's curiosity and desire.

*Picnic on the Hudson* was shown to a packed house every evening at eight o'clock, while *The Ballroom* continued to be displayed daily to diminishing audiences. By early summer, when evening attendance at the Phantoptic Theater showed signs of falling off, a rumor began to circulate that Crane had already started a new work, which would usher in an age of wonder; and it was said that if you listened closely, in the theater, you could hear the artist-showman moving about in the basement, pushing things out of the way, hammering, preparing.

A single anecdote survives from this period. In a dockside restaurant with a view of the Brooklyn ferry across the river, Crane told W. C. Curtis that as a child he had thought he would grow up to be a ferryboat captain. "I like rivers," he said. "I thought I'd travel a lot." Curtis, a well-traveled man who had spent three years in Europe in his twenties, urged Crane to go abroad with him, to Paris and Munich and Venice. Crane appeared to consider it. "Not far enough," he then said. Curtis had also spent six months in China; he immediately began to sing the praises of the Orient. Crane gave "an odd little laugh" and, with a shrug of one shoulder, remarked, "Still not far enough." Then he lit up his pipe and ordered another dish of Blue Point oysters.

We know very little about *Terra Incognita*, which was shown only a single time (February 6, 1885). From the foyer of the Phantoptic Theater, visitors were led down a flight of steps into a dark room illuminated by a few low-burning gas-jets in glass lanterns suspended from the ceiling. Gradually the viewers became aware of a painting rising up on all sides—a continuous twelve-foot-high canvas that stretched flat along all four walls and curved at the wall junctures.

The vast, enclosing composition seemed at first to be painted entirely black, but slowly other colors became visible, deep browns and blackish reds, while vague shapes began to emerge. Here the evidence becomes confused. Some claimed that the painting represented a dark cavern with rocks and ledges. Others spoke of a dark sea. All witnesses agreed that they gradually became aware of shadowy figures, who seemed to float up from the depths of the painting and to move closer to the surface. A woman screamed—it isn't clear when—and was harshly hushed. At some point several figures appeared to pass from the surface into the dark and crowded room. Precisely what took place from then on remains uncertain. One woman later spoke of a sensation of cold on the back of her neck; another described a soft pressure on her upper arm. Others, men and women, reported "a sensation of being rubbed up against, as by a cat," or of being touched on the face or bosom or leg. Not all impressions were gentle. Here and there, hats were knocked off, shawls pulled away, hands and elbows seized. One witness said, "I felt as though a great wind had blown through me, and I was possessed by a feeling of sweetness and despair." Someone screamed again. After a third scream, things happened very quickly: a woman burst into tears, people began pushing their way to the stairs, there were cries and shouts and violent shoving. A bearded man fell against the canvas. A young woman in a blue felt hat trimmed with dark red roses sank slowly to the floor.

The commotion was heard by a janitor sweeping the aisles of the upper theater. He came down to check and immediately ran outside for a policeman, who hurried over and appeared at the top of the stairs with a lantern and a nightstick to witness a scene of dangerous panic. People were sobbing and pushing forward, tearing at one another's bodies, trampling the fallen woman. The policeman was unable to fight his way down. Shrill blows of his whistle brought three more policemen with lanterns, who helped the terrified crowd up the narrow stairway. When it was all over, seven people were hospitalized; the young woman on the floor later died of injuries to the face and head. The painting had been damaged in many places; one portion of canvas showed a ragged hole the size of a fist. On the floor lay broken fans and crushed top hats, torn ostrich plumes, a scattering of dark red rose petals, a mauve glove, an uncoiled chignon with one unraveled ribbon, a cracked monocle at the end of a black silk cord.

Regrettably, newspaper accounts concentrated more on the panic than on the painting. There were the usual attempts at tracing the motions of the figures to hidden magic lanterns, even though not a single visitor reported a beam of light in the darkened, gas-lit room. The penetration of the figures into the room was explained either as a theatrical stunt performed by concealed actors or a delusion stimulated by the heightened anxiety of a crowd in the dark. In truth, we simply cannot explain the reported effects by means of the scant evidence that has come down to us. It is worth noting that no one has ever duplicated the motions produced in the Phantoptic Theater. On strictly objective grounds, we cannot rule out the possibility that Crane's figures in *Terra Incognita* really did what they appeared to do, that is, emerge from the paint and enter the room, perhaps as a result of some chemical discovery no longer recoverable.

By order of the mayor, Crane's theater was closed. Three weeks later, when he attempted to open a second theater, city authorities intervened. Meanwhile the parents of the trampled woman sued Crane for inciting a riot. Although he was exonerated, the judge issued a stern warning. Crane never returned to public life.

In his cramped studio and in neighborhood chophouses we catch glimpses of him over the next few years: a thin-lipped, quiet man, with a clean-shaven face and brooding eyes. He is never without his big-bowled meerschaum with its cherrywood stem and its chewed rubber bit. W. C. Curtis speaks of his melancholy, his long silences. Was he bitter over the closing of his theater, over his brief notoriety that failed to develop into lasting fame? Only once does he complain to Curtis: he regrets, he says, that his "invention" has never been recognized. When he is mentioned in the papers now and then, it is not as an artist or an inventor but as the former proprietor of the Phantoptic Theater.

He is often tired. Curtis notes that Crane is always alone in the evenings when he visits; we hear no further mention of Annie Merrow, who vanishes from the record. For a time Crane returns to his old invention, the Phantasmatrope, attempting to solve the problem of the shutter but abruptly losing interest. He no longer takes photographs. He spends less and less time in his studio and instead passes long hours in coffee shops and cheap restaurants, reading newspapers slowly and smoking his pipe. He refuses to attend art exhibitions. He likes to stroll past the East River piers and ferry slips, to linger before the windows of the sailmakers' shops on South Street. Now and then, in order to pay the rent, he takes a job that he quits after a few weeks: a toy salesman in a department store, a sandwich-board man advertising a new lunchroom. One day he sells his camera for a dollar. He takes long walks into distant neighborhoods, sits on benches at the water's edge, a lean man beside wavering lines of smoke. He appears to subsist on apples and roasted chestnuts bought in the street, on cheap meals in ale houses and oyster bars. He likes to watch the traffic on the East River: three-masted barks, old paddlewheel towboats and the new screw-propelled tugs, steamboats with funnels and masts.

Suddenly—the word belongs to W. C. Curtis—Crane returns to his studio and shuts himself up day after day. He refuses to speak of his work. At ale houses and night cafés he picks at his food, looks restlessly about, knocks out his pipe on the table and packs in fresh tobacco with slow taps of his fingertip. Curtis can scarcely see him behind clouds of smoke. "It's like the old days," Curtis notes in his diary, adding ruefully, "without the joy."

One evening, while Crane is raising to his mouth a glass of dark ale, he pauses in mid-air, as if a thought has crossed his mind, and mentions to Curtis that a few hours ago he rented a room in an old office building on Chambers Street, a few blocks from City Hall Park. Curtis starts to ask a question but thinks better of it. The next day a flurry of hand-lettered signs on yellow paper appears on hoardings and lampposts, announcing a new exhibition on November 1, 1888.

In the small room with its two dust-streaked windows and its roll-top desk, a single painting was on display. Only W. C. Curtis and four of Curtis's friends attended. Crane stood leaning against the opposite wall, between the two windows, smoking away at his pipe. Curtis describes the painting as roughly four feet by five feet, in a plain, varnished frame. A small piece of white paper, affixed to the wall beside it, bore the words SWAN SONG.

The painting depicted Crane's studio, captured with Verisimilist fidelity.

Crane himself stood before an easel, with his long legs and a buttoned-up threadbare jacket, gripping his palette and a clutch of brushes in one hand and reaching out with a long, fine-tipped brush in the other as he held his head back and stared at the canvas "with a look of ferocity." The walls of the studio were thickly covered with framed and unframed paintings and pencil-and-chalk sketches by Crane, many of which Curtis recognized from Crane's Verisimilist and Transgressive periods. There were also a number of paintings Curtis had never seen before, which he either passes over in silence or describes with disappointing briskness ("another pipe-and-mug still life," "a rural scene"). On the floor stood piles of unframed canvases, stacked six deep against the walls. One such painting, near a corner, showed an arm protruding from the surface and grasping the leg of a chair. The painting on the easel, half finished, appeared to be a preliminary study for *Picnic on the Hudson*; a number of seated figures had been roughly sketched but not painted in, and in another place a woman's right arm, which had been finished at a different angle, showed through the paint as a ghostly arm without a hand. The studio also included a zinc washstand, the corner of a cast-iron heating stove, and part of a thick table, on which stood one of Crane's magic lanterns and a scattering of yellowed and curling photographs showing a young woman in a chemise, with one strap slipping from a shoulder and her head turned at many different angles.

From everything we know of it, *Swan Song* would have been at home in the old Verisimilist Exhibition of 1874. Curtis notes the barely visible tail of a mouse between two stacked canvases, as well as a scattering of pipe ashes on a windowsill. As he and his friends stood before the painting, wondering what was new and different about it, they heard behind them the word "Gentlemen." In truth they had almost forgotten Crane. Now they turned to see him standing against the wall between the two windows, with his pipe in his hand. Smoke floated about him. Curtis was struck by his friend's bony, melancholy face. Weak light came through the dusty windows on both sides of Crane, who seemed to be standing in the dimmest part of the room. "Thank you," he said quietly, "for—" And here he raised his arm in a graceful gesture that seemed to include the painting, the visitors, and the occasion itself. Without completing his sentence, he thrust his pipe back in his mouth and narrowed his eyes behind drifts of bluish smoke.

It is unclear exactly what happened next. Someone appears to have exclaimed. Curtis, turning back to the painting, became aware of a motion or "agitation" in the canvas. As he watched, standing about a foot from the picture, the paintings in the studio began to fade away. Those that hung on the wall and those that stood in stacks on the floor grew paler and paler, the painting on the easel and the photographs on the table began to fade, and Crane himself, with his palette and brush, seemed to be turning into a ghost.

Soon nothing was left in the painting but a cluttered studio hung with white canvases, framed and unframed. Blank canvases were stacked six deep against the walls. The mouse's tail, Curtis says, showed distinctly against the whiteness of the empty canvas.

"What the devil!" someone cried. Curtis turned around. In the real room, Crane himself was no longer there.

The door, Curtis noticed, was partly open. He and two of his friends immediately left the rented office and took a four-wheeler to Crane's studio. There they found the door unlocked. Inside, everything was exactly as in the painting: the easel with its blank canvas, the empty rectangles on the walls, the table with its scattering of blank printing paper, the stacks of white canvas standing about, even the ashes on the windowsill. When Curtis looked more closely, he had the uneasy sensation that a mouse's tail had just darted out of sight behind a canvas. Curtis felt he had stepped into a painting. It struck him that Crane had anticipated this moment, and he had an odd impulse to tip his hat to his old friend. It may have been the pale November light, or the "premonition of dread" that came over him then, but he was suddenly seized by a sense of insubstantiality, as if at any moment he might begin to fade away. With a backward glance, like a man pursued, he fled the empty studio.

Crane was never seen again. Not a single painting or sketch has survived. At best we can clumsily resurrect them through careless newspaper accounts and the descriptions, at times detailed, in the diary of W. C. Curtis. Of his other work, nothing remains except some eighty engravings in the pages of contemporary magazines—mediocre woodblock reproductions in no way different from the hurried hackwork of the time. Based on this work alone—his visible oeuvre—Harlan Crane deserves no more than a footnote in the history of late-nineteenth-century American magazine illustration. It is his vanished work that lays claim to our attention.

He teases us, this man who is neither one thing nor another, who swerves away from the history of painting in the direction of the cinema, while creating a lost medium that has no name. If I call him a precursor, it is because he is part of the broad impulse in the last quarter of the nineteenth century to make pictures move—to enact for mass audiences, through modern technology, an ancient mystery. In this sense it is tempting to think of him as a figure who looks both ways: toward the future, when the inventions of Edison and the Lumières will soon be born, and toward the remote past, when paintings were ambiguously alive, in a half-forgotten world of magic and dream. But finally it would be a mistake to abandon him here, in a shadow-place between a vanished world and a world not yet come into being. Rather, his work represents a turn, a dislocation, a bold error, a venture into a possible future that somehow failed to take place. One might say that history, in the person of Harlan Crane, had a wayward and forbidden thought. And if, after all, that unborn future should one day burst forth? Then Harlan Crane might prove to be a precursor in a more exact sense. For even now there are signs of boredom with the old illusions of cinema, a longing for new astonishments. In research laboratories in universities across the country, in film studios in New York and California, we hear of radical advances in multidimensional imaging, of mobile vivigrams, of a modern cinema that banishes the old-fashioned screen in order to permit audiences to mingle freely with brilliantly realistic illusions. The time may be near when the image will be released from its ancient bondage to cave wall and frame and screen, and a new race of beings will walk the earth. On that day the history of the cinema will have to be rewritten, and Harlan Crane will take his place as a prophet. For us, in the meantime, he must remain what he was to his contemporaries: a twilight man, a riddle. If we have summoned him here from the perfection of his self-erasure, it is because his lost work draws us toward unfamiliar and alluring realms, where history seems to hesitate for a moment, in order to contemplate an alternative, before striding on.

The diary of W. C. Curtis, published in 1898, makes one last reference to Harlan Crane. In the summer of 1896 Curtis, traveling in Vienna, visited the Kunsthistorisches Museum, where a still life (by A. Muntz) reminded him of his old friend. "The pipe was so like his," Curtis writes, "that it cast me back to the days of our old friendship." But rather than devoting a single sentence to the days of his old friendship, Curtis describes the painting instead: the stained meerschaum bowl, the cherrywood stem, the black rubber bit, even the tarnished brass ring at the upper end of the bowl, which we hear about for the first time. The pipe rests on its side, next to a pewter-lidded beer stein decorated with the figure of a hunting dog in relief. Bits of ash, fallen from the bowl, lie scattered on the plain wooden tabletop. In the bowl glows a small ember. A thin curl of smoke rises over the rim.

# TERMINAL

*by* J. ERIN SWEENEY

SAY A RISING movie star visited a children's hospital and a little boy fell in love with her and decided that she was his destiny. Say the nature of his disease mattered. Say it also mattered that she had received no guarantees about the future of her professional success. Say the industry is fickle. Say bad things can happen to innocent people. Say good things, too. Say the story ends neither happily nor sadly because it is not always the privilege of stories to know when they are about to end, are ending, or have ended.

Say the movie star looks over a small sea of small faces and decides that, as there is a time for every purpose under heaven, it is now time for humility. The movie star is a sensitive person in many ways, and this realization has the power to crush some of her composure. But not all of it, and she is in the act of curbing the humility in order to salvage the remaining composure as her eyes move to the boy. She places her long hand on his head. On the side of his head, rather, and the back of it. She is both caressing the boy—humility—and pushing him away in order to stabilize herself in a world of complex and unanswerable questions. Many of the questions are sad. The boy has no hair and his scalp is smooth and warm.

She is surprised at how alive it feels, in spite of everything.

*　*　*

Consider this: that every time a last thought is repeated, a story comes to an end. People need clarity, and that is what stories are for. Our own lives are complicated—nothing is ever resolved because nothing is ever over. But stories end, so they can be pure. The joy is pure and the suffering is pure and even the questions that can't be answered are precise and clear.

A lost dog has finally found his family, and they're shouting his name and they hold their arms out and he jumps into them...

It is the end of an argument, and they are more in love than ever...

The criminal has been caught at last, and punishment is waiting...

Here is the baby, born finally, healthy, and the mother is sweaty but she's okay too...

These are ends, but they are also beginnings, and in life they will end and begin again and again. Every time something happens a world of possible action opens up, and possible meanings. But in fiction every story is an end, because we are only reading the end. Its last notes are sonorous and beautiful and final. They are beautiful. They are final.

Say a marriage is tragic. Say that the people close to the couple can find no words for the things they have done. Say at every point where the body of the world touches their bodies, people have bad dreams and lose their faith and turn their eyes away from things they once trusted. Even if this is true, it doesn't matter: it isn't the end.

There is a journalist standing behind the movie star. The journalist watches the movie star touch the boy's head and recognizes this gesture for exactly what it is: a lucky person surrounded by the unlucky and in the midst of a vanishing revelation. The journalist knows better than to try to articulate this in a one-paragraph piece for a glamour magazine so shallow that its appeal is limited even among its target audience of middle-class preteens. So he will keep his thoughts to himself. He will use the paragraph simply to praise her humanity.

The journalist speaks later to a little girl, one who had been standing beside the caressed boy with the naked scalp.

"Would you say," prompts the journalist, "that she is as kind as she is beautiful?"

"Yes," says the little girl.

The journalist waits. He touches his notepad with the tip of his pen.

"She is as kind as she is beautiful," says the little girl.

The journalist smiles. So does the girl.

They are satisfied with their work and with each other. Both of them have the same thought: it has been a good day.

Meanwhile, the little boy makes a decision. He will marry her.

Every part of the little boy, and every part of the rest of the world that touches a part of him, has aligned behind a single purpose. His decision is as true as any he has ever made. He will marry her. He will marry her. He will marry her.

# EXECUTORS OF
# IMPORTANT ENERGIES

*by* WELLS TOWER

**M**Y SISTER WAS under her house again, at 6:00 a.m., calling me up. "Do you ever think about all the ones who you didn't let them relish you? I wish I could get another crack at all of them, even the nastiest ones."

She said she felt undesirable. I threw a pencil and it made a tiny blue chevron on the wall. I told her plenty of people desired her.

"Well, nobody desires me to my face," she said.

"How is your dear husband, by the way?"

"He's like those microbes in the Amazon that rocket up your urine stream. Touch him in even the littlest way, and *zthhhhht!* He's all over you."

The day was beginning to pale. I'd been looking at the inside of this room for three years and still I couldn't have drawn a picture of it. What a sorry little warren it was—one hundred and fifty square feet—an indescribable waste-shape of crannies and recesses left over when the rest of the building had been sectioned off into more reasonable places to live.

"Anyway," she said. "Even though I *knew* it was bulljive you were coming down tonight, I stayed up till two for the train."

"Don't give me this, Lucy. I very clearly told you Wednesday."

"Sure you did. So I went over to the platform and you weren't there, and then I kept walking around all night. Except for the man in that glass thing on Person Street, I was the only sign of life in this entire town. I was thinking of you and I walked all the way over to the orange light zone, and I sat on some wood until the sun came up, which is now." She was talking about a giant gravel freight lot near our old house, where an orderly forest of vapor lamps went on forever. We spent evenings there as children because the light was alien and monstrously orange and had a way of making you feel good.

"Things are going to turn around for you, Lucy, I know it."

"What's your proof of that?"

"For one thing," I said, "keep doing like you're doing out there, all night long on Person Street, and somebody's going to relish you to a pulp."

The man who invented the sonic pest dispeller is one of our wealthier citizens, which is a sorrow to me. I bought his machine from a catalog, and for a time I took comfort in its honest ruby eye, glimmering from the dark corner by the stove, where a Norway rat patrolled. The rat found comfort in it, too. The vibrations did something pleasing to his brain. He would pick his way through a maze of traps just so he could cozy up to the speaker and sail into a mellow high. I knew the man who came up with this terrible box. He had condominiums in Manhattan, Malibu, and Dubrovnik, and young action on the couch. Yet he was obliging and decent and frustratingly hard to despise. His secretary was a sardonic beauty with an underbite and a hairless golden sacrum. She made her living murmuring into his ear, assuring him of his genius.

I had just received a royalty payment for an item of mine, a novelty silo that melted down your spare plastic grocery bags and poured them into interchangeable molds (golf tee, pocket comb, flatware, etc.). What would you think the take might be, in dollars and cents, for an appliance featured in a nationwide, full-color circular? $430.42. I could hardly bear to show such a melancholy check to the good girls at the bank.

I did not leave for my sister's house on Wednesday. Instead I took the Icepresto to a trade show in Connecticut. I snugged a foam shipping sleeve around it and boarded the morning train. There was an atmosphere of worry on the platform in Westport. The clouds' upholsteries had ruptured badly, and citizens were fleeing what would surely be an awful rain.

I lingered for a moment to arrange my things at a sheltered bench where two men were sitting. One was wearing a T-shirt of the New Mexico license plate.

"*Land of Enchantment*," said the man's friend. "Now what exactly do they mean by that word 'enchantment'?"

"You don't know 'enchantment'? Now that's ridiculous," the first man said. He sighed. "You know what 'charm' is?"

"Yeah."

"Well, it's about like that."

The second man gazed at the violent green immensity above the trees and power steeples. "*Land of Charm*," he said.


My booth cost me three hundred dollars, and I stood at it for six hours with very little luck. My Icepresto was essentially a commercial coffee cistern with a copper heat-transfer coil in the base so that freshly brewed tea or coffee came out tepid. Today, I planned to sell the prototype and patent for several tens of thousands and hurry to the Gulf to cram an inexpensive boat and a big-titted stranger into the hollow places in my heart. All day long I had poured cool tea for men from large concerns. They drank of the Icepresto and kept one hand in their pockets so I couldn't snap my card into their palms. At five o' clock, with the hubbub of dealmaking dying out, and the rain falling thickly on this great glass cavern, I slid the Icepresto back into its sleeve.

I went to a party in the Fo'c'sle Lounge. Everyone there was in a good mood already, except for a walleyed little ladybug from the Beatrice Corporation. She was complaining about how somebody had stolen her glass of drink, and I took the opportunity to recommend an item of mine: a Styrofoam cooly-cup fitted with a clap-triggered alarm for just this sort of difficulty. "You might have seen it around," I said. "They've got it all over QVC."

She said it was the stupidest thing she'd ever heard. Three seconds later she was up on a table eating a hot wing and beaming a shit-eating grin at all who cared to glance her way.

Good ideas sell and bad ideas sell. Ask the fellow with the rat beguiler. In Japan they have a method for turning turds back into food.

\*   \*   \*

Tim called to say he and Wendy hadn't heard from me in a while and they were worried. I wouldn't have worried about Tim if I'd seen him eating an ember, and also, who was Wendy?

I woke up in the afternoon, and the rat was sprawled in front of the dispeller, whose merry pomegranate seed still blinked in vain vigilance on and off and on. I rose from the bed for the first time today, and tiptoed toward him with a hammer in my hand. I nearly had him in murdering range when someone opened the door, and the rat flowed back into the wall. It was my good friend Aubrey Brunious. He said, "Gyah!" when he saw me. "I was thinking you were gone."

I put the hammer down. "I was getting ready to be, Aubrey," I said. "But then a couple of ducks slipped out of line on me."

"Yep, yep," he said. He bit off a kernel of pinky nail and worried it with his front teeth. He began making a little wheedling noise.

"What's wrong?" I asked him.

"Ah, jeez, well I'm not going to dress it up for you," he said, galloping his fingers on his clipboard. "There's this thing with the apartment." Aubrey was part-owner of a small-potatoes real-estate firm, and he part-owned my terrible apartment as well. His brother, Wes, was Aubrey's partner, and because of the largeheartedness of the Brunious boys, I had not paid rent here in some time.

"Oh, jeez," Aubrey said. "I was thinking you'd left town, and Wes's got some guys coming in pretty soon to do some things around here."

"When, soon?" I asked. "What kind of things?"

Aubrey pursed his lips.

"A couple of things, tomorrowish, I think."

I looked around at all my stuff spread out everywhere. "Wow, tomorrow. Interesting."

"You know how it is with Wes," he said apologetically. "'Hey, Aubrey, ASAP! ASAP!' Don't sweat it. We'll work something out."

He would have been within his rights to order me off the premises right then, but he was an old friend, and he understood he owed me something for having endured his company when things had not been so fine for him. There are plenty of stories that illustrate what an unpalatable person Aubrey used to be. Here is one example:

He was a sophomore in college when a tiny patch of blemishes sprouted on his cheek, and he somehow thought that these were responsible for every difficulty he'd ever had with the human race. He more or less quit eating, and you never wanted him to come across you during a meal because he'd make you drop everything so that he could sit there and smell your lunch. Yet the problem persisted. He begged dermatologists to punish his skin with a laser, but his acne was so minor that all they would give him was liquid soap. At last Aubrey convinced a psychiatrist that he was going to blow his own head off unless his condition improved. The psychiatrist wrote him a prescription for some drastic curative tablets, known now to cause feeblemindedness and suicide. The pills cleared up the acne and at the same time turned Aubrey's face into a brittle, cracked disaster, crazed chin to forehead with little crimson wounds. He spent two semesters avoiding well-lit places and lathering himself with so many creams and unguents that he looked as though he was sweating lithium grease.

I remember I was crossing the campus with him one day when a member of the groundskeeping staff, a man I liked, who was moderately stricken with Down's syndrome, made the mistake of asking Aubrey to explain the mystery of his face. Aubrey was gingerly carrying a brand-new lightbulb back to his dormitory room. It took a moment for Aubrey's fury to gear up, but when the man was still not quite a sporting distance down the path, Aubrey turned the lightbulb loose. Aubrey was craven even in a rage and fled for the bushes as soon as the lightbulb left his fingers. It flew more purposefully than you might think. It shattered musically against the man's canvas jacket. He turned around unharmed. Then he peered at his feet and browsed the airy lightbulb flak with the toe of his rubber shoe. He looked at me as though we were sharing a great discovery. "Well, well," he said happily. "How is this for snow?"

There were worse, weirder stunts Aubrey pulled, both on me and near me. For years it nagged at me that I had stayed friendly with him in those ugly days, unlike wiser friends of mine. We were both glad, I think, that he'd been able to pay me back a little bit with a free apartment, even if it was this awkward little belfry.

"Yeah, I don't think anybody can come in here tomorrow," I said. "There are a couple of packages I'm trying to roll out before I split."

"Oh, they can work around you," Aubrey said. "They're Wes's people. Oh, they're awesome. They can do anything."

Tim explained that Wendy had a sister who was wanting to get dated. I said I would date her within an inch of her life, if that's what she was looking for.

Tim said she was free on Friday. Would that work? Frankly it wouldn't. I needed to be gone from here by then. But in recent years the episodes where I'd been allowed to touch a woman had been getting farther and farther apart. This was a pattern that worried me. I had to strain to remember the last time. What I did recall was a lot of talk and hard work and a sunrise beside a stranger who was quaking with loneliness. I reserved a table for Friday at Red Morocco.

Sister Lucy on the phone again, back under her home, down in the hideout, inhaling bongloads. Her husband forbade her habit, with good reason. Under the fevered clarity of reefer, her favorite thing was to savor his inadequacies—the girlish overdrive of his singing voice, his moist, offended silences, his delicate heron-manner in bed. Still, tough luck if he thought Lucy was going to listen to anything he said. Times that I had visited, I'd found it strange to be among them. Whenever he'd leave the house, the second the door shut behind him, she'd go, "Move! Move! Move!" We'd hustle down into the hole, turn very rapidly on, and douse ourselves with Visine and Binaca, which she'd hidden down in the earth. She was like the Navy SEALs when it came to running deceptions on her husband.

"What are you doing?" said Lucy's voice, close in the clay and soft stone.

"Just sitting here breathing."

"You're somehow still not here."

"Yeah. Sorry. Tomorrow for sure."

"Well, I'm fucking hurting."

"I gave you an apology," I said. "I'm doing my best here, Lucy."

"No, I mean my head, my skull is hurting. Big Iranian girl on my volleyball team. Absolute sasquatch. Most ungraceful bitch you've ever seen. Stuck her finger down my eye and touched me on the mind. Seeing double now."

I said I was sorry to hear it.

"Beer helps. Anyway, is all your shit packed up? You're not going to screw me on this, are you? If you flake out again I'm going to lose it on you in a major-type way."

"I promise, mostly," I said. "In fact, I've got a woman I'm supposed to catch up with. I'm going to see what she has and then get the late train."

It turned midnight, and all up the street security shields rattled down over shop windows.

"You better. This is really sucking down here. Bart and Joanie Duene are still upstairs with Dennis. I know they're popping shit. Hey, did I tell you I saw another armadillo come in here? They are the craziest things. I really, really love 'em. All they care about is digging. They've got these shovelish-type whatchacallit—tallions—and they only dig and dig. At least that's all I've ever seen 'em do."

"Bart and Joanie who, now?"

"Oh, Duene. The *Duenes*—if you asked me for the two biggest rod-ons in the state and I gave you the Duenes, you'd owe me back some change."


First thing in the morning, Wes Brunious was in my face. "Okay, what the fuck is this?" he said. "Aubrey, can you explain what this asshole is still doing in my property?"

In my opinion, Wes was one of those people who more than anything needed somebody to come along and break him down with a piece of steel cable. That kept not happening and every time I saw him he needed it more.

I stood up in my underpants. "All right, Wes, just take a breath. Let's just try and figure out how to handle this."

"Shut your fucking mouth," Wes said. "Now look, Aubrey, I don't know what the hell you're doing, but I'm trying to run a business here. I don't have time to stand around jawing with some washout friend of yours. Tell him to get his shit and get out."

A handyman appeared, grunting under the burden of a sleek black commode. Then another guy shouldered in with a sawsall and a bucket of joint compound. A third fellow was out in the hall. I couldn't see him, but

I could see the end of some long lumber bobbing around through the door.

Aubrey did his old tic, a trembling reverse-yawn, as though he was gnawing at a washboard. "Hey, Wes, come on."

Wes kicked at a box on the floor. Something inside made a chimey fracturing sound. "Okay," I said. "Now you're starting to get me a little mad here. What I want you to do—"

Wes put a big brown finger in my face. "I said for you to shut your mouth. Now, Aubrey, this is on you."

Aubrey was going red as a cranberry. "You get this joker together and get him out of here," Wes said. "However long it takes, it's coming out of your ass. The crew's getting what, a hundred fifty an hour? That's coming out of your end."

Aubrey punched the wall. A wound in the plaster a few feet away coughed out a spray of dust. Wes glanced at Aubrey and chuckled. He checked his watch and gave me fifty minutes. He explained that they were going to attach one of those refuse chutes to the window. Whatever I left was going down it. His mood seemed to lighten when he talked about the chute. Then he nodded at his handyfolk, and they all thundered down the stairs.

Aubrey went over to the sink and poured himself a drink of water.

"Well, that wasn't all that cool," I said.

"He's fine most of the time," Aubrey said. "It just sucks when he gets a bee in his bonnet." He rubbed his thumb and forefinger together and flicked something away. "Do you have anywhere you can go?"

"Sure," I said. "I've got a couple of options, but thanks," even though he hadn't offered anything. He hung around the sink for another moment, trying to work up a goodbye. At last, he just dropped his glass into a shoebox on the counter, nodded at me, and jogged off to find his brother.

I filled my large duffel-pack with clothes, specs, a chef's knife, a photograph of my mother holding a leggy ten-year-old who was unknown to me, and a jar I knew contained at least two hundred dollars in small change. I thought of calling Tim to cancel this evening's get-together, but then it registered that I might not get a crack at anything else for quite some time. I jammed the bag into a secret cubby space above the closet where I could come and get it later. There was no room for the Icepresto, so I carried it in my arms.

It was 11:00 a.m., and a cowl of pale clouds was receding over the river. I walked past a vest-pocket park where young people were making a movie. It revolved around a single special effect: a skinny youth with a mail of birdseed glued to his nude chest. Cameras were poised but the pigeons were not cooperating. Too much free seed was falling off of him, and none of the pigeons wanted to bother pecking him on the skin. I walked for three hours north, then three hours south again. The Icepresto was so cold that it turned my palms gray. Frost was growing on the street. I bought hot almonds cloaked in sugar. I peered into a plastic barrel and watched huge green frogs striving on each other in the waning sun. Then I went to Red Morocco. I stashed the Icepresto in the cloakroom and awaited Wendy's sister.

She arrived on time. Wendy's sister must have once been very lovely, but she was still perfectly all right. Strong bones, thick hair, lipstick bleeding into hairline crevasses around her mouth. She was of higher quality than any woman I'd sat down next to in an awfully long time. She made me uneasy. I cannonaded her with foolish questions.

She replied:

"Anything? I think I would wish that my psyche were divided into twenty or thirty different, wholly realized egos scattered all across the planet. We would all be distinct, but we'd be able to share a common fund of knowledge and experiences, so that at any time I could slip into another ego totally capably and let someone else take over mine for a while. Either that or shrimp where you didn't have to remove that disgusting poo-vein."

"Anywhere but Maryland."

"I don't think I've seen that channel, though it sounds like quite an achievement." She continued: "Interestingly," she said, "it was an uncle of mine who designed the Lippes Loop, the I.U.D. He's a fairly famous man."

I mentioned an idea I'd been thinking of, and immediately wished I hadn't. It was not one of my better ones: a broad-coverage prophylactic, thigh to belly button. You applied it like a spray-on bedliner for a pickup truck.

She listened patiently. "With an aerosol can? Actually, I try to not to have much to do with aluminum—you know, Alzheimer's."

"Do you want to hear a funny story?" I told her about my grandfather, the last time I saw him. He lived in Florida and he'd been married to my grandmother for sixty-five years. I didn't know what his aluminum appetites had been, but when he got old, Alzheimer's struck him suddenly, and soon a day came when he didn't recognize his wife. To him, she was just a strange lady who'd shown up on his property. He kept calling the police to come and take her to jail. My sister had sent me down there to check on him. He'd looked fine to me. "You look all right," I said.

"I am all right," he said. "Fine in every way, except the doctor says I eat too much calabash. Also, there's a crazy woman who's moved herself in here with me."

"I heard about that," I said.

"Yes, well, can I tell you something in the strictest confidence?" he said.

"Sure," I said.

"I've been thinking this one over," he said, his voice full of fever, "and I believe I'll try and fuck her."

Wendy's sister's face assumed the puzzled, faintly terrified look of someone anticipating a sneeze. She said, "Oh. Oh, no."

We sat in silence for a while. "Tim says you have a book coming out," I said. "Tell me the name so I can look for it. I'm a very big reader."

Wendy's sister said: "Oh, that? It's embarrassing. Okay, well I called it *Now You're Talking: Toward a Pedagogic Praxis of Dialogue-Constitutive Universals*, if that gives you any idea."

"Sure, sure." Then I said, "You see, the thing about my work—as I see it, the human appetite for convenience is a force of nature, a massive, tectonic power. Our longings, our wants—they shape the world to fit their own exigencies. People who do what I do, we're the executors of important energies, the energies of human desire."

I kept filling up my wine glass, hoping that if I drank enough, I might find a way to shut up. If she noticed, she didn't say. She was eager, as I was, to get us to a point where we could start behaving like animals with each other.

Together we labored to steer the conversation toward a topic with some erotic promise. I asked her to relate a memory from summer camp, something her parents never knew. She grew melancholy and talked about a gorge in New Hampshire with rocks as smooth as water. Walking barefoot along the creek she'd come across a livid trail of fresh blood and followed it across a beach of white stones to a thicket of dark junipers, into which she didn't want to go.

I put my hand on hers, which seemed to make us both unhappy.

We stood on the pitted sidewalk and shivered in the unyielding December wind. We lost the flickering instant where we might have grabbed each other by the face, and instead watched a child working his fingers up the change slot of a newspaper machine. No cordial kiss, just a crisp goodbye and the morbid clasping of cool hands. When she left, I went back inside, and retrieved my machine.

I rummaged in my pocket, where I found a goofball that had once belonged to my sister. I ate it, and then my brain began to marble up with fat white veins of optimism. I headed east and then west. I stopped into a number of establishments, and I must have cut a suspicious figure with the Icepresto because people looked at me and drew into themselves, as though it would be bad if I found out anything about them.

I stopped for an orange hand pulsing at a crosswalk. I waited beside a man with a dirty bag on his back and a less dirty bag on his front. Along came a squad of guys in leather car coats and skinfade haircuts, hooking their thumbs in their pockets and grinning at one another with asymmetrical longshoremen's grins. Their broad, braying camaraderie was exciting for me to hear. They moved in close around us, giving off the eye-watering store-bought whang of north New Jersey malehood. "Let me ask you a question," one of them said to me. "Does he suck your dick, or do you suck his?"

"They think we're friends," I said to the man beside me.

"You people better vaporize," he said. "Unless you want to see a nigger go nuclear."

Perhaps something exciting would have taken place, but police cars came rolling down the boulevard at one mile an hour, escorting a sirenlight parade of oversized loads. The men sauntered off, sneering and bawling loud New Jersey swears as they bumped along the street.

Now it was just the man and me, the two of us together. "Jack, you are looking out of shape," he said. "And what is that, a tin watermelon?"

"This is part of my business," I said.

"Yeah, cool," he said. "Well, let me tell you this. I'm the victim of some unforeseen hassles at the moment. I'm not proud to tell you that I will be staying on the street tonight, but those are the facts of the situation. What I'm wanting right now is maybe fifteen or twenty dollars for transportation and other expenses, if you could help me out."

I gave him four quarters from my pocket, which lingered in his palm for half a second before they vanished into his jacket. "That's it," I said. "That's a hundred percent of my resources."

"As long as it spends," he said. "I bless you for it, because to look at you, I can tell you don't have too much to spare. You seem to me like Li'l Abner. I mean, look at me. Talking 'bout Girbaud, Karl Kani, Gucci, Dick-Knee. You see, no matter the condition of my circumstances, I always present myself with respectable style."

I said, "You've got something on your chin, a snot-booger or some filth, it looks like."

He wiped his chin with his fingers. "C'mon, now, be nice," he said. He reached out with his wiping hand, and I shook it.

"All right," I said. "Kenneth is my name," I told him, although this was a lie.

I asked what I should call him, and I heard him say, "Jarmoos."

Jar*what?* I wanted to try saying the word but I wasn't sure what would happen if I did.

Two human greyhounds in immaculate white jackets stepped from a restaurant door, hatchet heads swiveling in their fur collars, estimating the chill. The man went and spoke to them and they gave him eighty cents to make him leave.

"Don't cross your eyes at me," he said to me. "Just because I know a few hustles, that doesn't affect my value as a human being. You are in the presence of an artist, a musician. I blew horn for Kenny Loggins on a European tour. I blessed his outfit with very beautiful backing vocals. I know the private number of his home telephone. Call him up and he'll tell you how it was."

He mimed a flurry of saxophone riffs and his fingerings looked fairly professional.

He said he lived a ways away, but he was visiting here on business. "I'm here to get my masters from Aristedes. You know this man? He's young, but he gets respect as a producer, so I shared some compositions with him. But at this point in time, it's become necessary for me to terminate our relationship. He sold three hooks for me, but he's delinquent on my dividends, which puts me in a bad understanding of his character. We are going to get into a problem about all this. I'm an artist, and I don't hurt people, but I'm afraid when I find this Aristedes, I will whip his ass until the Lord tells me to lay off of him."

"I understand," I said. I offered to buy us something at a bodega. I got a thing of gin and a beer and he got a bottle of liquid yogurt that cost four dollars. We sat on a narrow lip of concrete below a row of iron palings. He sipped the yogurt and sighed. Then he began to talk about his music. He said he'd written a lot of songs, but he had one in his head right now that was making him miserable. He didn't know the words or the notes, but he knew the shape of it, he said, and the way it made him feel. "I been trying to creep up on it all week, but the vision is so strong that it always whups my ass." He pointed at his temple. "I always got a war going on up here. That's just how it is in the mind of a genius."

I told him what I did, and he immediately interrupted me with an idea he'd been working on.

His idea, he said, was that a cell in the human body was like a circuit in an electrical matrix. He said this meant that people could actually withstand electrical shocks of infinitely high voltages. If you modulated the shocks correctly, the electricity would let you live forever, he said, and enable all sorts of extraordinary new organ transplants, even brains or entire living hides.

"But if nobody dies," I said, "the world is going to be completely clogged with people."

He said, "No, it won't, because human beings are still gonna be killing each other and whatnot."

"But I thought that with the electricity and the organs you could cure every injury known to man."

"Yeah, but look at it like this," he said. "All that modulation and such ain't gonna do nothing for you when somebody hits a lick with a durn machete and chops your head off."

"Why is somebody going to chop my head off?"

He said, "Because in this age I'm talking about, they are really gonna want to *kill* you, man!"

Jarmoos sucked the last of his yogurt into his mouth with a brusque mucosal clatter. He shook my hand and said he was going his own way, out to Queens to settle his score.

"Look," I told the man. "I'm going to help you out, but I don't want you to kill me. You can come over to my house. The heat's good. They crank the boiler. We could have a conversation. I wouldn't mind doing that, but if you think you might want to make it or rip off my things, just tell me up front. That's what that dollar was for, and that drink I got you, the truth."

He shut one eye and looked at me. "All right, now you starting to vex me. Why am I gonna try do some stuff to you? How do I know what type of shit you might be wanting to do to me?"

I said he didn't, and yet he came along.

The air in my room had a high clean reek of fresh solvent and spackle. I mashed a brand-new rheostat and hidden halide lamps threw cold blue light into the room. The Bruniouses had made a new apartment here, sumptuous and germ-resistant: white lacquer cabinets; beige granite counters; a hard milky polymer had been sprayed over the ruined wooden floors and was perfectly slick and dry. Everything I owned had gone down the refuse tube, which yawned in the window and bellowed traffic sounds and voices from the street.

Jarmoos sat and leaned against the wall. The workmen had left some saws and things. Jarmoos rummaged in a bucket and found a nail puller. He slicked his thumb along its pudgy cleft and grinned. "Know what this reminds me of?"

A flurry of rat's nails whispered in the new ceiling tin and then fell silent.

"I used to have a wife who I loved deeply with my soul. Everything about it was the way it was supposed to be, except one thing."

"Hm?"

"Man, there was something hectic with her rig. I was allergic to it, and that got me mixing with other girls. Bless her, she went and took it to a friend of mine who was better built to hack it, I suppose."

A woman's screaming blared up through the tube. On Fridays, they had "faggot bingo" two blocks up the avenue. Afterward, it was a regular thing for the lesbians to stop by and use the west wall of my building to beat each other up against. They broke each other's hearts on schedule, always in the same indigo half-hour of the morning.

Jarmoos dozed under the bright light. The soft tissues in his throat bleated faintly. His hands lay in his lap, forefingers hooked together. This was something pretty good. How long had it been since this man had been between four walls? You could see from the asphalt texture of his cheeks and the tall, sun-nourished moles around his eyes that he'd spent a lot of uncomfortable time out of doors. But no alleyways or steam grates for him tonight, no sir. I got a good feeling in my chest—a painful feeling, actually, as though a sea urchin was swelling there. I felt suddenly fierce with it, and let me tell you this: anything I owned, I would have given it to that man right then. Was this not something rare? Hadn't we stolen something back from this uncharitable town tonight? Two good people coming together with no secret greeds or intrigues in either of our minds—that was a triumph. A *minor* triumph, one that no one would remember a week from now, but at this spot, for these brief hours, a tiny human victory was taking hold. I could see that Jarmoos knew this as I did. The corners of his broken lips were hoisted in a dozy smile, and I was overcome with the urge to give him something valuable. Instead, I reached over and touched his shoulder. His eyes snapped open. "*Watch your business!*" he yelled. I had made a mistake.

It was late, and I did not feel well. I went to sleep, and I woke up a minute or an hour later to the sound of singing. It was Jarmoos going into "How She Boogalooed It," but at a third the tempo. He hummed an overture, and even that hum was good, trembling with a kind of ethnic insouciance, spiralling around the homely old melody. He got into the words, and it filled up the whole room. You could hear an entire crowd of people singing in his one voice—a husky, howling tenor up front, a brassy feminine volume chiming in the chorus, and a gang of weary men who grumbled in the gaps between the phrases. Music this good had never happened so close to me before. I opened my eyes and he stopped.

"No, man, please keep going."

"I'm gonna need about three dollars," he said. "This is how I make my living."

I threw up into the new toilet. When I came out of the little cupboard where the bathroom was, he was standing in the middle of the room, watching me.

I slept again. When I stirred, he was close, staring at my face.

"You still breathing?" he said. "You starting to worry me, man. You need to sleep more careful. Roll over on your side."

That didn't sound too smart to me. "I'm going to stay like this," I said. "Why don't you go over there and lay down."

"Nah," he said. "I already did my resting. But I'm not trying to disturb you, man. I'm just gonna sit here and consider some lyrics, turn some things over in my mind."

When I heard him head for the john, I grabbed my bag from the cubbyhole. I laid my head down on it, but first I got the chef's knife out and held it in my fist.

When Jarmoos came back out, I was straight with him. "So I'm hitting the hay. I'm sleeping on everything I want, but if you want to take those tools or whatever, I don't care."

He started to laugh. "Kenneth. *Ken-nay*. Right now, I'm reminded of a song written by a colleague of mine called 'Killing Me Softly,' because you are hurting me with this."

"I know. I was just saying. Also—" I waved the knife at him, "—I've got this, just in case you're waiting to rob me or do whatever. I don't mean anything by it, but just to let you know."

I started nodding off. Then I felt the toe of his shoe nudging my ribs. "Open your eyes, motherfucker," he said. He was standing over me with a huge bulge of money in his hand, a five-dollar bill on top. He held the money so tightly his hand shook. He seemed to wish there was a way of killing me with it. "You see this? This is two hundred and seventy dollars, you ignorant piece of shit."

"What am I supposed to do about it?" I asked him.

"Respect it," he said, and the door clicked shut behind him.

I slept poorly. All night long a sharp splinter of streetlamp light was sticking straight into my eye.


When the buzzer rang, it was dawn, and the carpentry dust floating in the room was turning blue. I was instantly afraid. The buzzer bleated in steady bursts and got me off the floor. I went to the box and pressed listen. I heard the gruff gray static of the street and the warning song of a reversing truck.

"Kenneth!" a voice said. "It's Craig."

"Who?"

"Fuckin' *Craig*, man, from last night. Buzz me in. My gear's all up in there."

The man called Craig was looking rough today. The whites of his eyes were so yolky and pebbled up with broken capillaries it seemed as though his eyelids would make a scraping sound going over them. On the side of his neck was an inch-long gash where his ear met his cheek. A dark varnish of blood had dried on his neck, but he was in a sprightly mood. He hoisted his bags. "All right, my man," he said. "I am square with Aristedes, and today I'm on the move," he said. He claimed to have a car, and he said he was going to drive it immediately to Dinwiddie, Virginia, a town whose name I was happy to hear, and which was not so far from where I needed to be. I thought of my sister, down in the dirt, and of the Bruniouses advancing. I asked Craig, "What would you think of helping me out with a lift?"

"That'd be a big inconvenience to me," he said. "I have some things to think about, and I couldn't have you disturbing me with a lot of extra chatter. But what kind of cash have you got on you?"

The car he had was a brand-new white Mercedes with deep leather seats, but when I tried rolling up my window, a crumbling horizon of broken glass rose in the pane. Outside, the gray winter was viciously underway. I said, "I'm going to freeze to death riding like this."

The mouth of the tunnel gaped in front of us. Craig touched his ear, put his finger to his tongue, and told me, "This is how we roll."

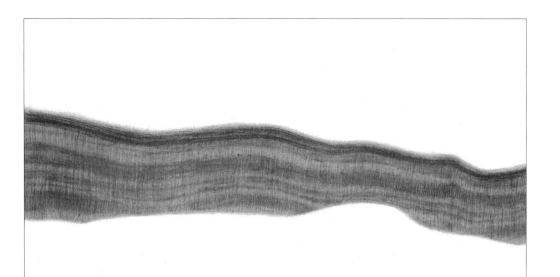

# THE GREAT DIVIDE

*by* SHANN RAY

*The train moves west on the highline outside Browning, tight-bound in an upward arc along the sidewall of tremendous mountains, the movement of metal and muscle working above the tree line, chugging out black smoke. Smoke, black first against the grayish rock, the granite face of the mountain, then higher and farther back, black into the keen blue of sky without clouds.*

1

THE BOY FIVE YEARS OLD, and big, bull child his father calls him, and bulls he rides, starting at six on the gray old man his father owns, then at nine years and ten in the open fields of neighboring ranches. He enters his first real rodeo at thirteen in Glasgow and on from there, three broken fingers, a broken ankle, broken clavicle, and a cracked wristbone. Otherwise unharmed, he knows the taste of blood, fights men twice his age while attending bars with his father. When he loses his father grows quiet, cusses him when they get home, beats him. When he wins, his father praises him.

Work, his father says, because you ain't getting nothing. People are takers. As well shoot you as look at you.

At school he has high marks. He desires to please his mother.

Home, he smells the gun-cleaning, the oil, the parts in neat rows on the kitchen table. The table is long and rectangular, of rough-hewn wood she drapes in white cloth. He sees the elongated pipe cleaner, the blackened rags, the sheen of rifle barrel, the worn wood of stock. He hears the word Winchester and the way his father speaks it, feels his father's look downturned, his father's eyes shadowed, submerged in the bones, the flesh of the face. The family inhabits a one-room ranch house, mother, father, son. There is a plankwood floor, an eating space, a bed space, cook stove. A small slant-roofed barn stands east of the house where the livestock gather in the cold. Mom is in bed saying, Don't make a mess. The boy's father, meticulous at the table, says, Quiet woman. Outside the flat of the high plains arcs toward Canada. To the south the wild wind blows snow from here to a haze at the earth's end. A rim of sun, westerly, is red as blood.

The boy's mother reads aloud by lamplight. Looking up, into his eyes, Mind your schooling, she says. She touches his face. The words she reads go out far, they encompass the world, and in the evening quiet the boy and his father curl at her feet on the bed listening. Before I formed you in the womb I knew you, she reads, and before you were born I set you apart.

In town the boy witnesses a drunken Indian pulled from his horse by a group of four men. Hard rain falling, the boy standing on the boardwalk staring out. The man has wandered from the Sioux reservation, Assiniboine, day ride toting liquor, empty, seeking more. They throw his body to the ground, his head they press down. Their hands are knotted in his hair and into the wet earth they push his face until it's gone. They throw loud words from white-red mouths while the Indian's body lurches and moves beneath them. The man's lathered voice seeks life and they laugh and champion one another before they rise and spit and walk away. The Indian turns his head to the side and breathes. The boy waits. Directly, he walks and lifts the man, positions him on his horse. He puts his hand on the round flank and horse and rider continue on. He watches, cleans his hands on his pants, and when he turns he is violently struck down in the street.

His father stands over him. He holds the shovel, the long handle he put to the boy's head, the father's countenance as misshapen as the mud that holds the boy, the boy's blood. Sir? The boy says. You helped the Indian, his father says, and lifts the handle again, fine circular motion that opens a straight, clean gash above the boy's cheekbone. The boy lowers his head. He touches the wound, dirtying it, feeling it fill and flow. His eyes are down. He keeps silent. Next time finish it, his father says. The father leaves him lie. The boy follows him home. Voiceless, they work the land, the boy in his father's shadow from the dawn, walking. The sound of his mother is what he carries when he goes.

Sixteen years old, the boy walks the fenceline in a whiteout. He is six foot seven inches tall. He weighs two hundred and fifty pounds. Along a slight game trail on the north fence he is two hours from the house at thirty below zero. He wonders about his father, gone three days. His father had come back from town with a flat look on his face. He'd sat on the bed and wouldn't eat. At dark he'd made a simple pronouncement. Getting food, he said, then gripped the rifle, opened the door, and strode outside long-legged against the bolt of wind and snow. Gone.

Walking, the boy figures what he's figured before and this time the reckoning is true. He sees the black barrel of the rifle angled on the second line of barbed wire, snow a thin mantle on the barrel's eastward lie. He sees beneath it the body-shaped mound, brushes the snow away with a hand, finds the frozen head of his father, the open eyes dull as gray stones. A small hole under the chin is burnt around the edges, and at the back of his father's head, fist-sized, the boy finds the exit wound.

When the boy pulls the gun from his father's hand two of the fingers snap away and land in the snow. The boy opens his father's coat, puts the fingers in his father's front shirt pocket. He shoulders his father, carries the gun, takes his father home.

They lay him on the floor under the kitchen table. At the gray opening of dawn the boy positions old tires off behind the house, soaks them in gasoline and lights them, oily-red pyres and slanted smoke columns stark in the winter quiet. The ground thaws as the boy waits. He spends morning to evening using his father's pickaxe, then the shovel, and still they bury the body shallow. He pushes the earth in over his father, malformed rock fused with ice and soil, and when he's done the boy pounds the surface with the flat back of the shovel, loud bangs that sound blunt and hard in the cold. The snow is light now, driven by wind on a slant from the north. His mom forms a crude cross of root wood from the cellar and the boy manipulates the rock, positioning the cross at the head of the grave.

The boy removes his broken felt cowboy hat, his gloves. His mom reaches, holds the boy's hand. Their faces turn raw in the cold. Dead now, she says. He saw the world darkly, and people darker still. May his boy find the good. She squeezes the boy's hand, Dust to dust. May the Good Lord make the crooked paths straight, the mountains to be laid low, the valleys to rise, and may the Lord do with the dead as He wills.

Already inside the boy is a will he does not see but feels, abstruse, sullen, a chimera of two persons, the man of violence at odds with the angel of peace. Find the good, the boy thinks, a burden that resides in the cavity of his chest.

The next day, sheriff and banker come and say I'm sorry and the four ride in the cab of the Studebaker back to town. Papers and words, the ranch is taken, some little money granted, and the two move thirty miles to Sage, farther yet toward the northeast edge of Montana, the town joined to the straight rail track that runs the highline. Small town, Sage, post office, two bars, general store. They room with an old woman near dead in a house with floors that shine of maple, neat-lined hardwood in every room. At night the boy hears a howling wind that blends to the whistle of the long train, the ground rumble of the tracks, the walls like a person afraid, shaking, the bed moving, the bones in him jarred, and listening he is drifting, asleep, lost on a flatboard bunk near the ceiling in a sleeping compartment, carried far into forested lands. Within the year the boy's mom dies. He finds her silent in the morning under cover of cotton sheet and colored quilt. In her hair the small ivory comb given by the boy's father nearly two decades before. The boy places the comb in his breastpocket. In her hand a page torn from scripture, Isaiah in her fingers of bone, the hollow of her hand, the place that was home to the shape of his face. He lifts the page, finds her weary underline, Arise, shine, for your light has come. And the glory of the Lord has arisen upon you. Behold, darkness covers the earth, and deep darkness its people, but the glory of the Lord has arisen upon you.

The boy waits. He stays where he is, not knowing. Behind the Mint Bar past midnight, he beats a man fresh from the rail line until the man barely breathes. When it started the man had cussed the boy and called him outside. The boy followed, not caring. The man's face was clean, white as an eggshell, but the boy had made it purple, a dark oblong bruise engorged above the man's neckline. She has been dead one month now.

The boy lies on the hardwood floor at the house in Sage, watching the elderly landlady as she enters the front door. She is methodical, working the lock with tangled fingers. Welcome, Ma'am, he mouths the words. Same to you boy, she answers. Same hour each day she returns from the post office. It is dusk. The boy sees the woman's face, the boned-out look she wears. They have their greeting, she passes into the kitchen, he notices the light. He feels it as much as he sees it, a white form reflected left-center in the front window of the old woman's house. The house faces away from the town's main street. The thing is a quirk, he thinks, a miracle of fluked architecture that pulls the light more than one hundred feet from across the alley and down the street, from the pointed apex of the general store and its hollow globe-shaped street lamp beneath which the night-people ebb and flow on the boardwalk. The light comes through the aperture of a window at the top of the back stairs. From there it hits a narrow gold-framed mirror in the hallway and sends its thin icon into the wide living room. The light is morphed as it sits on the front glass, an odd-shaped sphere almost translucent at dusk, then bright white, bony as a death's head by the time of darkness. The boy hears the woman on the stairs, her languid gate, the creaking ascent to her room. As her body passes, the light disappears then returns. She is never in the front room at night and the boy rarely looks at her during the day, done as he is over his mother, over the loss of all things.

A man will be physical, he thinks, forsake things he should never have forsaken, his kin, himself, the ground that gave him life. Death will be the arms to hold him, the final word to give him rest.

The boy curls inward, lies on the floor for days. The greeting remains the same, the woman leaves him his space. He pictures the round bulb over the general store, pictures himself beneath it in the dirt street, standing in the deep night, looking up. He beholds the bloom of light as he might a near star, a sun. Then he sees himself above it, behind it, clenching the roof between his knees as he would a circus horse, his chest upraised, his father's big sledgehammer lifted overhead. He pulls down sky with arms like wedges. He blasts the light to smithereens. He floats in shards of glass and frozen light, soft, and softer, the wind and the powdery glass like dandelion-white parachutes adrift through the opening, through the window and down, angled from the hall mirror and pulled inward to the living room, falling soft, clumsily, full-bodied onto the hardwood floor. He has returned to the space he keeps. It is dark. The light's reflection shines white in the night of the front window, the outline complete, precise. He sleeps. Outside, he hears the loud confidence of the engine, the steel wheels of the cars at high speed along the rails. In the early morning the old woman puts a hand on his shoulder. The touch awakens him. Yes, he thinks, I will leave this place.

The next day he rises, moves south and west to Bozeman. No jobs, but big he gets work in a feed store. He passes a placement exam and enrolls in the agricultural college in Bozeman. He rides bulls in every rodeo he can find. Nearly every Saturday night he fights in bars. He doesn't drink. He seeks only the concave feel of facial structure, the slippery skin of cheekbones, the line of a man's nose, the loose pendulum of the jawbone and the cool sockets of the eyes. He likes these things, the sound they make as they give way, the sound of cartilage and the way the skin slits open before the blood begins, the white-hard glisten of bone, the sound of the face when it breaks. But he hates himself that he likes it.

Still he returns. In the half-dark of the bar in the basement of the Wellington Hotel outside White Sulpher he opens the curve of a man's head on the corner of a table. A small mob gathers seeking revenge, the man's brothers, the man's friends. He throws them back and puts out the teeth from the mouth of one. He breaks the elbow of another. You'll leave here dead, he says, and the group recedes, the power in him vital and full and he walks from the open door alone into darkness until he sits off distant wrapping his knees in his arms, weeping. He seeks to turn himself and he turns. He fights less. He wanders more, dirt streets of rodeo towns when the day is done, the lit roads of Bozeman in the night after his reading. It is the sound of gravel beneath his boots he seeks, a multitude of small stones forming a silver path under the moon and sky, leading nowhere. He graduates college, barely passing, a first in agribusiness, a second in accounting, Depression on, jobs scarce. He builds roads, digs ditches, dams, gets on at Fort Peck, his home a hillside cut-out, tarp angled over woodstove, single three-leg stool, small lamp of oil, he smells the earth, he sleeps on dirt. North still but jobless, he waits overnight in a line of one hundred men. The head man sees his size. He gets on as a workman with the railroad. He'll earn some money, buy himself some land. Perhaps buy back the land they lost. Plant a hedge of wild rose, he thinks, for his mother. He is six feet nine inches tall now and weighs over three hundred pounds. He works the Empire Builder, the interstate rail from east to west. He works with muscle and grit. He shovels coal. He keeps his own peace.

Alone in the late push across the borderlands they ride the highline of Montana and he stops for a moment and rests his hands on the heel of the shovel, rests his chin on his hands. He feels the locomotive spending its light toward the oncoming darkness, toward the tiny crossings with unknown names, the towns of eight or ten people. He feels the wide wind, sees the stars in their opaque immensity. He hears the long-nosed scream of the train, bent in the night, and he pauses, considering how fully the night falls, how easily the light gives way, then he returns to his work.

Late he lies himself down in his sleeping berth. He stinks of smoke and oil, the sweating film of his body envelops him and he falls toward sleep as one who has come from the earth, who has molded it with his hands, who has returned again. In his place in the dark, always he hears his mother. Mind your schooling, she says. It is after dinner. She lays him down. He is a child sleeping, and in the half world between night and morning, waking him she speaks her elegant words, presses her cheek to his small cheek, whispers, Awake, awake O Zion, clothe yourself with strength. Put on your garments of splendor. She smoothes his eyebrows with a forefinger. You can get up now, she says. She touches his face with her hand.

It is not yet dawn. He lies on his side, sees on the hard shelf before his eyes the ivory hair comb bright as bone. He takes the comb in the curve of his hand. He lies still. He puts the comb to his lips in the half-light. He breathes his deep and holy breath. He remembers the clean smell of her hair. Along the spine of the comb he moves his index finger, then he eyes his finger for a moment, coal and dirt deep set in the whorls. He draws his hand to his mouth and licks the tip of his finger. The sun has broken the far line of the world. His tongue tastes of light.

He works the train and travels to places he has not yet known, where day is buoyant and darkness gone, and when death comes seeking like the hand of an enemy he gives himself over, for it is death he desires, and death he welcomes, and the spirit of his good body is a vessel borne to the eternal.

2

He is born into this world, he is named. He is made of dirt and fight and the grace of his mother's sacred words. He is one. He is caught in the mass of many. The earth bends beneath him and he listens to the whistle of the train, the notes like a voice of reason in the early dark that wakens him and returns him, takes him weary back to the loaded pull of the cars, the sound of the push and the steel of the tracks.

He rises. He begins again.

The older men on the line call him Middie because they've heard talk of him breaking the back of a bull that wouldn't carry its weight. It was at a rodeo he entered when he was nineteen, up in Glendive. The bull was old and skinny, put in by a local farmer as a joke. The bull didn't show enough verve so the boy bucked the animal himself.

Bent its middle like a bow, the vet said. Sprung its spine.

The bull had to be put down. The boy had both hated and delighted in this, delighted in undoing the farmer's intention, hated that the animal was hard done by. The railroaders laugh their heads off and Middie has to listen to them nearly every stop. They sit behind their counters at each station chewing fat with Prifflach, the conductor, telling and retelling what they've heard. Middie doesn't like them. When they speak they look through him, just as Prifflach does. He sees he is nothing to them. He lets them think they own him. He has a job, he bides his time.

The railroad furthers the chasm between father and mother. Something lower down is revealed, something more sedentary and rooted than even the earth that had opened and closed, closing over him the darker image of his father alongside the subtle light of his mother, the stiff shock of his father's hair under snow, the gray, grainy look of his mother's teeth long after the last exhalation, after he'd found her in her bed.

Riding the highline he is mostly unseen by the passengers, hauling freight, working coal. But a change in duty comes, a change he doesn't welcome. He'll provide muscle for the bossman, the conductor, Ed Prifflach. Three times tossing drunks to local sheriffs at the next stop, twice tracking rich old lady no-shows still wandering after the all aboard. Then the real trouble begins. Just past Wolfpoint, when the first theft is discovered, Middie is put in charge of public calm. He keeps to the plan, following Prifflach's words though it is distasteful to him and he begins to feel in the eyes of others he is becoming the conductor's efficacy, an outline of Prifflach's power, a bigger, more mobile expression.

Things aren't what they seem, Middie thinks. Danger, for reasons a man doesn't comprehend. On his first trip east a workman at the round-house in St. Paul threw himself between the cars of an outgoing train. When Middie got word he went to see. The man was severed in two at the chest. Middie isn't afraid to die, and when he dies he wants it to be hard and without any hope of return, as physical as rock and water so he can feel the skin give, the bones in the cavernous weight of his body broken, and blood like a river moving from the center of him, pooling out and away and down into the earth, to the soil that receives him and sets him free.

In the first compartment Prifflach leans toward him, nonchalant in body in order to avoid alarm, yelling at him to surmount the noise. First seat, worst position, thinks Middie, while Prifflach sets the course with regard to the thief. Get some leads, he says. Prifflach's face is wolflike, a man with large buttocks, hairy arms and hands. Middie dislikes him, his sunken eyes, the haughty tenor of his voice. Happening nearly every stop now, Prifflach says. Bad for business. Under a long, narrow nose his mouth tightens. The line ain't gonna like it, guaranteed. Give me the tally.

Five people, says Middie.

Tally his take, says Prifflach.

Middie uses a small piece of paper, a gnawed pencil. Near four hundred dollars, he says, four hundred ten to be precise. His face feels colorless, his body breathes in and out.

Get going, Middie, Prifflach says.

Middie stares at the double doors with their elongated rectangular glass, two top squares open for the heat. Prifflach said he'd picked him because Middie had thighs like cottonwoods and thick arms.

Look alive, Middie.

He hears the words, notes Prifflach's face. Wet lines in a wax head, he thinks. Then he looks at the people.

A weight of soot covers everyone. Their eyes are swollen and bloodshot. They have stiff red necks. On their laps they hold children and bags, grip-ping them as if to ward off death. Middie peers at the faces, and farther back, through more doors at the end of the car, more elongated squares of glass into the second car where expressions breathe the same contempt, the shadow of a shadow, the same self-preservation, the same undignified desire. They are on the upswing through great carved mountains and though Middie has worked the round-trip St. Paul to Spokane five times, he still feels unlanded here, awkward under the long slow ascent of the train, the sheer drop of landscape, of trees and earth, and way down, the thin, flat line of the river.

Side windows remain mostly shut, frozen in place by the interlock of the moisture inside and the frigid temperature of early winter outside. The air in the compartments, especially those closest to the heat of the locomotive, is heavy, thick to the lungs, and lined with body odor.

Middie has succeeded, through a forceful combination of the billy club Prifflach issued him and a jackknife he carries, in slightly opening the casement adjoining his seat. Air slides through the sliver of space he's created and Middie can feel it, even if the chug of the train taints it all, he feels the clean blade of pine, the rich taste of high mountains, the snicker of winter, windy and subliminal. He feels Bearhat Mountain and Gunsight out there, the draw of Going to the Sun Road lining the opposite side of the valley, spare of people now, the park locked in the grip of September, closed to visitors but for the oil and punch of the train, and the Blackfeet nation in the expanse below the great rocks.

Looking out he feels the calling an eagle might feel in the drafts over the backbone of the continent, that something of light and stone and water, perhaps fire, has created him and breathed life through the opening of his lips, and there is a violence in that, he thinks, and a tenderness, and he sees as if with the eyes of a child the wings of the eagle thrown wide over the body of the beloved, the scream of the bird in the highborne wind.


Yet a dark pall covers Middies' eyes; he stares at everyone suspiciously. When Prifflach rises, Middie follows. They walk a few steps and sit down again in another couplet of chairs, aimed back down the corridor, to the next car, and the next. People are seen in a long line, from compartment to compartment, bumped by the small clicks and turns of the train, jilted forward, hitched to the side, bumped back. The people say nothing. They clutch their bags.

The scenario sickens him. Too many people. Too public. If he were alone, or in the dark of barrooms, he'd feel clear, free to do as he wished, but here the fray of his mind annoys him. He brushes the tips of his fingers over his left shirt pocket, the cloth there housing his mother's comb, he feels the form of it, the tines like a small alien hand, the spine simple and hard. He's already checked them all three times by order of Prifflach. Once each after the last three stops: Wolfpoint, Glasgow, Malta. The first time he apologized, comforting an older woman on her way to see her son in Spokane. Prifflach had sent a wire out at Glasgow, inquiring what to do. The second check more of the same, this time soothing the worry of a young gal off to the state agricultural school in Pullman. Prifflach called it coincidence—two different burglars, two different towns, a little over three hundred dollars missing. But after the third stop, at Malta, when an elderly man was found dead, his head askew, a small well of blood in his right ear, the rumors poisoned every compartment.

He had money, said the help in the dining car. Paid for his meals in crisp new bills. But when Middie checked the body, Prifflach looking over his shoulder, there was nothing, no money, not even any silver. Middie felt the minds of the people beginning to hum and move and he sensed the interior of Prifflach, angry as if cornered, pushing him to take action. Middie hated it, but the line chose him, and he was big.

On the first check, the "just checking" check, no one resisted; everyone simply wanted the thief caught. The second check, the "only a coincidence, folks" check, people remained polite, grimacing some while Middie displaced their bags and Prifflach went through them. Middie had to pat the people down, check their coats, their clothing, have them empty each of their pockets. It took far longer than he wished, but mostly the people smiled and tried to be helpful. On the third check the death had changed things. The women whispered and shrank back from him. The body itself, alone in a sleeping car until the next stop, was like an evidence, an imprint of the predator among them. Middie felt the tension of it, the people's thoughts in fearful accord, like a dark vein of cloud swept into the bank of mountains, collecting, preparing.

Prifflach had declared all must hand over their weapons, and declared Middie the one to gather them. The men looked boldly at Middie as Prifflach rifled their bags. Some were openly angry. Many, he thought, suspected him, or Prifflach. Only a few gave up their arms, and unwillingly, a cluster of pistols, four Colts, two Derringers, along with one rifle. Other men lied directly, though Middie felt their weapons, in a bootleg or under the arm, the stock of a gun, the handle of a knife. He decided not to push and Prifflach silently colluded, the potential threat subduing the conductor's zeal. What Middie retrieved he stored in the engineer's cab. Returning, walking the aisles, he felt weary. People don't like being pushed, he thought.

The next stop, Havre, town of locked-in winters, town of bars. At last, the removal of the dead man, to be shipped back to Chicago. Not dusk or dawn but day, not night as Middie would hope, nor the color of night. The body is well blanketed, taken off from the back of the train. Middie carries it across the platform and it feels light to him, almost birdlike in his arms. He turns his back to shield the view. Prifflach holds the door for him and as Middie enters the station he catches over Prifflach's shoulder the faces of passengers in the fourth car, most of them pale and dumb-looking, not meeting his eye. But one, the Indian man he'd noticed on his passenger checks, a crossbreed, looks right at him. The eyes are black from where Middie stands. He imagines round irises among the slanted whites; it reminds him of how people had stared at this man during the checks, a few uttering quiet threats while the man stared back at them as if taunting them to put meaning to their words. Despite the fact that the Indian was well dressed, Middie had had to quiet the car twice as they searched him.

Inside the station Middie hears Prifflach tell the attendant the death is nothing. Old man died in his sleep, Prifflach says. Line informed the family; they'll meet the body in St. Paul. The attendant is a potbellied bald man, chewing snuice. Prifflach orders Middie back to the train to watch the passengers. No sheriff, thinks Middie. Line saving its own skin. Close-mouthed, he looks at Prifflach, but the conductor waves him on and Middie does as he is told.

He sits on the train, puts his head in his hands, runs his hands through his hair. He rises, he disembarks, rounds the platform and crosses the dirt street. He approaches the front door of the Stockman Bar. Door painted black, oiled hinges, inside a dim small room and three tables, dark marble counter with five stools, the place is clean, a lone bartender wiping things down. Help you? he says. No, Middie answers, the murmur of his voice barely audible. He needs a chair to sit in, a space to calm his mind. The bartender spits in a tin cup on the counter. You don't drink, you don't stay, he says. Middie feels things shutting down, his insides are heavy and tight, the center of him like an eclipse that obscures the light, three quick steps to the barman and one fist that rides the force of hip and shoulder, the man laid cold on the hardwood floor. Not dead, but still, and flat-backed, and Middie, seated in the chair he desires, watches the blood curl from a three-inch line over the man's eye, elliptic down his face to his neck, to the floor. Orbital bone still sound, eyes rolled back in the head, the man lies motion-less and Middie considers him. Should've been Prifflach, he says aloud. But saying it Middie feels broken. He can't go back. His eyes are grave, dark as his father's. Darkness covers the earth and deep darkness its people. It is a darkness he feels he cannot undo. But he must, he thinks, he will. Prifflach comes cursing, and Middie walks in the conductor's shadow, back to the train, the people.

Three quick halts at Shelby, Cutbank, and Browning. East Glacier next, the station at the park's east entrance, the one with the Blackfeet Agency greeting in which three Indians wait on the small gray platform in full regalia. An elder in full eagle-feather headdress gives out cigars. Two women in white deerskin dresses sell beadwork. Only a handful of white passengers gawk this time, not all as is customary. Most remain sub-dued, brooding, sitting in their seats. Then on the track past East Glacier, climbing the high boundary toward the west side of the park and the depot at Belton, two more reports of impropriety, two more thefts, lesser, but significant, one of sixty dollars, the other forty. Not counting the unknown amount stolen from the dead man, the total, as Middie said, had reached four hundred and ten.

Middie loathes the thought of checking bags again. He thinks the people, all of them, close and far, dislike him. Some of the faces are full of disdain.

So? says Prifflach.

Yes? says Middie.

So start another check, says Prifflach. He speaks like a crow, thinks Middie. He watches Prifflach pull a small piece of paper from his vest pocket, the wire retrieved from the Havre station in answer to his plea at Glasgow. Prifflach turns the paper to Middie, these words: keep quiet—no police—security man finds thief—or loses job.

No good, says Middie, awkward, aloud, using a tone he'd seen his mother use to calm his father. Look at them, Middie says, motioning with his eyes to the people around him.

Prifflach turns on him, sharp-faced, and what he says makes Middie desire to kill him. It's your own good, boy. Line's takin' you out if you don't get it done. Move.

Middie sees it coming, and he wishes against it, but he knows no other alternative. All that college, he thinks, up against the wall with book learning, and nothing now for real life. Heavy shouldered, he rises from his seat. He begins the procedure again.

Pardon me, may I see your bag? and, Pardon, sir, I have to look through your personal effects. The words are graceful in Middie's mind, his mind electric, his body like ether around his words.


But people are openly hostile. A woman in the first car, one in the second, and one in the third make a scene and won't unhand their bags. He pulls the bags from the first two, and lets Prifflach search the contents while he quickly pats the people down, pushing his fingers in their coat pockets. When he approaches the third woman she claws a bright hole in his cheek. His mind thinks terrible things. Ugly, he tells himself. Ugly. Has to be done though, he thinks. Other passengers help him do it too, they hold the woman back while he searches her and while Prifflach gives the bag a thorough inspection. Idiots, Middie thinks, all of them, and me with them. They see it too, the people. They all admit inwardly the logic is imprecise, but better than doing nothing. Check everyone or it's no use. Futile, Middie thinks, a man can hide money anywhere. When he returns the third woman's bag she curses him. Then she looks him in the face, says God curse you, and turns her back.

Middie can't remember ever having heard a woman speak like that. He walks from the third car toward the fourth, opens the double doors at the end of the compartment, closes the doors behind. He stands on the deck, he hears the raw howl of the train, the wind. Something will happen now, he thinks. To his left a wall of wet granite undulates, hard and dark, blurred by the train speed. He looks up and sees the great face of it arching, reaching up and out, thousands of feet of rock, jagged and pinnacled at the top, swept up and out over the roof of the train. Beyond this, the gray sky is low and thick. The look of it gives him vertigo and he turns his head down, gripping the handrail, seeing his worn boots on the grated steel. His mother, he thinks, he can't remember her face.

To his right he can feel the valley out there, spread wide in a pattern of darks and lighter darks, filled from above by the distant pull of fog and rain. Sleet falls in wide diagonal sheets, descending into massive rock blacks and rock grays far on the other side of the valley. Along the bases of the mountains forests are spread like cloaks, and everything bleeds to a river that glistens coal like the curve of a gunbarrel, choked by the runoff of the storm. The river is the middle fork of the Flathead, past the summit of Marias Pass and past the great trestle of Two Medicine Bridge. They've crested the great divide and the train's muscle pumps faster now, louder on the down westward grade. The river runs due west from here, seeming to bury itself into the wide forested skirt of a solitary mass of land. The flat-topped tower of the mass is obscured, mostly covered over by wet fog and cloud, but visible in its singularity and the ominous feel of something hidden in darkness, something entirely individual, devoid of any other, accountable to neither sky nor storm. At the mountain's height a black ridge is barely detectable in among the gray fog. The hulk of the land feels gargantuan. Is it Grinnell Point or Reynolds Mountain, Cleveland or Apikuni? He can't make it out. Here in Middie's reverie, muffled shouts are heard, faint like the far-off cry of a cat. He looks up to the doors of the fourth car, the final passenger car. Slender windows frame what he sees and suddenly the words, though disembodied, come clean. I've got him! yells a fatty-faced man, sealed up there in the box of the car. I've got the mother-hatin' rat!

Middie leaps forward, opening the fourth car, shouting, Stop! Wait! About midway up the car the fatty-faced man, and now four others, have thrown a man to the floor in the aisle. The man wears a brown tweed suit, he makes a vigorous struggle with his assailants.

It's him! cries the fat one. We caught him red-handed.

To avoid the wild flail, passengers press back against the walls. Women push their children in behind them, children with wide eyes, lit with fear.

Let go, says Middie, staring at the fat man, and the men heed his word quickly and without complaint. An understanding strikes Middie, a remembrance of the fear men harbor, bigger than a child's, and Middie recalls the pure sway he holds because he is big, over people, over men.

The captive stands in the aisle now, brushing wrinkles from his suit, his hair flung forward, black and thick over his face. The Indian, thinks Middie, as he draws nearer.

When the man pushes his hair back, the bones of his face appear, cheekbones driven up as if by hammers, chin chiseled like stone, and dark aggressive eyes, the skin a thin casing for all the intrepid want in him. Thin as a sheet of newsprint, thinks Middie, ready to tear open, ready for it all to rush out. The man tucks in his shirt and realigns his belt. He straightens his vest, then the lapels of his jacket, visibly pulling the tension back in and down, breathing. He is silent. He views his captors with contempt, each one.

Middie remembers seeing him board the train in Wolfpoint. Assiniboine-Sioux he'd thought. But after pulling his bag and questioning him four times he'd found him to be a Blackfeet-White cross, Blood in fact, a Blackfeet sub-tribe (and Irish on the other side, he'd said, one clan or another). He was on his way to his family's home south of West Glacier after a "work-related" trip to Wolfpoint. Middie had checked him once more than all the rest. The man said he taught at the college in Missoula. In education, he said. They locked eyes when Middie carried the dead man at Havre, but Middie had dismissed it, and other than the agitation of the crowd during the checks, an agitation Middie felt always accompanied whites and Indians, he had found nothing unusual. The man carried no weapon.

What is it? Middie asks the man with the fat head.

A short man, a man with slick hair, one of the others who had held the accused, speaks up vehemently. This man—he points in the Indian's face—this man has been lying! He's the one. He took all the money.

Slow, says Middie. Say what you know.

I have not lied, says the prisoner.

Shut up! the slick man yells.

Middie puts a forearm to the slick man's chest. Settle yourself, he says. Sit down.

The slick man obeys, whispering something, glaring. He's lying, he says. Hiding something.

How do you know?

Check his side, see for yourself. He's had his hand there in his jacket from the start.

The fat man butts in, edging with rage, He won't show us what he's got in there.

Is it true, sir? asks Middie, heightening his politeness. Is there something hidden in your vestcoat?

Yes, he states, looking into Middie's face, but that makes me neither a liar nor guilty of the offense in question.

We will check it, sir, Middie replies, but he feels aggravated. He doesn't like the uppity tone the Indian has used. What have you concealed? Middie asks.

My money belt, says the man.


Middie hardens his look. His hands sweat. He wipes them on his pantlegs as he stares at the man. Probably had it on his waistline, Middie thinks, concealed under the clothing, probably thin as birch bark. He remembers Prifflach muttering under his breath at the Indian, checking the man's bag, a small cylindrical briefcase made of beaten brown leather, sealed at the top by a thin zipper that ran between two worn handles, the word MONTANA inscribed on the side. Mostly papers in the bag.

You have searched my briefcase and my wallet, says the man, and me once more than the others. I saw no need for you to search my money belt. And if I had shown you my belt, would that not become a target for the robber if he were present in this compartment during the search?

Don't listen to him, the slick man says in a wet voice, he's slippery.

The crowd murmurs uneasily. Middie notes that outside, the fog has pressed in. Nothing of the valley can be seen, and nothing of the sky. The mountains will be laid low, Middie thinks. He hears the words soft and articulate in his mother's voice. Outside is the featureless gray of a massive fog bank, and behind it a feeling of the bulk of the land.

Check his belt, the fat face says.

Then the crowd begins. See what he's got, says a red-haired woman, the fat man's wife by the look of it, the small eyes, the clutching, heavy draw of the cheeks about the jowls. She says the words quietly but they are enough to hasten a flood. Do it now, hears Middie. Make him hand it over, Take it from him, Pull up his shirt, Take it—all from the onlookers, all at once, and from somewhere low and small back behind Middie, the quiet words, Cut his throat.

The conductor arrives and Middie exhales and feels his body go slack; he stares outside. The gray-black of the storm leaks moisture on the windows. The moisture gathers and pulls lines sideways along the windows, minuscule lines in narrow groupings of hundreds and wide bars of thousands, rivulets and the brothers of rivulets, and within them the broad hordes of their children, their offspring, all pulled back along the glass to the end of the train, to the end of seeing.

You will have him hand over that money belt directly, says Prifflach, his nose leading, his face pinched, set like clay. Pressure builds in the bodycage of Middie, a pressure that pushes out against his skin like a large child caught inside, big feet placed on the ribs, forcing out as if to crack the ribs wide and emerge leaping from the open ribwork. Middie reaches out, grabbing the accused man's wrist, gripping the flesh with frozen fingers, red-white fingers latching on.

To Middie's relief the man responds. With one arm in Middie's grip, the man uses his free hand to untuck the front of his shirt. He slides the money belt to a point above his waist and undoes the small metal clasps that hold the belt in place. His fingers are so meticulous, thinks Middie, so dexterous and sure. His eyes as clear as the sky before they reached Glacier, cold and steely black. Middie looks again to the window. He thinks his own reflection is not unlike the gray outside, and behind it the unpeopled weight of land, the emptiness. He notes he has left his billy club in the last compartment, on the floor near a seat where he'd checked a man's ankles, his socks. Middie's fists feel big, hard as the stones of a landslide. He doesn't need it, he tells himself.

Give up the belt, Prifflach says, though already the man is pulling the belt free.

He holds it out to the conductor. Nothing out of the ordinary, he says. I'm simply a man carrying my own money. His hair is still bent, his shirt poorly tucked. He does not look away from his accusers.

At once, the fat man and his wife shout something unintelligible.

We'll see, says the conductor, interpreting their words. We'll see if it's his money. At the corners of Prifflach's mouth the skin twitches. Prifflach takes the money belt and hands it to the slick man. Count it up, he says, watching the Indian's face.

The slick man thumbs the money once, finding an unfortunate combination of bigger and smaller bills. How much is there? asks the conductor. The slick man counts again, slowly. Five hundred ten dollars, he says. Exactly one hundred more than the amount stolen. Middie knows a desire has gripped them, and that they all, silently, hastily, have calculated the old dead man's loss at a clean one hundred. Middie has done the same.

I could have told you that, says the accused.

Prifflach tells the man to shut up, then says, A hundred dollars more than the total. He folds the money belt in half, and half again; I'll take that, he says, placing it in the chest pocket of his coat.

It comes clear to Middie now, the look of the onlookers, the way of their eyes and their bodies, how they've all torn loose inside, all come unspun. He remembers what he'd read in a pamphlet at the West Glacier station a month ago. Something of a hidden passage west, close to the headwaters of the Marias, a high mountain pass that according to Indian belief was steeped in the spirit world, inhabited by a dark presence. Decades back, when the line first wanted to chart its track through here, no Indian would take a white man through. Death inhabited the place.

Middie sees the demeanor of the Blackfeet man change. The man's face loses expression, his body pulls inward and a gathering is felt in the space between them, Middie senses it, the surging, up through the flesh of the Indian's forearm. Middie tightens his grip.

The crowd moves.

Suspected him back in Glasgow, a stout man pipes up. I should have known, says another, and from the slick man, He ain't gettin' outta here. Low again, deep back in the crowd, a voice says Slit his throat.

The movement begins in words and rustling, then leaps upward like a mighty wave that breaks upon the people and the man all at once. The Blackfeet man jerks free and jumps the chair back next to him, seeking to flank the men and escape from the rear of the compartment. The men scramble after him, Prifflach leading, the others following, all of them livid with hate.

Middie vaults a set of chairs and lands on the Blackfeet man, slamming him bodily against the sidewall of the car. The man rights himself and spits in Middie's face and Middie, fueled now, lifts him, encircling the Indian's neck in the crook of his left arm, positioning him. He props him up, left hand on the man's shoulder, holding him an arm's length away. Then he levels a blow with the right that bounces the Blackfeet man's head off the near window, flings his hair like a horsetail, and leaves a grotesque indentation where the cheekbone has caved in. Four other men, along with Middie, jerk the prisoner from the wall, shake him hand over fist to the aisleway. They surround him and proceed to drag him toward the back of the car. The shoving lurches the Indian forward and makes his neck look thin, snaps his head back, throws his eyes to the ceiling.

What are you doing? he cries out, I'm innocent, and straining from the hands that grasp at his upper body, turning his face to the window, to the gray valley beyond, he says, I have a wife. I have a child.

With shocking swiftness the Indian throws his forearms out and lunges forward with his head in order to strike someone. But now his flailings are as nothing to the weight of the accusers: there are many men now, their arms entangled in his limbs, controlling him easily. They punch him in the back and in the back of the head. Keep your head down! they say; You'll lose your teeth in a second. The group is packed in, forming a tight untidy ball in the aisleway and among the spaces between the seats. A thick odor is in the air.

The prisoner's head is near the floor. Reaching for the Indian's waist, Middie sees a look of resignation, a look of light among the features of his face. The man stares at Middie and whispers something Middie cannot hear or understand.

Amid the tumult a smaller voice says, Wait! It comes from behind Middie, up near the front of the car. Turning, looking up and back through the moving heads, back behind the bending, pressing torsos, Middie sees the source of the voice, a small man, adolescent in appearance, thin-boned in a simple two-piece suit. The man has fine blonde hair and oval wire-rimmed glasses.

Wait! the man says, I know him.

A large man at the back of the mob turns to the boyish man and says, You shut up.

The small man's face goes red, he shrinks back to his seat. Middie sees this and turns back to the mob. The people are grabbing the Blackfeet man's clothing in their hands and shaking his body like a child's doll. Men are emerging from their seats, running the aisles like ants, joining the mob. The man's limbs appear loose in the torque of the crowd. The arms move as if boneless, the elbows seem disconnected from the shoulders.

From his vantage Middie turns and sees the little man with his head down now as the people swirl toward the rear of the car, down to the doors they have already pulled back and the opening tilted like a black mouth from which the wind screams. Middie hears the accused grunting, cursing. He sees the little man rise and walk directly to the rear guard of the mob. Unable to get through, the little man sidesteps the knot of people, climbing over three or four seats, repositioning women and children. He travels awkwardly but consistently, like a leggy insect, toward the back of the compartment, toward the opening and the landing beyond. He goes unrecognized by all but Middie and when he reaches the far wall of the car he stops, and stares. The prisoner is held about the neck by the thick hands of Prifflach, clinched about the waist by Middie, and on both sides by bold, angry men.

The small man positions himself, mounting the arms of the last two aislechairs so that he stands directly before the mob. He straddles the aisle, the land a blur in the open doorway behind him, around him the live wind a strange unholy combustion. He draws his fists to his sides, billows his chest as he gathers air, and screams, Stop! A wild scream, high and sharp like the bark of a dog.

The little man's effort creates a brief moment of quiet in which the people stand gaping at him. Seizing this, he strings his words rapidly. I know him. I spoke with him when he got on in Wolfpoint. He has a three-year-old daughter. He has a wife. He has a good mother, a father. He will be dropped off at the stop on the far side of Glacier where they are waiting for him. He will return with them by car to the Mission Range.

Shut up, says the fat man.

I won't, says the small man. He told me precisely.

He lied, says the slick man.

Let me speak, the small man pleads. He touches his hand to his face, a gesture both elegant and tremulous.

We won't, the mob responds, and in their movement and in the pronounced gather of their voices the prisoner is lifted by the neck and shoved forward toward the door.

Out of the way! someone yells, and Middie watches as the small man takes a blow to the side of the head, a shot of tremendous force that lifts him light as goosedown, unburdened in flight to where his body hits the wall near the floor of the car and he lies crumpled, his face lolling to one side. Thickly now the small man says, He told me precisely. His words are overrun but he continues, slow, distinct. He told me precisely, in Wolfpoint. Before all of this, he had five hundred ten dollars of earnings. He meant to do what he and his wife dreamed. Middie's fists are bound up in the clothing of the Blackfeet man, his forearms are bone to bone with the man's ribs. The little man is speaking, He meant to buy land, off the reservation. The voice seems small, down between the chairs, He meant to build a home.

The opening through which they pass is wide, the small man's body a bit of detritus they have cast aside, the landing now beneath their feet solid and whole, like a long-awaited rest. Middie hears the velocity of wind and steel as he flows with the crowd to the brink. He feels the rush, like the expectancy of power in a bull's back when the gate springs wide, like the sound a man's jaw makes when it breaks loose.

Also he feels sorrow; he wants to cry or cry out. He wants to reach for the ivory hair comb but a weight of bodies presses him from behind and his hands are needed to control the captive. He feels the indent of the guardrail firmly on his thigh. He hears the small man's voice, back behind him. He told me at Wolfpoint—precisely five hundred ten dollars. Five hundred ten.

The landing is narrow, the people many, and they are knotted and pushed forward by a score more, angry men running from other cars, clogging the aisle to get to the man. Those at the front grab the railing, the steel overhead bars, they grab each other, the Indian, the enemy. Noise surrounds them, the train's cry, the wide burn of descent, the people's yells are high and sharp above everything, shrill as if from the mouths of predatory birds. The Indian's suitcoat and vest are gone. His slim torso looks clean in his worried shirt, a V-shaped torso, trim and strong. In the press of it Middie is hot. Oxlike, he feels the burden of everyone, borne at once in him, and he bends and grabs the man's leg. Other men do the same, there are plenty of hands now. He wants to hold the man fast but instead the crowd shoves the man aloft, tipping him upside down, clutching his ankles, removing his shoes. They tear off his shirt, then his ribbed under-shirt. They throw the shoes down among the tracks. The clothing they throw out into the wind where it whisks away and falls deep into the fog of the valley, rolling and descending like white leaves.

From here the man is lowered between the cars. He becomes silent. Below the captive, Middie sees the silvery gleam of the tracks, a line in the black blur of the ties, the line bending almost imperceptibly at times, silver but glinting dull like teeth. With his elbows he tries to hold the people back. He feels the oncoming force of the crowd behind him, the jealousy, the desire. A woman's voice is heard, a voice he knows but does not recognize. He bows his back, groaning, trying to draw the man forth. The words are like a song, simple and beautiful in his mind: Put on your garments of splendor. He smells the oil of the train, the heat, the wet rock of the mountain.

He sets his jaw and strains, he would pull the people and the man and the whole world to the mercy of his will; he gains no ground.

In the gusts of wind, the mob squints their eyes. Leaning forward, their hair is blown back, it swirls some, it blows back again. The speed of the train and the noise of the tracks, the scent of high sage and jack pine, the fogged void of gray as wide and deep as an ocean, but foremost the wind, which rushes up against the mob creating an almost still-life movement into which they carry their considered enemy. Then the wind dies. The river of men, flowing from the compartment, bottlenecks in the doorway. Bodies from the choked opening to the guardrail twist and writhe and a vast shouting commences. Middie says No! This must stop! He grips the Blackfeet man's belt with both fists and pulls him upward. His big body is a counter-movement against the rise of all around him but angry yells issue from wide red mouths and the mob grows to an impossible mass that pushes and swells and breaks free in a sudden gush. Middie finds himself with the Indian airborne, cast into the gulf without foot or handhold, he has lost everything, and falling he sees a shaft of blue high in the grey above him and he is surprised at how light he feels, and how time has slowed to nothing. He reaches back seeking a purchase he will not find, and in the singular sweep of his arm he takes people unaware—Prifflach, the fat man, his wife, the slick man—and they fly from the edge, effortless in the push of the mob, unstrung bodies and tight faces, over the lip of the guardrail and down between the cars, down to the tracks, the wheels, the black pump of the smoking engine, the yell of the machine.

# THE NEUTERED BULLDOG

*by* RACHEL SHERMAN

WHEN MY TEACHER first began her affair, she told me about it on the rug where it had happened. We were in the second-floor study of her house—above her husband's office—where she had first kissed Brian Wojowsky.

The floor was hard with only a thin rug on top of it. She had a couch but they hadn't used it, and while she told me, neither did we. I sat on the wood part, facing her bookshelves, while she leaned against the wall and smoked one of my cigarettes. It was the afternoon, during lunch hour, and soon we would both have to be back at school.

"Brian is in my gym class and in my math class next period," I told her. I took the cigarette from her thin freckled fingers and blew smoke into the dusty light.

"Really?" she said. She took the cigarette back and stubbed it out in the ceramic ashtray she hid from her husband, Ed. "I didn't know that." I got up and pulled my jeans down on my waist. If I was late for math I could get a detention, and my teacher had already written me a bunch of notes. She couldn't write too many more. Boys were already saying things.

"What does Brian wear in gym class?" she asked, getting up and looking in the mirror that was next to her computer. She ran her fingers around the rim of her lips.

I had never thought about Brian in gym class before. He was not someone I noticed. He was small, for one, and not attractive in the way I liked boys I couldn't have. If I couldn't have any of them, I saved my fantasies for the best. Brian was thin and quiet and didn't play sports.

"I don't know," I laughed, walking down the stairs to the living room where she had lined the windows with rocks and shells and beach glass she had found. "Shorts and a T-shirt, probably."

My teacher followed me and we walked out the door together.

"See you tomorrow—third period," she said, getting into her car. "I'll be busy tonight," she said, and winked.


On the first day of school, in the beginning of fall, I called my teacher "Mrs. Holly." She wasn't my teacher then the way that she is now. On the first day of school she wore glasses and her hair pulled back. She wore a pleated skirt that was too long to show her perfect calves that tapered into her knee in exactly the right place.

The desks were already in a circle when everyone got to class so we all sat around and tried not to look at one another. Mrs. Holly was a new teacher, and no one told her that we weren't used to sitting that way. "I'd like to go around the room and have everyone tell a little bit about themselves," she had said. She pointed at me. "Starting with you."

"Moldy," one of the boys whispered loud enough so everyone could hear. I rolled my eyes and ignored him.

I had been nicknamed "Moldy" because my last name is Gold and it rhymed. Sometimes they called me "Moldy Matzoh" because I am Jewish.

I had been drawing in my notebook, making circles inside of circles. I did not want to go first.

"Um…" I said, "My name is Sarah… I'm sixteen years old… I don't play any sports."

"Okay," Mrs. Holly said, smiling, "Tell us a dream."

"A nighttime dream?" I asked. My dreams were filled with colors and boys and people without any genitals rubbing up against each other.

"No, a daytime dream," Alec Ryerson said and there were laughs around the circle.

"I pass," I said, that first day.

I handed in my first poem to Mrs. Holly after our second class. The poem, "P is for Prozac," was about a girl who commits suicide. It did not rhyme.

When I read it in class, Mrs. Holly smiled and asked me to stay afterward.

She told me that I had talent, like her.

After class we both sat at the desks, next to each other.

"You remind me of me," she said.

I blushed because she was beautiful. She was tall with reddish hair and I was tall but did not look like her. I looked at the width of her freckled wrist and compared it to my own.

"I would love for you to come over sometime," she said. "It's important for poets to stick together."

I nodded at my teacher and looked away from her eyes.

"I'm a person too, you know," she said, tilting her head so that I had to look at her. She laughed and invited me to her house. She told me that when we were alone, she didn't like to be called "Mrs. Holly."

Brian is not the best poet in the class. I am. That is why my teacher likes me. That is why, after I handed in my first poem, she invited me over to her house.

On the first visit I met her husband, Ed, who is handsome and nice, and who shook my hand. He looked the way I imagined a husband should look, with dark hair parted to the side.

"She's my best student," my teacher told him.

They stood there in their hallway together, he taller than she, and I imagined them making love.

When Ed went to work, she told me he didn't like to fuck.

"Really?" I asked. My teacher was beautiful and I thought that everyone wanted beautiful women. If I were beautiful I was sure things would be different.

"So why don't you get a divorce?" I asked her. It was the first time I had been to her house.

"I don't know. I don't know why we even got married. It just seemed like a good idea at the time."

I watched her purse her lips. We were in her study smoking cigarettes.

"Ed will be done soon," she said, taking my cigarette from me and taking a drag, then putting it out in the ashtray.

I looked at the floor where, beneath us, Ed was working.

"He seems nice," I said.

She shook her head. "He doesn't like it dirty. We're not compatible."

My teacher told me about an ice sculptor she had met, a man who knew how to make love. She said they went into his freezer to cool themselves down, and she watched as he carved things: birds and bowls for restaurants and a naked woman made of ice, who, when she melted, dripped water from her crotch, for his art.

She wrote a poem about the ice sculptor. He wasn't as tall as she was, but he had thick arms that made her feel small.

We left her study and I followed her up the stairs to the bedroom. We lay on her big bed and looked at ourselves across the room in the mirror on the vanity.

"How old do you think I look?" she asked.

I did not know.

"Thirty," I said, "Twenty-eight?" I was not good at telling people's ages.

"Really?" she said, pursing her lips. Her lips were shriveled in a strange way that reminded me of brains.

"I think so, yeah," I said.

She squinted and reached over to feel my face. I worried her hands felt each acne bump on my skin, but she smiled. She pushed my hair behind my ear.

"Wow," she said, "And you don't even own your face yet."


After class, the next week, my teacher pinched me under the table and wrote on her notebook, "I need to show you something. Stay after class."

When class was over we sat on the desktops and closed the door. My teacher opened her folder and took out a sheet of paper that was typed. "Read this," she said.

I read the poem. It was short, about a neutered bulldog who was sad and thought no one would ever love him.

I looked up at my teacher, who was looking at me, watching me read and smiling.

"I think I'm missing something," I said.

"Really?" she asked. "I thought it was so obvious. Brian must feel inadequate. He must feel inadequate as a man."

"Brian Wojowsky wrote this?" I asked, looking again at the neat type-writing, definitely from a real typewriter.

"Yeah," she said, taking the page back. "He gave it to me this morning during homeroom. Who would have thought? I mean, he never says anything, right? So talented… And how great that he can express himself this way. It's kind of sexy, even though he's admitting he might not be able to satisfy a woman."

She wasn't looking at me when she said this. She had her skirt bunched up at her knees and her feet on the chair. Someone could look in on us through the small rectangular window on the door. "Yeah," I said, pretending I understood. It did not surprise me that I was missing something, since the way she told me things, sometimes, made me think everyone knew things I didn't. It was as if all the secrets people whispered to one another, all the books I hadn't read, were the things that I most needed to know.

"I wonder if he knows how good he is…" my teacher said, placing the page back in her folder, being careful not to crease it. "I should tell him," she said, nodding to herself.

My teacher is a poet, and that means she gets a faraway look sometimes. I wonder if I will get that way when, someday, people will watch me stare. She is a poet, so sometimes everyday words, words unphrased and boring, are beneath her to hear. She was thinking about Brian's words, I could tell. Words on paper were stronger than anything. My simple word, the squeak of my leaving, was not enough for her to come back to me that day, and I wondered if I was really a poet too. It worried me that I might just be a girl with too much time, when I heard myself say "Goodbye."

My teacher calls me in the middle of the night. She whispers into the phone.

"I did it!" she says, "I saw it!"

"Saw what?" I say.

"The neutered bulldog!" she says and laughs.

I am still half-asleep, warm in my bed.

"Can we talk tomorrow?" I ask, even though I love her.

"OK," she whispers and puts down the phone.

*　*　*

When I am at home, in my own house, I go upstairs and lock the door to the bathroom where I lie on the thin bath carpet on the tile floor and try to think only about the things I can see. I look at the dust beneath the sink cabinet and the underside of the toilet bowl and up at the red heat lamps I turn on. I look out the top of the window at the black branches against the gray sky and inevitably feel sad and lonely.

Twice I have showered in the bathroom with all my clothes on, which felt strange and warm, but in a good way, until I turned the water off. Then I felt cold and disgusting, and my jeans stuck to me in a thick and heavy way. Usually I get in the shower without my clothes and sometimes I shave different parts of myself I hadn't before, like the backs of my hands and my toes.

On the floor with the heat lamps on, I can only think about what I see until I think of something else. No matter what is in front of me, it seems, it never keeps all of my attention.

I imagine Brian and my teacher, using up all the space on her bed. I imagine Brian so small next to my teacher.

Brian is just a boy in my class, and I don't know how to make her see that everything that is in front of him is probably just there, and that she, so big on her own bed, makes him focus on her. It occurs to me then, sadly, that maybe this is what she wants.


It is Saturday so I drive to my teacher's for brunch. She mixes up a salad dressing from balsamic vinegar and mustard and pours it over lettuce. She makes us chamomile tea.

My teacher is still wearing her nightgown. Her husband has been away for the week on a business trip. We sit alone at her sunny table and pick at our salads.

"So, I did it," she says.

"With Brian?" I say.

"Yes. And he has nothing to worry about," she says, shaking her head, "It won't be a problem for him. I think he'll be fine."

My teacher doesn't know that I am still a virgin. When I tried to do it, once, with a boy with huge feet I met last summer, it hurt too much and he couldn't get it in. It did not feel good and I can't imagine it ever feeling any way but sore. I am told that once you start you will not want to stop, and I pretend to my teacher that I have started, with boys in other school districts that she doesn't know.

"Did you like it?" I ask.

"I think we're going to have to work on it," she says, swiping her highlighted hair from her face and letting the strap of her nightgown fall so that I can see the start of her nipple.


In math class, I watch Brian walk in. He does not look at me. He sits down across from me, his shaggy hair in his face, and begins to draw in his notebook. He has acne on his neck that it looks like he picked, and his shoelaces are untied. He does not look full, the way my teacher looked in the morning. His cheeks look like he is sucking on a straw.

I draw in my notebook. I try to picture how lesbians do it. I draw two vaginas squeezing each other with their lobes. This must be the way.

I ask to go to the bathroom and sit in the stall and smoke a cigarette. Brian is a loser, I think, and no one in our class wants to date him. Everyone loves my teacher. The boys that see me leave with her ask if I ever lick her pussy.

I put my head between my legs to get a head rush and try to picture Brian with his neutered dick. I picture my teacher on top, her freckled body astride small Brian. I picture them lying in the sheets afterward, looking at their reflections in the same mirror that my teacher and I did and laughing.


I go to my teacher's after school. She is sitting in the backyard on one of her lawn chairs, her eyes closed and her face up to the sun.

"Come tan with me," she says, but I hate the sun. I pull a chair into the shade of her house.

Her garden is lined with bricks she put there herself. I've seen her some days, shovel in hand, trying to grow things. She wears a hat, like a woman with a garden in the movies.

"Where did you learn to garden?" I ask her.

Her past seems like something unreal, something that would never happen to someone like me. The way she talks about things seems so easy, like she slipped out of a bed somewhere faraway, already a woman with a husband and lovers, already with a past.

"My dad," she says, "He used to make us help him plant things."

She keeps her eyes closed and I stare at her. It is like she is asleep and I am spying, or that she is dead and I am examining her, so close, in a way that nobody would let anyone else look at them.

My teacher is wearing tight white jeans and a striped T-shirt. Her skin looks papery around her eyes and I can see the creamy cover-up she has on her face. There are white hairs on her cheeks, fine hairs that look soft. For a moment I wonder what would happen if I sat on her lap with my arm around her neck.

My father does not plant things. He makes me mow the lawn every weekend on a small tractor. He makes me wear headphones so that I don't lose my hearing from the loud noise the mower makes. He has a way I am supposed to mow: around and around in one big oval, then in smaller circles when I get to the two big trees in the middle of the yard.

"I like to garden," she says, "It distracts me, you know?"

I don't know, but I nod. It is hard for me to get distracted that way. When I mow, all I can think of is the next circle, and then the next, and how when I am done I will be able to go inside and lie on the bathroom floor.

My teacher's eyes are still closed, and she does not see me nod. She opens one eye and smiles.

"Brian is coming over tonight," she says.

"Again?" I ask.

"Again," she says.


At home, in the bathroom, I lie on the floor and turn on the heat lamps and close my eyes. I think about my grandparents' old bathroom with its bidet that my mother once washed my underwear in when I peed in my pants.

"What's it really for?" I had asked.

I had never tried the bidet then, and now that I am old enough my grandparents have moved to a less fancy apartment.

I love the idea of being that clean after I go to the bathroom, hardly having to wipe. I love the idea of all that mess disappearing.

Someone knocks and my father's voice says, "What's going on?"

He must see the sliver of red glow beneath the door and worry.

"Nothing," I say.


In math class, on Monday, Brian's shoelaces are untied. I wonder if he slept over at my teacher's or if he drove home late, listening to loud music down the long roads in the dark. I wonder if he is like me, and can only think of other things while he is in math class. I draw a woman with a long white skirt on my math test margin.

Mr. Hall, our math teacher, calls on Brian.

"And what did you get for number nineteen?" he asks. Mr. Hall wears wide ties with bright patterns on them. To get our attention, he says.

"Um," Brian says, shuffling through his papers.

"Dork," Alec Ryerson coughs into his armpit.

"Enough," Mr. Hall says, pointing at Alec. "Brian?" he asks.

"Um. I didn't get that far," Brian says.

Brian's face is flushed. He is in the moment. He doesn't know what I know about him, that I know what he is thinking. That I know, I know. I didn't even have to be there.


My teacher holds up a pair of plaid boxer shorts.

"They're his!" she says.

"Whose?" I ask.

"Brian's," she says, laughing.

Before I met my teacher, I thought only teenagers acted this way.

"Oh," I say.

Ed is on a business trip again and will be returning tomorrow. I wonder what she will tell him she did while he was away.

We sit on her couch in front of the fire place and drink tea. I look through a photography book on her coffee table. It is a photo book of trees.

"How are you going to see Brian when Ed gets back?" I ask.

"Oh, well," she says, sipping, "I have it all planned out. When Ed is at work Brian can come over and we can have our rendezvous in my study."

"Wow," I say. "Right above him?!"

"Yes," she says. "It turns me on."

I did not know that cheating was so easy. It is all a matter of time and space, it seems: When one person leaves a space, another person can fill it. When one person comes back, the other person leaves. Just like that.

If I squeezed over in my own bed there would be room for one more. There is also another bed in my room for sleepovers, but no one has slept there since eighth grade. Sometimes I switch beds for a few weeks and sleep in the empty bed. I wake up in the night and wonder where I am. The room is in the wrong place, and I can see what every girl that ever slept there saw: my mother's old doll collection she passed down to me, the slant of the ceiling in stucco white, and my own empty bed, looking more cozy than it did before. After a few days, I crawl back into my own bed and wake up only to pee.

"Do you think my breasts are sagging?" my teacher asks me in the afternoon while she is changing into her bra. We are in her bedroom and I am sitting on the bed where she sleeps and does it with Brian.

It had not occurred to me that there was anything wrong with my teacher before. She had been a model. She is a poet, and after a new man makes love to her, she has a new poem in the morning.

"No, not at all," I say. I sit on my teacher's bed and watch her.

"You should try this on," she says, taking out one of her dresses from her closet. It is long and navy blue and goes out where her hips must have pushed it.

"I'll try it in the bathroom," I say, taking the silky dress off the hanger.

"Don't be silly," she says, catching me and pulling at the other end of the dress. "Try it on here."

I sit on the bed and take off my jeans and then my shirt, covering myself up quickly by putting the dress under my chin and then over my head. My teacher watches me and laughs.

"What are you doing?" she says. "You silly."

"Stand up," she says, and I do.

First my teacher pulls the dress all the way down. It is a bit big, but in the three-way mirror she turns me in front of, I can tell that it fits in the back.

"Look how nice you look," she says, and then she turns me around to face her. She looks into my eyes and I laugh because for a moment I forget who I am. Then she lifts the dress above my head so that she can see everything but my face.

"Stop," I laugh. I try to pull the dress down with my hands but my teacher is tall and strong. She holds the material above my head so I can only see the outline of her through the fabric, and not what her mouth is doing.

I stop trying to bend over. I hold my hands above my head and surrender.

My teacher lets the dress fall back down.

"You're lovely," she says, pointing her finger at me.

"Shut up," I say. I wonder if she is teasing me. Or if she feels bad for me. I also wonder, enough to make me blush, if maybe she is telling the truth.


In gym class we have to run the entire field. The gym teachers are all old men—stupid old men—who wear shorts that go down to their old men knees. They are tired old men who have been here too long. They don't even coach sports teams, they just watch us run in gym.

A bunch of kids go into the woods at the edge of the field and smoke pot. You can see through the trees when the gym teachers are calling them in and you can hear the whistles in the woods. These kids depend on the other kids, the nerds, to run around and around the field for the whole gym period. I usually go into the woods alone or else stand near the other kids and smoke cigarettes. When there is a big group, sometimes they don't notice me.

Today Brian is there, smoking a cigarette between two fingers like a girl, not like the other boys who hold it with their thumbs and look sexy. He looks stupid smoking; he has always been one of the runners. I wonder if he has only taken up smoking since he has taken up sex.

Alec Ryerson walks over to me and asks me for a light. He has blond hairs on his legs that are thick on his thighs. He has a joint.

"Hey," he says, "Hey, Sarah." He talks as if he is just remembering my name.

"Hey, Alec," I say.

I slump down and lean against a tree and light the joint for him. He leans over and looks down, and in the flame his eyelashes are dark and long.

Alec stands back and blows the pot smoke in my face.

"Brian says you eat Mrs. Holly's pussy."

I look over at Brian, who is looking out at the field.

"Shut the fuck up," I say to Alec.

"Brian," Alec calls over to him, "didn't you say you saw Mrs. Holly and Sarah in a 69?"

Brian looks at me and blushes. It seems to be the first time we have ever looked at each other. His eyes are small like mine.

"Yes," Brian says. He needs no coaxing from Alec. He is set on his lie, the way he insisted the neutered bulldog was about his "friend's brother" to my teacher before she got it out of him and then inside of her.

I look down at the ground where onion grass is growing up from the dirt.

"Jaime Dwyer says he saw you two at the movies once too."

It was true my teacher and I had gone to the movies once, two towns away. We shared popcorn and a large diet soda and sat near the front, silently. We both cried—it was a sad movie about two people in love. During one scene, while the actors had sex, my teacher pinched my leg and twisted. I wanted to tell her I didn't like that, that I was sensitive.

I hadn't seen Jaime Dwyer there. I often missed other people when my teacher was around. When I was alone, I was always looking at people—kids in the halls who were trying to walk quickly without tripping, mothers who looked like their sons, picking them up in their vans after practice. With my teacher I felt safe, like I had a blindfold on and she was leading me, her manicured hand pushing and pulling me.

"Whatever, asshole," I say.

I realize how much I hate Brian. I hate his smallness and his stupid poems. He is unremarkable and I notice everything.

"You stupid bitch," Brian says, out of nowhere. He flicks his cigarette like some tough guy and folds his arms across his chest.

Kay Simon, the class slut, pulls down her belly-shirt so her breasts are flattened. "Fight!" she says, walking over to where we are from where she was, wherever she was. "Fight!" she says.

Other kids start to come out from behind the trees like dwarfs who were hiding in *The Wizard of Oz*. Where were all these people before? They surround us, and for once it seems like Brian and I are popular.

I feel like I am in the middle of things, and I start to get a ringing in my ears. Brian and I are inside a group in the middle of the woods and in the center of my world. I can see his pores.

"Come on, "Alec says, clapping his hands like he's trying to get a dog to come to him.

"Dyke," Brian whispers.

I get close to him like I will spit on him, but instead I say, "Neuter."

No one else can hear us, but Brian's face turns red.

The whistle blows. A gust of wind hits us. Brian and I can only see each other.

"Shit," Alec says, walking back to the field. Everyone else starts to follow. If we are not back by the second whistle we get detention.

I watch as Brian walks with his head down, his hands in his pockets. I walk behind him, staring at the back of his greasy head. I walk in the footprints he makes in the misty field, noting that my footprints are bigger.


At home, my teacher calls.

"I want you to come over for dinner," she says, "and wear the dress."

The dress has been in my closet, hanging there as if it is waiting in the shape I hope to fill.

"Eight o'clock," my teacher says.


In the bathroom, after my shower, I lie on the floor and think of how I will tell her. I will move over to her side of the table and sit on her lap. I will stroke her hair off her face and put my finger to her wrinkled lips.

"Him or me," I will say. "Choose."

Then she will answer me with her hands or her tongue and I will find the words in her mouth, without her having to say them.

*       *       *

I smooth the dress on my hips outside my teacher's front door. I look down at the pouch of my stomach and suck it in. In my backpack are two packs of cigarettes and wine from my parents' cabinet.

I ring the doorbell and put one hand on my hip. I wonder where her husband is tonight.

When my teacher opens the door she is smiling. She is wearing a tight black minidress that hangs off the shoulder, and her hair half-up, half-down. In the light, she looks like a Club MTV dancer. I have never seen her so beautiful.

"Come in," she says, kissing me on the cheek. "You look fabulous."

"You do too," I say, putting down my backpack, and I walk into the living room. There, on the couch, sits Brian, in a sweater and khaki pants, as if he thinks he is grown up. He holds a glass of red wine and motions it to me as if he is giving me a toast. He is smirking.

"You know Brian," my teacher says, "and I want you to meet Michael. He's the ice sculptor I was telling you about."

Michael is leaning on the fireplace mantle, looking at the photo book of trees. His blond hair is tied back in a ponytail, and I can see the veins in his big arms.

Michael shakes my hand and I start to feel a ringing in my ears.

"Good to meet you," he says, and I am surprised he does not have an accent.

I sit on the arm of the couch. I want to put my head between my legs but I don't. I feel like I am sweating through my dress.

"Want a cigarette?" Brian asks, opening his pack toward me. My teacher has gone into the kitchen and I wonder what everyone was talking about before I arrived.

I take one of Brian's cigarettes. He takes out a lighter and flips it open on his knee. He is stupid, and I think he must have practiced that move over and over, the way I mouthed to my mirror, "Him or me?" I hate him.

"Here's some wine," my teacher says, pouring me a large glass.

Brian and I watch my teacher walk over to Michael. She puts her arm around his low waist and opens her legs. He puts his hand on her ass and moves it with his stubby fingers.

"Come up to my study," she says to him, "Let's pick out some music to dance to."

I have an urge to look at Brian and smirk, as if I am saying "We know what that means," but we have shared enough secrets, and we both know, without looking at each other, what we know.

I listen to my teacher's laughter while I trace the patterns in her rug with my foot. I hear the door shut, then a thump, then muted laughter, and then nothing. I wonder if Ed hears sounds like these and thinks she is bumping around her office, just writing poems.

"Oh God," Brian says, putting his head in his hands.

There is a space on the couch next to Brian, between us, that needs filling. I lean from the arm of the couch and slide my butt down. It feels easy moving this way, the red wine making me ache.

My hand touches Brian Wojowsky's back and I rub it in circles—first big and then smaller and smaller to the center of his back, as if there was something there that needed kneading. In the center of Brian Wojowsky there must be something like that, but I do not say anything, because we are not writing poetry. The poem, it seems, is where my fingers go, on the tiny bone I come back to each time the circle becomes a dot. It is not something we say in my teacher's house. It is not something we will write down.

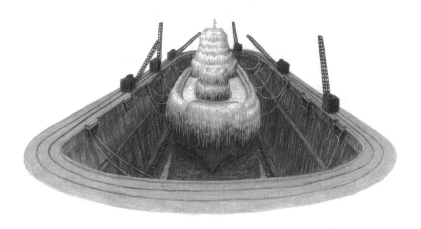

# WHAT KEELER DID TO HIS
# FOOT IN THE NAVY

*by* SEAN WARREN

This is about Keeler, not me, so I don't want you thinking anywhere down the line that I ever did anything to my foot like what
he did to his, even though we were both boot squids on board the
USS *Constellation*.

Actually, I was just going to turn over a year in the Navy when Keeler
showed up, and no one was really calling me a boot anymore since I'd
been on the Connie for eight months. When I first saw him in the berthing, sitting in a busted bottom rack that didn't have a privacy curtain
and with his stuffed sea bag lying on the deck in the middle of the aisle
so that I couldn't get to my rack, I kicked it a little and told him to get
it out of the way—like he was a real peon, because that's how it had been
for me when I'd first come on board. But really, deep down, I was feeling
like a bastard because a dog wouldn't have to put up with half the shit a
boot squid puts up with at sea, and I felt like an even bigger bastard when
Keeler didn't come back at me with any attitude or snarling at all after I'd
kicked his sea bag. He'd been reading a book, a fat paperback, and after
I got on him he just sat there with it still open in his hand and sighed,
looking down at his sea bag like it was a dead body someone had chained
to his ankle. Then he stood up and bent down and started tugging on the
strap. But it was stuffed with his whole damn life and hardly budged,

and finally when I got tired of him not getting the sea bag out of my way, I stepped on the damn thing to let him know I could be just as big an a-hole as anyone else if he didn't do what I said. When I put my foot down something inside the bag snapped really loud like I'd just broken its back. That made me feel the worst of all, but I didn't want to make an idiot of myself apologizing all over the place to a new squid, so I went straight back to my rack without saying another word and climbed in and commenced to try to take my nooner.

It was during lunch and the berthing lights were bright enough that I could see Keeler's fuzzy shape standing there through the blue cloth of my privacy curtain, not coming after me or working the sea bag or moving at all. Finally I had to look out to see what he was doing because of how quiet he was. I thought for some reason he might be about to cry, but he was back reading again. I figured the book to be one of those Tom Clancy or Stephen King bricks that floated around the ship on cruise, but it was about philosophy. *The History of Western Philosophy*, by Bertrand Russell. I didn't know what to make of that, but after a while of me looking at him reading really steady like I wasn't there, like he was in a world that was way above mine where nobody could touch him, I told him to move that fucking bag before I moved it for him. Keeler was a skinny tall guy, taller than me, but when I saw the word *Philosophy* on that book and how his eyes wouldn't come off the page when I was staring at him, it set me off. No way could you get out of doing boot squid hard time on the Connie by reading a philosophy book.

I was still in my rack and had cooled off enough to start feeling drowsy when I started asking myself why anyone who read philosophy books would volunteer to have their ass kicked by the Navy. After I fell asleep for a while and woke up, I looked out of my curtain to see if Keeler was still there. He was gone, but he hadn't unpacked his sea bag, he'd just pushed it back up onto his busted rack. I could see why he wouldn't want to live there. The Connie was an aircraft carrier, not a cruise ship, and even though it looked humongous tied up to the pier and had eighty planes stacked up on the flight deck like dinosaur warhawks when we were out steaming, there were five thousand squids squirming around below decks and we each had maybe two square feet of living space, including the lockers under our mattresses, and no fucking privacy at all except for that little curtain pulled across your rack.

Like I said, Keeler's rack was broken. The metal shelf that the piss-
and splooge-stained mattress laid across it was out of its grooves and bent
down toward the floor, and he didn't have any curtain at all. I was lucky
in one way when I first came on board—I damn sure wasn't lucky any
other way, being sent to the Connie—because the ship had been working
up to deploy over in the Western Pacific and Indian Oceans, and there'd
been some extra money to buy new mattresses and sheets and even stand-
up lockers for the first-class lifers. But Keeler's rack had been vacant the
whole time I'd been on board and nobody'd done a damn thing with
it, and we all looked at it like it was this busted-out crack house in our
neighborhood that nobody would be crazy-desperate enough to live in.

Too bad they had to fly Keeler out to the ship right then, because we
were all in a lousy mood and sick like hell of looking at each other after
floating around together in the Arabian Sea for over three months. What
chance did a new guy, especially a boot squid, have of us taking him in
and showing him the score?

The Joint Chiefs had sent us out there from the Philippines after
Saddam Hussein had popped a couple of shots at our aircraft, or maybe
he'd overflown the no-fly zone, or he could have just farted and our sat-
ellites had picked it up as him detonating a nuclear bomb. And I know
you're probably thinking I must be some kind of unpatriotic bastard for
saying this, after 9/11, but this all happened before that, and even if it
hadn't, there's no way I can fake it and tell you how great it is to be out
to sea on a man-o-war for over three months, when it's really the most
tedious fucking thing ever invented. It melts a man down, turns him into
one of the living dead. We worked twelve on, twelve off, but there was
really only enough work in most spaces belowdecks to keep us busy for
the first four or five hours, and anywhere else that's what you lived for,
to finish your work early so you could maybe get off and... But where
were we going to go, what were we going to do? We were used to beer
and women in the PI, so you think we're going to be all revved up over
playing video games or poker or looking for skin shots in R-rated movies
with a few thousand of our squidly shipmates? That was the kind of shitty
attitude Keeler was up against. It was like, We been out here for three
months while you been Stateside all that time living the high life, so we
ain't doing a goddamn thing for you, and if you whine about it we'll just

make it colder for you or ride you harder, piss on your mattress, whatever. It kind of gives me the creeps to think back about it, because I wasn't ever a bully or the sort of person that got off on being cruel to people.

I didn't see Keeler again for a couple of days. His sea bag sat in his rack the whole time, and made me wonder if they'd given him a rack somewhere else. But if they had, why hadn't he come back for his sea bag? Putfark, one of the compartment cleaners, asked me if I knew where Keeler was, like the rack was a prime location, and I guess it was for him because he used to take naps in it when the Berthing Petty Officer wasn't around. After I told Putfark I didn't know where Keeler was, he started dragging the sea bag out of the rack. When I told him to just leave it, he looked at me like he wanted to fight, this scrawny little peahead from some part of Louisiana or Mississippi where the kids eat possum taters and wear raccoon-claw necklaces. But then he threw down the sea-bag strap and mumble-fucked me and walked away.

Next thing I heard, Keeler was working for Adolfson in the ID Card Shack, and that started me feeling bad for him all over again. Adolfson was only a third class, but he hadn't joined the Nav until he was thirty-five—they must have given him the biggest age waiver of all time—and I used to think he must have been pissed about being that old and having to go through boot camp and being such a junior weenie, because he made damn sure that anyone who worked for him was more miserable than he was.

The ID Card Shack was a little dungeon off by itself that was stuffed in a fan room up by the anchor windlass. Working there had to be the worst job on the whole ship. All you did was take pictures and do a little typing and print out ID cards all day, the same thing over and over, a hundred ID cards a day. And when you weren't doing the cards, all the Ship's Company service records were over there, more than three thousand of them in all, and there was always stacks of paper to be filed in them. But you could never catch up because of the ID cards. That was the reason Squids were always bitching about their records not being up to date.

Adolfson never helped out, never did ID cards or filed anything. He just sat at his desk, which took up half the little office and had this nasty mini-mart plastic coffee mug as big as an oil drum on it, and had himself a good ol' time grinding on whichever seaman was working for him about why the fuck all the filing hadn't gotten done and kissing the asses of any officer or chief who came around for an ID card (but never, ever doing one for them himself). My big moment with Adolfson came one time when four or five of us were watching an R-rated Jennifer Lopez movie down in the berthing lounge. We all knew Jen'd take her clothes off eventually, and we were sitting there watching and thinking Goody-goody, here it comes, and she pulled off her halter and we started getting stiffies and leaning away from each other and maybe thinking of going back to our racks for a little log-flogging when Adolfson lost it, got up holding his crotch through his dungarees, and started yelling, "I got to get me some of that! Suck my dick, bitch!" A couple of the squids told him to cool it, but he kept on holding his biscuit and hollering and ruining it for the rest of us. I finally blew up and told him to sit the fuck down and shut up. Since he was a third class and I was just a peon seaman he went off on me like a little old bitch about how he was going to write me up for insubordination. He actually did write me up, but when the Legal Officer heard the whole story he threw it out. Adolfson acted like a dick every time he saw me after that, told me he'd get me humping stores for him down the line on a working party.

So Keeler had it bad. He was catching it every which way—he was jammed in the ID card craphole twelve hours a day with Adolfson, and when he got off everyone could see him reading his philosophy book or logflogging or picking his nose, because he didn't have a privacy curtain. Except that, like I said, he didn't come back to his rack for the first couple of days he was working with Adolf Hitlerson. I wasn't really thinking much about Keeler at all then, except for when I went down to the berthing and saw that sea bag stuffed in his rack like it hadn't been touched, and then I thought, He's got to be pulling stuff out of the sea bag, skivvies and stuff to take a shower and brush his teeth, otherwise he's stinking bad. Or he jumped over the side. A couple of times after that, when I was making my rounds dropping off paperwork from the Old Man for the Legal Officer or the XO, I went by the ID card window and looked in to make sure Keeler hadn't jumped. He'd be in there bent over a filing cabinet drawer with a service record open and looking up at Adolfson standing over him making a lot of noise like he was the Main Man, the Head Motherfucker, when all he was really was this a-hole they'd shitcanned to ID cards because nobody could work with him. I probably would have jumped over the side if I'd had to spend as much time as Keeler did with that idiot.

But I didn't know how much everything was working on Keeler until one night when I went to the head to take a shower. There was a movie playing on TV and most everyone was still watching it except me, because I thought it was junk, and because with everyone glued to the TV I wouldn't have to stand in line for a shower stall. And maybe I could get away with taking a Hollywood shower, just let the water come down on me for a whole five or ten minutes. If there were other squids in the head when I was showering, I could never tell if they were timing how long I'd been in there, scarfing up all the fresh water, and getting ready to report me to the Master-at-Arms. At sea you're supposed to take a Navy shower to conserve fresh water: turn it on, then off, lather up, then on again to rinse, then get out. Some hardcore lifers said you were gay if you took a Hollywood, like you were taking a pink bubblebath, but that's pure BS. Any American should be able to take a shower for as long as he wants, anytime, anywhere. But anyway, there I was in the head thinking I was all by myself and with all four shower stalls wide open for me, not just the one that had the busted head that dribbled water, and then I heard this grunting in one of the shitters behind me, like a squid was working hard to pass that assham the cooks had fed us for dinner. I wasn't going to listen to anyone taking a dump, so I jumped in the shower and turned on the water. It took a couple of minutes to really warm up and then I was cooking, man. But when you're at sea a long time and they're always beating it into you about conserving water, it's hard to just let the water run without thinking the water police are just about to lower the boom, yank you out bare-assed and drag you straight up to the Old Man for a dose of Military Justice. So I opened the plastic curtain a crack to make sure there weren't any finks around timing my shower. What I saw were two big feet under a stall curtain—the shitters were right across from the showers in our head—and one foot was bleeding on top from fingers rubbing something, some kind of razor blade across the top of it.

There's a lot of nutty stuff that goes on at sea when you're floating around with five thousand squids, but seeing the fingers working this blade and jerking back like it hurt like hell and then the blood oozing out of the cuts was the craziest thing I ever saw—until I watched the fingers lay the razor aside and take a little smoky brown bottle and dribble some liquid into the cuts. When the liquid hit the cuts, whoever it was inside the stall hissed off a GODDAMN! real loud and started jumping around like his foot was burning. I could almost hear the toes on the foot squealing like little animals by how they were flexing. Then Keeler crashed out of the stall and hopped around with his mouth clutched open. Once he saw me peeking around the shower curtain, it was like the whole Navy had found out what he'd been doing. He hopped out of the head looking scared shitless and furious at the same time, slamming the hatch behind him so that the squids out in the lounge must have been wondering what the hell was going on. I made sure I stayed in the shower with the water running as long as I could after that, so the only thing they might ask about was if I was taking a Hollywood. That would be okay, as long as they didn't ask me about what I'd seen Keeler doing to his foot.

I couldn't stop thinking about Keeler and the way the toes on his burned-up foot had been squealing at me. The only answer I could come up with for him cutting and burning his foot was that Adolfson was driving him crazy and him not having a privacy curtain was making it worse. When you're at sea, that privacy curtain is like the front door to your house. I know I've already talked about it too much and probably bored the crap out of you, but that's the way it is. I couldn't do anything about Adolfson, but maybe I could get Keeler a curtain. Putfark and the other compartment cleaners wouldn't do shit when I asked them about it—they were miserable, so why should they help anyone not to be miserable, that was their attitude—so I decided to go on a mission to find Keeler a curtain.

It wasn't as easy as it sounded. I was on board the Connie a couple of weeks before I got *my* curtain, and that was only because I had pestered the hell out of everybody, asked at least twenty people, even dropped a hint on the Old Man himself (I worked for him). Then, one day, there it was on my mattress. And this was just after I'd asked Styles, the Berthing Petty Officer, for about the tenth time for a curtain and he'd told me they weren't even in the supply system.

The only way I could think of to get Keeler a curtain without asking every swinging D on board again was to snag one off another rack. No way was I going to lift one out of my own berthing, so I'd have to go around to other berthing compartments until I came across a vacant rack that had a curtain. I didn't think it could be that hard—there had to be at least one empty rack with a curtain somewhere—but I was big-time wrong about that. And another thing I learned was that when you're trolling through a berthing compartment other than your own, it's like landing a plane in Afghanistan and not speaking the language. I got looked at funny a lot, but the worst part was seeing a rack that didn't have a sheet and might be empty and lifting the curtain and then finding this big, hairy body lying there asleep or with the squid actually waking up and staring at me like I'd just busted into his house and raped his girlfriend. That happened to me twice, and the only way I got out of it was to say I was looking for someone who had to stand a watch.

I finally found some empty racks with curtains in the back of the mess-crank berthing. A mess crank is a brand-new boot squid who gets sent down from his department, Weapons, Deck, Air, wherever, for ninety days to the Mess Decks to bus tables or wash dishes in the scullery or clean out the galley kettles or do whatever shit job the lifer cooks don't want to do. The crank berthing was no doubt the worst on the ship, because the cranks were moving in and out all the time like in one of those crappy neighborhoods where nobody owns the homes and they're all pissed off at the landlords (lifer cooks) about not owning anything, and that pissed-off way of looking at everything builds up with each crank coming and going until all the smells and darkness and squids not having enough room to live make it fucking unbearable.

I'll admit, I was scared as hell poking around down in the crank berthing. The cranks had busted out most of the little bulkhead nitelights because they worked all shifts, so I was walking between the racks in the dark without seeing a damn thing, stepping on piles of clothes, never once hitting down on a clean piece of deck tile, and breathing in all this BO and misery and old food and angry cig smoke, and then suddenly a light yawned on and it was this black dude coming out of the head with a towel wrapped around him and looking at me and saying "Fuck you going?" like my white ass was soon to be hamburger. But I kept moving, got tangled up in a huge pile of clothes, saw another light and went for it, and then stepped into the cleanest, shiniest, brightest berthing I'd ever seen. It was really small, only one cubicle with six racks, but there was a big lounge area with a couple of old couches and a nice card-table setup for Mah Jong.

The racks all had curtains and fat mattresses like the kind the officers have in their staterooms. I couldn't believe I was standing there by myself—it was like whoever controlled that little piece of heaven should have posted a crank with an M-16 on watch to keep an eye on it. None of the racks had sheets, which made me think they were all empty. But while I was trying to untie one of the curtains I saw an old Filipino cook sleeping in a bottom rack through a crack in *his* curtains. At that point I thought Hell with it, clipped the curtain cord with my Leatherman instead of fumble-farting around anymore to untie it, and got out of there, stumbling and bumbling back through the dark and getting tangled up with more piles of stinky-ripe clothes and almost falling on my ass about ten times.

I had the curtain stuffed into my shirt like a sackful of money when I came out of the crank berthing. Then I went back to my own berthing and was going to tuck it under Keeler's sea bag, or his rack, but I didn't want to leave it there unprotected, knowing that another squid would boost it if I did. And also I wanted Keeler to know that you didn't have to be a lifer to get things done, you could get along okay if you were smart and not willing to swallow every piece of garbage the Nav tried to jam down your throat.

That's when I had a crazy idea about giving the curtain to Keeler personally. I walked around the ship for a while with it still tucked in my shirt, but kind of nervous about delivering it. What if he didn't want it? Then I decided to walk down to the ID card shack. Adolfson was leaning out of his little window on his elbows, smiling like he was running for mayor or maybe had just let some officer sodomize him. Once he saw me coming toward him, I never saw the look the look on anyone's face change so fast. He looked like he wanted to spit out a roofer's nail at me right between the eyes. I went up to him and he pulled back because his style was to bullwhip you from six feet away, he didn't like anyone getting up in his face. Keeler was back behind him in the office with his head down, filing service-record papers like a dog. Seeing him working that way gave me the little extra push I needed to lean through the window enough to clear Adolfson out and get Keeler's attention and pull the curtain out of my shirt. I didn't expect him to act grateful, especially after he knew I'd seen him cutting his foot in the stall. But he just slid his chair over to the window without getting up and took the curtain from me like it was no big deal. That disappointed me. I didn't need him to be my friend, but if he'd known the hell I'd gone through… Adolfson knew. He'd probably been counting on Keeler not getting a curtain and that that was somehow going to keep him under his thumb. But then Keeler went from not having any kind of reaction at all to folding and unfolding the curtain on his lap a couple of times like a little old lady. Finally he looked up at me and said "Thanks." His eyes were moist, not like he was going to start blubbing, but just that it had finally hit him how important having a curtain was for anyone on that goddamn birdfarm. We connected so strongly just then that I could feel my own eyes getting moist. Suddenly it was like there were two of us fighting all the BS, instead of just one.

I didn't want to see Keeler again after that, not ever, probably because I didn't want a boot squid thinking I was going to be his buddy, helping him out all the time when nobody had ever helped me. I stayed away from our berthing for the rest of the day, until it was past midnight and I was too tired to give a shit about anything anymore. Then I walked back to my rack and saw that Keeler had hung his curtain. A thousand-volt charge of pride shot through me when I saw that curtain that kept me lying awake for a long time after I'd hit my rack, like someone had just made me the goddamn CNO and I could do anything I wanted. I didn't sleep hardly at all, but still felt good in the morning after I took half a Hollywood and went up to my office on the third deck. This corpsman named Hernandez dropped off the daily sick bay muster for the Old Man later on. I was looking over the muster to see if I knew anyone who'd been admitted or if there were any crazy diseases listed. Down at the bottom of the list I found Keeler, admitted for cellulitis.

We'd done a lot of marching in boot camp, and a bunch of squids in my company had come up lame with blisters. Some of them had gotten infected; that's how I knew what cellulitis was. Could you get it from cutting open the top of your foot and pouring poison into the cut? I sat there thinking about it for a while, about Keeler cutting himself open to get away from Adolfson. I would have just blown a hose on him, told him to fuck the hell off, but that was probably because I'd already gotten away with doing it, when we were watching that movie down in the berthing. Maybe I needed to tell Keeler not to sweat Hitlerson, that it was a damn shame to be hurting himself on account of that old squid being such an a-hole. But what kept me from going straight down to sick bay and talking to Keeler was remembering him rubbing that razor blade on his foot, and the toes barking when he poured the poison into the cut. I didn't want Keeler latching on to me if he was a hardcore nutcase.

All this was still blowing around inside my head when Hernandez called me from Medical and said that Captain Crawford, the Senior Medical Officer, wanted to see me. I knew it had to be about Keeler. I was really nervous because even if Crawford just wanted to talk about the weather, it's impossible for a seaman to get a call from a full bird like that and not think he's in the shitsoup, especially since I knew Crawford was good buddies with the Old Man, and anything we talked about would go straight back to him.

But I could only take being all nervous and trembly for so long, and then I went down and Crawford's office. His door was open a crack and a little tinkle of classical music was coming out that made me feel easier because even though I didn't know anything about classical music, I liked it from hearing it on all the old Warner Bros. cartoons I used to watch when I was a kid. Crawford must have seen me through the crack, because he told me to come in before I'd even knocked on the door. His office was good-sized, about what you'd expect for a captain on ship. There were some framed museum posters up on the bulkhead, and his rack was behind him, so it was probably also his stateroom. Crawford stood up and shook my hand man-to-man and said "Welcome, Tom Powers, I've heard good things about you." That about knocked me over, not him saying he'd heard good things about me, but just saying my first name. There he was, one of the big boys on that monster ship, he could have sent me straight down to bread and water in the brig if he'd wanted to, and he was the first officer in my almost one year of being in the Canoe Club to use my first name.

It probably sounds stupid to say it, but I would have done anything for Crawford after that, even though he had funny, heavy-lidded eyes that never seemed to blink, and gave me the feeling that he could look right down to the bottom of what I was thinking and see all kinds of little white mice running around crazy and confused. Crawford was tall and his hair was going gray, but he didn't have any gut or love handles at all. He had to tuck his khaki shirt in all the way around to the back so that it didn't bunch up in front.

"You getting Keeler that curtain for his rack really meant a lot to him," Crawford told me after we had sat down. "He's having a rough time with some things, being on ship for the first time... You know what I'm talking about. You're doing all right—he could probably learn from you. The Skipper says you're doing a great job running his office by yourself."

I just sat there listening, but I could almost feel my feet and ass lift off like I was about to start floating around.

He stretched out in his chair. "You know Keeler's on the ward now down here." he said. "I think he just got overwhelmed with everything, but I know he's got what it takes to be a good sailor. I don't want to see him Med Boarded out. That'd be a shame. What he needs is a young guy his age who's making it to tell him that there's more to the Navy than this, just this floating around. You've been in the PI, and I bet that keeps you and a lot of the other sailors going around here. I'd like you to talk to him about that. You don't have to get raunchy about it, just tell him this isn't going to last forever."

I wondered if Crawford went around in the PI. He could probably buy a whole island on his Captain's pay. But no way, he probably had a gorgeous wife and huge house back in San Dog with golden retrievers in the backyard. It was embarrassing to think about him, a Navy doctor and a full bird, catting around Olongapo or Subic with some bar slut. I wanted to talk more, give him some regular-guy chatter to pay him back for how he'd stroked me. But then he cut me off by standing up all of a sudden, like he thought I was going to say something not nice about Keeler. "Why don't you go over to the ward and visit Keeler?" he said. "I'm sure he'd like to see you."

Crawford walked me across the p-way to the ward. It was really small compared to a regular hospital, with only six racks, but next to any berthing compartment it looked as clean and bright as a big suite at the Hilton. The racks weren't even stacked three-deep like they were in the berthing, they were single-tier and spread out and painted blue and had fat mattresses. All six of the the racks had a laid-out squid who didn't look very sick at all.

It took me a while to get over seeing everyone looking so comfy and tucked in and notice Keeler lying in bed behind a book. His foot was sticking out of the blanket and wrapped in about sixty layers of bandages that made it look like this big invisible-man head was growing on the end of his leg. He was reading the same *History of Western Philosophy* book that I'd seen him reading the first time in the berthing. He was so into it that his eyes didn't come off the page until Captain Crawford moved up closer to him and started checking over the bandaged foot. Keeler got a happy shine on his face when he saw Crawford, like he was his sea daddy. But when he saw me behind the Doc his eyes went panicky-mad, the same as when I'd seen him in the stall, like he thought I'd told Crawford the real story about his foot. No way would I ever rat someone out that way, and Keeler thinking I did made me want to get out of there and not ever do another thing for him.

But Crawford brought me around like I was Keeler's friend. We both knew, Keeler and me, that it was BS. Then Crawford left us alone and that just embarrassed me more than anything else, because we hadn't ever really talked at all and I'm sure Keeler still thought I'd ratted him out for being a malingerer, the word I'd found for him when I was looking through the Uniform Code of Military Justice to see if there was an Article there that covered someone hurting themselves to get out.

Keeler thinking I'd ratted kept working on me, until I told him, "You're nuts if you think I told Crawford anything."

He acted like he didn't know what I was talking about. But then he shrugged like it didn't matter anyway, and tried to go back to reading his book. I was going to leave it at that, but something kept me from breaking all the way off.

"Why would you want to come in the Navy if you read philosophy books?"

"I'm a pantheist," Keeler said.

"Is that some kind of religion where you cut your feet open?" I didn't know what the hell a pantheist was and thought he was trying to make me look stupid, when he was the one who couldn't hang being at sea for a week.

Keeler's eyes flashed around. Then he eased up, shrugged again, and said, "It's not that I want to act snooty, but that's how people are around here when they see you reading. Like they hate you or something. I don't know what the fuck's up with them."

"Probably hard to work for Adolfson and not think everybody hates you. But he's just a jackass. Keep your head down—they don't make anyone work for him for long, at least not if they got anything going for them."

"I ain't never going back there," Keeler said. His eyes were starting to steam. "You live like an animal, they treat you like a fucking animal. I must have been crazy, dropping out of school to join."

"Why did you?"

"Because everyone there dumped on the military. It's a college thing, that the only people who join, the enlisted people, are poor white trash or minorities. But then the fucking professors would go on about how we had to do more for the poor and people of color, and some kids'd do a pro-test... but if they joined the military it was the worst thing in the world. Slavery and—and fascism. Why'd you join?"

"I guess I got tired of living at home and not making enough with shit jobs to get my own place. Plus, I was sick of school. Sitting in a class-room was just useless to me. Now I wouldn't mind, put me in a classroom. But I still got three years left on contract."

"I'm gonna get out, but after that... I don't know if I'm going back to school right away."

"It's the pits floating around out here, no doubt about it, but maybe you ought to wait 'til we get back to the PI and you can see what that's about. The PI's crazy, man, women and beer up the yazoo. Not like San Dog at all."

"What's the PI?"

"Philippine Islands, man. Did you get any time there on your way out?"

"They flew me through Guam and Diego Garcia."

"There you go. Hang on 'til the PI, I'm telling you. Get you a girl..."

Keeler shook his head. "I'm finished, man. This ain't no way to live. Treat you like an animal, spit on you because you read. Those college fuck-ers may be soft, but this is crazy, it's just about hate and mindless control. How the fuck does democracy work, with the college fools and the ass-holes around here hating each other? You ever wonder about that?"

Too bad he didn't want to hear about the PI. But he was hardcore against the Canoe Club at that point, didn't know anything except Adolfson and floating around, so nothing I could tell him was going to change his mind.

*   *   *

Believe it or not, that same day I talked to Keeler in sick bay, the Joint Chiefs came out with a message ordering us out of the Arabian Sea and back to the Philippines for upkeep. Nobody went to sleep that night after the Old Man announced it. The crew played poker or video games or watched the movies that the station ran all night in honor of us heading back. I sat out on the catwalk that was outside my office and under the island and watched the sun cracking up through the dark ocean in the morning like this blazing huge bubble, thinking so hard about my girlfriend Linzi back in the PI that I might have flogged my log right out there if flight ops hadn't started all of a sudden with Hornets screaming off the deck over my head.

The crew sleepwalked through the next six days, but it was a good kind of sleepwalking, with a little cushion of air under us, not like when we'd been out forever and didn't know when we were going home. I'd be walking around or standing in the chow line with everything kind of blank, and then *zap!* this little jolt would hit me out of nowhere to remind me that PI was only five, four, three, or however many days away. Even though there were flight ops, nobody did much work. We'd been working twelve on, twelve off for over a hundred days out there, defending democracy and all that happy shit, and there wasn't much left that we wanted to do except get our asses back to Subic. But I'll tell you one bunch that was working hard on the way back: the squids down in sick bay. They were working to make sure they weren't locked up on the ward when we pulled in. The sick bay muster moved up to being the first thing I looked at in the morning after Keeler went in for his foot. There were five squids down on the list with him on his first day, and after we turned around and started to steam back east, one guy would drop off the muster every day. First the suicidal squid, then the squid with appendicitis, then the squid with a kidney stone. Then there was a day when nobody got out, but the next day the Docs discharged two squids with hernias.

Then there was only Keeler left on the list with this squid named Hagan who had hemorrhoids. It was starting to look like Captain Crawford might not let Keeler out in time for the PI, and I had mixed feelings about that because I didn't want him to lose a foot trying to get out, or even be separated with a wacko discharge, and I really thought that if he made it to PI and found a woman that he'd have something to look forward to besides working for Adolfson. But I also felt like he'd gypped the system, only been out to sea a week and then wimped out when all the rest of us non-philosophy-reading slobs had put up with the worst of it for a lot longer. The last part kept me from going down to sick bay to see Keeler until he called me up.

I figured he was probably getting desperate about missing the PI. Keeler wasn't reading when I walked into the ward; he was staring up into the overhead with his arm flopped across his forehead like he'd been blinded by all the crazy PI stories that were flying around the ship. He jackknifed straight off the bed when he saw me, and threw his bandaged foot down on the deck like he was going to walk right out of there.

"Powers, maaaaaaan." He shook my hand and looked at me like one of those squids who had to pull duty our first night in Subic and was paying two hundred bucks to anyone willing to stand their watch for them. "You gotta do something for me," Keeler said. "Captain Crawford says he'll let me off the first day we pull in, as long as someone comes with me on the buddy system, in case, you know, because of my foot."

That was worse to me than a squid asking me to take his duty, because I was a free ranger in the PI, I never buddied up with anybody over there. Nobody'd ever shown me around, and now that I'd been out a little and figured to have a girl waiting for me, I didn't want this clubfoot boot squid slowing me down. A picture of me and Keeler going down the afterbrow popped into my head.

"I can't be pushing you around in a wheelchair when I got a woman to hook up with," I told him.

"You crazy? I won't be in a fucking wheelchair. Look." Keeler tried walking around on the bandaged foot like it was good as new, but he was really hobbling. I couldn't see him making it ten feet off the gangway without me going back for help.

But, shit, in the end he talked me into it. It was probably just me feeling sorry for him again, but also he asked me a couple of questions about the PI, where I went, were there really as many girls out there as everyone said, that sort of thing. After I told him I went up to Subic City instead of Olongapo like most of the other swinging Ds on board, his eyes went buggy like I was some kind of PI God, like he'd give up all his books and college to have one night of what I'd had up in Subic City. When you're a peon like I was, you can't believe how far you'll go for somebody who suddenly treats you like a big man.

I left the ward and went over to tell Doc Crawford that I'd take Keeler out. But he wasn't in his office, which was a huge relief for me. I shot out of there like I was off the hook, a free man. But Keeler called me up later in my office and said he'd told Crawford I'd buddy up with him. Even though I didn't say anything to this, I was smoking mad. All of a sudden the Nav was expecting me to be Keeler's nurse, a fucking nurse, when all they'd done up to that point was treat me like I was seven years old. And that was how I talked myself into ditching Keeler when the Connie finally made it back to Subic. If Keeler had just asked me himself, I would have gone along with it. But with Crawford acting like it was my job to keep Keeler in the Canoe Club… I'd just given the Nav a hundred and ten days at sea, and now I was going to let them bust up my liberty?

I brought my civvies up to my office the night before the Connie pulled into Subic, so Keeler wouldn't find me in the berthing in the morning. Then he called me a couple of times to try and get me to set up where we could meet before leaving the ship. I told him I had to do some work for the Old Man and didn't know what time I'd be able to get off. After the second time Keeler called and I didn't commit, the panicky little tremble I could hear in his voice suddenly went bitter because he knew, even though he didn't say it, that I was dodging him. After that he kept calling, telling me I was his only hope of getting off that damn ship in the morning. When I couldn't take talking to him anymore, after taps, I left the office in the middle of the phone ringing again and pretty much wandered around the ship for the rest of the night.

We moored in the morning and everybody went nuts. It sounded like a cowboy had just opened a gate and fired off a round and a million cattle were stampeding out of a corral. I jumped through a hatch and ran across the Hangar Bay not even thinking about Keeler and pushed through the crowd and saluted the ensign at the top of the brow and then piled down and whooped like a goddamn hyena when I hit the pier, and took off running. I couldn't believe how fast I was moving, like the speed of freedom was faster than an F-18 screaming up into the blue sky after clearing the flight deck when you've been cooped up in a birdfarm forever. It didn't matter if I was riding in a taxi or changing my Andy Jacksons into pesos or walking out the Naval Station main gate and over the Shit River bridge, I felt like I was blazing along. Then I caught the very first jeepney up to Subic City, and the driver didn't even wait the way drivers usually did, until there were so many squids jammed in you could see the wax in the ear of the joker next to you, he just took off down the road and up around the steep hill that had this blue view of Subic Bay right near the top that made you want to get out and dive off the hillside and down into the water just to see if it felt as good as it looked, and then through this jungle where I'd seen some kids once with sticks chasing a monkey with arms twice as long as its legs, and then, finally, Subic City, just this dirt road running between some crappy saloons under a hot blue sky, no neon at all, just wood and a some stucco and no sidewalks except for two-by-fours or sometimes sheets of plywood laid out between the bars, and muddy as a swamp when it rained, and with girls in bikinis or little terry robes standing outside yelling at us, outnumbering us ten to one probably, when we rumbled into town.

My girlfriend Linzi was the bookkeeper at a bar called Caligula's. Even though we'd only been together a few days before I left the last time, I was sure that she'd be waiting for me. Linzi was down on Americans when I'd first met her at Caligula's, she'd had a couple of kids with a Marine who'd wound up marrying an Americana back in the States. I wasn't big on her either in the beginning, there were other girls around who were better looking or had bigger scoobs and who were ready to jump in my lap. I thought that I might want to shop around, but then I found out that I liked being with Linzi after we'd talked all night at the bar. She was the smartest girl I ever met in the PI, told me her dream was to become an accountant. After we bar-hopped and did some banging, I told Linzi I wanted to get a place for us out in town, so she wouldn't have to live in her piece-of-shit room over the bar that only had a grungy mattress on the floor for a bed. We got up one morning, not knowing it would be our last time together, and Linzi rode back down to the base with me. There were hot rumors flying around that the Connie was getting underway that night for a long stretch and I felt desperate, told Linzi I wanted to marry her, like that was going to get her on ship with me. We hugged and she ran away back over the bridge like me leaving was as tough for her as it was for me, and…

Because of what I'd been through, being at sea over a hundred days, I never, ever thought Linzi wouldn't be waiting for me at when I walked into Caligula's. But of course she wasn't. Four other girls were sitting around the bar drinking Coke and playing pool on two tables and waiting for the rest of the squids to come in. They came up to me, tugging on my clothes and stroking my face, wanting me to choose between them, until I started asking questions about Linzi. One girl who hadn't come up to me and was still playing pool said Linzi'd gone back to Baguio because her boyfriend on the Connie had been gone so long that she knew he butterfly on her. Then the girl looked up from her shot and stared at me. She knew I was the boyfriend. I thought that might make her mad at me, like Linzi was her friend, but she came over and handed me a cue and ran her hand through my hair like she was definitely interested. But I couldn't shake this feeling that Linzi would walk in any second, and that I had to be a straight arrow for her after leaving her behind for so long. That's how I acted up to when other squids started coming into the bar and the pool-shooting girl knew I was a lost cause. She took her cue back and moved on. I started downing San Miguels after that and playing pool and losing a few bucks to the girls and some of the squids, because I didn't want to be sober and by myself with this huge sucking chest wound from knowing Linzi wasn't coming back.

The last thing I remember was being in a jeepney and talking to a squid and his girlfriend who were the only other people on board with me. I didn't know them or what they were thinking, but they were acting scared, like I was some drunken menace. When I stood up to show them what a friendly guy I was, someone, probably the driver, hit me square between the shoulder blades and knocked me flying out the back of the jeepney. I landed on a dark dirt road. I crawled around for a while, not knowing where I was, and then all the beer I'd drunk pulled me under and I didn't care anymore. I lay down and felt my cheek press down against all the sharp little pebbles in the dirt... Then I was back on the Connie in my muddy civvies with a headache like a throbbing light bulb stuck behind my eyes and some squid eyeballing me through a crack in my curtain and yakking in my ear.

It was Keeler. He would not shut up. Finally I told him to get the fuck out like I wanted him to leave, but he thought I'd said it because

I didn't believe what he was saying, so he went on, telling me that Crawford had let him off after all and he'd met some girl out in town. With Linzi gone, the last thing I wanted to hear, was that Keeler had gotten laid, But underneath what he was saying, it sounded like Keeler was trying to thank me for telling him about the PI, like I was his PI godfather. Then he started pinging on me to go into town with him and meet his girlfriend, and shit, I didn't even know what day it was, but finally I told him I'd go after I slept a little bit longer. He left and I fell asleep. When he came back and I woke up, I could only see his one blue eye staring at me through the crack in my curtain. I knew then that I wasn't going to get rid of him again. At least the light bulb that had been throbbing behind my head was turned off.

I told Keeler I'd go out with him, but figured I could get rid of him if I took my time. I showered and put on some fresh civvies and changed the sheets on my rack and then I went down to the Mess Decks to get some chow. But Keeler hung on, kept talking the whole time, never took the hint that me not talking might mean that I wouldn't have minded us just being fucking quiet. All he did was talk about his girlfriend, on and on. Finally I just turned on my jamming frequency, hardly heard a word of it, until we were off the boat and walking down Magsaysay, out in Olongapo.

It was late afternoon and the sidewalks were full of squids trolling around with beers in their hands. It was the last situation I wanted to be in, walking around town with a million other squids, but it actually wasn't that bad because there were just as many women out. I don't mean bar girls, just regular women who had places to go, work and shopping. A lot of the young ones were wearing plaid Catholic school dresses and holding hands for protection, but also slipping squids these sly little side looks, like they were trying to figure out who the good guys were, who they could trust, even though they'd probably have run like hell if any squid had actually stopped to talk to them. I must have made eye contact with fifty women out there that way, and that's what finally woke me up and made me aware of things, especially that I still hadn't gotten laid since we'd pulled in. I looked at Keeler walking next to me and thought Shit, he's still around, and started listening to him, hoping we were heading to the bar where he'd found his girlfriend. He was walking without much of a limp and wearing a big basketball shoe with the laces pulled out on his bandaged foot, and he was also toting a carton of Marlboro Reds. When we were way down Magsaysay and had passed most of the big bars and there weren't many squids left around us, I asked him about the bar where his girlfriend worked.

"I told you she doesn't work in a bar," he said, sounding pissed at me for not listening to him.

"Where does she work?"

"Man, she doesn't work, I just told you."

That made me mad, made me feel like a dumbass, but Keeler was just rattling on. Anyone who'd listened to even ten percent of what he'd been saying would have wanted to stuff a sock in his mouth by then.

Finally we cut off Magsaysay and started hiking up a steep road that turned to dirt half way up. I knew a couple of squids who'd wandered drunk off the main drag and gotten rolled. There was no else around and it was getting dark I was starting to get worried. After we finally made it to the top of the road, we were standing across from five or six dark gray concrete shells without roofs that looked like little houses in the middle of being built. But since they were deserted and there wasn't any lumber or building materials around, I thought that they could have also been abandoned. And then in a couple of the shells I saw some blankets laid out and a lot of San Miguel bottles lying around like it was some kind of skid row, PI style. I told Keeler, "You got women all over the place back in the bars, and you bring us up to this dump?" Keeler gave me a smug smile, like he had a surprise waiting for me.

We walked around the edge of the site, under a big sign that said KEEP OUT in English and a bunch of stuff in Tagalog that I couldn't read. It was almost dark now and in a couple of the concrete shells I could see the glow from fires and smell the burning. Keeler turned into one of the shells. A tall Filipino stepped in front of us with a mean look. He had a mop of straight black hair and a big ugly sore on his cheek and a cig blazing from his mouth. The mean look he was giving us only relaxed after Keeler slipped the carton of Marlboro Reds into his hand. Then he stepped aside. Keeler pushed into the shell while I kept staring at the Filipino. For some reason it looked like he was only half there. I kept staring at him until I saw the right sleeve of his shirt lying flat, like he was missing an arm. He didn't like me looking at him so hard and bumped past me out of the shell, hiding his armless side and smoking and with his meanness looking pathetic now that we both knew he only had one arm.

I don't know exactly what I expected to find in the shell behind the one-armed guy, but I know it wasn't a gorgeous woman breast-feeding a baby and an old granny sucking a cig in her caved-in mouth and staring flat ahead with shiny little black button eyes like she was blind. They were sitting around a fat candle and there was some food spread out on a blanket in front of them on the floor, bread and gallon water jugs and Oscar Mayer sandwich meat and ketchup and a veggie tray and four boxes of Pop-Tarts that Keeler must have picked up for them from the commissary on base. They hadn't made but a couple of sandwiches by the look of how much bread and meat was left, but the Pop-Tarts were almost all gone. I was thinking it was some kind of crazy college Peace Corps thing that Keeler was doing, taking food to a needy family, and taht how they were living was awful, but all I wanted to do was get laid and the gorgeous woman breastfeeding the kid was turning me on and making me feel like a perv. I told Keeler I didn't have time for this Peace Corps crap, that's exactly what I told him, even though I know I should have just choked back the words, even if they'd poisoned me.

Keeler flashed back at me as angry as I ever saw him. "This is my family, man. Bonnie's my woman and this is my family."

He bent over and kissed Bonnie. They looked at each other and she gave him a tiny, surprised, embarrassed smile that was still like someone turning a light on. She gently pulled the baby from around her nipple and Granny reached to take him. Then Bonnie stood up with a beautiful dignity, smoothing her blue dress and trying to ignore me, but not completely able to do it, and enjoying how amazed and knocked out I was that you could find that kind of woman in such a shithole. Then she went with Keeler around the corner into another room. They lit a candle. I looked at Granny, who had given the baby a Pop-Tart to gnaw on. I wanted to get the hell out of there to avoid Keeler throwing any more guilt on me, but I figured that one Americano trying to get back to the main drag by himself might be tough with all the stew bums around.

Then I heard them, Keeler and Bonnie, banging away in the other room, both of them moaning and groaning, but most of all that beautiful *thuk-thuk-thuk* sound of the mamba filling the joyhole. Just thinking of a woman like Bonnie getting the snot banged out of her was enough to give me a stiffy right there in front of old blind granny and the baby. Fucking Keeler! I'd ditched him and look what he'd come up with while I was getting stupid drunk over Linzi. I wanted to go around there with him banging her and say Fuck you, pal, I'm out of here, and have fun taking care of the whole family—Granny, the kid, One Arm, whoever he is. But I couldn't do it, I didn't know what I'd do if I saw him getting laid with me so hard up. I might have beat his ass and taken her away from him. Bonnie was that gorgeous.

All of that finally made me mad enough to get out of there, fight every bum in Shit City on the way back down to Magsaysay if I had to. I charged out through the doorway and bumped against the one-armed guy. He fell down and flopped on the ground and then acted like he was having a hard time getting up. I wasn't going to help him at first, but then I heard him crying like he was hurt. That took all the juice out of me, and I had to go back. I was trying to pull him up by his arm when out of nowhere these lights, big floodlights, blazed on all over Shit City. Then Filipinos in military or cop-blue uniforms were running all around us, clutching machine guns and talking in low, hard voices like it was a drug raid.

I was scared shitless, I thought it really was a drug raid, that Keeler, the college-puke druggie, had gone up there to buy his stash from the bums and had hooked up with Bonnie along the way. It flashed on me how the cops were probably going to throw me into a little bamboo cage for twenty years and feed me fish heads and rice through the bars. Most of the cops were on my left, so I turned right to run. I saw that they had gotten a hold of One Arm and were yanking him around with surgical gloves on their hands. One Arm fell down again and the cops dog-piled on top of him. The cops still standing had their machine guns trained on One Arm like he was a murderer. When I thought they were going to start blazing away on him, this pathetic one-armed guy, I stopped dead and yelled at them, "Holy shit! Don't shoot him! Don't shoot!"

Two cops came up and shoved me back, clutching their guns sideways and up around their chins so that all I could see was their eyes. I was trying to hold my ground and watch between them to make sure the other bastards didn't kill One Arm when one of my cops brought the butt of his gun up on my temple and tried to turn my head away. I grabbed the butt and pushed it down on him so that the barrel hit him in the face. It was a stupid thing to do, but who the fuck did they think they were, doing that to an American who was just trying to make sure they didn't kill a pathetic one-armed guy? Then the partner of the cop I had hit in the face with the barrel swung his gun butt down into into my side. He knocked the wind out of me, but in the middle of sliding down to my knees and gasping for air, I was stabbed by this knife-pain in my side, like he'd also broken a rib or two. The pain was so bad that I couldn't even stay up on my knees. I rolled over onto the dirt clutching my side.

Then I heard Keeler roaring. I had sat up, and was holding my side and trying to breath through the pain. I looked up and saw a bunch of cops locked on Keeler's arms and dragging him out of the shell in his skivvies. The fight he was putting up made me feel useless. Then the cops must have smacked him hard, knocked him out or something, because he stopped suddenly right in the middle of yelling. They threw him down next to me and he hit the dirt and slithered around. I heard people whimpering behind me and I turned around and saw Bonnie moving in the middle of all these cops, holding her baby and kind of crouched down to protect it, her beautiful face all seized up and crying at how her whole world, that shitty, awful world, had been turned upside down.

I couldn't do squat to help her. I was just trying to figure out how to breathe with that broken sword of a rib sliding around inside me. I kept figuring that the cops would drag us away next, take us to those bamboo cages and tell the Navy we'd been busted for drugs. But they all left, and when it finally felt like they'd really gone I started talking to Keeler to see how he was, telling him we had to get out of there. He was laid out flat on his stomach and didn't answer me. I thought he was really hurt. The cops had left on a couple of floodlights and dust they'd kicked up was still floating in the air so thick that I wondered how I could breathe without choking. I crawled over to where I could see Keeler's face. His eyes were wide open and at first I thought he was dead, and that made me forget the pain and stand up, because I'd never been around a dead person, not even at a funeral. But then Keeler blinked. I'd never felt so relieved in my whole life, it was like maybe I'd been dead myself. The cracked-rib pain didn't bother me for a while after that.

But it was hell trying to get Keeler up on his feet and going. He acted like he wanted to be dead, with Bonnie gone. He kept saying her name whenever I told him how our asses were going to be grass even if the cops didn't come back, because I could still see some bums sliding around the shells out of the light with these hungry looks on their faces, like they were trying to see if we were hurting enough for them to take us. Why the fuck hadn't the cops dragged them away?

I got so mad at Keeler for not wanting to get out of there that I started to act like I was leaving without him. "I'm not getting killed up here for you being mixed up in some drug deal," I told him.

That brought him all the way up like a rocket and he grabbed me by the collar with both hands. I hurt too bad to fight back much, so all I could do in the end was glare at his face from four inches away, like he'd have to kill me if he didn't want me coming after him when my rib healed. Then he knew I was hurt, but it didn't stop him from starting to yell at me with wet eyes and his hot breath and spit spraying all over my face. I went blank when I put together what he was saying.

"The cops said they were lepers, man! That's why they took them away with those gloves on their hands. They told me they're taking them to this fucking island where the lepers go."

"Shit." I couldn't hold the word *leper* anywhere near a woman as gorgeous as Bonnie. But finally I asked Keeler, "How'd you... meet her?"

"They needed me." Keeler's eyes wandered off over my shoulder. "Bonnie was standing in front of this dusty little food shop down in town looking at stuff in the window. Everything else... everybody else was moving fast, they were walking along past her or going in or out of the shop. But she was just stopped in the middle of them. I stopped to talk to her and she didn't want to for a while, like she was embarrassed, but then she said she wanted to buy some of the canned milk that was in the window. She didn't say she didn't have the money, but I knew, man, I knew. I bought some cans for her and followed her back up. Here."

Keeler let go of me and I slid down to my knees and that rib must have speared my heart, it hurt so bad. I don't know how long I was on the ground, but after the pain had laid down a bit I told him that he'd done the right thing for Bonnie, even though I couldn't help thinking about how his damn mamba was probably going to fall off from her having leprosy.

Keeler didn't answer, he just went back into the shell and walked around. He was limping when he came out, like the foot was really bothering him again. "She should have told me," he said. "I wouldn't have cared." He stared at me. "I wouldn't have fucking cared!"

Long story short, we finally made it out of there. We started out walking with me in the worst shape, walking real slow to keep that rib from sticking through my chest. But after a while Keeler was complaining like hell about his foot. By the time we were close to the main drag again he could hardly walk. He had to loop his arm around my neck to hold himself up until a jeepney picked us up out on Magsaysay.

Captain Crawford put Keeler back in sick bay the next day. Even though Keeler had told me he was going to get out and find Bonnie, wherever she was, he never made it off the Connie again. Then he started reading Bertrand Russell again down on the ward. One day, when we were still in the PI, I asked him if Crawford was going to let him out before we got underway. Keeler set his book down on his chest and stared at me. "You know what, Powers?" he said to me. "You're a real ignorant fuck." Then he went back to reading.

That was the last time I saw him. A week later the Nav flew him back to the States for a medical discharge.

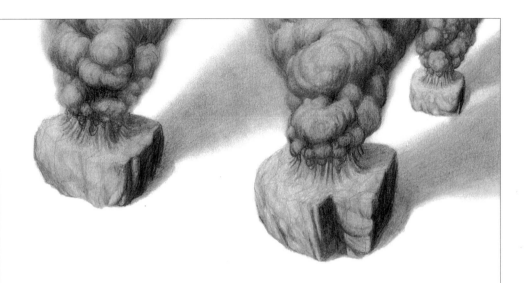

# HADRIAN'S WALL

*by* JIM SHEPARD

WHO HASN'T HEARD by now of that long chain of events, from the invasion by the Emperor Claudius to the revolt of Boudica and the Iceni in the reign of Nero to the seven campaigning seasons of Agricola, which moved our presence ever northward to where it stands today? From the beginning, information on our campaigns has never ceased being gathered from all parts of the province, so it's easy to see how historians and scribes of the generation before me have extended the subject's horizons.

In my father's day, before my morning lessons began, I would recite for my tutor the story of the way the son of all deified emperors, the Emperor Caesar Trajan Hadrian Augustus, on whom the necessity of keeping the empire within its limits had been laid bestowed by divine command, had scattered the Britons and recoverd the province of Brittania and added a frontier between either shore of Ocean for eighty miles. The army of the province built the wall under the direction of Aulus Platorius Nepos, Propraetorian Legate of Augustus.

I would finish our lesson by reminding my tutor that my father had worked on that wall, and my tutor would remind me that I had already reminded him.

The line chosen for the wall lay a little to the north of an existing line of forts along the Stanegate, the northernmost road. The wall was composed of three separate defensive features: the first a ditch to the north, the second a wide, stone curtain-wall with turrets, milecastles, and forts strung along its length, and the third a large earthwork to the south. Their construction took three legions five years.

I have memories of playing in freshly dug material from the bottom of the ditch. I found worms.

The ditch is V-shaped, with a square-cut ankle-breaker channel at the bottom. Material from the ditch was thrown to the north of it during construction to form a mound that would further expose the attacking enemy. The turrets, milecastles, and forts were built with the wall serving as their north faces. Double-portal gates placed front and rear at the milecastles and forts provide the only ways through.

The countryside where we're stationed is naked and windswept. The grass on the long ridges is thin and sere. Sparse rushes accentuate the hollows and give shelter to small gray birds.

The milecastles are situated at intervals of a mile, and between them, the turrets, each in sight of its neighbor, ensure mutual protection and total surveillance. The forts are separated by the distance that can be marched in half a day.

Here then is the aggregate strength of the Twentieth Cohort of Tungrians whose commander is Julius Verecundus: 752 men, including 6 centurions, of which 46 have been detached for service as guards with the governor of the province, under the leadership of Ferox, legate of the Ninth Legion. Of which 337 with 2 centurions have been detached for temporary service at Coria. Of which 45 with 1 centurion are in garrison in a milecastle six miles to the west. Of which 31 are unfit for service, comprising 15 sick, 6 wounded, and 10 suffering from inflammation of the eyes. Leaving 293 with 3 centurions present and fit for active service.

I am Felicius Victor, son of the centurion Annius Equester, and I serve in the Twentieth Cohort as scribe for special services for the administration of the entire legion. All day, every day, I'm sad. Over the heather the wet wind blows continuously. The rain comes pattering out of the sky. My bowels fail me regularly and my barracksmates come and go on the bench of our latrine while I huddle there on the cold stone. In the days before his constant visits, my father signed each of his letters *Now in whatever way you wish, fulfill what I expect of you.*

My messmates torment me with pranks. Most recently they sent off four great boxes of papyrus and birch bark for which I'm responsible in two wagonloads of hides bound for Isurium. I would have gone to get them back by now except that I do not care to injure the animals while the roads are bad. My only friend is my own counsel, kept in this Account. I enter what I can at day's end while the others play at Twelve Points and Robber-Soldiers. I sit on my clerk's stool scratching and scratching at numbers, while even over the wind the bone-click of dice in the hollow of the dice box clatters and plocks from the barracks. Winners shout their good fortune. Field mice peer in at me before continuing on their way.

Our unit was raised in Gallia Belgica according to the time-honored logic concerning auxiliaries that local loyalties are less dangerous when the unit's not allowed to serve in its native region. Since spring, sickness and nuisance raids have forced the brigading of different cohorts together to keep ourselves at fighting muster.

Scattered tribes from the north appear on the crests of the low hills opposite us and try to puzzle out our dispositions. The wind whips through what little clothing they wear. It looks like they have muddy flags between their legs. We call them *Brittunculi*, or "filthy little Britons."

Even with their spies they don't fully grasp how many of the turrets and milegates go undermanned. Periodically our detachments stream swiftly through the sparsely guarded gates and we misleadingly exhibit strength in numbers.

The governor of our province has characterized us as shepherds guarding the flock of empire. During punitive raids all males capable of bearing arms are butchered. Women and children are caravanned to the rear as slaves. Those elderly who don't attempt to interfere are beaten and robbed. Occasionally their homes are torched.

Everyone in our cohort misses our homeland except me. I would have been a goat in a sheep pen there, and here I contribute so little to our martial spirit that my barracks nickname is Porridge. When with some peevishness I asked why, I was dangled over a well until I agreed that Porridge was a superior name.

Every man is given a daily ration of barley. When things are going badly and there's nothing else about to eat and no time to bake flatbread, we grind it up to make a porridge.

I was a firebrand as a brat, a world-beater. I was rambunctious. I was always losing a tooth to someone's fist. My father was then an auxilia conscripted in his twenty-first year in Tungria. Later, after his twenty-five-year discharge, he was granted citizenship and the privilege of the *tria nomina*—forename, family name, and surname. I was born in the settlement beside the cavalry fort at Cilurnum. My mother worked in a gambling establishment with an inscription above the door that read DRINK, HAVE SEX, AND WASH. My father called Cilurnum a roaring, rioting, cock-fighting, wolf-baiting, horse-riding town, and admired the cavalry. My mother became his camp wife, and gave him three children: a sickly girl who died at birth, Chrauttius, and me. Chrauttius was older and stronger and beat me regularly until he died of pinkeye before coming of age. Our father was on a punitive raid against the Caledonii when it happened. He returned with a great suppurating wound across his bicep and had a fever for three days. When my mother wasn't at work in the gambling establishment, she attended to him with an affectionate irritation. She dressed and bound his wound with such vigor that neighbors were required to hold him down while she flushed the cut with alcohol. His bellows filled our ears. When he was recovered he brooded about his elder son. "Look at him," he said to my mother, indicating me.

"Look at him yourself," she told him back.

He favored a particular way of being pleasured that required someone to hold his legs down while the woman sat astride him. Usually my mother's sister assisted but during his fever she feared for her own children so I was conscripted to sit on his knees. I'd been on the earth for eight summers at that point, and I was frightened. At first I faced my mother, but when she asked me to turn the other way, I held my father's ankles and pitched and bucked before he kicked me onto the floor.

At the start of my eighteenth summer I armed myself with a letter of introduction from him to one of his friends still serving with the Tungrian cohort. My father's command of the language was by no means perfect, and since my mother had had the foresight to secure me a tutor for Latin and figures, I helped him with it. *Annius to Priscus, his old messmate, greetings.*

*I recommend to you a worthy man...* and so on. I've since read thousands.

I then presented myself for my interview held on the authority of the governor. Though I had no citizenship, an exception was made for the son of a serving soldier, and I was given the domicile *castris* and enrolled in the tribe of *Pollia*. Three different examiners were required to sign off on a provisional acceptance before I received my advance of pay and was posted to my unit. Attention was paid to my height, physical capacity, and mental alertness, and especially my skill in writing and arithmetic. A number of offices in the legion required men of good education, since the details of duties, parade states, and pay were entered daily in the ledgers, with as much care, I was told, as were revenue records by the civil authorities.

Thus I was posted to my century, and my name entered on the rolls. I trained for two summers in marching, physical stamina, swimming, weapons, and field-service, so that when I was finished I might sit at my stool and generate mounds of papyrus and birch-bark, like an insanely busy and ceaselessly twitching insect.

I have a cold in my nose.

We're so undermanned that during outbreaks of additional sickness, detachments from the Ninth Legion are dispatched for short periods to reinforce our windblown little tract. And there are other auxilaries manning the wall on either side of us. Asturians, Batavians, and Sabines to our east, and Frisiavones, Dalmatians, and Nervii to the west.

My father's agitating to be put back on active duty. He's discovered the considerable difference between the standard of living possible on a officer's pay as opposed to a veteran's retirement pension. He's tried to grow figs and sweet chestnuts on his little farm, with a spectacular lack of success. He claims he's as healthy as ever, and beats his chest with his fist and forearm to prove it. He's not. The recruiting officers laugh in his face. Old friends beg to be left alone. He's asked me to intercede for him, as he interceded for me. He believes I have special influence with the garrison commander. "Oh, let him join up and march around until he falls over," my mother tells me, exasperated.

Every day he rides his little wagon four miles each way to visit my clerk's stool and inquire about his marching orders. The last phrase is his little joke. It's not clear to me when he acquired his sense of humor. Even when the weather is inclement he presents himself, soaked and shivering, with his same crooked smile. His arms and chest have been diminished by age. "This is my son," he tells the other clerk each day: another joke. "Who? This man?" the other clerk answers, each time. There's never anyone else in our little chamber.

Sometimes I've gone to the latrine and he waits, silent, while the other clerk labors.

Upon hearing that I still haven't spoken to the garrison commander, he'll stand about, warming himself at our peat fire while we continue our work. Each time he speaks, he refashions his irritation into patience. "I've brought you sandals," he might say after a while. Or, "Your mother sends regards."

"Your bowels never worked well," he'll commiserate, if I've been gone an especially long time.

On a particularly filthy spring day, dark with rain, he's in no hurry to head home. Streams of mud slurry past our door. The occasional messenger splashes by; otherwise, everyone but the wall sentries is under cover. The peat fire barely warms itself. The other clerk and I continually blow on our hands, and the papyrus cracks from the chill if one presses too hard. While I work surreptitiously on a letter to the supplymaster in Isurium, asking for our boxes of letter material back, my father recounts for us bits of his experiences at work on the wall. The other clerk gazes at me in silent supplication.

"We're quite a bit behind here," I finally remind my father.

"You think *this* is work?" he says.

"Oh, god," the other clerk mutters. The rain hisses down in wavering sheets.

"I'm just waiting for it to let up," my father explains. He gazes shyly at some wet thatch. He smells faintly of potash. He re-knots a rope cincture at his waist, his knuckles showing signs of the chilblains. His stance is that of someone who sees illness and hard use approaching.

"Were you really there from the very beginning?" I ask. The other clerk looks up at me from his work, his mouth open.

My father doesn't reply. He seems to be spying great sadness somewhere out in the rain.

"Without that wall there'd be Britons on this very spot at this very moment," I point out.

The other clerk gazes around. Water's braiding in at two corners and puddling. Someone's bucket of moldy lentils sits on a shelf. "And they'd be welcome to it," he says.

The wall was begun in the spring of his second year in the service, my father tells us, as the emperor's response to yet another revolt the season before. The emperor had been vexed that the Britons couldn't be kept under control. My father reminds us that it was Domitius Corbulo's adage that the pick and the shovel were the weapons with which to beat the enemy.

"What a wise, wise man was he," the other clerk remarks wearily.

Nepos had come from a governorship of Germania Inferior. Three legions—the Second Augusta, the Sixth Victrix Pia Fidelis, and the Twentieth Valeria Victrix—had been summoned from their bases and organized into work parties. The complement of each had included surveyors, ditch diggers, architects, roof-tile makers, plumbers, stonecutters, lime burners, and woodcutters. My father had been assigned to the lime burners.

Three hundred men working ten hours a day in good weather extended the wall a sixth of a mile. He worked five years, with the construction season running from April to October, since frosts interfered with the way the mortar set.

The other clerk sighs and my father looks around for the source of the sound.

Everything was harvested locally except iron and lead for clamps and fittings. The lime came from limestone burnt on the spot in kilns at very high temperatures. The proportion of sand to lime in a good mortar mix was three to one for pit-sand and two to one for river sand.

"Now I've written *two to one*," the other clerk moans. He stands from his stool and crushes the square on which he was working.

"Water for the lime and mortar was actually one of the biggest problems," my father goes on. "It was brought in continuously in barrels piled onto gigantic oxcarts. Two entire cohorts were assigned just to the transport of water."

The other clerk and I scratch and scratch at our tablets.

As for the timber, if oak was unavailable, then alder, birch, elm, and hazel were acceptable.

While I work, a memory-vision revisits me from after my brother's death: my father standing on my mother's wrist by way of encouraging her to explain something she'd said.

Locals had been conscripted for the heavy laboring and carting, he tells us, but everyone pitched in when a problem arose. He outlines the difficulties of ditch-digging through boulder clay. Centurions checked the work with ten-foot rods to insure that no one through laziness had dug less than his share, or gone off line.

The rain finally lets up a bit. Our room brightens. A little freshness blows through the damp. My father rubs his forearms and thanks us for our hospitality. The other clerk and I nod at him, and he nods back. He wishes us good fortune for the day. And you as well, the other clerk answers. My father acknowledges the response, flaps out his cloak, cinches it near his neck with a fist, and steps out into the rain. After he's gone a minute or two, it redoubles in force.

On my half-day of rest I make the journey on foot to their little farmstead. When I arrive I discover that my father's gone to visit me. He never keeps track of my rest days. A cold sun is out and my mother entertains me in their little garden. She sets out garlic paste and radishes, damsons and dill. My father's trained vines to grow on anything that will hold them. There's also a small shrine now erected to Viradecthis, set on an altar. It's a crude marble of Minerva that he's altered with a miniature Tungrian headdress.

I ask if he's now participating in the cult. My mother shrugs and says it could be worse. One of her neighbors' sons has come back from his travels a Christian. Worships a fish.

She asks after my health. She recommends goat cheese in porridge for my bowels. She asks after gossip. It always saddens her that I have so little. How did her fierce little wonderboy grow into such a pale little herring?

She smiles and lays a hand on my knee. "You have a good position," she reminds me proudly. And I do.

It would appear from my father's belongings that a campaign is about to begin. His scabbards are neatly arrayed next to his polishing tin. The rest of his kit is spread on a bench to dry in the sun. His marching sandals have been laid out to be reshod with iron studs. A horsefly negotiates one of the studs.

She tells me that periodically he claims that he'll go back to Gallia Belgica, where the climate is more forgiving to both his figs and his aches. Having returned from service in Britain as a retired centurion would make him a large fish in that pond. But he has no friends there, and his family's dead, and there's ill feeling bound to be stirred up by the relatives of a previous wife who died of overwork and exposure.

Besides, there's much that the unit could do with an old hand, she complains he's always telling her. Sentry duty alone: some of the knot-heads taking turns on that wall would miss entire baggage-trains headed their way.

She asks, as she always does, about my daily duties. She enjoys hearing about my exemptions. A soldier's daily duties include muster, training, parades, inspections, sentry duty, cleaning our centurions' kits, latrine and bathhouse duty, firewood and fodder collection. My skills exempt me from the latter four.

She wants to know if my messmates still play their tricks on me. I tell her they don't, and that they haven't in a long while. I regret having told her in the first place.

When I leave she presents me with a wool tunic with woven decorations. I wear it on the walk back.

During training, recruits who failed to reach an adequate standard with a particular weapon received their rations in barley instead of wheat, the wheat ration not restored until they demonstrated proficiency. While I was quickly adequate with the sword, I was not with the pilum and could hit nothing no matter how close I brought myself to the target. Even my father tried to take a hand in the training. My instructor called me the most hopeless sparrow he'd ever seen when it came to missile weapons. For three weeks I ate only barley, and have had the shits ever since. On the one and only raid in which I've taken part, I threw my pilum immediately, to get it over with. It stuck in a cattle pen.

Night falls on the long trek back to the barracks. I strike out across the countryside, following the river instead of the road, the sparse grasses thrashing lightly at my ankles. At a bend I stop to drink like a dog on all fours and hear the rattle-trap of my father's little wagon heading toward the bridge above me. When he crosses it his head bobs against the night sky. He's singing one of his old unit's songs. He's guiding himself by the light of the moon. It takes him a long while to disappear down the road.

*    *    *

By any standards, our army is one of the most economical institutions ever invented. The effective reduction and domination of vast tracts of frontier by what amounts to no more than a few thousand men requires an efficiency of communication that enables the strategic occupation of key points in networks of roads and forts. Without runners we have only watchfires, and without scribes we have no runners.

In my isolation and sadness I've continued my history of our time here. So that I might have posterity as a companion, as well.

More rain. Our feet have not been warm for two weeks. We are each and every one of us preoccupied with food. We trade bacon lard, hard biscuits, salt, sour wine, and wheat. When it's available, we trade meat: ox, sheep, pig, goat, roe deer, boar, hare, and fowl. We trade local fruit and vegetables. Barley, bean, dill, coriander, poppy, hazelnut, raspberry, bramble, strawberry, bilberry, celery. Apples, pears, cherries, grapes, elderberries, damsons and pomegranates, sweet chestnuts, walnuts and beechnuts. Cabbages, broad beans, horse beans, radishes, garlic, and lentils. Each group of messmates has its own shared salt, vinegar, honey, and fish sauces. Eight men to a table, with one taking on the cooking for all. On the days I cook, I'm spoken to. On the days I don't, I'm not. The other clerk runs a gambling pool and is therefore more accepted.

The muster reports worsen with the rain. Eleven additional men are down with roundworm. One of the granaries turns out to be contaminated with weevils.

For two nights one of the turrets—off on its own on a lonely outcropping here at the world's end, the wall running out into the blackness on each side—contains only one garrisoned sentry. No one else can be spared. He's instructed to light torches and knock about on both floors, to speak every so often as though carrying on a conversation.

It's on this basis that one might answer the puzzling question: how is it that our occupation can be so successful with so few troops? The military presence is by such methods made to seem stronger and more pervasive than it actually is. We remind ourselves that our detachments can appear swiftly, our cavalry forts never far away.

This tactic could also be understood to illuminate the relationship between the core of the empire and its periphery. Rome has conquered the world by turning brother against brother, father against son; the empire's outer borders can be controlled and organized using troops raised from areas that have just themselves been peripheral. Frontiers absorbed and then flung outward against newer frontiers. Spaniards used to conquer Gaul, Gauls to conquer Tungrians, Tungrians to conquer Britain. That's been Rome's genius all along: turning brother against brother and father against son. Since what could have been easier than that?

Peace on a frontier, I've come to suspect, is always relative. For the past two years of my service our units have devoted their time between small punitive raids to preventing livestock-rustling and showing the flag. The last few days we've noted our scouts—lightly armed auxiliaries in fast-horsed little detachments—pounding in and out of our sally ports at all hours. Rumors have begun to fly around the barracks. Having no friends, I hear none of them. When I ask at the evening meal, having cooked dinner, I'm told that the Britons are after our porridge.

My night sentry duty comes around. I watch it creep toward me on the duty lists the other clerk and I update each morning so no one's unjustly burdened or given exemption. The night my turn arrives it's moonless. The three companions listed to serve with me are all laid low with whipworm.

At the appointed hour I return to the barracks to don my mail shirt and scabbard. As I'm heading out with my helmet under my arm, one of my messmates calls wearily from across the room, "That's mine." At the duty barracks I'm handed a lantern that barely lights my feet and a small fasces with which to start the warning fire. All of this goes in a sack slung over my shoulder on a short pole which I'll carry the mile and a half through the dark along the wall to the turret. Before I leave, the duty officer ties to the back of my scabbard a rawhide lead with two old hobnailed sandals on the end of it, so I'll sound like a relieving party and not a lone sentry.

"Talk," he advises as I step out into the night. "Bang a few things together."

The flagstone paving along the wall's battlement is silver in the starlight. With the extra sandals and my kit sack I sound like a junk dealer clanking along through the darkness. Every so often I stop to listen. Night sounds reverberate around the hills.

I'm relieving a pair of men. Neither seems happy to see me. They leave me an upper story lit by torches. Two pila with rusted striking blades stand in a corner. A few old cloaks hang on pegs over some battered oval shields. A mouse skitters from one of the shields to the opposite doorway. There's an open hearth for heat in the story below. Up here two windows afford a view but with the glare from the torches I'm better off observing from outside. With the moonlessness I won't have much way of tracking time.

After a few minutes I find I haven't the heart to make noise or clatter about. I untie the rawhide lead with the sandals. I don't bother with the hearth and in a short time the lower story goes dark. The upper still has its two torches and is nicely dry though a cold breeze comes through the windows. I alternate time on the wall and time inside. It takes minutes to get used to seeing by starlight when I go back out.

Some rocks fall and roll somewhere off in the distance. I keep watch for any movement in that direction for some minutes, without success.

My father liked to refer to himself as stag-hearted. He was speaking principally of his stamina on foot and with women. "Do you miss your brother?" he asked me on one of those winter fortnights he spent hanging about the place. It was only a few years after my brother's death. I still wasn't big enough to hold the weight of my father's sword at arm's length.

I remember I shook my head. I remember he was unsurprised. I remember that some time later my mother entered the room and asked us what was wrong now.

"We're mournful about his brother," my father finally told her.

He was such a surprising brother, I always think, with his strange temper and his gifts for cruelty and whittling and his fascination with divination. He carved me an entire armored galley with a working anchor. He predicted his own death and told me I'd recognize the signs of mine when it was imminent. I was never greatly angered by his beatings but once became so enraged by something I can't fully remember now, involving a lie he told our mother, that I prayed for the sickness which later came and killed him.

"I prayed for you to get sick," I told him on his deathbed. We were alone and his eyes were running so that he could barely see. The pallet around his head was yellow with the discharge. He returned my look with amusement, as if to say, Of course.

Halfway through the night a bird's shriek startles me. I chew a hard biscuit to keep myself alert. The rain's a light mist and I can smell something fresh. My mother's wool tunic is heavy and wet under the mail.

When I'm in the upper story taking a drink, a sound I thought was the water ladle continues for a moment when I hold the ladle still in its tin bucket. The sound's from outside. I wait and then ease out the door and stay down behind the embrasure to listen and allow my eyes to adjust. I hold a hand out in the starlight to see if it's steady. The closest milecastle is a point of light over a roll of hills. My heart's pitching around in its little cage.

Barely audible and musical clinks of metal on stone extend off to my left down below. No other sounds.

The watchfire bundle is inside to prevent its becoming damp. In the event of danger it's to be dumped into a roofed and perforated iron urn mounted on the outer turret wall and open-faced in the direction of the milecastle. The bundle's soaked in tar to light instantly. The watchfire requires the certainty of an actual raid, and not just a reconnaissance. You don't get a troop horse up in the middle of the night for a few boys playing about on dares.

There's the faint whiplike sound of a scaling rope off in the darkness away from the turret. When I raise my head incrementally to see over the stone lip of the embrasure, I have the impression that a series of moving objects have just stopped. I squint, then widen my eyes. I'm breathing into the stone. After a moment, pieces of the darkness detach and move forward.

When I wheel and shove open the turret door a face, bulge-eyed, smash-toothed, smeared with black and brown and blue, lunges at me and misses, and a boy pitches off the wall and into the darkness below with a shriek.

Behind him in the turret, shadows sweep the cloak pegs between me and my watchfire. A hand snatches up my sword.

So I jump, the impact rattling my teeth when I land. When I get to my feet, something hits me flush in the face.

On the ground I hear two more muffled blows, though I don't seem to feel them. I'm face down. Pain pierces inward from any mouth movement and teeth loll and slip atop my tongue. I'm kicked around. When my septum contacts the turf a drunkenness of agony flashes from ear to ear.

When it recedes there are harsh muted sounds. One of my ears fills with liquid. There's commotion for a while, and then it's gone. In the silence that follows I make out the agitated murmur of the detachment mustering and then setting out.

Fluids pour across my eyes. Lifting my head causes spiralling shapes to arrive and depart. I test various aspects of the pain with various movements. At some point, silently weeping, I stop registering sensations.

In the morning I discover they'd been pouring over the wall on both sides of me, the knotted ropes trailing down like vines. Everyone is gone. Smoke is already high in the sky from both the milecastle and the fort. When I stand I teeter. When I look about me only one eye is working. The boy from the turret door is dead not far from me, having landed on rock. His weapon is still beside him, suggesting he was overlooked.

The rain's stopped and the sun's out. My mother's wool tunic is encrusted and stiff. I walk the wall, throwing back over those ropes closest to my turret, blearily making my dereliction of duty less grotesque. It requires a few hours to walk across the heather past the milecastle, and then on to the fort. I can't move my jaw and presume it's broken. Two of the fort's walls have been breached but apparently the attack was repulsed. Legionaries and auxiliaries are already at work on a temporary timber rampart. Minor officers are shouting and cursing. The Brittunculi bodies are being dragged into piles. The Tungrians' bodies probably have already been rolled onto pallets and carried into the fort.

My head is bound. A headache doesn't allow me to raise it. My first two days are spent in the infirmary. My assumption about my jaw turns out to be correct. I ask if my eye will be saved and I'm told that that's a good question. A vinegar-and-mustard poultice is applied. Two messmates come by to visit a third dying from a stomach wound. They regard me with contempt, tinged with pity. Over the course of a day I drink a little water. My father visits once while I'm asleep, I'm informed. I ask after those I know. The clerk who shared my little room died of burns from the barracks fire. He survived the night but not the morning. Somehow the location of the raid was a complete surprise, despite the rumors.

It takes all of six days for four cohorts of the Ninth Legion, with its contingents of light and heavy horse, supported by two of the tattered cohorts of the Tungrians, to prepare its response. The Romans suffer casualties as though no one else ever has. There are no speeches, no exhortations, among either the legions or the auxiliaries. The barracks ground is noisy only with industry. The Romans, hastily camped within our walls, go about their business as if sworn to silence and as if only butchery will allow them to speak.

I live on a little porridge, sipped through a straw. No one comments on the joke. On the fifth day I report my ready status to my muster officer. He looks me up and down before moving his attention to other business. "All right, then," he says.

On the sixth day of our muster my father appears over my pallet, the first thing I see when I wake in the barracks. He's wearing his decorations on a harness over his mail and the horsehair crest of his helmet sets some of our kitchenware, hanging from the rafters, to rocking. He's called himself up to active duty and no one's seen fit to argue with him.

It's only barely light. He tells me he's glad for my health and my mother sends her regards and good wishes and that he'll see me outside.

At the third trumpet signal the stragglers rush to take their positions in the ranks. A great quiet falls over the assembled units, and the sun peeks across the top of the east parapet. The herald standing to the right of a general we've never seen before asks three times in the formal manner whether we are ready for war. Three times we shout, *We are ready*.

We march all day, our advance covered by cavalry. The sun moves from astride our right shoulder to astride our left. By nightfall we've arrived at a large settlement with shallow earthen embankments and rickety palisades. Are these the men, or the families of the men, responsible for the raid? None of us care.

Their men are mustering themselves hurriedly into battle order before the settlement, unwilling to wait for the siege. They wear long trousers and have animals painted on their bare chests: Caledonii. Is this their tribal territory? I have no idea.

We are drawn up on the legion's left. At the crucial time, we know, the cavalry will appear from behind the settlement, sealing the matter. On this day with my father somewhere lost in the melee off to my right, we will all of us together become the avenging right arm of the Empire. We will execute what will be reported back to the provincial capital as a successful punitive raid. I will myself record the chronicle with my one good eye. I will write, *When we broke through the walls and into the settlement we killed every living thing. The women, the children, the dogs, the goats were cut in half and dismembered. While the killing was at its height pillaging was forbidden. When the killing was ended the trumpets sounded the recall. Individuals were selected from each maniple to carry out the pillaging. The rest of the force remained alert to a counterattack from beyond the settlement. The settlement was put to the torch. The settlement was razed to the ground. The building stones were scattered. The fields were sown with salt.* My comrades-in-arms will think no more of me than before. My father and I will continue to probe and distress our threadbare connections. And what my mother will say about her marriage, weeping with bitterness in a sun-suffused haze a full summer later, will bring back to me my last view of the site after the Twentieth Tungrians and the Ninth Legion had finished with it, pecked over by crows and studded with the occasional shattered pilum: "We honor nothing by being the way we are. We make a desolation and we call it peace."

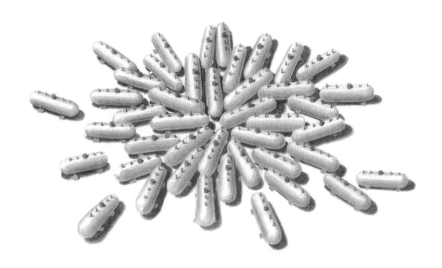

# PIGS IN SPACE

*by* CLAIRE LIGHT

FROM WHERE I SIT, strapped down in this seat, I can see most of the Earth through the porthole. Daryl has on his Sunday face: part complacency, part celebration, no calculation. He's bouncing, naked, hands free, around the quarters, singing his Making the Omelette Song. The Making the Omelette Song is pretty much the same as the Strap on the Toilet Song or the Mix the Slurry Song or the Wait for the Rations Song: it comprises two notes, as many words as the title, and endless repetition.

In the midst of Daryl's endless singing I am playing a game of my own: nod your head up and down, up and down, fast. Now shake it back and forth, back and forth. If you go fast enough, the truncated marble of the Earth blurs to white. Now blink rapidly and the white clears into high-contrast white and blue splotches and blotches. The splotches and blotches seem to get bigger every day, although we aren't approaching rapidly enough to see a daily difference. Now hold a fixed stare without blinking, until your eyes dry out. At some point in all of this, the marble loses its familiarity, an alien thumbnail without a thumb, brighter than reality and approaching like the end of a dream.

I blink and shake and nod while Daryl collects four eggs from stasis storage, a pat of butter, and a pan. We should eject everything in stasis storage and shut it down. It burns two units per hour. But I don't say anything. He swoops into the kitchen-area he's rigged—one hundred units worth of materials—and pulls the switch. A hiss and a suck and his feet hit the ground. A simultaneous tiny skittering sound from the entire floor in a perfect radius of two feet around him. He threw dry semolina into the air an hour ago to punctuate the Semolina Song. It ricocheted off the walls for several minutes before becoming inert all over the quarters. Some if it will be in my covers when I get in tonight. Something my mother used to say about attractive young men when I was very small that I never understood back then: "He can eat crackers in my bed anytime!" Even in the golden past, was there always some small price to pay for the kind of thing we did last night?

Fifteen units cooking semolina. Should leave the semolina in dry storage. Should really eject the semolina. Should never have brought semolina in the first place. But I don't say anything. I keep expecting to see semolina sticking to Daryl's broad moon face and clustering around his opaque eyes. I expect that he generates his own small gravity field out here and that he will inevitably draw the results of his mistakes and his scattering of spirits back to himself.

He wastes gas turning on the gravity, heating the skillet, reconstituting the water, boiling it. Fifteen units per minute on his jury-rigged range. Should at least use the cooker. Five units per minute in the cooker. He says it doesn't taste the same in the cooker, live a little. Should eject the cooker when he's not looking, along with the pan and the range. He uses butter from stasis storage to cook with. Should eject everything in stasis storage when he's not looking.

Barring any further accidents—I've done and redone the figures every week for ninety weeks now—barring accidents, these once-a-week skillet fests will deliver us back to the company's door when the two-year cycle is through with our pigs nearly dead, our tanks empty, and our fuel drained to the last drop. Without batting an eyelash, the manager will say "good job" tonelessly, hand us credit scrip and a document of our cancelled indenture, and we'll be free to sign up for another round or kiss our futures goodbye. It's a game, an experiment for them, but not a game that they play against us. They play the game against chance and their own skill in choosing crew members. We're just the players, with no players in reserve. If we fuck ourselves up, they'll retrieve the data and the cattle and put the information toward the next cycle. They'll inform our families and hand over the bodies, or in my case, cremate and recycle. If we fuck ourselves up, we're fucked.

I put that at the bottom of every fuel inventory I've written for the past nine months, which Daryl never reads. It says, "Please God, no more or we're fucked." It's intended as a reminder to myself. I whisper to myself on the long week's approach to Saturday when I do the fuel inventory, "No more or we're fucked." I tell myself to just try, for one week, to make up some units. And every Saturday night, when I hear him coming to me, I tell myself to tell him no. Even once a week is too much; he takes too much for granted; I have to think for us both. No more or we're fucked. And every Sunday, he wakes up singing and I say nothing.

Eggs don't smell like anything, but when they hit the butter with that fractured smack, the browning-butter smell changes and slicks the air. My mouth doesn't water, my eyes do. The dry gold dust of the air we make out here becomes morning all at once, the morning of our week: wet, moist, greasy, and full of things that still need to be done. The smell of things comes close for a moment on plastic plates and cold forks. I walk into Daryl's circle of gravity and am sucked down. The smack on the soles of my feet is better than coffee. We eat standing in a two-foot radius, warmed by each other's bodies.

Less than a half hour later, I'm suited up and in the pigpen. The molded interior is a nonreflective white that glares off our masks but doesn't blind us. Near the entrance is what I call the pigfirmary, a small room with a transparent door so that Daryl can isolate a sick pig but I can still see in. Inside are two pig-sized stasis chambers, one containing the body of Liz, our first herd mother, or rather, containing what remained of Liz's body by the time Daryl reached her that morning. As well as being all-around stupid, the herd is vicious to other sick pigs. Daryl hoped to study Liz's physiology when back on ground to discover what exactly had caused her sudden incapacitating colic when she'd been so consistently healthy before. This colic is a major killer of higher-bred pigs and the constant threat hanging over herd mothers' otherwise proverbially healthy heads.

They're bred to produce gas; sometimes it gets trapped in their abdomens and no one knows how, what triggers it, or how to prevent it. Daryl's answer is his new feed, but it's experimental. He was feeding it to Liz, too. Another major waste of units, that stasis chamber. But sick and dead pigs are not things you argue about with Daryl.

Whenever I come in here, I check in with Liz first. It's my way of paying respects and my little fuck you to Porkbella, the second herd mother who replaced Liz. Unlike Liz, who was installed by the company, Porkbella is one of Daryl's own. He designed her and sequenced her DNA himself at the last laboratory he worked at before he was fired. He grew her and birthed her and trained her up from a piglet through adolescence. He made sure she was in top condition when he put her in stasis. He had a stable of six adolescents and seventeen piglets when he signed up for this cycle. He picked Bella, his favorite, to bring. When Liz burst from colic, it only took Bella a week to recover from stasis, and four days to whip the herd into shape. We only lost eleven days of fuel production and she made it up within three months. She significantly improved efficiency, no doubt about it, and significantly encouraged Daryl's profligacy.

Anyone would treat such a pig well, but Daryl loves her with a passion that enclave boys usually reserve for their pet raptors. Not that Bella isn't a predator. He brought his own feed for her, cases full of flat, hand-sized green pellets, using the storage reserved for his extra clothing and books. He insists that if the company had given him storage room enough to bring feed for both pigs, we'd never have lost the first one. He insists that if we could feed it to all the pigs, they'd produce almost as high a yield as the cattle. He insists that efficient feed and care could make up for inefficiency in absolutely everything else. I insist to myself that if he'd used his space as it was meant to be used, we'd never have run out of books, or clothes, and I wouldn't be letting him distract me from saving up units. But I don't say anything.

After paying my respects to Liz, my recent habit is to locate Bella and greet her with a kick. She hates me. She's jealous. I have to watch out for her. She's stopped going for my lifeline; I've foiled her at that too many times. But once, six months ago, she caught me in an explosion in the mint which lost us three hundred units, destroyed my second-to-last suit, and gave me third-degree burns over half my body. Daryl wasted another thousand units regenerating my skin tissue while I was unconscious. An utter waste of units, something he did for himself, not for me, although I'm sure he convinced himself otherwise. He still believes that it was an accident. But I saw the look on her face.

The moment I leave the pigfirmary, she makes a beeline for me, moaning with pig joy as she trots over, the way she does with Daryl. She starts rubbing herself against my legs and I can feel a vague sort of roughness from her bristle through the soft legs of my suit. I am immediately suspicious. Normally she ignores me, and when the shit starts hitting the fan, sometimes literally, she's as far away as she can get. I still don't know how she can tell me from Daryl, unless it's the height difference. With our masks and gloves and suits on, with the anti-odor seals and the shuffle we use to get around in the pens, with glare making our masks opaque from their point of view, we look like the same faceless creature. Daryl says they just know, just the sort of faith-based-belief mumbo-jumbo with which he approaches everything from shoveling pig shit to genetic sequencing.

He spoils Bella to the breaking point. She does her job well and it's a job even Daryl can't do. The herd pigs fight him, even when he's in the pen scratching their backs to a chorus of piggy moans. They've become unmanageable with breeding. He tells me pigs used to be among the smartest of domestic mammals, but no more. Herd pigs are unimaginably stupid. Bred for only one thing, with "unnecessary" characteristics bred out without forethought, they won't work for anyone or anything but a bred, trained herd mother. I know all the stories about the early days of the company, when they sent harvesters out for five years with only one herd mother and the installation would be towed in at the end of the cycle with the depressurized quarters haunted by dessicated human bodies. The herd pigs, minus the herd mother, whose bones would often be found in the rig, would be mostly alive and nearly buried in their own shit.

Bred for intelligence and aggression, a good herd mother like Bella can keep a herd of over three hundred in line. They won't shit without her permission and they eat what and when she orders them to. She lines them up at the food dispenser, cutting out the ones that have displeased her. They eat by her leave, then she trots them in groups of ten to the manure trough exactly forty-five minutes later. They shit by her grace. The herd is like her hive-cum-harem, with her queen bee and sultan. Without her, they're almost too stupid to eat, shit, or even go to sleep. With her, they're a well-oiled, fuel-producing machine. If Daryl butters her up enough, she'll even hit the switch that washes the slurry into the tank. She dances to the beat of the Porkbella Song.

I don't know enough about pig farming to understand the intricacies of Bella management, but she's thriving. I've never seen that pig whole. She's so enormous she can't get far enough away from me in the pen to fit her entire body into the view within the flat front plate of my mask. Her long snout or her hindquarters always end up bending around the peripheral plates. I think of her as permanently bent. As she plays at affection for me this morning, I wonder if she knows our lives depend on her ability to make pigs shit.

I kick her away and enter the tank, holding my breath for a second even though the gas can't penetrate. Bella actually tries to climb in after me and I have to kick her away again. That's twice now. I close and seal the hatch behind me, and immediately the pressure reasserts itself, making it difficult to move through the air. Probably three units lost opening the tank. Bella, strangely, starts bumping the outside of the tank, calling to me. It's a petulant, demanding squeal I know from the times I've been in the pen with Daryl to work and he was ignoring her. I ignore it, too. The slurry, a simple mixture of pig manure and reconstituted water, is a sludge today, not a soup, which means that either the pumps are clogged or the mixers are. Probably the mixers. I just fixed them last week, though. They warned me of this in the training. Wear and tear on machinery is simply higher in space, and near the end of the cycle breakage accelerates and maintenance begins to become a constant issue.

As I clean and scrape, clean and scrape, my mind wanders away. Out here, where away from night and day your senses grow sharp from deprivation and lights, every sound, new smell, or uncommon phrase strikes you with pungency, like oleander in the first summer rain after a long, dry spring. In the thick silence of the tank, my mind's ear returns to what Daryl, smiling ruefully, said before he went off to the pens. I pull my mind back, and clean and scrape. But it escapes again, circling the sound of my name, toying with what "Yayoi" sounds like spoken with an accent, spoken for the first time in months. In his voice "Yayoi" sounds over and over again. Clean and scrape, Yayoi, Yayoi. My mind dances with me, offering this rhythm, like an errant child wanting to distract me with song so it can go examine the forbidden treasure box. I pull it back. It reaches again.

Then I'm standing in the first summer monsoon on ground and I'm thirteen and the rain is purifying me and I look up for the first time into weather, realizing that there's nothing up there but water and pressure. I should be alarmed that I've left the ship in my imagination and returned to ground. I do not permit this, ever. I should be alarmed by Bella's squealing, or by my distance from the fact that I'm knee-deep in disease-ridden slurry and surrounded by toxic, explosive gas. But all I can see is the gray-white sky above me letting fall rain and, out of the corner of my unwary eye, the long-haired boys standing under the eaves of a rare, abandoned house, waiting for me as I raise my arms to the rain and celebrate my freedom from everything. They stand there in a line, five of them, two more than I can handle by myself, slightly bigger than I am now, as will happen when boys start to grow. I can see now, they are not animated by the devil, they are just boys. But, unfortunately, I am a girl.

When the bells sounds for lunch, I am still in the tank. Normally I keep time better. With ten minutes from the bell until the food is dispensed, and only another ten minutes until the food is recycled—I set the limits myself—I can feel lunch coming on by the lurch of my stomach and I'm usually half out of my suit by the time the bell goes off. But today I'm full of omelette and there's something wrong with my mind and with my body. I feel like I've failed in some essential way and I can hardly move at all.

I rush out of the pen into the airlock and try not to hurry cleaning my suit. It doesn't do to rush, ever. That's how accidents happen. Daryl isn't in the quarters when I get there, but I assume that he's at prayer in a corridor somewhere. He's extraordinarily sensitive about some things. He decided it would be better not to force me out of the quarters five times a day, so he finds a spot—a different one each time—to lay his prayer rug and mostly manages to avoid me doing it.

Our food is turning to slush in the dispenser as I leave the corridor, which is weighted during work hours (ten units per hour), and push off into the atmosphere of the weightless quarters. I palm myself forward faster and faster. I can see the two ration cakes disintegrating and I have one minute at most before the sieve opens and the food gets sucked out. I arrive with one hand on the pole, just in time. The blue one, with Daryl's meds, is nearest, but I grab my pink one just before both would've been sucked out. Daryl's cake goes. Two units. My cake is just together enough to hold. It's cold and the gelatinous consistency is breaking down rapidly into liquid. I slurp it fast to get it down before it melts.

I palm over to my porthole seat to digest and strap in to wait for him. I feel like I owe him an explanation for missing his food, although in reality, I don't owe him a damn thing. He owes me for getting his food for him most days. Owes me period. You can tell what kind of family he's from, on ground, someone who thinks prayer is more important than eating because he's never had to choose between the two. Someone who can take for granted that his food will be there when he's finished communing with his god. A long-haired boy, his eaves following him wherever he goes. I never thought that I would stand shelter over someone like him, not willingly. He doesn't understand the game. No, that's not true, he understands the game as a *game*, something to be played, something with no stakes. He thinks we're the players, not the playing pieces. He thinks he has a right to lose. He bounces around out here breathing air wrung out of space dust, air he's hardly earned, playing pig like the god of some pork-eating race.

My mind slips again and I'm ten years old and my mother is standing in a doorway, the doorway to our house, and a man is trying to come in. She says no to him and closes the door. She walks around, barring the windows one by one and rechecking them, finishing by checking the door again. "We'll go now," she says to me. "I've had enough." And I'm afraid, in spite of everything she has said about a better life and about safer neighborhoods and food, food all the time. I go to the window to see if the man is gone and I lean into it to see out into the darkening yard. It's empty, the yard, but I know he's out there and the fear grows in me, knowing this, and grows and grows until I have to shriek from sheer pressure. Instead, I open my eyes.

The distant marble is half cut off in the porthole, just like this morning, but less vivid. Not much time has passed. Daryl is still missing, probably decided to skip lunch. I unstrap and palm over to his locker and pick the lock. I haven't done this in months, but suddenly I need it. I open the cheap, rattling door and the smell of him comes out. He keeps all his torn and worn clothing in here, meaning to sew it back together, but never getting around to it. It's so much easier for us to be naked in the installation and save the fuel it would require to clean our clothes and the energy to mend them. I am so used to the sight of him naked now that it almost doesn't turn me on anymore. I grab a pile of cloth and press it to my face. I could easily go and find him and press him to my face. In fact, I *should* go find him. It's protocol. We're supposed to check in with each other at lunchtime and again at dinner. But after what he said this morning before escaping to his pigs, I can't. If I go to him now, in this bizarre mood, I don't know what I'll say, what I'll do. I'm going to have to let him go, permanently. Thank god we're only here for three more months. I put one of his shirts on, or what used to be a shirt. It hangs off me in rags. Cheap material. I can almost imagine that I'm him, I suddenly smell so much like him.

Thus armed, I go through his locker. I have a ritual here. First I find the family pictures and go through them one by one, counting off his store of family members, so many, all alive and well-fed and cared-for: his father and mother, his two older brothers and three sisters, his wife, his first son, his second son, his daughter. They are all married now, his children, married in adolescence, like he was. He is now a grandfather—he found out right before we launched—a grandfather at thirty-one. It is so strange to me, I still get a delight from it.

There is nothing about his life that is familiar to me, nothing about his background. We didn't move to a traditional enclave like the one he grew up in. We moved to one of the few "open" enclaves that accepted Christian families—or didn't exactly accept them, but didn't ask for proof of religious affiliation with one's application. So we never came into contact with any traditional, wealthy old families like Daryl's. It's hard to understand someone who doesn't know what wealth a family is. And I must close the locker on that.

I am startled awake by the dinner bell and struggle against an incomprehensible restraint to get up. It's a moment before I realize that I'm still strapped to the seat. I unstrap myself. I float over to the dispenser and grasp the pole lightly with one hand. If I inflate my stomach and then blow a puff gently downward, I can rise slowly, a few inches per minute. My hand dragging on the pole slows my progress and stops me after an inch. Inflate. Blow. Rise. Inflate. Blow. Rise.

The dispenser whirrs and spits out two double rations. It's detected the food recycled at lunch and is making up for it. It doesn't always; I just fixed it last week. Thirty units spent testing. Four units each for double rations. It's another endless arrhythmic beat out here—when the food dispenser's sensors go out. I take the food out immediately: Daryl's in my right hand, my own in my left. Daryl would never eat anything I'd touched with my left hand, and for some reason I am unwilling, or unable, to lie to him about such things.

The cakes are firm and oaty and I eat them slowly, in nips, pretending that I'm a pig. A neat pig. They're still warm, and if I hold my breath I can almost imagine myself eating a real oatcake, or, almost, an oatmeal cookie. Little bits crumble onto my lips and then cool and turn to droplets there, that are just beginning to run when I lick them off. Daryl doesn't come. Finally, I put his cakes in a baggie and seal it to the wall over his bunk. He's definitely not coming. Suddenly it occurs to me that there must be an animal down if he's missing two meals. Shit.

I go for the cattle pens, quickly now. My feet smack the weighted floor of the hallway. It hurts. I curse my feet. I curse the gravity. I curse my stupidity in not going after him right after lunch. We've already lost more than our quota of units today. Knowing Daryl, he's probably sitting in a pen mourning a lost cow with the slurry going cold in the tub behind him and a thousand capital units dissipating into the pen air. He has no sense at all.

The whole installation is arranged so that the harvest from the cattle pens—the capital units—never comes under our control at all. We can't convert any capital units into fuel for our own use. They go directly into hull-exterior holding tanks, which explode if tampered with. Only the units from the tanks in the pigpens are for our use. But there'd be nothing to keep us from collecting manure from the cattle pens before it goes into the tank and taking it out to the pig pens and running it through the tank there. So they set the moderator to calculate the number and weight of the cows and amount of their feed, and then estimate a weight and volume of slurry per day. If the slurry falls more than 5 percent below the estimate, the moderator begins to replace it with the harvest from our pigpens, i.e., our fuel. That runs life support, the food dispensers, our own gravity and light. Daryl's lost us up to fifty units at least twice through sheer stupidity. We're already down I don't know how many units today.

The weight warning sounds, dammit. Five seconds later the weight lets go and I lift into the air on a long stride and bump my head against the ceiling. I have to pole all the way to the cattle pens. I'm so certain it's a burst calf that I actually put my cattle gear on without checking the com to see if he's there. He's not in the first pen, nor in the second, though, like an idiot, I run around both calling to him through my mask. Do I have to search through all hundred? I finally calm down and hit the com. He doesn't answer. I hit it again. No answer. It must be a pig down this time.

I don't know why I have to get there. There's nothing I can do. I know what comes next. But in my eagerness I almost forget safety and have to remind myself—I hurry out of my suit (never rush, ever) and pole like a maniac toward the pig pen. I should've gone there first. We can afford to lose a calf. Down into the weighted room, into my suit, boots, gloves, mask, check, calm down, check again. Adjust.

The pen is much as I left it for lunch. I can't distinguish most pigs. Bella is obvious but not the others. Daryl knows every one by name, weight, feeding patterns, and trenchant personality points. I turn into to the pigfirmary and there they are, Bella lying on her side, not squealing but breathing heavily, her abdomen distended, Daryl holding her head on his lap and a scalpel in his hand, his right hand. It's Bella. I almost smile.

I can only hear a low murmuring sound through his mask and mine, but I can tell by the rhythm and the relaxed set of his shoulders and the slight rocking of his upper body that he's praying. By the rhythm of his rocking I can pick up the place—I never learned Arabic but the sounds of the words, so familiar from my school days, the five times a day, the intervention of the word "Allah" every so many syllables—the sounds I can remake with the mouth in my mind, never forming with my lips, ever. I'm struck, with an irony more bitter than usual, by what stereotypes we make: the Christian mechanic, the Muslim shepherd. Only the Muslim is butchering a pig, and the Christian is standing while someone prays, mouthing "Allah" in her mind, eyes wide in the white light with eagerness for what comes next.

Daryl lowers the scalpel and cuts an incision into her abdomen. She is awake but numbed. His hand returns to the incision and cuts another one, this one deeper, just as the blood starts. Her blood is darker than black and runs down to the floor, whitening the room around it, clinging to what gravity there is. It is now the only thing in the room. The third incision breaches the wall of her stomach and the gas is released, deflating her. I move forward to help but Daryl has all his implements within reach. He adds a clotting agent, waits two minutes, then cleans the wound and clamps its lips together and sprays a disinfectant over the whole. Shifting sideways, he lays her head on the floor and moves to mop up the mess.

Daryl turns and sees me then, as I see that his mask is fogged. He must not be able to see too well. I take the gauze from him and finish mopping up. The gauze is made alive by the color. I wipe some of the blood onto my sleeve, then push it into my arm. I almost wish it would penetrate the seal and the blood and gas could reach my skin. The blood is a tear in the pressure of this room, releasing it, leaving emptiness. He returns the scalpel, clamper, and chemicals to the disinfecting bins. Then he goes back to Bella and tries to sit down. I throw the gauze into bio-waste and grab him. I gesture eating. He lets me lead him out.

I have to wash him and take his suit off and then pole us both back to the cabin, dragging him with my right hand while I pole with my left. His dinner is a liquid in its baggie. The sight of it animates him again. He rips it off the wall as I pull the weight in the whole cabin. Ten units. He hits the floor with a thud, dropping the food as he hits. I go to pick it up but he gets there first, tearing the bag open in one corner and sucking it down in one long slurp. The baggie is ruined but tonight seems a night reserved for waste. I let him rest for a while.

"What are her chances?" I ask finally.

"About 20 percent for recovery. She probably can't rejoin the herd."

"Why not?"

He looks at me in surprise. "You saw what they did to Liz before I got to her."

"Can't you grow another?"

"In three months?"

"Can't you herd them yourself?"

He doesn't answer. Stupid question. Stupid. Wake up.

I immediately stand up and check the gauge. Stupid. I know what it says. I sit back down and pull the nearest monitor to me and call up the fuel inventory. We're just where we should be at this point in the cycle without interruption. But we've just been interrupted, permanently. If we turn off the weight everywhere, turn off the lights in the quarters and reduce its air volume, turn off our dispenser and live off of Bella's rations, this three months' loss will still deliver us to the company one and a half months dead. I crunch numbers again, close the quarters, put Daryl and me into the hallway at night. We still fall one month short. I close the hallways, restrict us to a small area near dry storage. It still leaves one week. I put us in suits, attached to the air valve—put us in restraints, buckled to the wall for the next three months. It still leaves three days. Reduce the amount of air. Two days. Reduce again, to the point we might die anyway. One day. I check, I recheck. One day. One day. It's the two pairs of lungs. That puts us over.

Daryl begins to pray. I am shocked. I've never heard prayer before, right in front of me, with no walls or mask to muffle it. I think that he should damned well pray before I realize that it's a prayer of mourning. He's grieving for that pig.

Then the fear grabs me down like into a weighted room. I've never felt such a desire to live before—not since I've been out here. Not since I left the enclave. Never. Going on this cycle always seemed like a step toward death or forgetting. Now the humiliation of what we do, the littleness of Daryl's loves and comforts, my free rein to my paranoia, and the terrible distance from safety, it all suddenly appears as the hair shirt it is. I don't want to die. I don't want to forget. I don't want to wait to live. I want to live now.

I am staring at what remains of the Earth as it sets over the prideful horizon of the ship's hull. I'm naked but I'm not cold yet, even though the temperature of the quarters has dropped since I cut life support down. My body is still warm. Every irony comes to me from a distance, cobwebbed.

I've restricted life support to a small area and programmed it to turn off permanently in twelve hours. By then I'll have rigged a small tank to my suit and will only have to create atmosphere inside it, and I'll still be mobile. I'll liquefy Bella's rations, put them in another tank, and run a tube to my mouth. Food and drink. I've cut gravity entirely—in fact, smashed the gravity controls in the quarters to protect myself from myself, and my learned habit of luxury. I've reprogrammed every control, set every gauge on conserve mode. I've counted and recounted every unit I have. It should be enough. I have a little leeway now. Just enough. I'll have to be careful with that. I need to consider mixing some sedatives in with my food-slurry. It will be a long three months.

Just the thought of it makes me drowsy, but I can't doze off yet. Daryl's body is still floating in the main section of the quarters, the part I've cut out of the atmosphere. There was relatively little blood, but every few minutes I hear a dull, mild pop from a droplet that floats into my little circle of air and explodes from the pressure. My skin is covered with tiny pinpoints of black blood. I'll have to find something absorbent to remove it with. Or maybe I'll just leave it there to be absorbed by my underclothes. I'm concerned about the energy I'll waste collecting and removing the blood, but I'm more worried about how its constant presence will affect my mental state over the next few months. I need to get up now and clean up, remove his body. I'll put it in the pigs' tank, with Bella and Liz. The human body isn't much good for gas, but every little bit helps. I wonder how many units he's good for? Surely no more than thirty.

I made sure there was a second scalpel near to his hand, one the same size as mine. He saw it, but didn't reach for it. I wanted him to leave some scars on me—proof that I had acted in self-defense. I wanted the opportunity to die fighting, too. But he came to me full of grief and looked up at me and let me decide for both of us.

His blood entering the room was no different than any other blood, no darker, no brighter, no more real. The release of pressure, the dissipating of blood throughout the room he had inhabited and dominated for so many months, lasted only a moment. It did exhaust me. I wish he had earned this exhaustion with me. I wish he could understand that there are no mistakes in writing such stories except that when you write in blood you have to conserve enough ink later to underline and re-underline the word *life*.

# LIE DOWN AND DIE

*by* SETH FRIED

**M**Y FATHER WAS shot and killed the day after I was born. He was in St. Louis, Missouri, at the time and I am forced to assume that things did not go well for him there. I am forced to assume a great deal about my father: that he was tall, that he shaved against the grain, or that his death was tragic and undeserved—and while I have never been one to give in to superstitions, I am also forced to assume that somehow he knew he would never live long enough to see me alive.

For instance, he took me to a baseball game when I was still in the womb. There is a photograph of my mother leaning back uncomfortably in Tiger Stadium, a baseball cap propped at a careful angle on her stomach. This seems, to me, the act of a man who had serious doubts concerning his ability to survive the nine months it would take for his son to be born.

My mother never explained why my father had been shot or by whom, which even as a child I regarded as strange—a strangeness which was complicated by the fact that when I was thirteen years old my mother was abducted on an unannounced, impromptu trip to Niagara Falls and was never seen again.

My family was full of stories like that: dubious suicides, sudden disappearances, the police always suspecting foul play. An uncle would vanish only to be found mangled in farm equipment miles away from home, a cousin would run away, turning up weeks later with her wrists slit in the cargo hull of a ship bound for South America. It was as if our family tree had been written in invisible ink, names and branches disappearing as quickly as they were written.

Even things that were attached to our family by the simple means of possession seemed doomed: pets would burst into flames, appliances, fresh out of the box, would eerily fail to work.

I remember watching my Aunt Loyola one summer afternoon as she plugged a brand-new blender into the wall of her cream-colored kitchen and held down the button marked pulse. She listened intently to the unnatural whirrs and clicks as the blades refused to spin and then, suddenly, as if the hum of the blender's failing was the sound that marked all our dooms, she burst into tears.

Six months later she was struck and killed by a rust-colored Buick in the parking lot of Blessed Sacrament Church after Saturday night mass.

These deaths, of course, were difficult to grow up around, and to this day when I leave my apartment it is not without a certain amount of consternation. I see vans with tinted windows, crop threshers and wood chippers placed inexplicably in the middle of busy streets; there are suspicious sounds, angry-looking strangers, reckless people everywhere, all bent toward some yet-unknown harm—and at these times, when I see the moment coming, streetlights flickering out the second I step under them, the moment of my certain, untimely death, I tend to think of my mother and father in terms of fate and possibilities.

I think about the possibility of a foul ball hitting my mother in the stomach that day at Tiger Stadium and the subsequent miscarriage. I think about my father dodging the bullet meant for him in St. Louis and beating his assailant within an inch of his life. I think about my mother going over the Falls in a barrel, narrowly escaping abduction and explaining her story to rescuers after being fished out of the foaming waters and pried out of the barrel; I see her, standing on the deck of a stunned ferry, damp and breathless.

My mind drifts and the moment passes and then I'm never dead—and all at once the idea that the world is a history of sad and preposterous deaths seems almost comforting.

What happens after that can be different. Sometimes afterward the moon looks big or there's the faraway sound of a train or I might hear a dog bark or locusts so loud it hurts.

# ASUNCIÓN

*by* ROY KESEY

IT IS A BEAUTIFUL CITY: flowering jacarandas, old yellow streetcars, Sunday afternoons in the plaza rich with heat and birdsong. It is also an excellent city in which to be mugged. By this I mean that on the whole the muggers here are extremely inefficient.

I have been the intended victim of five attempted muggings thus far during my three years in Asunción. Though my Spanish is perfect and most of my clothes are made locally, it is clear what I am, even from a distance; muggers note my pale skin and the lack of grace in my straight-backed walk, and they know immediately that I was born elsewhere, in a country where salaries are high and jobs are plentiful, where the streets are swept and the air is clean. Do they resent this? Do they rage at my good fortune? I don't believe they do. I believe their only thought is this: Here is another foreigner, another soft victim.

*Blanco*—in Spanish it means both "Caucasian" and "target," among other things. But there is a difference between spotting a target and hitting one. I have never been mugged successfully, because I am far stronger than I appear, and because I am not afraid.

They do not like confrontation of any kind, these criminals. When they work in groups it is generally in groups of four, and this is how it will happen: Muggers one and two will start an argument in front of you, hoping to distract your attention; mugger three will push you from behind, and mugger four will tug violently at your purse or briefcase. If you do not let go, they will almost always scatter.

There is of course the slight possibility that instead of scattering they will stand their ground and puff out their chests and demand that you give them what they have tried and failed to rip from your hands; in this case, in general, you have only to puff out your chest as well. If you do, they will most likely slink away—slinking, it is precisely what they do, the slinking of dogs that have been kicked—and you will be left alone, sweaty and victorious.

But of those few who do not run at the first sign of confrontation, there is a small percentage, a very small percentage, who will likewise not slink away once you have puffed out your chest. Instead they will smile. When you meet a mugger such as this, you must swing as hard as you can and you must pray not to miss. If you miss he will pull a knife from his belt, will stab you in the chest, will kill you. That is the only rule.

Of course I detest all muggers, but there is a constant roil inside of me, the struggle between acid and base, perhaps, the latter seeking to neutralize, the former to overwhelm: I was taught as a child to hate the sin and love the sinner. I have never been very successful at this, but now at least I know that it is possible. This last scenario, wherein you are accosted by one of the very, very few muggers who smile and do not run, it is how I met the latest great love of my life.


I was on my way home from work, striding through the dense summer dusk, the heat at last relenting. A young woman was twenty or thirty yards ahead of me, walking in the same direction. The moment I saw her, I began to speed up.

It was not that I wanted to speak to her, to compliment her eyes or her smile, to undress her slowly and spread her across my bed—I did not desire any of this. I wanted only to be close to her for a moment. This is something I have felt so many times, man or woman or child—it is all the same, the need to be close. Sometimes it is all that one requires.

This was not, I think, the first time I had seen the young woman.

That night she was dressed neither poorly nor well, but cleanly: pressed black trousers, smooth white blouse, low black heels that clicked as she walked. She smelled of jasmine and moved through her own quiet music as I closed in.

Then he came from the side, he was slender and lithe, and he went for her purse but she held to it just long enough for me to reach them. I shoved him in the back, and he sprawled; she gaped at me, her mouth ever so slightly open, her purse on the ground at her feet.

I retrieved the purse and set it in her hands. Now she was not watching me. She was watching the mugger, who stared up at us from where he lay.

—Just go, I said to her. Go now, go quickly, fly.

She nodded, turned away, turned back. The mugger was getting to his feet. I stepped toward him and he raised both hands. The woman turned away again and started walking, faster and faster, and at last she disappeared around the far corner.

If the mugger had taken off just then, he could have caught her in the space of two or three blocks. Of course I would have followed, would have arrived soon enough. But he did not pursue her, not at all. Instead he squared his shoulders and puffed out his chest.

—Your wallet, he said.

I puffed out my chest as well, and he smiled. It was a beautiful smile. I knew that it was time, time to swing as hard as I could, praying not to miss. As long as I didn't miss, one punch would have been sufficient, I think. But I didn't. I couldn't. His smile was so beautiful.

There was movement, one hand flitting to his belt, still the smile, still I could not swing, the smile, my hands at my sides, but something failed, something caught, he pulled and tugged and his smile waned and finally I was free of him. I set my feet and drew back my fist, something flashed at his belt and I swung, the blow starting in the strength of my legs, surging up through my back and chest, through my shoulder and arm and into my fist, his hand was rising and again the flash as I hit him and he flurried and collapsed face-down across the curb.

I waited for him to rise, but he did not. His body trembled in that low light. There was a more distant movement then, and I looked up, saw the young woman standing at the corner. I motioned, and my motion was unclear even to me, meant for her to stay or to go, I have no idea.

When she disappeared again I stepped to the mugger and flipped him over, thinking to kick him in the face, to show him that mugging is wrong, that it makes an already hard world still harder. As he slumped onto his back I saw his hand held tightly to his stomach. I saw the blood that bubbled up through his fingers. I saw that what had flashed at his belt was a knife now buried to the hilt in his abdomen.

I bent over him, the knife, his thin chest heaving, his kind and delicate face. One of his eyes was swollen nearly shut, and there were scrapes across his forehead, a gash at one temple. He would not be getting up for some time.

I could have walked away and been done with it, but leaving him there was not possible, not in any real way. He looked up at me and smiled again, that smile. His one open eye was a wonder, long black lashes, a warmth of brown. And at that moment I began to believe he could be taught, to hope he could be saved.


Rafael is his name. I nursed him here in my apartment. We were fortunate that the knife had not pierced his diaphragm, that his internal bleeding was not unmanageable. I set him on my bed, the knife still in place: From films I had learned that if I pulled it out too soon he would bleed too much too fast, would be lost to me.

I fed him only liquids, my own dinner blended until smooth, and I brought him cups of warm herbal tea whenever he complained of thirst. I bathed his scrapes and daubed antiseptic cream on the gash at his temple. I even consulted a pharmacist and bought everything he recommended, the gauze and tape, the antibiotics and painkillers.

I noticed that the ringing of the telephone often disturbed Rafael's rest, so I had it disconnected. And on the morning of the third day, as he lay sleeping, I called a locksmith, who came and put locks on the windows, the interior doors, the kitchen drawers. I try to think only the best of the people I meet, but there is no sense in taking unnecessary risks.

I sat with Rafael each afternoon as heat thickened the air and the city went still. I tried to amuse him with stories of finance and scandal in Brussels and Baghdad, Bombay and Buenos Aires. Always he turned his face away.

Then for nearly a week a fever came and went, came and went; hallucinations took him and he sobbed in Guaraní. When he woke from his frothing fear I asked what he'd seen. He claimed not to remember. Slowly I cured him, and at last he began to reveal himself to me, but his stories came in fragments: the name of a cousin he hadn't seen in years, the title of a book his mother had once read aloud, and then he'd fall silent again.

Through all of this, the fever and shards of past, I eased the knife out as gently as possible, half an inch per day. Soon the knife threatened to fall of its own accord, and I was unsure what would result if it fell, if the bleeding might resume or additional damage might be done. I braced the knife with damp towels and forbade Rafael to move.

Finally I was able to slip the tip of the blade from his smooth brown hairless skin, and we had a small celebration: champagne, strawberries, candles. Our first kiss. He struggled against it, but not, I think, with much conviction.

A few days later he tried to escape. My downstairs neighbors called me at work to say that it sounded as though some kind of animal was trapped and dying in my apartment, and I came home to find claw marks on the inside of the bedroom door, a broken window, blood smeared along the ledge to where he sat. But the ledge is far too high, the fall too much for anyone who wished to live; as well, the streets below are noisy enough that no distant shout would be heeded. I repaired the window, painted the door, and punched him once, as hard as I could. Then I kissed him, his forehead and cheeks and eyelids, his soft and bloody mouth.

It is difficult to know how much is enough. For a week I kept him bound and gagged in my bedroom. The neighbors complained once or twice of thudding sounds coming through their ceiling, but I calmed them with stories of construction. There is no point in worrying those around you.

The last few days of that week there were no more complaints, and from the depth and gentleness of his gaze each time I entered the bedroom, I came to believe that he now understood. I removed the gag, unbound his feet and hands, massaged his wrists and ankles. I told him of my apartment's many comforts, and promised he would learn them all.

The following day a rasping cough took hold in his chest. I went back to the pharmacist for decongestants and more antibiotics, but the cough grew hollow and deep—bronchitis or pneumonia, I never learned for sure.

It was almost a month before he was healthy again, and in that time I grew ever more certain I could trust him and his love for me. Sponge bath and hot compress, mentholatum and lemon tea, and bit by bit he told me all I wished to know. His home in Bahía Negra on the bank of the Lateriquique, and the brothers and sisters he'd left there. The fortune he'd come looking for and now knew he'd never find. The garbage he pawed through for food, the bridges under which he slept, the alleys where he laid in wait.

He told me so much, and I could only trust him. When the sickness finally burned itself out, I gave him keys to all the doors of the apartment. He had earned them, I thought. That evening I came home to find him waiting on the living-room sofa. He presented me with gifts: a gold watch and a beautiful leather briefcase. They were stolen, of course, and I beat him unconscious. There is no point in making a hard world still harder.

We had no further problems for the next several days, and on Sunday afternoon I took him to the plaza. It was still very hot, though autumn had begun. We watched the old men sipping their cold tea, the ornate cages at their feet filled with canaries and finches. Rafael begged me to buy him a songbird, and I let him choose. The old man set an unreasonable price, but was not difficult to persuade, and Rafael and I walked slowly home, carrying the cage between us.

Though the canary was a female, Rafael insisted on naming her Teodoro; he cared for her with great tenderness, and of course she sang splendidly. When I returned from work four days ago, I found him leaning over her cage, whistling something pleasantly serene, a folksong of some kind, perhaps in the hope that she would learn it.

I came to stand beside him, asked if the words to the song were in Spanish or Guaraní, and Rafael turned, kissed my mouth, held me. He drew back and something flashed at his belt and this time I was not quick enough. Love slowed me, I believe. The knife hit me where his knife had hit him on the day we met, or very nearly so. He must have spent hours sharpening the blade, or it would not have slipped in with such grace, such warmth.

I have been lying on the couch since then, drawing the knife out half an inch per day. By the end of next week I will be able to remove it entirely. And how long after that must I wait for full recovery? A month or so, perhaps less.

The pain is only a nuisance; far more troubling is the manner in which Rafael left me. As I slid down the wall he kissed me again, the softest kiss. He drew my wrist to his face and kissed my hand. He stepped over me and walked to the door. Do you see? Instead of setting Teodoro free, he left her caged, and in so doing surely meant to send me a message. But what does the message mean? There is precisely one way to find out.

Rafael should not be too hard to find. As soon as I am well I will begin my search for him, in the alleys and under the bridges. If he has left Asunción I shall track him, to Esteros or Villarica, to Horqueta or back to Bahía Negra. He may even have left the country: Bolivia, Brazil, Argentina. It will make little difference.

I will find him lying in a hammock beside a slow jungle stream, wild parrots eating guava from his hand; or in a shack above the tree line in the mountains, rain thrashing at the roof; or in a small dirty house on the outskirts of some major city, cinderblock walls, a poster of the Virgin curling up at the corners. I will find him and take him in my arms. I will trace his lips with my fingertips. I will teach him the indefatigable strength of love, the rippling force of forgiveness.

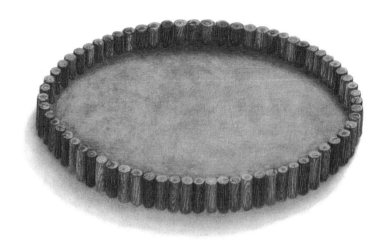

# THE DOCTOR OF
# MENTAL HEALTH

*by* MIRANDA MELLIS

I AM A FIFTY-YEAR-OLD vegetarian man in decent health, though somewhat sedentary. I've recently come into possession of ten pounds of raw red meat. Since I live alone, I am either going to have to give up vegetarianism, give away the meat, or let it sit in my freezer indefinitely. (Of the three, I imagine the last is the likeliest scenario.) I got the meat from my ex-therapist.

I've managed to get through life largely unscathed. On the whole, I have been grateful for my lot. Nonetheless, about a year and a half ago I began to wonder if I was too stable. In order to investigate this matter I went into therapy, on the advice of my friend Carolette.

From the start, I was put off by the therapist's office.

I am no interior decorator; my apartment is a simple affair. It is probably almost austere, a well-lit place with minimal furniture. From my building there is a pleasant view of what is reputed to be the best private girls' school in the country. My furniture is modern yet well built; my linens are gray and white. As my friend Carolette will have it, I have "no pizzazz."

On the other hand, my first, and as it happened my last, therapist, recommended to me by Carolette, was full of pizzazz. She saw fit to hang wind chimes and mobiles in her windowless office. We sat across from each other in fat faded purple chairs. On my right was a tray of

"Star Magic" wands. Early on, I sometimes gamely tilted a stick or two, which caused the viscous sparkling glitter to ooze around in its little trap. Directly in front of me was a large, cheaply framed, slanted photograph of a pair of sandals in a forest. Possibly whoever had last been wearing the sandals was caught in a noose just above. If the frame were a little larger you'd be able to see the feet dangling there. Or maybe the wearer of the shoes had just evaporated.

The room was less a therapist's office than a portal into a trick dimension not unlike those terrifying false-bottom suburbias conjured in occult mystery movies of which I have seen my share. In such films, typical middle-class environs and good-looking, conservatively dressed protagonists in normal-looking houses are just one red theater curtain away from an altogether unreasonable place, where small men talking backward control time and space and cause you to actually murder yourself and then wake up in your own bed with an entirely different set of teeth.

It wasn't just the room, though. The therapist's get-ups were more assemblage than ensemble. It was not uncommon, come my weekly three o'clock Tuesday afternoon appointment, to find her in a long yellow dress decorated all over with leering, contorted frogs. Because she accessorized surrealistically, it required several minutes to take her all in. With the dress in question she wore earrings of outstretched enamel (napping? dead?) frogs. Once, she wore a glistening fly on a brooch with a necklace of hands holding hands.

I remember another day when she wore a short mustard cape, black stirrup tights, and a yellow crochet tunic. The tunic did not provide sufficient cover and should have been worn with a slip of some kind. It exposed the crotch of her tights as well as the hairs around her areolae, which timidly protruded like the nascent swirls of a young fern. And always she wore the moist-looking shoes that, where I am from, are considered slippers. Her hair was a maze of static; her eyes sagged like a basset hound's. The sprouts on her chin were stiff quills and on the one occasion that we hugged I was stabbed in the face. None of these repulsive aspects would have troubled me, however, if she did not also behave, even for a therapist, so uncannily.

Dressed as she was, one might conjecture that my therapist was developmentally stunted. The ramifications were troubling. In turning myself over to her for treatment, was I putting myself in the care of a child?

Gradually I became convinced of it when, regardless of what topic I introduced, she insisted that I play in a sandbox and have imaginary conversations with my relatives.

I would leave her office in a state of agitation and paranoia. She said it was part of the "healing process," that I was getting "triggered." I told her I felt like I was "going crazy." "Men are so necessarily mad," she quoted, while pointing inexplicably at the photograph of the sandals, "that not to be mad would amount to another form of madness." She then pulled out the sandbox, with all the figurines, seashells, toys, and plastic flowers I had come to dread.

The things I found myself saying and doing with those objects can only be attributed to the sadistic influence of the therapist.

One day she brought in a box of plates and bade me smash them with a hammer. In another session I flogged my chair with a strangely heavy pillow. I turned hysterically toward her and she was stifling a yawn. The therapist was never satisfied until I was either in a state of roiling mania or boneless inertia, at which point I was summarily dismissed to stagger home, undone, to my cat, who appeared accusatory, or scarily insubstantial.

My therapist, upon learning of my emotional dependency on my cat, mentioned the possibility that he was the reincarnation of my mother. She later said she had done some poking around about the matter on her own and was now fairly sure of it. "I did not talk about you," I would say to my mother, the cat, from the door. What had he been doing while I was gone? I'd never wondered before. I searched the house for signs of paranormal activity. If I found vomit, or a dead sparrow, I didn't know how to take it.

I could never have ended therapy on my own, as frightening and confusing as the experience was proving to be. Fortunately, she just disappeared one Tuesday. I came back the next week, and again she wasn't there. I gladly put the whole episode behind me and resolved to avoid therapy and the examined life in general from then on.

It had been eleven months since I'd last seen her when she called, she said, with an offer I wouldn't want to miss: she was selling inexpensive hunks of red meat. The meat, she informed me, came from a very recently killed cow. It was hanging at present in a cooler at her friend's house. She was selling the meat for five dollars a pound and could bring it to me as soon as tomorrow. But there was a minimum purchase of ten pounds for fifty dollars. It was the same amount she used to charge me for our sessions.

I asked if she was still practicing as a therapist. "Not really," she said. I could hear her breathing.

Unable, as before, to say no to the doctor, I agreed to buy ten pounds of the meat, although I am a vegetarian and I live alone.

# ONE DAY THIS
# WILL ALL BE YOURS

*by* PHILIPP MEYER

**M**Y FATHER GREW UP in a mining town in West Virginia; baths outside in a coal-fired tub, missing strikers found buried in the slag piles, the vein giving out and the whole town with it. His father and twelve others died in a shaft collapse.

I went to see him after my mother left, ten years after the rest of us. My brother and sister still wouldn't talk to him. My sister got pregnant in college and married a banker; she must have played up the family saga because he treated her like a rescued bird, though she'd gotten off easiest of the three of us. I'd visited her in the Keys and she was nervous, and then the banker scolded her in front of my face for leaving the children alone with me. I headed back to Georgia that night, but my appetite was ruined and my face went gray for weeks and I told everyone I had a virus. I'm a big man. I could have wrecked that banker's jaw with one swipe.

My brother lived in Canada; he and I were on good terms. We spoke often and he asked me to visit and I wondered what he'd told his new family about me. I decided it was better if I never found out.

As for my father, he'd been alone a week before I called him. I had to work up to it. None of the others would even consider it.

"Nice to hear from you," he said. "I mean your timing."

"I was wondering how you were holding up."

"Been working on the house all week."

"Maybe you should be around people."

"Thank you," he told me.

"I was just saying."

"Did you know about this?"

"I didn't know anything," I said.

"You two didn't talk much, I know that."

"She and Melanie talked, mostly."

Melanie was my sister.

"Melanie probably knew."

"It doesn't matter," I told him.

"Things don't get easier. I thought they would, but I was wrong. In fact, they go downhill, generally speaking."

"This is just a rough spot," I said. "You'll get over this."

"My loyal son."

"Maybe we can just pretend to be nice people."

"There are things about us," he said. "There are things I've learned and you're not going to know them until it's too late."

"Come off it," I told him.

"I named Bud Mitchell executor."

"Pop."

"I'm just telling you."

"You don't even talk to him anymore."

"I called him last week. Everything is straightened out."

"Are you sick?" I said. "Tell me. Mom didn't say anything."

"I don't want your mother to find me. At first I thought I did."

We were quiet. I could hear him breathing.

"I'm calling the cops," I finally said.

"That would be best. I don't want your mother to be the one."

I had trouble staying between the lines on the road and finally I pulled over. My skin was cold and I was damp everywhere and my hands were tingling, and in my ears I could hear my blood. When I was a kid I shot a groundhog with a deer rifle from ten feet. I thought about that and how my father would look. Then I was sick.

Afterward I lay on the hood and took off my shirt to dry. The sun felt close and bright and the hood burned my back but I was shivering. I touched the padding on my gut—the softest it had ever been. Trucks went by and the air shook but I didn't hear anything.

I called my father to tell him I was on the way.

"You're not coming," he said. "I knew it before you called."

"I just had to pull over a minute."

"Sure."

"Are you outside? It sounds like you're outside."

"The neighbors are all looking at me. These people are afraid of everything."

"Wait for me," I told him. "I'll be there in ten minutes."

When I was younger I would hold broken glass in my hand and squeeze it until I couldn't think about anything else. Even now I can spin a carving knife into the air and catch it by the handle. In college I went to a palm reader, and she took one look and refused to say anything.

I pulled back onto the highway and called my brother and sister but they didn't pick up. *I know you're there*, I said into their machines. I thought about calling my mother and decided against it. She would go back if she knew. She was the only one of us who deserved better.


Their house was a rancher. All the windows were closed and it was stale inside. I started sweating and the blood came back to my ears. There were unwashed dishes in the kitchen, which my mother would not have allowed. In the living room, there was a sheet on the couch and a pillow, empty beer bottles on the side table, a dirty magazine, unopened and still wrapped in plastic. The dining-room table was bare except for a piece of paper with my address and phone number in careful print. *Son*, it said. My father was outside, at the edge of the pond with a skeet gun across his lap.

He didn't look up when I walked out.

"Pop?"

There were dozens of new homes. I could see the faces of the people inside. Their fences ran to our lawn. Long rectangles of orange dirt lay where the sod in their yards had died, and the sky beyond our house looked immense and empty where it had once been blocked with trees.

"Sorry about the lawn," he said.

I looked around for a sign that the gun might be unloaded, but there was a box of shells on its side in the grass, half scattered.

"You mind if I hold that?" I said.

"I lent the mower to the woman down the street and she drove it off a curb. It's at the shop."

"Have you called Tim or Melanie?"

"You can't trust women with complex machinery," he said. "Their brains get all haywired."

"A riding mower isn't really a complex machine," I told him.

"All you're doing is agreeing with me."

"I'm not trying to fight."

"You didn't have to come over. You haven't come over for nine years and all of a sudden here you are."

"Let me hold the shotgun," I said.

He didn't let go of it, but he didn't tighten his grip, either.

"Notice anything different about the yard?" he said. "Other than the woods are gone."

"No."

"Look carefully."

I thought I could wrestle the gun from him. I looked around the yard. It was the nicest part of the house, an acre with the pond at the center, a white pergola running up one side, dogwoods and apple trees. There were tulip beds around the pond. When my father was a kid, he'd seen something like it in a magazine. We pulled the weeds by hand, cut the grass around the flowers with scissors, watered sunup and sundown. There were gophers, and the poison killed our dog. When my brother left for college he filled his truck with rock salt and was going to dump it everywhere. My sister and I stopped him.

But, standing there with my father, I noticed something new. There was a sandbox, as if for children.

"Where'd that come from?"

"You guys all seem to be spawning. I thought it might come in handy."

My sister's four children, the oldest nearly twelve, had never met him. My brother and his wife had their third on the way but they'd insisted he not know.

"You need to talk to someone. I'm worried about you."

"You bought a house yet?"

"No. I put in for a transfer to Denver."

"Shack up the road just went for two hundred thousand. Believe that?"

"You'd probably get half a mil with all the land. Move someplace smaller."

"The house would be full enough if it weren't for your mother."

"Don't."

"She doesn't know how stupid she looks," he said. "Running around at her age."

"Let's not do this."

"Be glad you never married."

"I'm thirty-two."

"Your grandfather passed when he was thirty-four."

"That's a nice thing to tell someone."

"I keep thinking about that Cadillac I bought her. She drove it right out of here."

"She could have taken more," I said.

"I'd kill her before I let her have this house."

I didn't say anything.

"She's a whore. I'm not afraid to say it."

"I'm going home now."

"Come on. I've got steaks in the freezer."

"You are fucking impossible."

"I'm just lonely, Scotty. I worked so hard to make her happy."

"You don't really think that."

"I gave her that car last year. And a goddamn plumber. It burns me up, that guy riding around in my Caddy."

"Actually," I said, "he's a steamfitter."

"What?"

"Not a plumber."

"What the hell," he said.

"I want to stop this," I said. "I'm sorry."

"You know I took baths in an outdoor tub that we heated over a coal burner? That's how much we had."

"I know you had it rough, Pop."

"You had everything you asked for."

"Pop," I said.

"Your grandfather could do a hundred pushups. He'd cuff me and my ears would ring all morning."

I didn't say anything.

"It's in the blood."

"That doesn't mean anything," I told him.

We watched football for two hours without speaking. My father correctly predicted the final score. I'd been a guard at Michigan for a season, then quit to spite him.

As for the shotgun, I'd unloaded it and pocketed the shells.

"Plenty more where they came from," he said about the shells.

"Clemson is on fire this year," is what he said about football.

"They seem fine," I said.

"They're a lot better than fine."

"You need someone to talk to. Other than the guys at the trap range."

"Let me ask you a question, Scott."

"Probably not."

"Are you mad at your mother?"

"Dad."

"Well. Are you?"

"Off-limits," I said.

"Do me the favor," he said. "For ten years of not seeing you."

"That's not on me," I said. "That's on all of us."

"Just answer it. I want to hear you say it."

Of course I was mad at her. At eighteen you can look at your father and know you'll never be anything like him. At thirty it's a different story. All three of us blamed her for not seeing it when she married him, but in the end we'd paid her back. We'd escaped to colleges in different states, stayed away summers and holidays. I was the youngest and the last to leave and my mother couldn't look at me when she dropped me at the airport. *I guess I won't be seeing you much*, she said. *I guess not*, I told her. Then I disappeared like my brother and sister. I've always known it was the worst thing I've ever done.

"I'm not mad at Mom," I told him.

"Sweet Jesus Christ," said my father. "Now I've heard it all."

He picked up the remote to turn the TV back on, but I stopped him before he could.

"I used to think you did everything on purpose," I said.

"Everything what?"

"But now I'm not sure. I think it comes from someplace you don't understand."

He didn't say anything.

"I liked it better when it was on purpose."

His fists balled up like the old days and his face got dark.

I left him on the couch and got a case of beer from the kitchen.

"I'm going outside," I told him.


The sun was going down when my father came onto the patio. I don't know if he saw all the neighbors. I watched him load his gun. Then I looked away.

Where the people stood with their children and fences I imagined everything as it had been before, land unbroken all the way to the river, pigeon hawks hunting the clearings, foxes and deer, owls at night. When we were kids we would camp in those hills, my father and brother and I, and I thought about the feeling of the cold air on my face and the warmness inside the sleeping bag and the sound of my father's soft breathing as he slept.

I threw my beer into the pond. I could feel him watching me. I threw the rest of the bottles one by one. They skittered across the grass, cracked on the slate path. I expected to hear a shot. When the case of beers was empty I went into the garage and dragged back a trashcan full of bottles. I aimed them against the rocks in the pond, against the pergola and the flagstone in the yard.

The neighbors stood at their fences and watched.

"Do you want us to call the police?" one of them said.

My father didn't answer. I kept throwing. The sun was getting lower and the glass on the lawn was glowing like embers from a wreckage.

"You can stop now," he said.

I barely heard him.

"Scotty," he said.

Then there was a noise, a gunshot, and a bottle cracked apart in the air. Something cut me on the face. The neighbors started away from their fences. My father had the gun shouldered and the pieces of the bottle were spinning and falling over the yard and I touched my check and it was sticky hot. We're even, I thought quickly, but then I knew we weren't and that we couldn't be. I watched him and he couldn't hold my eyes, and I saw the thinness in his arms and legs, the slouch in his back.

"That's enough," he said, but it was a whisper. It was so quiet I could barely hear it. I didn't know what it meant, or what he wanted me to do.

Then he was leaning and I caught him and held him up. I was lifting him from under his elbows and he was sagging back against me.

He doesn't want me to see him like this, I thought, but after that we didn't move. The sun was in our faces. I could hear the sound of his breathing, soft like I'd remembered it, and the light was spread across the hills and trees as if the land had been set on fire.

CONTRIBUTORS

CHRIS ADRIAN is a Fellow in Pediatric Hematology-Oncology at the University of San Francisco. Farrar, Straus, and Giroux will publish his third novel, *The Great Night*, next summer.

TOM BISSELL is the author of *Chasing the Sea*, *God Lives in St. Petersburg*, and *The Father of All Things*. His new book, *Extra Lives: Why Video Games Matter*, will be published in 2010. He lives in Portland and teaches in Portland State University's MFA program.

RODDY DOYLE lives and works in Dublin. His next novel, *The Dead Republic,* will be published in June 2010.

BEN EHRENREICH is the author of the novel *The Suitors*.

BRIAN EVENSON is the author of nine books of fiction, most recently the novel *Last Days* and the story collection *Fugue State*. His novel *The Open Curtain* was a finalist for an Edgar Award and an IHG Award, and was one of *Time Out New York*'s top books of 2006. A limited-edition novella, *Baby Leg*, will be published by New York Tyrant Press in late 2009. He lives and works in Providence, Rhode Island, where he directs Brown University's Literary Arts Program.

SETH FRIED'S first published story appeared in *McSweeney's* 15, when he was twenty-one years old. Since then, his stories have appeared in the *Missouri Review*, *One-Story*, *Vice*, and many other magazines.

ROY KESEY had no idea it would come to this.

ADAM LEVIN's first novel, *The Gurionic War*, will be published by McSweeney's in 2010. *Hot Pink*, a collection of stories, will follow. His fiction has appeared in a number of publications, including *Tin House*, *Ninth Letter*, and the *New England Review*. He lives in Chicago, where he teaches writing at Columbia College and the School of The Art Institute.

CLAIRE LIGHT is a Bay Area freelance writer. She has a chapbook of short stories appearing at the end of 2009 from Aqueduct Press.

MIRANDA MELLIS Miranda Mellis is the author of *The Revisionist* and *Materialisms*. She is an editor at The Encyclopedia Project, and teaches at Mills College and California College of the Arts.

PHILIPP MEYER has worked as a derivatives trader, a construction worker, and an EMT, among other jobs. His first novel, *American Rust*, has been published in twelve countries, and was recently named one of *Newsweek's* "Best. Books. Ever." He currently splits his time between Texas and upstate New York.

STEVEN MILLHAUSER is the author of eleven works of fiction, including *Edwin Mullhouse, Martin Dressler*, and T*he Knife Thrower and Other Stories*. His most recent book is *Dangerous Laughter*, a collection of stories.

KEVIN MOFFETT is the author of *Permanent Visitors*, a collection of stories. He lives in Claremont, California, and teaches in the MFA program at Cal State University San Bernardino.

YANNICK MURPHY lives in Vermont with her husband and three children. She is the author of *Stories in Another Language, The Sea of Trees, Here They Come, Signed, Mata Hari, In a Bear's Eye, Ahwooooooooo!*, and *Baby Polar*.

SHANN RAY grew up in Alaska and Montana. Currently a professor of leadership at Gonzaga University, he has also served as a research psychologist with the Centers for Disease Control. His book, *The Spirit of Servant Leadership*, edited with Larry C. Spears, is forthcoming from Paulist Press. He lives with his wife Jennifer and three daughters in Spokane, Washington.

JIM SHEPARD is the author of six novels and three story collections, including *Like You'd Understand, Anyway*, which was nominated for the National Book Award and won the Story Prize. His short fiction has appeared in *Harper's*, the *Paris Review*, the *Atlantic Monthly, Esquire, Granta, Tin House*, the *New Yorker*, and *Playboy*. He teaches at Williams College.

RACHEL SHERMAN is the author of a novel, *Living Room*, and a book of short stories, *The First Hurt*, both published by Open City Books. Her stories have appeared in *Fence*, *Open City*, and *Conjunctions*, among other publications; *The First Hurt* was short-listed for the Story Prize and the Frank O'Connor International Short Story Award, and was named one of the 25 Books to Remember in 2006 by the New York Public Library. She teaches writing at Rutgers and Columbia Universities, and lives in Brooklyn.

ALISON SMITH is the author of the memoir *Name All the Animals*. Her writing has appeared in publications including *Granta*, *Gunzo*, the London *Telegraph*, and the New York *Times*. She lives in Brooklyn, New York.

SUSAN STEINBERG is the author of *Hydroplane* and *The End of Free Love*. She teaches at the University of San Francisco.

J. ERIN SWEENEY lives and works in Philadelphia. Her stories have appeared in *American Short Fiction*, *Spork*, the *Licking River Review*, and elsewhere.

WELLS TOWER is the author of Every*thing Ravaged, Everything Burned*, a collection of short fiction.

SEAN WARREN recently retired from the Navy after twenty years, seven of which he spent in Europe. Hia stories have appeared in *Washington Squar*e and *The Writer's Block*, and he is at work on his second novel. He currently lives in Reno, Nevada.

# STORIES: ISSUES 11 – 20
Alphabetized by author